SAVI
THE S

DELORES FOSSEN

AND

COWBOY SWAGGER
BY
JOANNA WAYNE

MILLS
BOON

SAVIOUR IN THE SADDLE

BY
DELORES FOSSEN

All the characters in this book have no existence outside the imagination of the author, and have no relation whatsoever to anyone bearing the same name or names. They are not even distantly inspired by any individual known or unknown to the author, and all the incidents are pure invention.

First published in Great Britain 2012
by Mills & Boon, an imprint of Harlequin (UK) Limited,
Eton House, 18-24 Paradise Road, Richmond, Surrey TW9 1SR

© Delores Fossen 2010

ISBN: 978 0 263 89493 6

46-0112

Harlequin (UK) policy is to use papers that are natural, renewable and recyclable products and made from wood grown in sustainable forests. The logging and manufacturing processes conform to the legal environmental regulations of the country of origin.

Printed and bound in Spain
by Blackprint CPI, Barcelona

Imagine a family tree that includes Texas cowboys, Choctaw and Cherokee Indians, a Louisiana pirate and a Scottish rebel who battled side by side with William Wallace. With ancestors like that, it's easy to understand why Texas author and former air force captain **Delores Fossen** feels as if she were genetically predisposed to writing romances. Along the way to fulfilling her DNA destiny, Delores married an air force top gun who just happens to be of Viking descent. With all those romantic bases covered, she doesn't have to look too far for inspiration.

To my daughter, Beth

Chapter One

Austin, Texas

They had found her.

Willa Marks saw the proof of that when the man stepped from the black four-door Ford that had just pulled into her driveway.

He had a badge clipped to his belt.

She pressed her fingers to her mouth to silence the gasp that nearly escaped from her throat and she eased down the blinds that she'd lifted a fraction so she could peek out.

Oh, God.

This couldn't be happening.

Willa hurried away from the window and to the wall next to the door. Her shoulder brushed against the trio of yellow sticky notes that she'd left there, and one of them fluttered to the floor.

Don't Trust the Cops, the note said.

She no longer needed the reminder. At least, Willa didn't think she did. But she'd left it there just in case. It was too important for her to forget something like that again.

"It'll be okay," she whispered to her unborn child, hoping she wasn't lying to the baby and herself.

She slid her hand over her pregnant belly, but she knew her hand wouldn't be much protection if this turned out to be the start of another round in the nightmare that just would not end.

The doorbell rang, the sound knifing through the room, and this time she wasn't able to muffle her gasp. Of course, she'd known they would ring the bell. And they wouldn't stop until she let them inside.

They had found her.

Well, by God, they weren't taking her back into their so-called protective custody. Look where that had gotten her the last two times.

She and her baby had nearly been killed.

There were ten notes around the house to remind her of that, and just in case that wasn't enough, the warning scrolled across the screen saver of her laptop: Don't Trust the Cops.

The doorbell rang again, and it was followed by a heavy knock. "Ms. Marks, I'm Lieutenant Bo Duggan from San Antonio P.D. I know you're in there."

Maybe he had seen her car in the garage. Or perhaps he'd even spotted her when she'd made a quick trip just a half hour earlier to the grocery store.

But how exactly had they found her?

She'd been so careful—using an alias, paying only with cash, leaving no paper trail. She hadn't wanted to dye her hair because of the chemicals, but she hadn't cut it in months and, with it pulled back from her face, she didn't resemble the photos that had been snapped of her four months earlier and splattered all over the news.

Apparently all those safety measures hadn't been enough.

"Lieutenant Bo Duggan," she repeated under her breath, and Willa hurried to grab her PDA from her desk next to the sofa.

There was another knock, and another, but Willa ignored them and scrolled through the pictures and names she'd assembled in case her memory failed her again. She found him. Bo Duggan's photo was there, and she'd added a caption: I Think I Can Trust Him.

It was the word *think* that kicked up her heartbeat an extra notch. But then, in the past four months, there was no one that she trusted completely.

Not even herself.

"We need to talk to you," Lieutenant Duggan said from the other side of the door. "We know you're scared, but there are things we have to ask you—important things."

Willa carried the PDA back to the window and peeked out again. The lieutenant's face matched the picture she had, but he wasn't alone.

There was another man with him.

The second man was tall and lanky. He wore jeans and a crisp, white shirt topped with a buckskin jacket, and he held a saddle-brown Stetson in his left hand. His dress was casual, unlike the lieutenant who had on a dark blue suit.

It was the second man that Willa focused on. Did she know him?

His face wasn't familiar.

He had thick black hair that was slightly long and rumpled, no doubt from the cold December wind that was assaulting them. With that Stetson, jeans and jacket, he looked like a cowboy from the *Texas Monthly* magazine she had on her coffee table.

His skin was deeply tanned, but she shook her head, rethinking that. The skin tone was probably natural. Those high cheekbones and features were Native American.

She frantically scrolled through the pictures again, but she didn't expect to find him. With those unique looks, Willa thought he might be someone she would remember without the prompts, pictures and captions.

"Ms. Marks," the lieutenant tried again. "Please, open the door."

The knocks got harder, and each blow against the thick wood sent her pulse racing out of control. She couldn't call the local cops. There were plenty of notes telling her not to trust them. So maybe she could wait out these two. Eventually Lieutenant Duggan and his Native American partner would get tired of knocking and leave.

She hoped.

Then she could gather her things and go on the run again.

The baby inside her kicked hard, as if protesting that. "Well, I'm not too happy about it, either," Willa mumbled.

She'd lived here at this suburban Austin rental house for two months now, and that was a month longer than the extended-stay hotel where she'd stayed in Houston.

Two months hadn't been long enough for her to settle in or to stop being afraid, but she had started to believe she might be able to remain here until after the baby was born. Or at least until Christmas, which was only three days away.

So much for her short-term dreams.

They were as fleeting as her short-term memory had been just weeks ago.

"Willa?" someone called out.

Not the lieutenant. Another look out the blinds, and she realized it was the other man who'd spoken. The man whose picture wasn't in her PDA. But he had said her name as if he knew her.

No, it was more than that.

He said her name as if he knew her *intimately*.

"Willa, it's me, Brandon. Look, I know you're probably still mad at me—I don't blame you. But I've been searching for you all this time so I could tell you how sorry I am about the argument we had."

"Brandon?" She repeated it several times, but it jogged no memory.

Who was he? What did he want? And what argument had they had? Better yet, just how badly did she need to know the answers to those questions?

Willa made sure all four locks on the front door were engaged, though she already knew they were. That was routine these days. The lights were green on the security panel box, meaning it was armed and ready to sound if tripped. Also routine. As were the window locks, gun and the multiple cans of pepper spray she had stashed around the house.

The lieutenant and his partner couldn't get in. Well,

not unless they broke down the door or smashed a window, but that could happen if she spoke to them or not.

"Do I know you?" she called out. And Willa prayed that merely asking the question wouldn't turn out to be a deadly mistake.

She watched through the blinds, and she saw the men whispering to each other. Both of them also fired glances all around the yard and street. Not ordinary glances, either. The kind that cops made when they were worried they might be ambushed.

Of course, it was also the kind of glances that criminals made to make sure they weren't being watched.

"You know me," the man, Brandon, assured her. He said it with complete confidence, but there was also a tinge of frustration in his voice. "Willa, open the door. I want to see you."

Willa didn't budge. "How do you know me?"

He hesitated. It wasn't just a pause. But definitely a hesitation. She'd lost so much after everything she'd been through, but she'd gained something, too. Willa had gotten very good at reading people.

Brandon was on edge.

"They told me you had memory loss from a fall you took at the hospital, and that you were in a coma for a while," Brandon finally said. "You still don't remember me after all this time?"

No, but she didn't intend to tell him that.

Truth was, she had no memories—*none*—before the nightmare that had happened four months earlier when she and about three dozen other pregnant women and medical staff had been held hostage at gunpoint for hours on the fourth floor at the San Antonio Maternity Hospital. Questioned. Verbally abused. And worse.

People had died that day, and those who had survived did not come out unscathed.

She was proof of that.

The gunmen had even forced her to help them retrieve some computer files in the lab. Or so she'd been told because part of the hostage standoff had been captured on a hospital surveillance camera.

Willa had no recollection of that, either.

No memories before that fall she'd supposedly taken when one of the gunmen had pushed her down during her attempted escape. No memories before or immediately following the coma she'd supposedly been in when her brain had swollen from a deep concussion.

And what she had remembered since was spotty in too many areas.

The head injury had given her both amnesia and short-term memory loss. That was the last diagnosis she'd received anyway. She hadn't seen a neurologist in nearly a month.

She had made some progress with the short-term memory issues but none with the amnesia itself. She could have indeed met this Brandon, but she knew so few details of her life that anything was possible.

For all practical purposes, Willa's life had begun two months ago when her short-term memory had started to stabilize.

She knew the basics. She was Willa Diane Marks, a computer software designer from San Antonio. Both parents were dead. No living relatives. She wasn't rich, but she'd had more than enough money to decide at the age of thirty-three that she wanted to reduce her hours at the business she'd started and have a child. Since she hadn't been involved in a relationship at the time, she'd used artificial insemination, which had been done at the very hospital where, three months later, she'd been held hostage.

Willa could thank a nurse at the San Antonio Maternity Hospital for filling her in on those few details. And just so she would remember them, Willa had put them in notes in a computer file. Notes she read daily in case she forgot. Heck, there was even a note to remind herself to read the file.

"Well?" Lieutenant Duggan prompted. "Are you going to let us in? Because I have a warrant and I can break down the door if necessary. I don't want to do that, and I don't think you do either. Am I right?"

She dodged the questions. "Brandon, how do you know me?" Willa countered.

More hesitation. More whispered conversation between the men. Finally, Brandon angled his eyes to the window. Right where she was. As if he'd known all along that she was there.

Brandon's gaze met hers. "Willa, I'm your ex-boyfriend."

Whatever she had expected him to say, that wasn't it.

Her heart went to her knees.

The baby stopped kicking and went still. So did Willa. Her breath lodged somewhere between her lungs and her throat, and she forced herself to exhale so she wouldn't get light-headed. She had enough things against her already without adding that.

"My ex-boyfriend?" she challenged. She had been involved with this man, but there was no photo of him in her PDA? No yellow sticky note with his name on her wall? And he darn sure wasn't in her memory. "Prove it."

"Open the door, and I will." It wasn't exactly a promise, but it was close.

Close enough for Willa to put her PDA aside and grab the .38 handgun she kept on top of the foyer table. Before she could change her mind, she undid the locks, paused the security system and opened the front door. There was still a locked screen door between the men and her, but even through the gray mesh, she could see their faces clearly.

Brandon's eyes were a dark earthy brown.

And much to Willa's surprise, she reacted to him. Or rather her body did. There was deep pull within her.

Attraction, she realized.

She was physically attracted to him. Strange, because it was a new sensation for her. She was certain at one time or another she had been attracted to a man, but she didn't remember this feeling.

"What proof do you have?" Willa immediately asked.

Those rich brown eyes combed over her face, but she couldn't tell what was going through his mind. His gaze dropped to her stomach. Since she was seven months pregnant and huge, it would have been hard not to miss her baby bulge. Then, his attention landed on the .38 Smith & Wesson she had gripped in her hand at her side.

"There's no need for that," Brandon said, his voice

mostly calm. There was still that edge to it. "Neither of us will hurt you."

"Forgive me if I don't believe you," she fired back.

"You have reason not to trust us," Lieutenant Duggan volunteered. "We didn't do a good job of protecting you while you were in the hospital recovering from your head injury."

She nearly laughed. "No. You didn't. A gunman got into my room just two days after the hostages were rescued, and he tried to shoot and kill me."

Willa didn't exactly have memories of that incident, either. Thank God. The memory loss was good for some things, and she didn't need that particular nightmare in her head. But she'd read the reports, over and over, and every time she would forget, she would reread them. She needed to remember that the cops hadn't protected her then. Or now.

The lieutenant nodded. "That gunman was caught. His name was Danny Monroe, and later that same morning when he tried to kill a police captain and another hostage, he was shot. He died in surgery. You don't have to worry about him now."

"Maybe not him. But that wasn't the only attempt made on my life," Willa reminded the lieutenant. "Someone tried to break into the safe house where you had me staying after I got out of the hospital."

"You remember that?" Duggan asked.

"No," Willa reluctantly admitted. "But I haven't had any short-term memory problems for the last two months. I remember everything that's happened during that time, and I remember all the notes I've read about the incident."

And that was the truth. *Almost.*

"We're not sure who tried to get into the safe house," the lieutenant admitted, "but it's still under investigation."

"Well, the investigation can continue without my help." She looked at Brandon who was staring at her. "You said you have proof that you're my ex-boyfriend?"

He nodded and shifted his head against the wind when another cold gust slammed into them. "Can we come in, and I'll show you?"

"You can show me what you have from out there. And you'd better have more than a going-steady ring or a picture from our high school prom."

Even though there was something that made her want to trust, and *believe,* the man. Willa groaned. Hadn't the last four months taught her anything?

Brandon mumbled something she didn't catch, and he reached into his pocket, prompting her to bring up her gun. Lieutenant Duggan's hand went to the butt of his own weapon that was tucked in a shoulder holster inside his jacket.

Brandon held up his hands in a calm-down gesture. "I'm not going for a gun."

But he had one. Willa saw it then. It was in a cowboy-style waist holster that rested low on his hips.

She also spotted the badge clipped to his holster, and she backed up a step.

"You're a cop?" she accused.

Brandon nodded. "Not SAPD though. I'm the sheriff of a small town, Crockett Creek. It's about a half hour from San Antonio."

He was still a lawman. The very people her notes warned her not to trust.

"You didn't remember that Brandon Ruiz is a sheriff?" Lieutenant Duggan asked.

"No," she snapped. "And I think there's a reason for that. You're trying to trick me. You figured if you could convince me that this man, this stranger, is my ex-boyfriend that I would let you in so you could talk me into doing whatever it is that brought you here."

Duggan and Brandon exchanged glances, and it was Brandon who continued. "It's true. We do have things to tell you. Things that could affect your safety—and the baby's." He paused, his gaze heading back in that direction again.

He swallowed hard. And looked away.

So, he couldn't even look her in the eye. Or the belly. He was lying.

"Get off my porch," Willa demanded. "And stay away from me."

"I can't," Brandon said. "I have the proof you want." He took a piece of paper from his pocket.

Willa already had her hand on the door, ready to slam it shut, but that stopped her. "What is that?"

"It's a medical report." Brandon took his time continuing that explanation. "You had an amniocentesis done after the hostage incident."

She had. There were notes about it on her computer. The doctors had been concerned that her injury might have affected the baby, so she'd had the test done to examine the amniotic fluid to make sure all was well.

"What does that have to do with anything?" Willa asked.

Brandon's mouth tightened a little. "We, uh, were able to compare the baby's DNA we got from the amniocentesis results that were on file at the hospital."

Now it was Willa who held up her hand. "Wait just a darn minute. Why were you comparing DNA? I had artificial insemination, and I used an anonymous donor."

"No," Lieutenant Duggan disagreed.

And that one-word denial was all he said for several heart-stopping moments.

"We had the nurse tell you that," the lieutenant explained, "because you were so upset—you were hysterical. The doctors couldn't sedate you because you were in the first trimester of your pregnancy, and they thought you might lose the baby if we couldn't calm you down."

"So, they lied," Brandon added.

Willa moved her hand to her heart to try to steady it. "Lied about what exactly?"

Brandon's gaze came to hers. "There was no artificial insemination, Willa. And that baby you're carrying is *mine*."

Chapter Two

Brandon waited for Willa Marks to grasp what he'd just told her.

It didn't take long. Within seconds, her eyes widened. She went pale, and she inched back farther away from the screen door, no doubt to put some distance between her and them.

She stood there, looking scared, lost and vulnerable in her maternity jeans and dove-gray sweater that seemed to swallow her. She was petite, barely five-three. Hardly big enough to be fighting off bad guys, but she'd had to do too much of that in the past four months.

From the corner of his eye, Brandon saw the lieutenant make another sweeping glance around the yard and street. Brandon did the same. Because it might not be safe for Willa or for them to be standing out here in the open like this.

"You're my baby's father?" Willa questioned. Despite her obvious surprise, there was still a Texas-size dose of suspicion in her expression and her tone.

Her memory might not be in full working gear, but her instincts sure were.

She had a reason to be suspicious.

But Brandon didn't want her suspicions to get her and the baby killed.

"We need to come in," Brandon insisted, and he tried not to make it sound like a question.

He immediately saw the debate in her wide blue eyes. She volleyed glances between Bo Duggan and him before she mumbled something under her breath. She went to the screen door, unlocked it and then stepped back.

She held on to the gun, and Brandon hoped like the devil that he didn't have to wrestle it away from her.

Brandon walked in first, and Bo was right behind him. Bo closed the door, and Brandon immediately felt the warmth from the central heating. But not from their guest.

Willa was glaring at them.

He glanced around. Old habits. He'd been a peace officer for eight years. That was eight years too long to let down his guard. Willa had given no indication that someone was inside holding her hostage, but he needed to make sure that wasn't the case.

The place was small so he didn't have to look too far to take it all in. They were in a living-dining combination area, and there was a modest kitchen through the double doorway near the dining table. In the center of the table was a potted plant that had been decorated with tiny foil Christmas ornaments. No wrapped gifts, and judging from Willa's situation, there probably wouldn't be any.

On the other side of the house, he could see directly into the two bedrooms and the bathroom, with all the doors wide open. Apparently, Willa was trying to minimize the chance that anyone could sneak in through one of the windows without her hearing them.

The place was neat as a pin except for the yellow sticky notes all over the walls and surfaces of the furniture. He spotted one on the hardwood floor and reached down to pick it up.

"Don't trust the cops," he read and passed it to Bo.

Bo glanced at it as well and then looked at her. "I thought you weren't having any more short-term memory loss."

"I'm not. The notes are leftovers from a time when I was having problems. I just haven't gotten around to removing them." Her chin came up, causing her long blondish-brown ponytail to swish. It brushed against her shoulder and settled on the top of her left breast.

Brandon quickly got his attention off that.

Should he go to her, he wondered? Should he try to hug or kiss her? That was something Bo and he hadn't discussed on the ride over, but Brandon wished they had. He knew what he had to say to Willa, what he had to do about her safety situation, but he hadn't given much thought to the personal aspect of this.

Willa held out her hand. "Let me see that DNA report," she insisted.

Brandon walked closer, halving the distance between them and gave it to her.

He watched her read through the report, and with each line her gaze skirted across, her forehead bunched up even more.

"It could be a lie," she concluded, handing it back to him.

"Why would we lie about that?" Bo questioned.

Willa opened her mouth. Then, closed it. She shook her head. "I don't know, but you just admitted you lied four months ago when you had a nurse tell me I was artificially inseminated."

"We did that only because we didn't want you to lose the baby. It worked," Bo insisted. "You settled down, quit asking for Brandon, and you started to heal."

"I asked for him?" She immediately wanted to know.

Brandon let Bo answer. "You did. You wanted to see him because he's your baby's father."

Her accusing gaze came back to Brandon. "Then why weren't you there at the hospital that day, when I was scheduled for my first ultrasound along with some other lab tests?"

"I didn't know about it," Brandon answered.

"SAPD thinks the ultrasound and lab tests were a ploy to get to you the hospital that afternoon because the appointment wasn't on the schedule," Bo explained. "We believe the gunmen called you with the bogus appointments because they'd researched the records of several of the pregnant women, and they knew you were a whiz with computers. They thought you could help them access some files."

"I know all of that," she snapped. "It's in my notes." She pointed to Brandon. "That doesn't explain why you weren't there."

Brandon lifted his shoulder, trying to shrug. "We'd had an argument about a month earlier, and you told me to get out, that it was over between us. I was out of the state at the time, and I didn't know you'd been taken hostage until two days after it ended. By then, you were in protective custody at a secret location."

"He asked for your location," Bo continued. "But there had already been an attempt on your life, and we thought it best if no one knew where you were."

And then there had been another breach of security. Another intruder. That had caused Willa to go on the run, leaving the safe house and not telling anyone where she was. It'd taken SAPD all this time to find her.

Without moving her gaze from Brandon's, she walked closer, her steps slow and deliberate. Until she was very close. So close he could take in her scent. There was some kind of floral fragrance in her hair. Roses, maybe.

She reached out and caught onto his arm. Brandon wasn't sure what she had in mind, but he didn't think she was about to launch herself against him for a welcome-home kiss.

No. Her suspicions were getting stronger.

She took his hand and placed it on her stomach. On the baby.

Brandon pulled in his breath before he could stop himself, but he did manage to hold his ground and not move away. He also kept eye contact with her, which was probably stupid.

Willa didn't say a word. She just stared at him.

The moments crawled by and because Brandon didn't know what the hell else to do he just stood there.

"Let me guess," Willa said, her words as slow and deliberate as her steps had been. "We argued about the baby. That's why we broke up. Because you weren't ready to be a father."

Brandon settled for a nod.

"What was I to you—your one-night stand?" she asked. No more of that slow and deliberate tone. She was riled now.

"No," he answered truthfully. "Willa, you weren't a one-night stand."

She studied his eyes. Then she studied him. Her gaze eased down the length of his body. Back up. And then she groaned, turned and sank down on the sofa. She put the gun on the coffee table, something that probably pleased Bo as much as it did him.

They'd made it past step one.

But they had a hell of a long way to go.

"I'll give you two some time alone," Bo said, hitching his thumb to the door. "I'll be in the car. But just don't take too long."

And Brandon knew why. This was not going to be a lengthy romantic welcome-home chat. They were in a hurry.

Bo opened the door, and the wind cut through the room again. The notes on the walls stirred, and two of them went flying through the air. One of them landed near Brandon's boots.

"Take prenatal vitamins," he read aloud and handed her the note. He eased down into the chair across from her. "Just how bad is your memory?"

"Just how much didn't you want this baby?" Willa countered.

So, her memory wasn't up for discussion. He wished she'd taken the baby talk off the table as well.

Brandon knew they had to discuss it, eventually. That was all part of the plan, but he hadn't counted on having the emotional reaction of touching Willa. And he sure as hell hadn't counted on this gut need to protect her. He'd planned on doing what SAPD wanted and then walking away.

Especially walking away.

He was good at that.

But he'd been in the room with Willa for less than fifteen minutes, and he was already having doubts about this plan. She deserved the truth.

The *whole* truth about why he was there.

"Tell me who you are," she insisted. "Not just your name. I want to know who you really are."

Brandon nodded and gathered his thoughts. "My full name is Brandon Michael Ruiz. Like you, I was born in San Antonio. I'm thirty-six. Never been married. I spent some time in the army before I came back to Texas and made it my home again."

She motioned for him to continue.

"I've been sheriff of Crockett Creek for eight years."

"And your bloodline?"

"My dad was—is," he corrected, "Comanche. My mother was part Irish, part Italian, part German. Guess that makes me a real American, huh?"

Willa ignored his attempt to lighten up the conversation. "How did we meet?"

Thankfully, he didn't have to pause to collect his thoughts. "At a restaurant on the Riverwalk in San Antonio. The place was crowded, and we shared a table."

She stared at him again. "I think you're probably lying about that. I don't know why." She waved him off before he could try to convince her otherwise. "It doesn't matter. It's obvious you don't want to be here so that means the lieutenant brought you to convince me to do something."

Well, he hadn't expected her to give him that kind of opening.

"But first, you're supposed to regain my trust," she continued. "And SAPD's theory is the reason I'll trust you again is that we have a child in common." She moved closer to the edge of the sofa. "But you and I both know how things really are, don't we, Brandon?"

Yeah, he thought, maybe they did, so Brandon stuck with the truth. "I gave up the idea of being a father not long after I got out of the military. Let's just say I didn't think my gene pool was worth passing along to an innocent baby."

She made a sound to indicate she was thinking about that. And he could see the doubt creep back into her eyes. "That probably has something to do with the *was* versus the *is* when you described your father's bloodline, but I don't believe you want to share that secret with me so I won't push."

Surprised, Brandon angled his head to the side and studied her. "Have you been taking deception-training classes since you've been in hiding?"

The corner of her mouth lifted, but the smile didn't make it to her eyes. "When I couldn't remember anything for more than ten minutes, I started relying on other things. Eye contact. Facial signals. My gut instincts," she added in a mumble.

Brandon tried his hand at it. "The way you said the last part—*my gut instincts*—does that mean you don't like what your gut instincts are telling you about me?"

Her glare returned. "Stand up," she said abruptly.

"Excuse me?"

"Stand up. *Please*." That last word was clearly an afterthought.

Brandon did stand, all the while wondering where this would lead. And Willa stood up as well. She went to him, hesitating just a second, before she reached up and caught on to the back of his neck. She pulled him down and touched her mouth to his.

It was a peck, hardly qualifying as a kiss, but it lit a very bad fire inside him that shouldn't be lit. A fire below the belt.

She pulled back and drew her tongue over her bottom lip. Yet something to stoke that blaze that he had to put out.

"Yes," she said, "I think I remember kissing you." Willa shook her head, stared up at him.

Brandon decided to do something to convince her to reconsider that *I think* part. His hand went to her back, and he hauled her to him.

And he kissed her.

Yeah, it was probably stupid, but he didn't keep it a peck or at some wimp level to be merely a test. No. He wanted this to be a kiss she'd remember. So, he pressed his lips against hers, moving over her mouth. Taking in her taste, along with that incredible scent. He got an even better sample of her when his tongue touched hers.

She jerked away from him and stepped back. Way back. Her breath was gusting now. Brandon realized his was, too. And she propped her hands on her hips and stared at him.

"I'm attracted to you," she said in the same tone as if confessing to premeditated murder.

The woman certainly knew how to keep him on his toes. "I'm attracted to you," he echoed.

Her stare turned to another glare. "I hate that I just told you that because it gives you leverage over me. But don't be fooled." Willa walked to the foyer table and grabbed her PDA. "I will never put anything I feel for you over the safety of my baby. That means I'm not going to let you talk me into doing anything I could regret."

Oh, man. Since they kept going back to that, Brandon figured it was time to move on to step two.

At least step two didn't involve kissing her.

"The baby is my priority, too," he clarified. "Yeah, I know. I said I'd dismissed fatherhood, but now that I know a baby's on the way—"

"It's a girl," Willa interrupted. "I'm having a daughter."

It took everything inside him not to react. He nodded. "A daughter," he repeated.

Brandon eased that information aside and got back to work.

Yes, he still wanted to protect Willa. He was sorry for what she'd been through. But the groundwork had been laid. She'd bought the story, and it was time to move on. However, before he could do that, Willa lifted the PDA and a second later, there was a small burst of light.

She took his picture.

She typed in something. Paused. And added something else. Notes about him no doubt.

Don't Trust Brandon Ruiz maybe.

Well, she would have to learn to trust him. At least temporarily.

"You're going to have to leave this place and come with me," he told her. Willa started to object, but Brandon talked right over her. "You don't have a choice. The baby's safety is at stake, and I won't let you endanger my child."

There. That was the gauntlet.

"*Your* child?" she said, mocking him.

"Oh, no, we're not going back to that part about my ambivalence toward fatherhood. We'll do what's best for this baby. And what's best is for you not to be here."

Willa didn't say a word, not even to demand more information. She was no doubt trying to figure out how she could escape. That attempt would probably come when she tried to excuse herself to go to the bathroom. Or to get something from the kitchen.

But that wasn't going to happen.

"We've received an intelligence report that there's going to be another hostage situation," Brandon stated as clearly as he could.

Her bottom lip started to tremble. "Where?" Her voice was all breath.

"We don't know that. Or when. Or who will be involved. All we have is that it'll take place at an undisclosed hospital and that the person responsible has hired two computer techs to break into some files."

She caught her bottom lip between her teeth to stop

the trembling. From what he'd been told, Willa didn't have any actual memories of the hostage situation she'd endured, but she had read reports. Heck, she'd probably memorized them and knew she didn't want any other person to go through what she had.

"You could put guards at all the hospitals," Willa suggested.

He shook his head. "Too many of them. We can put them on alert, of course, and warn them of the potential danger, but we're not even sure this attack will happen at a hospital in the state. It could happen anywhere."

She waited a moment. Mumbled something. "How can I help?" she finally asked.

Brandon took a deep breath. Even though he still had to be mindful of her attempted escape, step two had been a success. Now, it was time for the grand finale.

Well, part of it anyway.

The last step wouldn't happen until SAPD was sure this new hostage threat had been squelched.

"We think someone masterminded the situation with the maternity hostages," he continued.

"But you caught the two gunmen and the man who hired them. I read about it."

"Yes, his name was Gavin Cunningham, and last week he committed suicide in prison. In his suicide note he indicated he hadn't worked alone, that someone had helped him set up the entire maternity hostage situation."

The breath rushed from her mouth. "Who helped him?"

"We're not sure. That's where we're hoping you can fill us in."

"I get it," she said almost immediately. "You want me to resume my therapy so I can remember if the gunman who held me said anything about the identity of his boss."

"Yeah."

Among other things.

"But I might not remember," she pointed out. "Or maybe the gunman didn't say anything to me at all. I could be putting myself out there for no reason."

"You wouldn't be just putting yourself out there, Willa." Brandon tried to keep his voice level and calm. "I'd be with you. You'd be in my protective custody."

She rolled her eyes. "Let me guess—that wasn't your idea. It was Lieutenant Duggan's."

Brandon evaded that. "Bo Duggan lost his wife during that hostage situation. She died after giving birth to their twins. He's, well, eager to solve this case once and for all."

She stayed quiet a moment. Then, she said, "No."

"No?" Brandon challenged. Well, there went his calm and level voice.

"No," she insisted. "I won't go with you into protective custody. And I won't work directly with Lieutenant Duggan, SAPD or even you."

She pointed to her laptop. Don't Trust the Cops was scrolling across the screen in bold white letters on black background.

She had a reason not to trust cops, or anyone else for that matter. But he had to get her past that because she had no choice. Willa had to trust him.

Even if he didn't deserve that trust.

"I'll restart my therapy on my own," she continued.

"I can't take any memory-activating drugs because they might harm the baby, but maybe hypnosis will work if I try it again. I can do the hypnosis sessions here."

Brandon shook his head. "No, you can't."

That got her back on her feet. "Now, just a darn minute. You might be my baby's biological father and my former boyfriend, but that doesn't give you any say in my life."

He got to his feet as well. "This badge does."

She pulled back her shoulders and looked as if he slapped her. "You're pulling rank on me?"

"I don't have a choice, Willa." He'd practiced this on the drive over, but he didn't think practice would make it sound any better than it had when he'd first said it. "We didn't just get intel about another hostage situation. We learned from a deep-cover agent that an assassin has been hired."

Her shoulders went back even further. "An assassin?"

He nodded and relied on the words he'd rehearsed. "An assassin hired to come after you."

Oh, man. She didn't just pale, every drop of color drained from her face. Willa slipped her PDA into the pocket of her sweater, sank back onto the sofa and buried her face in her hands.

Brandon went in for the kill. He had to tell her the final part of this covert briefing. The detail that would put her back in police custody.

And maybe right back in danger.

"That's how we knew where to find you," Brandon said, hating the sound of his own voice and the words coming out of his mouth.

Words that were unfortunately true.

"We got your address from the intelligence report that the Justice Department agent had intercepted from the assassin." Brandon checked his watch, though he already knew time was running out. "If the intel is right, and we think it is, he plans to kill you tonight."

Chapter Three

Willa was glad she was sitting down.

She didn't speak—she couldn't—and she didn't look at Brandon. Instead, she forced herself to focus on what he'd just told her.

An assassin would come tonight to kill her.

Maybe.

The warning on her screen saver flashed in her head, and it was the reminder she needed to put this in perspective.

"Is it true?" she asked, with her eyes still turned away from Brandon. She wanted to listen for the inflection in his voice.

"It's true, an assassin plans to kill you. We think because his boss doesn't want to risk your memory recovering so you can tell the authorities his identity. But I'm going to protect you," Brandon quickly added. "Because you'll gather your things and come with me. I've already arranged a place for you."

Her emotions were like a whirlwind inside her, but she thought he might be telling the truth about the assassin. There was some kind of danger anyway. Brandon definitely wasn't lying about that.

Willa wasn't naive enough to believe she'd be able to keep out a professional killer. All the security precautions she had already taken wouldn't be enough, and the last thing she wanted was to go gun to gun with an assassin. The three-hour handgun course was her only training with a firearm, and she was betting the man coming after her would know how to kill with one shot.

She nodded, stood and rubbed her hands on the sides of her jeans. "Give me a minute, please. I need some time to gather my thoughts."

And her things.

She had an emergency bag already packed and stashed beneath her bed, and she'd practiced climbing out the window. She could cut through the backyard and walk to the train station, which was only four blocks away. That's one of the reasons she'd chosen this particular house to rent.

Willa headed for her bedroom, but she didn't get far. Brandon was right behind her. She whirled around, not realizing he was so close, and she knocked right into him. The contact was a reminder of that kiss, and the fact that he was going to be a hard man to shake.

"I can't let you escape," he told her.

"Who said I'm trying to escape?" Willa tossed right back.

He gave her a flat look to indicate he knew what she had in mind. Probably did, too. He was a cop, after all.

"Lieutenant Duggan is watching the back of the house, so you wouldn't get far anyway," Brandon added. "Now, get your things so we can leave."

Willa considered arguing with him, but he looked as stubborn as she was. Not a good DNA legacy to pass on to their daughter. A double dose of bullheadedness.

If he was the baby's father, that is.

She wasn't convinced he'd told her the truth about that, either.

"I'll get my things," she agreed. But that was the only thing she was agreeing to do. She wasn't going with them, and that meant she had to distract Brandon in some way so she could escape.

"What did you type about me on your PDA?" he asked, following her into the bedroom. There was barely enough space for one person, and she was quickly learning that Brandon had a way of monopolizing not just the room but all the air in it.

"Nothing," she lied. And she grabbed the packed overnight bag, put it on the bed and tossed in the PDA. The bag already contained a change of clothes, toiletries, meds, cash, a fake ID that had cost her dearly and a flash drive with duplicate files that were on her computer.

She also had a gun in there.

Willa didn't want to use it, but she would if it came down to protecting her baby.

Because she wanted to buy some time for that escape opportunity, Willa went through the dresser drawer and pretended to look for something to add to the bag. Maybe conversation would help, too. Besides, there was one thing she needed to verify, even though she wasn't sure a chat with Brandon would give her that proof.

"Are you really my baby's father?" she asked.

But he didn't answer. He walked across the room

and looked into the drawer to see what she was doing. He likely thought she had a gun and was maybe about to pull it on him. No gun. However, he took the tiny canister of pepper spray from the top of the dresser and cupped it in his hand.

Willa gave him a cynical smile. "You trust me about as much as I trust you. So answer my question. Are you really my baby's father?"

He looked her straight in the eyes.

And nodded.

"The DNA test is real," he said. "The child you're carrying is mine."

Everything inside her went still. Because that didn't sound like a lie.

"We were in love?" she pressed.

"No," he answered just as quickly.

That seemed to be the truth as well. Strange that he wouldn't have said yes and then used that love confession to convince her to cooperate with him.

"All right." For show, she took out several pairs of panties and shoved them into the bag. "So, we weren't in love, and I wasn't your one-night stand. What was I to you?"

"The same thing you are to me now." He didn't wait for her to respond to that puzzling answer. "Finish packing."

She added a bra to the bag and stuffed in a flannel nightgown. Willa lifted the bag and put the strap over her like a messenger's bag even though it was a tight fit over her belly. "I have to get some things from the bathroom. Prenatal vitamins," she added, knowing he wouldn't refuse to let her get those.

The bathroom window was small, but she knew she could squeeze through it. She'd have to hurry and hope that Lieutenant Duggan wasn't keeping watch on that particular side of the house. All she needed was two minutes, and she could be out of there. Away from the assassin, and away from the cops—including, perhaps, her baby's father.

And that gave her an idea.

With Brandon right on her heels, she went into the bathroom and took out a cotton swab from the medicine cabinet. It obviously wasn't sterile, but she thought it would give her a clean enough sample. After all, labs got DNA from toothbrushes and baby bottles. Once she had his DNA extracted, she could have it compared to the baby's amniotic fluid. Willa didn't have the fluid itself, but she had her baby's DNA profile in an online storage file that she could retrieve from any computer.

Of course, a comparison would take days. Maybe longer. Still, she would eventually know one way or another.

Her gut was already telling her the test was unnecessary, that Brandon was indeed her baby's father. But her brain wanted to know why her gut trusted this man when it was clear that he wasn't volunteering the whole truth.

"Open your mouth please." She added the *please* hoping it would get him to cooperate.

He did. Brandon swabbed the inside of his left cheek and handed it back to her. "It'll be a match," he promised.

"We'll see."

He glanced at the swab. "You'll want to put that in a plastic bag." And he pulled a small evidence baggie from his jacket pocket.

Willa eyed him and the bag with suspicion, and instead of using his bag that might be contaminated with his DNA or something else, she headed to the kitchen and got a plastic sandwich bag. She sealed up the swab, put it in the overnight case and snapped her fingers.

"Prenatal vitamins," she said as if remembering them. "I wouldn't want to forget those."

She took slow steps, trying to get the timing of this just right. She needed to get to the bathroom just ahead of Brandon so she could slam the door. Lock it.

And escape.

"I also have to use the bathroom," she lied when she was a few steps away. "As in, actually *use* the bathroom. I don't want an audience for that."

She went inside and pushed the door so it would close.

Brandon caught it.

"I don't want an audience," she restated.

"And I don't want you trying to escape. Don't worry. I'll close my eyes. But this door is staying partly open."

Great. Just great. She hadn't wanted to do this, but she was obviously going to have to give him a hit of the pepper spray. She reached into her bag to retrieve it, but he caught her wrist.

Then he grabbed the bag.

"I'll hold this for you. It can't be good for a pregnant woman to carry around this much weight."

"It's not that heavy." Willa glared at him and kept a firm hold on her bag. "Why don't you just back off?"

"Because I can't. Forget about the personal connection we have because of the baby, forget about how you feel or don't feel about me. Just remember, I'm a lawman, and I'm not going to stand by and let that assassin come after you."

She had to tamp down her anger so she could try to reason with him. "The last two times I trusted a lawman, I was nearly killed. You know that. You've read the reports. I've done a lot better on my own."

"But you've never come up against a hired gun like Martin Shore. He's not someone you can get away from without help."

For some reason having the name attached to the assassin made her heart pound even harder. "Martin Shore," she repeated. "How did he even find me?"

"Apparently Shore's boss has been trying to track you through neurologists all over the state. Nearly a dozen doctors have had their files hacked. Including Dr. Betterman, the OB you saw four weeks ago."

She shook her head. "But I didn't use my real name, and I paid him in cash."

"You did, but in your hacked medical record, Dr. Betterman had written your diagnosis of post-traumatic amnesia and post-concussional neurosis resulting in short-term memory loss. He also listed your age, the date of the onset of the symptoms. And that you were in your third trimester of pregnancy and therefore couldn't receive traditional medications."

Oh, God.

There wouldn't have been many patients who fit into all those categories.

Then, Willa remembered something. "I didn't give the doctor my street address. He said he needed to mail me the results from my latest EEG, so I gave him the address of the rental box at a private mail facility all the way across town."

Brandon nodded. "The clerk there was murdered about four hours ago. We're pretty sure after he was tortured before he gave up your physical address to someone who wanted to find you. Because it was about an hour later when a deep-cover agent intercepted the intel about Shore being hired to kill you."

Willa choked back another *Oh, God,* and the tears that threatened to follow. She wouldn't cry. It would only waste time because she knew what she had to do.

"Just let me go," she begged Brandon. "If this is really your child as you say, then please help me get away."

"It *is* my child. And I can't let you leave."

"Swear it," she said, sounding as desperate as she felt. "Swear on my life that the baby is yours."

Brandon put his fingers beneath her chin and lifted it to make direct eye contact. "I swear on your life. On mine. On our baby's life. The child you're carrying is mine."

He sounded so sincere. Looked it, too. Still, there was something, something she couldn't quite put her finger on.

"If you're lying to me—"

But Willa didn't get a chance to finish that threat.
There was no warning. No time to get down.

A bullet slammed through the bathroom window.

Chapter Four

Brandon latched on to Willa and pushed her out of the bathroom.

It wasn't a second too soon because there was another shot ripping through what was left of the glass in the small window. He drew his gun and maneuvered her into the living room and then to the kitchen. He wanted her as far away from those shots as he could manage.

Hell.

He hadn't expected the attack to come this soon. He'd hoped to have Willa tucked safely away before Martin Shore tried to kill her. Brandon obviously hadn't succeeded, and Willa might pay the price for his miscalculation.

Brandon used his phone to call for backup from the Austin P.D. He couldn't risk trying to ring Bo because his temporary partner might be trying to conceal his location from the shooter.

Willa grabbed a knife and a can of pepper spray from the counter and covered her pregnant belly with her hand. Neither her hand nor the items would provide the baby with much protection, so Brandon threw open the fridge and positioned her behind the door. That would give her an extra layer. He considered pulling out the fridge and placing her in the space behind it, but if Shore moved to that side of the house, the bullets might make it through the wall.

"You weren't lying," Willa mumbled.

Not about Shore, he wasn't. But he had told her lies all right. Later, much later, he needed to fill her in on the whole truth.

There was another shot, not through the bathroom. There was the sound of more glass shattering, and it seemed to be coming from Willa's bedroom.

Brandon waited. Listening.

Where the hell was Bo? And better yet, where had the lieutenant been when that first shot had been fired? Brandon hoped Shore hadn't managed to injure Bo or worse.

Another sound, not a bullet this time, sent Brandon's heart to his knees. Because this one had come from inside. From Willa's bedroom. It was the sound of footsteps.

The assassin was in her house.

Brandon glanced at Willa. Her eyes were wide, and her breath was gusting. She'd obviously heard the footsteps, too, and she knew the danger was bearing down on them.

He couldn't wait for word from Bo or for backup to arrive. Once Shore made it to the tiny kitchen, he would see them immediately. They would be sitting ducks, and that meant Brandon had to act fast to keep Willa alive.

"This way," he mouthed.

Brandon kept his gun ready and aimed at the opening

that led from the dining room and into the kitchen. No doubt that was where Shore was headed. He maneuvered Willa behind him so he could shield her with his body, and he started to back them out of the room. It wasn't the best of plans because Shore could double back or even have an accomplice who could come from the other direction, but Brandon had no choice.

He had to get Willa out of there.

Each step seemed to take minutes, but he led them across the kitchen and toward the tiny mudroom and the back door. He wasn't sure what was on the other side of that door, but hopefully it was a yard with some kind of cover. He needed to get Willa behind a tree or something to shelter her from the bullets that would come at them when Shore realized they were no longer inside.

They made it to the opening of the mudroom where they heard a plinking noise as if something metal had been dropped.

Brandon glanced back into the dining room and soon noticed something he didn't want to see: the small, dark green oval object on the floor.

A grenade.

"Run!" Brandon shouted.

Willa reacted fast, thank God. With the knife and pepper spray in her left hand, she pushed her messenger's bag out of the way, disengaged the locks and threw open the door. Brandon had one last look to make sure Shore wasn't about to gun them down from inside the house, and changed places with Willa, so he could be in front of her. Either position was a risk because it was possible the grenade was a decoy to get them to run. If so, they were about to run directly into a professional assassin.

They hurried out onto a small porch and down the steps that led into a yard. No trees, something that made Brandon curse. But there was a small storage shed. He grabbed Willa's arm and made a beeline for it.

There was no sign of Bo. No sign of backup, either, but then it'd only been a couple of minutes since he'd made the call requesting help. Bo had likely called, too.

Well, Bo would have if he wasn't lying dead somewhere.

Shore could have managed to take out Bo before he started the attack on the house.

Brandon hated to force Willa to run, but he had no choice. He prayed this exertion wouldn't hurt the baby. Of course, the stress couldn't be good for the child, either. But Brandon also pushed that aside. Right now, he had to keep Willa alive because it was the only way to save the child.

He positioned Willa to the side of the small wooden shed.

Just as the explosion ripped through the yard.

Brandon had considered that the grenade might be a dummy, but it obviously wasn't.

The debris from the blast came right at them.

Brandon tried to keep watch, to make certain Shore hadn't come into the yard for another attack, but it was hard to see anything. The left side of the house was literally a fireball, and bits of wood, the roof and even wads of fire were raining down on them.

His instincts and training were to protect his fellow

peace officer, but Brandon couldn't risk taking Willa closer to the house. There could be a secondary explosion, and he needed to put some distance between the burning building and her.

Thankfully, she still had the bag draped across her body, and she used it to shelter her face from the dangerous falling debris.

"Is there a gate on the back fence?" he asked her.

She nodded, tried to speak, but no sound came out. Willa was obviously terrified, and there was nothing he could do to assure her that he could protect her. Shore could have orchestrated this entire attack just to get them out in the open.

And the *open* was where they'd have to go to get to the gate.

Brandon checked the strips of grass and shrubs that made up the side yards. No one was there that he could see. No one was on the porch, either, and it was too much to hope that Shore had blown up with that grenade. No. The man was out there, somewhere, waiting.

"Let's go," he told Willa.

As he'd done in the kitchen, Brandon kept in front of her and backed her toward the gate. The debris continued to fall, and he could hear neighbors shouting for help. What he couldn't hear was Bo or the sound of sirens from backup. Until he had help, he had to do everything within his power to get Willa away from there.

Thick black smoke billowed out from the house, fanning out across the yard, and making it impossible for Brandon to see all the places where Shore could be hiding. He kept his gun aimed. Ready.

He saw the movement just at the edge of the smoke. It was a man. And it wasn't Bo. Brandon recognized him from intelligence photos.

It was Martin Shore.

The killer was there, coming for them.

Behind him, Willa fumbled with the gate to open it. She'd obviously put some kind of lock on it, and that lock was now a trap.

Brandon protected Willa as best he could, but he couldn't help with the locks. He kept his eyes and gun trained on Shore and was ready to push Willa to the ground if necessary. That wouldn't take her out of the line of fire, but it might shield her long enough until backup arrived. By now, all the neighbors and anyone for blocks around had probably called for help or come out of their residences to see what was going on.

And what was going on was that Shore was about to try to kill them again.

The man kept walking but lifted his gun, aiming it at them.

Willa cursed, but she must have finally gotten the locks to cooperate because she shoved open the gate. In the same motion Brandon pushed her through to the other side.

A bullet slammed into the fence.

The shot came so close to Brandon's head that he swore he could feel it.

He jumped out of the way, staying low and lunged out of the yard to join Willa on the other side. They made it to a sidewalk that was rimmed with a street and then another row of pristine suburban houses. They could try to duck into one of them, but that wouldn't stop Shore. He'd just fire into the place and possibly kill some innocent bystanders.

"We have to run," Brandon told her. He didn't wait for her to do that. He put his left hand on her shoulder to get her moving, away from the fence and away from her burning house.

Running might not even be possible for someone in the last trimester of pregnancy, but he had to get her to cover so he could try to make a stand against Shore.

Brandon headed up the sidewalk toward the cul de sac where a car was parked. That was their best bet.

Until he saw the kids.

There were three of them, all on skates, and probably no more than ten or eleven years old. If he went in that direction, so would Shore's bullets.

"Get down!" Brandon shouted to the boys. Hopefully they and anyone else in the area would do as he'd ordered.

"This way," Willa insisted, turning and leading him in the opposite direction.

She obviously realized the danger to the children, but she also had to know the danger of going past her house again. Shore had probably made it across the yard by now, and if he wasn't already at the gate, he soon would be.

Brandon adjusted his gun, and aimed, and they hurried past Willa's section of the fence. The smoke was thicker now, and the wind was carrying it right in their direction. Willa coughed, but she didn't stop.

He didn't want to think of the risk this might be

causing the baby. Brandon only wanted to get her out of there. Their best option was the intersection just ahead. Cars were trickling past, but if he could get Willa to that point, he could position her on the side of the last stretch of fence and perhaps get her out of Shore's line of sight.

Brandon heard the creak of the wooden gate and glanced over his shoulder just as it opened.

Shore came out, and he had his gun ready.

The assassin glanced around and spotted them. Brandon wanted to shoot him then and there, but he couldn't risk a stray shot hitting the children.

Shore obviously didn't feel the same. He reaimed, pointing the gun directly at Willa.

Brandon grabbed on to her waist and shoved her into the side of the fence.

A bullet flew past them.

God knew where it landed, and Brandon prayed it hadn't gone into one of the houses or a car.

"We can't stop," he told Willa, though he could hear her breathing hard.

They headed up the street toward a parked car, but then Brandon spotted the city bus. It was only about two blocks away and was lumbering in their direction. If he could get Willa on that bus before Shore saw them, they might be able to escape before the man could figure out where to aim more of those deadly shots.

Brandon kept Willa positioned behind him, and he hurried toward the bus. He also pushed back his jacket to reveal his badge.

"Get back inside!" he shouted to an elderly woman who opened her door.

Still hurrying toward the bus, Brandon flagged down the driver and hoped like the devil the man would stop. He didn't take his attention off the intersection where he knew Shore would soon appear.

The assassin wouldn't just give up.

The bus inched closer, and with Willa in tow, Brandon raced toward the vehicle. The seconds clicked off in Brandon's head. He wanted to make sure these seconds weren't their last ones.

The driver slowed even more as he approached them. Probably because he was concerned about the gun Brandon was holding.

"Open up!" Brandon told the middle-aged Hispanic driver. And he flashed his badge again.

The door swung open.

Just as Brandon caught a glimpse of Shore.

The assassin was at the intersection, barely a block away. Willa was still in Shore's kill zone.

Brandon pushed her onto the bus and was relieved that they were the sole passengers.

"I'm Sheriff Ruiz," he said identifying himself. "Drive!" Brandon ordered the man behind the wheel.

He dragged Willa to the bus's floor, praying that Shore hadn't seen him.

But he obviously had.

Because a bullet came crashing through the bus window.

Chapter Five

Willa covered her head with the bag when the glass spewed across the bus.

The nightmare wasn't over.

Shore was still after them, and if he managed to injure the driver, then the bus would almost certainly crash. The crash alone might not be fatal, but it would leave them wide open for another attack.

"Don't stop," Brandon warned the driver, "and stay low in the seat."

The driver was cursing and praying at the same time. Brandon was mumbling something as well, but Willa didn't think she had the breath to utter anything.

Her baby began to kick, hard, but Willa welcomed the movement. It meant her daughter was safe. *For now.* But they weren't out of danger.

The next bullet proved that.

It came through the back window, tearing the glass apart, and it exited through the front. Thankfully, it didn't come near them or the driver, and the driver slammed on the accelerator to get them out of there.

"Shore's on foot," Brandon reminded her. "He won't be able to come after us for long."

Willa held her breath, waiting and trying to brace herself for more bullets. But the shots didn't continue.

Brandon lifted his head and looked out the window. "He's gone," he let her know.

Willa still didn't move. She lay there and prayed the threat was truly over.

"Drive to the nearest police station," Brandon told the driver, and he took out his phone.

While Brandon punched in some numbers, he helped her from the floor and moved her onto one of the seats. He dropped down onto the seat directly across from her.

"Are you okay?" he asked.

Willa nodded, but she doubted he believed her. For one thing, she was still breathing so fast that she was close to hyperventilating, and she was trembling from head to toe. It might be part of Brandon's job to be on the business end of gunfire, but until the hostage situation at the maternity hospital, Willa had never known what it was like to face real danger.

Well, now she knew.

And it couldn't continue.

Somehow, she had to find a safe place for her and her baby. If there was such a thing as a safe place. This was the third attack in four months. Four attacks if she counted being taken hostage at the hospital. Part of her was furious that time after time someone or something had endangered her precious baby. She wanted answers. She wanted justice.

But another part of her only wanted to run and hide.

Willa looked back at the broken glass and damage

the bullets had done to the seats. She also looked out at the sidewalk that was zipping by. No sign of Shore, thank God. Maybe they had finally lost him.

She listened while Brandon gave an update to whomever he had called. He also asked about Lieutenant Bo Duggan, and then about Martin Shore. Brandon's forehead bunched up when he apparently got a response.

"We're on our way," Brandon said to the person on the other end of the line, and he snapped his phone shut.

"They got Martin Shore?" she immediately asked.

He shook his head. "But they're looking. Backup arrived, and there are officers fanning out all over the area."

The hopeful tone was tinged with doubt. And Willa knew why. From what Brandon had told her, Martin Shore was a professional killer, and he probably knew how to evade the police. He was no doubt on the run so he could regroup.

And come after her again.

"Bo Duggan was shot," Brandon added, his voice practically a whisper. He closed his eyes a moment but not before she saw the flash of anger mixed with pain. "He's on the way to the hospital."

"I'm sorry." Not that it would probably help, but Willa reached out and touched his arm.

That touch brought his eyes open, and he met her gaze. "So am I. Sorry for the lieutenant and sorry that I didn't get to you sooner so I could stop this attack."

Willa didn't intend to take the blame for this, but it certainly wasn't Brandon's fault, either. The problem was she didn't know where to place the blame.

"You were trying to talk me into leaving with you and Lieutenant Duggan," she reminded him. She groaned softly. "And I was trying to figure out a way to escape."

He glanced back at the street and shook his head. "I wish to hell you had gotten out there before Shore arrived."

So had she. But here they were. Seconds after nearly being killed. Willa wondered if she would ever have peace of mind again, or if she would have to stay on the run for the rest of her life. It was possible that she could never give her precious baby a normal life.

"The police station's just around the block," the driver told them.

Willa had to take a deep breath. A police station filled with people she didn't trust. But she couldn't very well jump off the bus. Shore could still be out there. And besides, she didn't even have a house to return to. Other than the meager items in the messenger bag, the only things she had were Brandon and her memory.

Both were somewhat suspect.

"Don't trust the cops," Brandon mumbled, repeating what he'd seen on her computer screen and notes.

"Yes. But as you can see, I had my reasons for that distrust."

"And you still do?" he asked.

It wasn't a simple question, and there seemed to be a Texas-size amount of emotion behind it.

"I think I can trust you," she admitted. "Because I believe you truly are my baby's father."

Other than his word and the DNA results that could be fake, she had no other reason to believe him. But she did. Willa only hoped that didn't turn out to be another mistake.

The driver took a left turn and she spotted the police station just ahead.

Brandon put his hands on her shoulders and forced eye contact. "Look, when we get inside, I have no idea where they'll take us or what SAPD will tell you when they arrive."

That seemed like some kind of warning and Willa stared at him. "What do you mean?"

He opened his mouth. Closed it. Opened it again. Then, shook his head. He pulled her closer to him and put his mouth right against her ear.

"Shore was hired to kill you," Brandon whispered. "That part is the truth. So is the part about another hospital hostage situation." He paused. "But almost everything else that Bo and I told you is a lie."

It took a moment for that to sink in, but when it did, it felt like a punch. She gasped, a sound of outrage, and she tried to pull back, but Brandon held her in place.

The driver hit his brakes and brought the bus to a stop directly in front of police headquarters. Officers poured out from the building and began to run toward them.

"What do you mean everything else was a lie?" Willa demanded.

Brandon looked her straight in the eyes. "I'm not your ex-boyfriend, Willa. Before today, I'd never laid eyes or anything else on you."

BRANDON DIDN'T HAVE TIME to soothe that look in Willa's eyes. It was a mixture of anger, confusion and hurt. He also didn't have time to try to justify the lies he'd already told her.

Besides, there was no justification for that.

After SAPD had come to him and explained what was going on with a possible new hostage incident, Brandon had agreed to help them, but the plan had felt wrong from the very beginning.

And look where it'd gotten Willa.

She'd nearly been killed today, and they weren't out of the woods yet. As long as Shore was alive, the threat would be there.

"What do you mean you lied to me?" Willa demanded.

Brandon heard her, barely. That's because several officers ran onto the bus, and the sounds of their voices and footsteps drowned her out. One was plainclothes, in his late thirties with sandy-brown hair, and the other was younger and in a uniform. Both had their weapons drawn.

"I'm Sheriff Brandon Ruiz," he said, showing his badge. He slipped his gun back into his holster. "Any word about Lieutenant Duggan?"

The older officer shook his head. "Nothing yet."

Hell. Bo had to be all right. Brandon barely knew the man, but on the drive from San Antonio, Bo had talked all about his four-month-old twins. He'd also talked about his late wife, who'd died shortly after the maternity hostage incident. If something happened to Bo, those babies would be orphans.

Willa latched on to his arm when Brandon stood. "What do you mean you li—"

Brandon stopped that question by pressing his mouth

to hers. The kiss was hard, rough and way out of line, but he didn't want her to say anything in front of the other officers. He wasn't sure how much SAPD wanted him to explain about Willa and what might end up being a second hostage situation.

"We'll talk later," Brandon whispered and hoped his tone was enough of a warning for Willa to stay quiet.

He wouldn't blame her if she refused to cooperate, but he prayed that she would.

"Are you hurt?" the uniform asked them.

Brandon took the overnight bag from Willa and pulled her to her feet so he could check her out. She was riled to the core and confused, but she didn't appear to be injured physically. That was something at least.

"Do you need to see a doctor?" Brandon asked, and he held his breath hoping that she wasn't having contractions or anything.

"No," she answered through clenched teeth. "I only need to talk to you." Her gaze drifted to the police building, and she swallowed hard.

Don't trust the cops was probably racing through her head right now.

"SAPD is sending up some officers," the older cop relayed to Brandon. "They're already on their way. You can wait inside headquarters until they arrive. Plus, we'll need to get your statements on the shooting and the explosion."

"Ms. Marks will need a safe house right away," Brandon informed them. "After what she's been through, she needs to rest."

"I can find a place on my own," Willa insisted right back.

He didn't argue with her, for now, but there was no way he could let her go off on her own. God knows how he would be able to convince her of that, though.

Brandon led her off the bus, and the officers hurried them to the far side of the building to the patrol entrance, probably because they were still concerned about Shore being at large.

"I'd like to go someplace private," Willa told the officer the moment they were inside. "Because Sheriff Ruiz and I need to talk. It's important, and it can't wait."

The officer volleyed glances between Brandon and her, and the man was no doubt wondering what this was all about. Brandon didn't intend to fill him in, at least not until he'd spoken with the officers from SAPD. Even if those officers had indeed already left their headquarters, they probably wouldn't arrive for at least another forty-five minutes.

"Follow me," the officer finally said. He took them through the maze of squad rooms and stopped outside a break room that had chairs, a sofa and some vending machines. "I hope this'll do," the officer commented. "And while you're talking I'll see about an update on Lieutenant Duggan."

Brandon thanked the man but didn't say anything else until he was out of earshot. Too bad there was no door so he could give them an extra layer of privacy.

They were going to need it.

"Why did you lie?" Willa demanded.

Since this probably wouldn't be a short or quiet conversation, Brandon placed her overnight bag on the floor and pulled her to the side of a vending machine.

"Because SAPD convinced me that the fastest way to stop another hostage incident was to get you to trust me."

Her eyes narrowed, but it didn't seem to be simply from anger. "And it worked. Well, partly. I *was* starting to trust you."

"You still can," he promised.

She looked at him as if he'd lost his mind. "You're a liar."

"About some things. It's true, I'd never met you before today." It was a risk because she might slap him, but Brandon placed his hand over her stomach. "But I really am your baby's father."

She blinked and then stared at him, examining his eyes. "You expect me to believe that?"

"It's the truth." And he blew out a long breath. It was actually a relief to tell her the truth. "Nearly ten years ago I was in the military and headed to a dangerous assignment in the Middle East. I was engaged at the time, and my then fiancée convinced me to store some semen in case I was injured. When I got back from the assignment, the engagement was over. And I knew I didn't need what I'd stored, so I signed a donor agreement, and it was sent to a sperm bank."

Willa continued to study him and was no doubt trying to decide if he was telling the truth.

"A sperm bank?" she questioned.

He nodded. "Obviously it was the one you used for your artificial insemination."

"Obviously." But there was still a lot of skepticism in her voice. "Why should I believe you?"

"Because it's true. The DNA test results I gave you

are real," he continued. "And it proves I'm the baby's biological father."

Brandon tried not to show what he was feeling. He didn't want Willa to mistake it for dishonesty. But that last word, *father,* had not come easily.

And probably never would.

He kept that to himself.

The staring went on, and on, and finally Willa's shoulders relaxed. A weary breath left her mouth, and she sagged against the wall.

Since she looked ready to drop, Brandon held on to her. Or rather he tried. But Willa pushed him away.

"My sperm donor," she mumbled. She shook her head. "How did SAPD find you?"

"Bo Duggan said they'd been looking at all the angles as to how to approach you, so they kept digging into your background. You aren't close to anyone in your family, so they widened the search. And finally got to your medical records. They traced the donor number for your insemination, and that led them to me."

"They knew you were a cop?" she asked.

"Not at first. But I think that ended up being a bonus for them." It had certainly given the police captain carte blanche to press him into cooperating. "SAPD knew you wouldn't welcome them with open arms, and they were desperate. They need your cooperation."

"They need me to remember," Willa corrected. "To remember what happened during the hostage situation so I can see if it relates to what might happen in another crisis. But I can't remember. I've tried and I can't."

He lifted his shoulder. "That's where I was supposed to come in. They want me to coax you into going through more therapy. You've already made so much progress. You said yourself that your short-term memory problems were over."

"I lied." She huffed and pushed her hair away from her face.

Brandon had to do a double take. "What?"

Willa dodged his gaze. "My memory's not nearly as bad as it was right after my injury, but sometimes I still forget. That's why I put your picture on my PDA." Her gaze snapped back to him and she scowled. "I typed in my PDA that I thought I could trust you. I need to change that."

"No. You don't."

Her scowl melted away, and tears sprang to her eyes. That's when Brandon noticed that she was still trembling. From the attack, no doubt.

Even though it was a risk on many levels, he pulled her to him. Willa fought him, struggling to break the embrace, but Brandon held on.

"That's my baby you're carrying," he reminded her. And in doing so, he reminded himself. "I'm not going to let you go through this alone."

Willa likely had no clue as to what it took for him to say that. She pulled back slightly and, even though she was still blinking away tears, she looked up at him. Her breath broke and she melted against him.

"Nothing bad can happen to this baby," she muttered through the sobs.

"It won't." Though it was a promise that would be hell to keep.

He touched his mouth to her forehead. Just a touch. But he felt the heat spear through him. Brandon definitely didn't want to feel that heat, but he couldn't deny it was there.

What the hell was wrong with him?

He wanted to believe the attraction existed because of the baby. Maybe some kind of primal DNA trigger so he'd feel compelled to protect the unborn child.

Brandon silently cursed.

This attraction didn't have anything to do with the baby. He was attracted to Willa. Plain and simple. And that attraction could cause some big-time problems for both of them.

Thankfully, his phone rang because Brandon was ready for both a distraction and news. After he glanced at his caller ID, he figured he would at least get the latter.

The call was from Sergeant Cash Newsome, a cop in SAPD and someone Brandon had known for years. They'd both been in the army together and had done a tour of duty in the Middle East. Since Cash was also Bo Duggan's right-hand man, Brandon hoped he would have an update about the lieutenant's status.

"I heard you ran into Martin Shore," Cash greeted.

"Literally," Brandon confirmed. "How's Bo?"

"It's good news. He has a non-life-threatening gun-shot wound to the shoulder. He'll be out of commission for a day or two, but he'll make a full recovery."

Brandon released the breath he'd been holding. "And what about Martin Shore?"

"Still no sign of him. We haven't given up," Cash quickly added. "We're searching the area, going door to door. We won't stop looking until we find him."

They might get lucky, but Brandon had to be realistic.

A hired gun that was gutsy enough to attack in a residential neighborhood in broad daylight probably had made arrangements for an escape. Shore was likely already out of the area.

And planning round two.

"Any idea why Shore came after Willa earlier than intel had indicated?" Brandon asked.

"Our best guess is that he had her house under surveillance and saw Bo and you arrive. He probably thought he should go ahead while he still had her in his sights."

That made sense, and it told him a lot about Shore. The man could and would improvise, and that made him even more dangerous.

"We've arranged a safe house for Willa," Cash continued. "It's local so you won't have to be on the road too long with her. I guess it goes without saying that she'll be in your protective custody."

Yeah. Without saying. Brandon was too deep into this to turn back now.

"Sergeant Harris McCoy and I will be there in about a half hour, and we'll take you to the safe house." Cash paused. "We'd also like Willa to see a therapist who specializes in recovering lost memories."

Brandon glanced at Willa. Even though she probably hadn't heard what Cash had just said, she could no doubt sense Brandon's own hesitation. He was hesitating not because he thought the therapist was a bad idea but because he wasn't sure he'd be able to convince Willa to trust anyone associated with the police.

Including him.

"I'll have to get back to you on that last part," Brandon told Cash.

Willa's left eyebrow lifted.

"Why?" Cash asked. "Have you talked her into cooperating yet?"

"No."

"Try harder. Because we've just gotten an update on what could be our next hostage situation."

"And?" Brandon asked when Cash didn't continue.

"And the news isn't good."

Chapter Six

Two days.

The short timeline kept going through Willa's head, stuck like a broken record, on the entire drive from Austin to the safe house. Two days.

Christmas.

That's when SAPD thought there'd be another hostage situation at a hospital. Or at least that's the information Sergeant Cash Newsome had relayed to Brandon while they were waiting in the break room at the Austin P.D. building. The authorities had two days to stop another nightmare from happening. But while the so-called intel had provided a time, SAPD didn't have a location. Or a motive.

They were counting on Willa to help them.

"Good luck with that," she said to herself. She huffed at that and the so-called safe house as it came into view.

Even if she could completely regain her memory before then, Willa wasn't convinced she actually knew anything that would help.

Two days.

And God knew how many women and babies would

have to go through the same kind of hell that she'd gone through for the past four months.

"You okay?" Brandon asked, bringing the car to a stop in the tiny garage of the safe house.

Willa considered lying but decided it was useless. "No."

He matched her heavy sigh with one of his own and hit the button on the automatic garage opener. He waited until the garage door was completely shut before they got out of the nondescript dark blue car that SAPD had provided.

There was a single light on in the laundry room situated just off the garage entrance, but there was enough moonlight filtering through the windows that she didn't have any trouble seeing.

Willa glanced around at the safe house. Well, what there was of it anyway.

It was small, much like her rental place that Shore had blown up on the other side of town. Except this place wasn't in the suburbs. It was in the country, halfway between San Antonio and Austin, and to get to it they'd used a rural road. Their nearest neighbor was more than a mile away.

She walked through the house, taking inventory. Two sparsely decorated bedrooms, one bath and a living-dining-kitchen combo. Though Brandon and she had already eaten dinner at police headquarters, the fridge had been stocked with plastic-wrapped sandwiches, bottled water and juice.

The cramped quarters and limited food options, however, meant nothing to her. The only thing Willa cared about right now was being as far away from Martin Shore as possible.

She watched as Brandon double-locked the door, and then he took out the codes that Sergeant Cash Newsome had given him so he could arm the security system.

"I suppose the windows and both the front and back doors are connected to the system?" she asked.

He nodded. "They are. There's also an alarm that runs around the immediate perimeter of the house in case anyone attempts a break-in. It's supposed to be safe."

She nodded as well. Then swallowed hard. Because no place might be safe enough to protect them from Martin Shore. Or the people who might be planning another hostage situation.

Brandon turned slowly and faced her. "I don't want us to sleep here inside the house."

Willa had thought he was about to tell her to get some rest. Maybe even give her another reassurance that nothing else bad would happen. She hadn't expected that from him. And her breath stalled in her throat.

"Do you trust me?" he asked.

The question hit her almost as hard as his bombshell about not wanting to stay there. She automatically reached for the PDA in her bag. But Willa didn't need to see his picture or the note she'd written to go along with it.

She remembered.

And what she remembered was that she *thought* she could trust him.

"What's this about?" she wanted to know.

Brandon scrubbed his hand over his face. "You know I made several calls after I got off the phone with Sergeant Cash Newsome?"

Yes. He'd stepped to the other side of the room for those calls, and he'd whispered so she couldn't hear. Willa figured he was discussing the therapy appointment that SAPD had made for her. An appointment that was supposed to happen at eight the following morning. Since it was already nine in the evening, that appointment wasn't far off.

"Cash is an old army buddy, and while I trust him, I wanted someone outside of SAPD," Brandon explained. "I contacted another old friend who runs a security company."

"Is that the person who dropped you off the duffel bag?" she asked.

"Yeah." Brandon had that particular bag slung over his shoulder, but he eased it off and set it on an over-stuffed fabric chair. "I asked him to bring me some supplies that I might need. I also asked him to see if he's heard anything about a possible leak at SAPD."

Her breath stalled again. Mercy, she hadn't braced herself nearly enough for any of this. "What kind of leak?"

"The worst kind for us. A leak in communication. I don't like the fact that SAPD's intel told them that Shore wouldn't attack you until tonight."

She thought about that a moment, and the conclusion she came to caused her heart rate to spike. "You think someone tipped Shore off?"

Brandon shrugged. "I don't want to believe it, but I

also don't want to put blind trust in people I don't really know."

Neither did she. "You don't think Bo Duggan could have done this?"

"Not him. But I don't know how many people in SAPD had access to the information about Shore." He made a sweeping glance around the room. "Or this place."

That didn't steady her heart. Willa slid her hand over her stomach. "So, what should we do?"

Brandon didn't answer immediately, and his forehead bunched up. "My friend sent me several portable security cameras and a monitor. I want to set the cameras up here, inside, but I want us to sleep in the car in the garage."

She instantly thought of the grenade that Shore had tossed into her rental. "Shore could try to blow us up again."

Brandon nodded. "He could. But I'll keep watch on the monitor. And the cameras are motion-activated and will sound if they're triggered. If anyone approaches the house, I can drive us out of here." He reached out, touched her arm and rubbed gently. "This is just a precaution, Willa."

He added the last part as if he expected her to challenge him, but Willa had no intentions of doing that.

She nodded. "I need to go to the bathroom, but once you have the camera set up, we can go back to the car."

It wouldn't be comfortable, but she still might be able to sleep there. Her fatigue was past the bone-weary stage, and she had no choice but to rest.

Willa took her toiletries from her bag so she could brush her teeth and take her prenatal vitamin. She also used the bathroom and hoped she wouldn't have to make too many treks back into the house because of her pregnancy bladder.

When she came back into the living room, Brandon had lowered all the blinds in the house and was setting up the tiny golf-ball-size camera in the front window. Since it was so small and white, it blended right into the window sill.

"There's a camera in the kitchen," he explained, "and the front bedroom. I'll put the other one just outside the garage door, and then I can monitor all of them with that." He pointed to a GPS-looking device with four split screens.

"We can take turns watching it," she suggested.

"No need. The monitor will beep if any of the cameras are triggered by motion. That means you can get some sleep. Think of the baby," he added before Willa could argue.

"I do, all the time," she mumbled. "Do you?" She instantly regretted that question. Brandon had only recently found out he was going to be a father, and he probably hadn't even come to terms with it yet. Added to that, he had the extra worry about keeping them safe.

Willa waved off the question and reached for her bag.

"I think about the baby," he said, his words soft and slow. He took the bag from her, keeping his attention focused on it and not her.

"It's okay," she assured him. "When the danger has

passed, I don't expect anything from you. In fact, I don't want anything from you."

That was a semi-truth. Her body wanted him. For sex. How ironic. She hadn't had as much of a sexual twinge since she'd gotten pregnant; yet near Brandon, in her last trimester no less, she kept feeling that tug deep within her.

"Good." And that was all he said for several moments. "Honestly, I'm not sure I can give you and this baby what you really need."

His eyes met hers for just a second, before he looked away and put the monitor in the equipment bag. He hoisted it over his other shoulder and headed for the garage door. Willa grabbed the pillow and cover that had been stacked on the sofa and followed him.

This was good, she assured herself. Brandon didn't want to be part of her or their baby's life. That's exactly the way she'd planned things. Heck, it was the reason she'd no doubt used artificial insemination. Because she hadn't wanted a man in her life.

So, why did his confession sting?

She barely knew the man and, other than the fact he was almost certainly the biological father of her baby, that was the only thing that connected them.

Well, except for the attraction.

And the danger.

And this entire bizarre connection she felt with him.

Willa huffed. She was talking herself into falling hard for Brandon, and that could be a fatal mistake.

Since the front seats of the car reclined, Willa got in on the passenger's side and prepared a makeshift bed.

Brandon eased the garage door open just a fraction and placed the camera outside. After closing it, he got behind the wheel and started his own preparations. Not for a bed, though, but for security. So that he wouldn't lose them, he put the keys in the ignition, set up the monitor on the dashboard and placed the bags on the backseat.

Willa turned, leaned over and retrieved the PDA from her bag. What she hadn't counted on was Brandon moving at the same time. He turned to adjust his holster, and they practically collided.

And then they froze.

Breath met breath, and Willa got an instant reminder of that attraction. It suddenly raced through her. Hot and wild. As if her huge pregnant belly wasn't a hindrance to anything sexual.

Brandon made a sound, deep within his throat. A sort of rumbling. That sound stirred through her as well. So did his scent. Something manly and woodsy. That scent alerted every part of her body that hadn't already been alerted.

"This can't happen," she whispered.

"Yeah."

But the single word had hardly left his mouth when he dragged her to him and put his lips on hers. His scent had caused a jolt, but the kiss created an avalanche.

Willa found herself sliding her arms around him and pulling him closer. She found herself deepening the kiss. And she found herself getting lost in the steamy maze of passion she immediately knew she couldn't control. She was on fire, and her body was urging her to keep pulling him closer, to keep kissing him, to continue this insanity no matter the cost.

If she'd thought his scent had her hormonal number, his taste was even more potent. That taste drew her in. And so did Brandon's embrace. His kiss was gentle and left her with no doubts that it was exactly what she wanted.

But shouldn't have.

Willa latched on to that thought and kept mentally repeating it. However, she wasn't the one to stop the kiss. It was Brandon. He eased her away from him and glanced at the monitor.

"I have to keep you safe," he said with a lot of regret and heavy breath in his voice.

Since safety was the main reason they were here in the car, Willa had no comeback for that. He did need to keep an eye on the monitor. He needed to protect her because that was the only way to keep her baby safe. Still, it was a battle to get herself to move away from him.

Willa settled into the seat and tried to level her breathing. Her body was still on fire, but her brain just kept reminding her that she had done the right thing by stopping the makeout session—even if it felt wrong.

"Are you sure we weren't lovers?" she asked, trying to keep things light.

"I'm sure." There was no lightness in his voice. It was strained, just like his expression. The need was still in his intense brown eyes. But the corner of his mouth lifted. "Trust me, I would have remembered having sex with you."

Yes. And even with her amnesia, Willa thought she

might have remembered, too. Brandon had a unique way of being unforgettable.

Well, maybe.

She glanced down at the PDA cupped in her hand and scrolled through the photos and information she'd stored there. She remembered everything she'd recorded for the past two weeks. Prior to that, her memory was spotty and prior to that, there were huge gaps. Two weeks wasn't nearly enough time for her to trust herself. So, Willa began making notes. About the attack from Martin Shore. About Brandon.

About everything.

She had to get everything down before she fell asleep, and that wouldn't be long. Despite the fiery kiss and Brandon's closeness, her body would soon have to rest.

"The night can be the worst time for me," she explained to Brandon as she continued to type. "Sometimes, when I wake up, everything in my memory is gone."

And she meant *everything*.

He stayed quiet a moment. "What should I do if that happens?"

"Run," she joked. But then she shook her head. "I'll be confused. I might even try to attack you because I won't know who you are. But just remind me that your picture is in here." She tapped her PDA.

Brandon looked at it, then at her. His gaze lingered a moment on her face, and on a heavy breath, he turned back to the monitor.

"Sleep," he insisted.

She nodded but didn't close her eyes. Willa pulled

the covers to her chin, snuggling them around her so she'd stay warm, but she fastened her attention to the monitor. Thanks to the four cameras, every angle of the house and attached garage were covered. Even in the darkness, they would be able to see someone approaching.

Hopefully, it would stay that way, but Willa had a bad feeling that things were about to get a whole lot worse.

BRANDON POPPED ANOTHER mint in his mouth and wished it were a big gulp of strong coffee. He needed a hit of caffeine badly, but he didn't want to go back inside the house to see if there was any. That would mean either waking Willa or leaving her alone.

He had no plans to do either.

Since the monitor for the security cameras would alert him to any movement around the house, Brandon had managed a couple of catnaps, but with each one, the nightmares had come.

He glanced at Willa who was sleeping soundly in the reclined seat. The covers had shifted, draping down below her left breast. Brandon eased the cover back in place. He noticed her PDA then. It had slipped from her hand and was now on the console between them.

Was there something stored in the PDA that would help the cops stop another hostage situation? Maybe. Maybe it also contained something that would help Willa restore her memory. At least that was the justification he used when he read the first page entry.

Your name is Willa Marks, and you have amnesia and post-concussional neurosis, also called short-term memory loss. Everything you need to know is on this PDA.

There was a list of places where she had cash stored and her doctor's phone number, followed by a list of rules. Well, two rules to be specific.

Number one: don't trust the cops.
Number two: stay in hiding.

Neither was a surprise. Twice Willa had nearly been killed when she'd trusted the cops. If their positions had been reversed, he might have written the same damn memos.

He scrolled down farther to the next entry that Willa had labeled Latest Update.

The man beside me is Sheriff Brandon Ruiz. My baby's father. Use caution. He has secrets.

"Secrets?" he mumbled. Yeah, he had them.

Well, one anyway. But it was a secret that could affect everything.

What the hell was he going to do about Willa and the baby?

She needed help, all right. But she needed someone with less emotional baggage than he had. He certainly didn't fit the bill.

Frustrated with that and the lack of news about the case, Brandon took out his phone and sent a text message to Cash to see if there was an update. The moment he hit the send button, he heard the beep. It was so soft that it was barely audible, but it went through him as if it'd been a shout.

Brandon's gaze flew to the monitor. He checked the feed from all the cameras and didn't see anything out of the ordinary. Well, not at first anyway. He moved closer to the screen, trying to pick through the pitchy darkness of the tiny images.

There.

Beneath the bedroom window.

He spotted the man dressed head to toe in black. His movement had obviously triggered the perimeter security sensor. Brandon watched as the man lifted his hand and bashed something against the glass in the window.

"Willa," Brandon whispered. "We have to get out of here now."

Her eyes flew open, and she gave the seat a quick adjustment so she was in a sitting position. Her attention went straight to the monitor.

"Is it Shore?" she asked.

"I can't tell." But Brandon would put money on the fact that it was the assassin. If not, then it was someone equally dangerous.

"Put on your seat belt," Brandon instructed. He did the same. "And stay down. The second I open the garage door, I'm driving out of here fast."

That was a risk, of course, because Shore could shoot at them, but Brandon knew that was a risk he had to take—especially when he saw the man toss something through the broken bedroom window.

Hell.

It could be another grenade. And if it was, the

explosion could easily destroy the garage, or at minimum, the damage from a blast could trap them inside.

Brandon started the car and hit the remote opener clipped to the visor. It seemed to take way too long for the door to lift, and with each passing second, he prayed that Shore wouldn't have time to make it to the front of the garage entrance so he could shoot at them head-on.

As soon as Brandon had clearance to get out of the garage, he jammed his foot on the accelerator, and the car bolted out into the darkness.

The shot came almost immediately and shattered the back windshield.

"Stay down!" he reminded Willa, though he knew that might not be enough. Bullets could go through seats as easily as they could through glass.

The sound of the second shot drowned out his repeated warning for her to stay down. The bullet tore through what was left of the safety glass, and the shooter quickly followed it up with a third and fourth shot. But that wasn't all. Behind them, there was an explosion, and both the house and the garage burst into fireballs.

Brandon didn't dare risk looking at Willa to make sure she was okay because he had to focus on getting them away from the shooter.

He headed for the road and glanced in the side mirror to see if the gunman was in pursuit. It was impossible to tell, but it was obvious the guy was still in shooting range because yet another bullet tore through the side of the car. Thank God the shots missed the tires or their chances of escape would drop significantly.

The shots stopped, and Brandon continued to tear his way down the country road. He had to slow down to take a sharp curve, but as soon as he could, he sped up again.

He saw the headlights then.

They flared on behind them, and even though Brandon couldn't see their attacker, he figured the guy had hidden his vehicle nearby. He'd probably killed the car lights so that they wouldn't be alerted. The plan might have worked, too, if Brandon hadn't suspected there might be an attack and set up those security cameras.

Beside him, he could hear Willa's heavy breathing, and from the corner of his eye, he could see that she had her hands splayed protectively over her belly.

"He's following us, isn't he?" she asked. Her voice was raspy and thick.

Brandon glanced in the side mirror and saw the headlights. The guy was definitely in pursuit. "Yeah," he confirmed. "Hang on."

He took the next turn faster than he should have, and Brandon fought with the steering wheel to keep his vehicle on the road. He hated putting Willa through this, but there was no other choice. With Willa in the car, he couldn't risk stopping to have a showdown with this SOB. Later though, he hoped he got the chance to beat this guy to dust.

The anger roared through Brandon, and he could feel the dangerous energy course in his blood. With it, came the flashbacks. Like the nightmares, they were always there, ready to rear their ugly heads. He pinned his attention to the road, to the curves, and forced the old demons to remain at bay.

"Where are we going?" she asked. She levered herself up just a fraction to check her side mirror, but Brandon caught onto her shoulder and shoved her back down.

"Once we get to the highway, I'll drive toward San Antonio. Maybe I can lose him on the interstate and if not, maybe the traffic will get him to back off."

Both possibilities were long shots, but they were the only shots that Brandon had.

"Should I call 9-1-1?" Willa asked. But she hadn't said it eagerly, more as a last resort.

It was a last resort they couldn't risk.

"No," he answered. He could have sworn he heard her sigh with relief.

He took another curve, then another, but the vehicle stayed behind them. Too close. And worse, it was gaining. The only good thing about their situation was that the driver wouldn't be able to fire at them while trying to maintain the speed. Still, that didn't mean they were safe.

Brandon reached a straight stretch of the road and was able to go faster. So did the other car, and it closed in. The driver had on his high beams, making it hard for Brandon to see, but he could tell the vehicle was an SUV. It was much larger and faster than the car he was driving, so the SUV quickly ate up the distance between them.

"Hold on," Brandon warned Willa.

Just as the SUV smashed into their rear bumper.

Brandon fought to keep the car on the road, and he

didn't let up on the accelerator. He continued to race toward the highway. If his calculations were correct, that was less than a mile away.

The SUV rammed into them again, and the jolt sent them both snapping in their seats. He bit back some profanity and prayed all this jostling around wouldn't hurt the baby or Willa. While he was praying, he added that he could get them safely out of there.

There was another sharp curve, and then the road stretched out again in a straight line. The SUV's driver took advantage of it and slammed into the back of their car again. Brandon kept a tight grip on the steering wheel, somehow managing to keep the car on the road.

Finally, he spotted the highway, and Brandon took the turn on what had to be two wheels. He quickly righted the car and took off.

Despite the late hour, it wasn't long before he spotted another vehicle just ahead of them. Brandon raced toward it and hoped there would be others to deter the SUV driver from another attack.

The SUV stayed close, and Brandon braced himself in case they were rammed again, but the guy stayed back.

Brandon passed the other vehicle but then slowed, hoping to keep the car between them and the SUV.

"Are we losing him?" Willa asked.

"Not just yet."

There were several other vehicles just ahead on the highway, and Brandon got as close to them as possible. The seconds clicked off in his head, and he held his breath until he saw the cluster of lit buildings at an exit.

He wouldn't leave the highway just yet, but only a few miles ahead was the exit for the county sheriff's office and the fire department. He would get off the highway there and, if necessary, he'd even pull into the sheriff's parking lot.

Willa sat up just a fraction and glanced in the side mirror. She stared back at the SUV that was now several cars behind them. "Shore came out into the open at the rental house so he could follow us," she reminded him. "Neither the neighborhood street nor the traffic stopped him."

Yeah. Brandon was aware of that. And that was one of the reasons the knot in his gut had tightened to the point of being painful. If that was Shore in the SUV, then why had he backed off? Of course, the answer might be that it wasn't Shore.

That thought caused Brandon to take a deep breath.

Willa shook her head. "I'm past being tired of this. All I want is for my baby to be safe."

Brandon wanted the same thing, but he was aware that the danger was far from being over.

He put on his blinker when he reached the exit for the sheriff's office, and when Willa saw where he was headed, she sat up even farther in her seat.

"I thought you didn't want to involve the cops," she questioned.

"I don't. We can't," he corrected a moment later. He pulled into the well-lit parking lot and stopped in the spot that was closest to the front door.

The SUV slowed to a crawl but didn't turn into the lot. Brandon watched as it crept out of sight.

The driver wouldn't go far. No. He would wait for them to make a move. For now, the only move Brandon intended to do was stay put. He could go into the sheriff's office, of course, as a final resort, but the sheriff would almost certainly contact the San Antonio Police.

He kept watch to make sure the SUV didn't circle back around, and he glanced at Willa to check that she was all right. She wasn't. She was pale and trembling.

Brandon put his arm around her and eased her closer. She welcomed the contact.

He tried to figure out how to word what he had to tell her and decided there was no easy way to spell out their situation. Basically, they were in the worst kind of trouble, and Willa needed to know that.

"Shore—or whoever just attacked us—had to have known how to find us," Brandon explained.

She pulled back, met his gaze. "This means there's a leak?"

He nodded and hated the fear he saw in her eyes. "You were right, Willa. We can't trust the cops."

She made a sound of agreement and blinked back tears. "What about Sergeant Cash Newsome? Can you call him?"

"Maybe." Brandon did trust his old friend and would try to contact him but not now. Not until he could figure out a way to make sure any conversation he had with Cash would be private.

"So what do we do?" Willa asked.

He put his hand over his gun and kept watch around them. "For now, we wait."

Brandon was sure it wouldn't be long before there would be another attempt to kill them.

Chapter Seven

The sound of someone talking woke her.

Willa forced open her heavy eyelids and realized it was no longer dark, and they were no longer parked outside the sheriff's office. The car was moving. And judging from the massive buildings around them, they were driving through downtown San Antonio.

She sat up, yawned and looked at the man behind the wheel. She recognized that dark hair and those steamy brown eyes.

"I remember you," she mumbled.

With the phone sandwiched between his shoulder and ear, Brandon glanced at her and nodded. The corner of his mouth lifted into a near smile. Thank God she didn't have to re-create her life and memories this morning. But then Willa remembered something else.

The danger.

That kicked up her heartbeat to an uncomfortable level, and she looked all around them to make certain Shore wasn't still following them. There were plenty of vehicles on the road, but she saw no signs of that SUV.

"We'll be there in a few minutes," Brandon told the person on the other end of the line. "Remember, this stays just between us."

He closed his phone and shoved it back into his pocket. "That was Cash."

Her breath went thin. "You're sure we can trust him?"

"He's given me no reason not to. Not yet anyway," Brandon added in a mumble. "Cash insists there isn't a leak at SAPD. He thinks Shore is tracking us some other way."

"How?"

"Well, it's not my cell phone because I know it has an anti-tracking device." Brandon glanced at her PDA. And her stomach knotted. It was her lifeline. Her security blanket. It had saved her life—literally.

"It's just a possibility," he added.

True, but Shore was finding them somehow, and maybe her PDA had some kind of GPS tracking system.

It made her physically ill to think of what she had to do, but she couldn't let her lifeline put her baby at risk. Willa opened the glove compartment and fished out a pen.

"Don't give me any reason to regret this," she warned Brandon, and Willa waited until he made eye contact with her before she scrawled the words across her palm.

Trust Brandon Ruiz.

He glanced at the sentence and then mumbled some profanity. Profanity he didn't explain as he brought the car to a stop in a hotel parking lot.

"Leave the PDA in the car," he told her and checked their surroundings. "We won't be coming back to this vehicle or the parking lot."

She glanced around as well, and her attention landed on the hotel. "Are we staying here?"

Brandon shook his head, grabbed her overnight bag and opened the door. "In and out. We'll be on foot for a few blocks."

Good. She didn't want to be anywhere near her PDA or the vehicle with the shot-out windows. "But I'll need to find a bathroom soon," she let him know.

Brandon took her request to heart and hurried them from the car into the hotel. They didn't stop in the lobby but went to the back and exited into another parking lot. They walked past two more buildings before entering another hotel. Willa expected them to exit this one as well, but she came to a dead stop when she spotted the sandy-haired man in the lobby.

He was almost certainly a cop.

Willa didn't know who he was, but he did seem familiar. About six feet tall, lanky build and green eyes. Cop's eyes.

Brandon stopped directly in front of the man. "Willa, this is Sergeant Cash Newsome."

She still didn't release the breath she was holding.

Brandon leaned closer to Cash and lowered his voice to a whisper. "If this puts Willa in any more danger, you'll be the one to answer for it."

Cash stiffened, and his friendly expression faded. "That doesn't sound like something an old friend would say."

Brandon scowled. "Friendship only gets you one

shot. If Shore finds us here, then I'm taking Willa into deep hiding where SAPD and their possible leak can't ever find her."

"Think of those women who could become the next hostages," Cash countered.

"I'm thinking of Willa and the baby. Right now, they come first."

That started a staring match between the two men, and Cash hitched his shoulder toward the elevator. He started in that direction. So did Brandon. Willa stayed put, but after glancing down at what she'd written on her hand, she cursed and caught up to the men.

They went to the fifth floor, and Cash directed them into a suite that was nearly the same size as the safe house they'd left hours earlier. There were massive windows revealing the city's skyline, but what snagged Willa's attention was the smell of bacon and eggs that was coming from the silver dome-covered plates on the coffee table. Her stomach growled, and the baby kicked as if sensing it was time to eat as well.

Brandon handed her the bag. "Go ahead to the bathroom and then I'll explain what's going on after you've had some breakfast."

She really did need to use the bathroom, but she didn't budge. "I'd like to hear now."

Cash and Brandon exchanged glances. Cash's expression was laced with skepticism, but Brandon looked as if he were bracing himself for an argument.

"We need your help," Cash insisted.

But she ignored him and stared at Brandon instead. "What do they want you to convince me to do?"

"They want you to see a doctor who might be able to help you recover your memory."

"A psychiatrist who's a friend of mine," Cash supplied. "Her name is Dr. Lenora Farris and she'll be here in about twenty minutes."

"A shrink?" Willa made sure she let her tone convey her displeasure, and she aimed that displeasure at Brandon. "I've already seen therapists."

"She's supposedly different." Brandon turned so that he was between Cash and her. "I thought if you could remember it might help us put an end to the danger. *All* the danger for both you and any other possible hostages. We might also be able to figure out who hired Shore to come after you."

Willa couldn't argue with that, but she still wasn't convinced this would help. Plus, they were in a hotel suite with a cop, and if there was a leak, they could be sitting ducks for another attack.

Brandon put his mouth right against her ear. "I agreed to two hours. That's it. And then we're getting out of here."

Willa still wanted to argue, but then Brandon brushed a kiss on her forehead. That took the fight right out of her. Of course, maybe the fatigue and her full bladder were partly responsible as well. She shifted the bag to her shoulder, huffed and headed for the adjoining bathroom.

She didn't dawdle, but she did take the time to freshen up and change her top. Thankfully, she'd packed a green sweater in her overnight bag.

When she went back into the main room of the suite, it was obvious she was interrupting a tense discussion—maybe even an argument. Whatever had been going on came to an abrupt halt when Cash and Brandon spotted her.

Brandon scrubbed his hand over his face. "Eat," he told Willa. And he headed to the bathroom, leaving her alone with Cash.

Since her stomach was still growling and she was getting light-headed, Willa sat and helped herself to one of the plates. There was even a glass of milk and a bottle of prenatal vitamins on the tray.

"You don't remember me?" Cash asked. He poured himself a cup of coffee from a gleaming silver carafe and took the chair across from her.

"No. We've met?"

He nodded. "I was the first officer to get to you after the hostage standoff ended."

Without her PDA, she couldn't confirm that, so Willa settled for making a noncommittal sound while she ate her scrambled eggs.

"I found you in the hall outside the hospital lab," he continued. "You'd fallen, or something. You were barely conscious."

That got her attention. Had she known that "barely conscious" part? She didn't think so. Willa was sure she had put in her notes that she regained consciousness not at the maternity hospital but in the medical center after she came out of a coma.

"Did I say anything when you found me?" she asked.

He shrugged. "You were worried about losing the baby."

Well, that was a no-brainer, but she got the feeling

that Cash was withholding something. Or maybe it was just her overactive imagination.

Brandon came out of the bathroom at the same moment there was a knock at the door. The sound sent both men reaching for their weapons, and it was Brandon who went to the door to peek out the viewer.

"It's a woman," he relayed to Cash. "Tall with auburn hair."

"Dr. Farris," Cash supplied. He confirmed that by looking through the viewer as well, and then opened the door to greet their visitor.

Since she wasn't always able to rely on her memory, Willa had gotten accustomed to reading people. There was usually something—a quick unguarded glance, a tightening of the mouth. Some small detail.

But not with Dr. Farris.

Cash made the introductions, but Willa still didn't get any clues when she shook the woman's hand. Dr. Farris seemed friendly enough but, more than anything, she was a blank slate. Maybe because of her psychiatric training.

"Willa," the doctor greeted, and she held on to Willa's hand for several seconds. "I'm here to help you."

Willa didn't try to hide her skepticism. "Others have tried. And failed."

The doctor nodded and calmly whisked a loose curl from her pale ivory face. "But those therapies were used early on after your injury. Sergeant Newsome tells me you've made improvements since then and that you're not having as many issues with your short-term memory."

Willa aimed a scowl at Cash. "And how exactly would you know that?"

Cash shrugged his shoulders. "Lieutenant Bo Duggan. I had a long talk with him before I set all of this up."

Then obviously the lieutenant was recovering. That was something at least, especially since he'd gotten shot while trying to protect her.

Brandon stepped even closer to Willa and caught her hand in his. However, he directed his attention to Dr. Farris. "How do you think you can help Willa?"

"Well, since we obviously can't use any drugs to induce an altered state, I want to use something called Neuro-Linguistic Programming—NLP—that incorporates video hypnosis. I plan to use triggers that might cue in other parts of her brain to unlock the lost memories."

"What kind of triggers?" Willa demanded.

The doctor offered her a calm smile. "Both visual and auditory. By using NLP, I want to re-create the environment of the maternity ward the way it was when the hostage situation started."

Willa felt a chill go over her. "I'm not going back to that hospital."

"You don't have to. In a way, I'm bringing the hospital to you." Dr. Farris extracted a shiny DVD from her purse. "My assistants and I have worked on this for hours so you can replicate the experience."

Willa didn't want to replicate it because her time as a hostage had almost certainly been terrifying. But she couldn't refuse the opportunity to regain her memory simply because she was scared. As Brandon had already pointed out, the information trapped in her mind could ultimately give them the name of the person trying to kill them and it could save those possible Christmas hostages.

"Is this safe?" Brandon asked.

"Absolutely." The doctor didn't hesitate, either. "And if Willa becomes agitated, I'll stop." She looked at Willa then and waited.

Willa went over everything the doctor had just told her. This, whatever this was, wouldn't harm the baby. And she could stop if it got too extreme. There was no way she could refuse, not with her risking so little and with so much at stake for the future hostages.

Willa finally nodded.

Dr. Farris didn't give a sigh of relief. She didn't show any emotion as she went to the large flat-screen TV and inserted the disk in the DVD player.

"You two should wait in the other room," the doctor told Brandon and Cash.

Willa felt as though someone had just taken her security blanket. Not good. Trusting Brandon was one thing but relying on him emotionally just wasn't very smart.

"I'm staying," Brandon insisted.

Cash said the same, and after staring at them, the doctor finally showed some emotion. She made a sound of mild annoyance and turned away from them.

Despite the little lecture Willa had just given herself about not leaning on Brandon, she was thankful that he would be nearby. After all, it was his name and his name only that she'd written on her hand.

"Should I lie down or something?" Willa asked.

Dr. Farris shook her head and started the DVD. "Just stay seated and focus on what you're seeing and hearing."

That sounded simple enough. Well, simple unless her short-term memory decided to take a hike. Since it'd been weeks since that had happened, Willa thought that part of this ordeal might be over, but she'd been wrong before.

The images started to appear on the screen. Someone was holding a video camera and recording their walk through the double automatic doors.

"We know from the exterior surveillance cameras that this is how you entered the building," the doctor explained. "Once you reach the fourth floor, your movements and what happens there are reenactments based on eyewitnesses." She kept her voice at a whisper and lowered the lights so that the only illumination came from the TV.

Willa forced herself to imagine that she was the one walking into the San Antonio Maternity Hospital. The greeting area didn't look familiar, but they quickly went through it and to the elevators. She pretended that it was her hand that pushed the button to take her to the fourth floor.

When *she* stepped into the elevator and the doors closed, Willa heard the music. There was nothing unusual about it, but it seemed familiar. The elevator seemed familiar, too. There were posters of mothers holding their newborns.

She felt her heart speed up a little when the doors swished open and she saw the fourth floor. Again, there was nothing unusual about it, and she guessed wrong about which direction she would take. The camera went to the left, past an empty waiting area. She saw the signs on the wall leading to the lab.

Why was she going there?

Because she was supposed to have some lab tests and then an ultrasound. That wasn't an actual memory, but she'd been told that by the police. Someone had called and told her she needed lab tests, but that had been a ruse to get her to the hospital.

The ruse had worked.

When the camera reached the lab desk, it stopped. Willa glanced around the corridor spread out in front of her and waited. She didn't have to wait long. She saw the ski-mask-wearing man racing toward her. He was armed.

"Don't close your eyes," the doctor insisted when Willa started to do just that.

It was a challenge, but she forced herself to watch as the man came closer and closer to the camera.

"Come with me," the man demanded, and he jammed the gun at her.

Willa didn't want to go with him. She wanted to run out of the hotel suite, far away from the camera and the nightmarish images, but she forced herself to stay put.

The gunman led her into the lab, past the cubicles where the techs drew blood. They went about twenty yards farther to a door with a sign that read: Authorized Personnel Only Beyond This Point. The man pressed in a code to get the door to open and led her into a room with computers and refrigerated storage containers.

They stopped moving, so Willa looked around as far

as the camera angle would allow. She took in as many details as she could manage. The glossy gray tile floor. The sterile white walls and ceiling. The way everything was arranged in precise order. The smell.

She froze.

The smell?

Did she really remember that?

Yes, she did. It wasn't the disinfectant odor like the rest of the hospital. This particular area smelled like some kind of lab chemical.

She felt the air-conditioning spill out from the overhead vents. The room was too cold, and she shivered. Willa waited for more sensations to come, and they did. They came at her hard and fast.

Willa gasped and pressed her fingers to her mouth. "Oh, God. I remember."

Chapter Eight

Brandon wasn't sure which of them looked more surprised, but he thought he might be the winner. When Dr. Farris had started that DVD, and Willa had started to watch, the last thing he expected was for Willa to remember anything.

But she apparently had.

She kept her gaze fastened to the screen where the hostage situation continued to play out. It seemed like such a simple exercise. Visual cues of a nightmare. But Willa kept repeating those two words as if it were a mantra. Or a warning.

I remember.

"What do you remember?" Dr. Farris asked, taking the words right out of Brandon's mouth.

Willa pressed her fingertips to both sides of her head and began to rock. Brandon went and sat beside her, then put his arm around her.

"It's okay." He tried to assure her, but he had no way of knowing if that was true.

"I remember the gunman taking me into the lab," Willa said. Her voice was barely a whisper, and he could feel her trembling.

Brandon tightened his grip, and her hands dropped to her lap. "What else?" he pressed.

Both the doctor and Cash moved closer, probably hoping they were all finally about to get answers. Brandon wanted those answers, too, but he hated that Willa was having to go through this all over again.

"The gunman took me into a secure area," she continued. "He pressed in some numbers on a key pad."

"Did he have the code written down?" Cash asked.

Willa nodded. "On a piece of paper he took from his pocket. He opened the door and pushed me inside. 'Go to the computer,' he told me. And I did. I went to the one where he pointed. It was on the far side of the room, sitting on a desk."

Cash leaned down so that he'd be eye level with Willa. "What did he want you to do?"

Before Willa could answer, Dr. Farris eased Cash out of the way. "No more questions, please. This will work best if Willa lets the memories come to her. And sometimes, these bits and pieces are all we'll get. To be honest with you, I wasn't sure it would even work this well."

Willa stared up at the doctor. "These aren't bits and pieces," she mumbled, her voice catching. "The gunman wanted me to hack into some secure files." She paused. "I did it because he put a gun to my head and said he would kill me and the baby if I didn't."

Brandon ignored the punch of anger he felt over what Willa had been through. He also ignored the doctor's no-question warning. "What files?"

"Ones that were being outsourced to the hospital,"

Willa readily answered. "The files belonged to the San Antonio Police Department, and they were biological samples that were to be used in several active cases. He wanted me to hack into the files and alter the data."

Definitely not bits and pieces. This was the sort of information that could blow this case wide open.

Brandon met Cash's stare. "Is it routine for SAPD to outsource tests to the hospital?"

Cash shook his head. "No. We usually use the Ranger lab in Austin, but there was a fire, and they got back-logged. I heard we were using some local hospitals to do some of the tests, but I didn't know it was this specific hospital."

"Dean Quinlan," Willa said out of the blue. "It was his name on the files. He was listed as the file manager. Do you know him?" she asked Cash.

"Yeah." Cash propped his hands on his hips and mumbled some profanity. "He's one of our CSIs. Well, he used to be anyway. He resigned shortly after the hostage incident to take a job elsewhere."

The doctor turned off the DVD and looked at Willa. "What else do you remember?"

Willa opened her mouth, hesitated, then closed it. "Nothing. That's all."

"You don't remember what specific files the gunman wanted you to hack into?" Cash demanded.

She shook her head. "No. I'm sorry. I remember sitting down at the computer, and I remember seeing Dean Quinlan's name as the file custodian, but that's it. Everything else after that is a blank." She started to tremble again, and Brandon pulled her closer to him.

Cash checked his watch. "I need to talk to Dean

Quinlan and anyone else who knew about those files being processed at the maternity hospital. I'll let you know what I find out." He took out his phone and headed into one of the suite's bedrooms.

"Your memory might continue to return," Dr. Farris told her. She paused to take Willa's pulse. "Sometimes, when you recall portions of the traumatic events, other details soon follow."

Willa nodded and pulled in a long breath. While that was good news for the investigation, Brandon knew this would be hell for Willa. After all, the gunman had likely been trying to kill her when she fell and injured her head.

"How are you feeling?" Dr. Farris asked.

"Exhausted." Willa adjusted her position and placed her head against Brandon's shoulder. "Could you give me a few minutes to gather my thoughts?"

Dr. Farris nodded, but she didn't look at all certain about leaving Willa. Finally, though, she walked toward the second bedroom, went inside and shut the door.

The moment the doctor was out of sight, Willa's head swooshed off his shoulder, and she stood. "I remembered some other things," she whispered.

Brandon froze. He didn't think her memory had returned just this instant. No. It had probably come with the other memories, but Willa had been smart not to tell all to the doctor. While Brandon still trusted Cash, he didn't know Dr. Farris and was glad Willa had withheld something that might put her in even more danger.

If that was possible.

"The gunman tried to call Dean Quinlan while we were in that secure area of the lab," Willa continued.

"He had Quinlan's name and number written on the back of the paper with the codes he used to get past the door."

"Did he actually speak to Quinlan?" Brandon, too, kept his voice at a whisper and stood so he could be closer to her.

She shook her head. "His cell phone couldn't get a signal in that part of the lab."

Probably because the walls had been reinforced for safety reasons, he thought. Labs and X-ray areas often have metal barriers to stop the harmful rays from getting into other parts of the building.

"The gunman was frustrated because he couldn't seem to read his notes," Willa explained. "He finally showed them to me, and that's when I saw the names of the files I was supposed to access. There were three of them—the first was Baby Martinez."

"That makes sense," Brandon concluded. "Misty Martinez was a San Antonio woman who was murdered, and her newborn was missing. Since Misty had stored the baby's umbilical cord at the maternity hospital, SAPD requested a DNA test so they could identify the biological father, who turned out to be her killer."

Willa's eyes widened. "Please tell me I didn't do anything to that DNA sample that allowed a killer to get away."

"No. The biological father, Gavin Cunningham, was arrested and got a life sentence."

She nodded but didn't relax. "The second name on the list was Jessie Beecham..." She paused, shook her head. "And Wes-somebody."

"Dunbar," Brandon provided. And he cursed.

Willa blinked. "You know these people?"

"I know *of* them. Jessie Beecham was a wealthy club owner with ties to the mob. He was murdered earlier this year, and the prime suspect was a rival club owner named Wes Dunbar."

SAPD had sent Brandon the initial reports of the investigation because Wes Dunbar had a country estate in Crockett Creek, Brandon's own town. At the time he'd read those reports, Brandon had no idea just how personal that case would become. Of course, the question was did the investigation into Jessie Beecham's murder have anything to do with Willa's situation?

Maybe not.

Maybe the culprit who'd hired Shore was simply someone who was tying up loose ends for the now-dead gunman who'd held her hostage. Maybe an unknown accomplice. What Brandon needed was more information, and that included a case update on Jessie Beecham's murder.

He glanced at the room where Cash had gone to make his call about the former CSI, Dean Quinlan. He looked at the room where the doctor was as well. And he got a really bad feeling about all of this. God knows who Dr. Farris had already told about Willa's regained memory, and Cash's calls and questions would almost certainly alert the wrong people.

"We need to get out of here?" Willa asked, obviously noticing the alarm on his face.

"Yeah." He grabbed her bag and her arm.

Brandon hoped to hell it wasn't too late.

WILLA WAS BEYOND TIRED of being on the run, but she knew Brandon was right to get them out of there.

Maybe both Cash and Dr. Farris were on the up-and-up, but that didn't mean someone, including Martin Shore, would get word that she had remembered what had gone on in the lab the day the maternity hostages were taken.

Brandon eased the suite door shut behind them and got them moving to the elevator. He had her bag slung over his shoulder and kept one hand on her and the other within easy reach of his gun. Willa held her breath until they were in the elevator and the doors slid shut. They weren't out of danger yet, not by a long shot, but she wanted to put as much distance as possible between the suite and them.

"What do we do now?" she asked and mentally cursed the fatigue and fog in her head.

She should have already figured that out for herself, but here she was again relying on Brandon. Once they were safely away from the hotel, she had to find some time to come up with a new plan—and a couple of backup ones.

"We need a vehicle and some cash," Brandon answered. "I have to get you to a safe place, and we can't get there on foot with Shore this close and every cop in San Antonio looking for us."

That "safe place" part certainly sounded good to her, but was it even doable?

"I have some cash in the bag," Willa let him know. "About five hundred dollars."

But she would need a lot more than that if she had to go into hiding for any length of time. Which she probably would. That meant making a trip to the banks in Austin or San Antonio, so she could get to one of her safety deposit boxes where she'd stashed more money.

Brandon stopped the elevator on the second floor. "It's too risky to go into the main part of the lobby," he told her.

So, they left the elevator and went into the stairwell. Brandon stopped long enough to look at the emergency exit route map that was on the wall. Willa looked as well and wasn't pleased that the stairs ended so close to the lobby. They would still be in sight of the front desk and entrance. But hopefully not for long. There appeared to be a back exit just off a coffee shop. She prayed the door there wasn't rigged with an alarm.

When they reached the bottom of the stairs, Brandon stopped and peered out through the glass insert in the door. "No sign of Shore or other cops," he relayed to her.

That didn't give her any sense of relief. Shore had gotten the jump on them before, and it could happen again.

They left the meager cover of the stairwell and stepped out into the back part of the lobby, which was just ten or fifteen feet from the coffee shop. They only made it a few steps before Brandon pulled her into a shallow recessed area that led to the ladies' room. He maneuvered her behind him.

"Shhh," he warned.

Her heart went to her knees, and she came up on her tiptoes so she could look over his shoulder. Willa dreaded what she would see.

There were several people milling around in the lobby and two hotel employees behind the check-in desk. She certainly didn't see the apparent threat Brandon thought was there, but she had no intention of leaving their hiding place, either. She stood there waiting with her breath held.

Two of the people in the lobby picked up their suitcases and headed for the front exit.

That's when Willa spotted the man.

He was on the other side of the check-in desk, partly hidden behind a massive plant.

Oh, God.

It was Martin Shore.

He was volleying glances between the elevator and the front door. And she recognized what he held in his hand.

Her PDA.

Willa clamped her teeth over her bottom lip so that her gasp wouldn't be loud enough to draw anyone's attention—especially Shore's. How had he actually found them? Had Cash or Dr. Farris alerted him, or had Shore merely followed her PDA and guessed their location? His presence could be a fishing expedition, but it didn't matter. He was there—so close—and that meant the danger was there again too.

The baby began to kick, hard, and since her belly was pressed against Brandon's back, he no doubt felt it. He glanced over his shoulder at her but then nailed his attention back on Shore.

They couldn't wait long in the alcove without someone noticing them, and it wouldn't be wise to try to hide out in the ladies' room where they would be trapped. Soon, if not already, Cash and the doctor would realize they were missing and would come looking for them.

That would no doubt confirm to Shore that they were still in the building. Besides, she didn't want anyone, including Cash and Dr. Farris, to find them. Willa only wanted to get out of there.

"We need to move fast when we get outside," Brandon whispered.

Willa nodded and hoped that *fast* would be fast enough.

Part of her wondered if it was best just to have a showdown with Shore. Here and now. After all, Brandon was a cop. He knew how to take down a killer. But Shore wasn't an ordinary killer. He wouldn't give up without a hard fight, and that would mean bullets flying. Innocent people could be killed. And once again, her precious baby would be in harm's way.

"Now!" Brandon ordered.

He turned, not abruptly though. He kept his movement unhurried. He also kept her in front of him so that he was between Shore and her. Brandon was protecting her yet again.

The dozen or so steps to the exit seemed to take a lifetime, but Willa knew it was only a few seconds. Brandon shoved open the door and got her outside.

The burst of cold air hit her in the face, but she didn't take the time to catch her breath. Brandon got them moving, not across the parking lot where they could easily be seen. He led her toward the back of the hotel, and they hurried past the service and delivery entrances. There were men unloading boxes, but none seemed to pay any attention to them.

Brandon kept watch behind them and then stopped when they reached the corner of the building. There was about ten yards of wide-open space between the hotel and the next building, which was a one-story chain restaurant.

"Let's move," Brandon insisted, and they quickly got across to the back of the restaurant.

They repeated that process for three more buildings, putting some distance between the hotel and them.

Willa heard the sirens, but it only heightened her fear. However, Brandon paused and looked out as if he were considering the possibility of going to the responding officers.

"Please tell me you're not going out there," she whispered.

"Not a chance." He grabbed her arm again and got them moving farther away from the hotel and from those approaching sirens.

"Then where are we going once we get a car?" Willa demanded.

Brandon lifted her hand so she would have a reminder of what she'd written there. "You have to trust me a little longer, Willa. Because I'm taking you to the one place I know where I can keep you safe."

Chapter Nine

They were *home*.

Well, they were at *his* home anyway, Willa amended.

It was apparently the one place he knew where he could keep her safe. Maybe he felt that way because of the two dogs. The minute they turned into the gravel driveway that led to the isolated house, two Dobermans came racing toward them. Neither dog looked very welcoming, and they barked and chased the car.

It wasn't exactly a friendly greeting.

The trek to his rural Crockett Creek house hadn't been a friendly one, either. It'd taken them more than an hour to get far enough away from the hotel and to a pay phone he thought might be safe to use. He'd called one of his deputies, Pete Sanchez, a fiftysomething-year-old man who had arrived to pick them up in San Antonio, so he could then drive them out to Brandon's place.

The drive had been long and tedious. Along with bathroom stops to accommodate Willa and the round-about route the deputy had used to get them to the small Texas town, the trip was more than three hours. Willa was beyond exhausted, and that was probably a good thing because the exhaustion numbed some of the fear.

Temporarily, anyway.

The fear returned when she studied the house itself. Despite the barking dogs, it wasn't a fortress, that's for sure. It looked more like, well, a home.

Deputy Sanchez pulled to a stop in front of the porch and steps.

"Are you sure we'll be safe here?" Willa asked, eyeing the cottage-style house.

With the iron-gray sky and the icy drizzle spitting at them, the house was the only spot of color in the winter landscape. It was a cheery shade of yellow and had dark green shutters and door. There were even flower boxes anchored beneath the windows. It wasn't what she expected from a dark and brooding small-town Texas sheriff.

"The place was painted like this when I bought it," Brandon mumbled, probably sensing her surprise. "Wait here," he told her.

Brandon drew his gun, and just like that, the fatigue could no longer numb the fear. Willa sat there on the backseat of the deputy's four-door black Ford and watched as Brandon got out. He didn't say anything to the dogs. He merely lifted his left hand, and they both went silent. The pair followed Brandon up the steps and to the door he then unlocked. However, they didn't go inside. The dogs waited for him on the porch.

"Please, don't let there be anyone in there," Willa mumbled. But she obviously didn't mumble it softly enough because the deputy eased around in the seat and looked at her.

"Butch and Sundance wouldn't have let anyone inside," Deputy Sanchez drawled. "Brandon's just being extra cautious. If the dogs are alive and kickin', then no one got near the place and remained in one piece."

Even though Willa didn't like the idea of being around attack dogs, it was better than having no outside protection against a professional assassin.

Pete kept the windshield wipers on, and they scraped away at the sleety drizzle, smearing the ice on the glass.

"I'm assuming Brandon doesn't need the dogs for security," she commented. "Because I'd figured Crockett Creek was a safe town."

"Don't worry, it is. I think the dogs help Brandon make sure his privacy stays private. It's probably why he lives all the way out here by himself. This place is a good ten miles outside of town."

That said a lot about the man whose baby she was carrying. A private man. A man she trusted, she reminded herself.

A man she wanted.

Willa quickly tried to push that thought aside, but it flashed right back in her head. She huffed. Her memory was still a mess in parts, and yet she could remember in complete, agonizing detail every twinge of attraction she felt for a man who placed a high value on privacy and keeping secrets.

"So, who takes care of the place and the dogs when he's out of town?" Willa wanted to know. It hadn't occurred to her until now that Brandon might have a girlfriend.

"His neighbor's boy does that for him."

"Neighbor?" she questioned. Not a girlfriend. Though she didn't see a nearby house or any other signs of a neighbor.

"Zach Grange," the deputy provided. "He raised the dogs from pups, and he's about the only one other than Brandon that they trust to get near them. I figure Brandon likes having 'em around. He worked canines for a while in Special Forces, you know."

No, she didn't know. That was another of the secrets he hadn't been ready to volunteer.

Brandon came back out and returned to the car so he could open her door and take her overnight bag. The wet, cold air came right at her, sending a chill straight through her clothes. Brandon thanked his deputy, and the man tipped his Stetson and drove away.

"Will the dogs bite?" she asked, eyeing them as they went up the steps. Even though it was freezing, literally, she didn't hurry because she didn't want to alarm them.

"They won't bite you." And he aimed a glance at both, one that was effective because the two remained docile on the porch as Willa went past them and into the house.

Her first impression was that the place was toasty warm. Thank goodness. And everything was neat and orderly. There were no clothes lying around, no clutter. The living room had been painted a soft cream color that complemented the slate-blue sofa and recliner. He had a flat-screen TV mounted on the wall above the fireplace.

Other than the winter weather outside, there were no signs of Christmas here. Like her place in Austin.

Hard to concentrate on the holidays when their lives were on the line.

"The kitchen's through here," he explained, pointing through a doorway.

Willa looked inside. Neat and orderly there, too.

"The bathroom's over there." He pointed to the first room off the hall that fed off the living room.

"Is it okay if I take a shower?" she asked.

"Of course." He handed Willa her overnight bag and walked into the kitchen. "Then I'll fix us something to eat, and you can get some rest."

All three of those—a shower, food and rest—sounded heavenly, and Willa headed to the bathroom. But then, she stopped.

"I want the truth," she told him, turning back around to face him. "Will Shore come here looking for us?"

Brandon had been about to open the fridge, but his hand paused in midair. He looked at her and then crossed the room toward her.

"He might," Brandon confessed. "The dogs won't let him get close, but he could try to neutralize them."

Neutralize. What a benign word for *kill.*

"I have a security system wired to all the windows and doors," Brandon continued. "It came with the house, and even though I've never had an occasion to use it, I will now that you're here."

"Good." And she heard herself repeat it several times. Because she suddenly felt shaky, Willa placed the bag on the floor and held the doorframe to steady herself.

Brandon caught onto her. "Are you okay?"

She managed a nod. "I'm not very good with this whole trying-to-kill-us thing."

"Few people are good at that," he mumbled. He pulled her into his arms. "And you don't want to be around them if they are."

Since that sounded, well, personal, she eased back and met him eye to eye. She'd done that so she could see his expression when she asked him what he meant by that. But the question faded from her mind when she stared at him.

Mercy.

There it was again. That damn attraction. An itch, some people called it. Willa just thought of it as an itchy nuisance. It was clouding her judgment and drawing her to a man she should be questioning. Instead, she was falling for him.

"What?" he asked.

She had no intention of telling him what she was thinking. A man like Brandon would likely turn and run—after he made sure she was safe, that is. He was a natural protector. An alpha male. And she instinctively knew that a pregnant woman falling hard for him would take him right out of his very narrow comfort zone.

Willa shook her head to try to blow off his question, but she found herself leaning in closer to him. Why, why, why couldn't she just back away?

Because she didn't want to.

Because she wanted Brandon.

He reached to brush a strand of hair off her face, but he didn't pull back his hand. His fingers stayed, touching her cheek.

"You've been through a lot," he said as if that explained the coil of heat that was simmering inside her.

She made a sound of agreement and leaned in. Willa only intended to touch her mouth to his. Just a taste of what her body was begging her to have. But Brandon made a sound of his own.

Not of agreement.

The husky sound rumbled in his throat, and his hand went from her cheek to the back of her neck. He snapped her to him.

And it wasn't just a touch.

BRANDON FORGOT ALL ABOUT the danger. About the fatigue. About all the other things he should be doing. However, he didn't forget about this need inside him. A need that only Willa seemed capable of satisfying.

Why the hell did he want her like this?

He didn't have an answer for that, and it didn't seem to matter to his mouth, or to the rest of his body. He just hauled her as close to him as she could possibly get, and he kissed her as if he had a right to do exactly that.

He didn't have that right, though.

Kisses and caresses would just lead her on. But that still didn't stop him.

He tightened the grip he had on the back of her neck and angled her head so he could deepen the kiss. She tasted like…Willa. It was a taste he'd already sampled, and while there was the whole forbidden-fruit thing going on here, his response seemed about much more than that. He'd had forbidden fruit before, and it'd never tasted this good.

She made that mind-blowing sound of pleasure deep within her throat and pressed as hard against him as he did against her. They pulled away, only to catch their breath and, as if starved for each other, went right back for another round.

Soon, though, the kiss and the body-to-body contact wasn't enough. Soon, certain parts of him started to demand more. That was Brandon's cue to pull away, and he tried. But Willa held on, and he didn't put up much of a fight.

"I'm on fire," she mumbled against his mouth.

That was something he didn't need to hear, but it wasn't something he could forget, either. It was a primal invitation to his overly aroused body, and his instincts were to scoop her up in his arms and haul her off to bed.

That couldn't happen, of course.

Brandon repeated that to himself but still didn't pull away. Instead, he dropped some kisses on her neck and cupped her left breast with his hand.

"Still on fire," she let him know, and she added more of those sounds of silky feminine pleasure.

Willa went after his neck as well and landed a few kisses in one of his very sensitive spots. Too sensitive. More of that, and a trip to the bed would happen whether it should or not.

Brandon forced himself to pull back.

Willa's breath was gusting now, and his wasn't much slower. They stared at each other, too close for him not to consider just jumping right back in. But he didn't. If a simple kiss was leading her on, then this was a dozen steps past that at a time when Willa was most vulnerable. She was pregnant and scared. And he was taking advantage of that and this attraction between them.

She ran her tongue over her bottom lip and made another sound of pleasure. Brandon's body clenched, and he took a huge step back.

"So?" she said. "What happens now?"

No way was he going to answer that. Because a response—any response—could get him in even hotter water.

"Ah," she mumbled when he glanced away. "I guess that means we aren't going to do *that*."

"No," he agreed. "Wrong time, wrong place. Hell… wrong everything." Brandon mumbled some harsher profanity under his breath.

"Wrong man?" she concluded.

"Especially that." He glanced away again and was sorry he'd said anything.

"You have that look again, as if I just poked a stick at a raw wound. You obviously have secrets you don't want to share."

She grabbed his chin and drew his gaze back to hers. "Since you've saved my life more than once in the past twenty-four hours, I would tell you my deepest darkest secret…if I could remember it."

She smiled.

He didn't.

"You don't remember your secrets?" he asked. This was the first time it had occurred to him that she hadn't regained her full memory after watching that DVD in the hotel suite.

Willa shrugged. "I'd like to say yes to that, but there are still blanks." She drew in a quick breath. "On the drive over, I kept trying to piece things together, but I don't remember how I ended up on the floor of that hospital."

Good. Maybe she wouldn't regain those horrific memories. She had remembered what files the gunman had forced her to access, and that had to be enough. Willa had already had enough stress without recalling an attack that had left her in a coma.

She touched his face again, turning him in her direction. "I sense you're pushing me away. That's probably for the best, if I were in a sane mode right now. I'm not. I'm in pregnancy mode where I need to protect this baby at all costs. I figure you're my best bet for that protection because you have a genetic link."

He stared at her. "Yeah," he settled for saying.

Brandon almost left it at that. Almost. But for some reason he decided that Willa deserved something better. A better explanation. And she certainly deserved something better than him.

"My birth father is a man named Wade Decalley," Brandon heard himself say. "My mother never talked about him much, and a few years ago, I found out why." He paused long enough to gather his breath. "He's a convicted serial killer, and he's spent the last thirteen years on death row."

Brandon realized it was the first time he'd said that out loud. The first time he'd actually told anyone the truth about his father.

Willa didn't blink. Didn't gasp. She merely put her fingers on his arm and rubbed gently. "I'm sorry."

"No need," he practically snapped. "I didn't know about him when I agreed to donate the semen I'd stored for my military tour in the Middle East."

Now she blinked, and she gave him an ah-ha kind of look. "Now, I get it. You don't want to pass on your DNA to a child because of your father."

"But I did anyway. I'm sorry for that, Willa. I'm sorry you didn't get the biological father you thought you were getting for this baby."

The corner of her mouth lifted, but she was also blinking back tears. "I think this baby girl has an amazing biological dad, one who would risk his own life to protect her." Willa leaned in and kissed his cheek. "I don't regret her having your DNA."

"You might," he mumbled.

She huffed, pulled away from him and fluttered her fingers in the direction of the bathroom. "I think I'll grab that shower now."

Brandon hoped it would help her relax, especially after their kissing session and his confession about his family *legacy*. He sure as hell could use something to help him relax, too, but he had too much to do. While he fixed Willa something to eat, he needed to call and try to get some information about Jessie Beecham's murder and the files that the gunman had wanted Willa to tamper with.

That meant contacting Cash.

Brandon took a prepaid cell phone from the kitchen drawer. A phone that couldn't be traced. He'd bought it on impulse, a throwback to his Special Ops days when he had been trained to be prepared for anything. At the time of the purchase, he had figured it would never be used, that he would spend the rest of his life as a sheriff, not doing anything that required a prepaid cell. But he needed to return to his roots in covert ops in order to keep Willa safe.

However, it would have to end there.

Once he had the answers they needed and Martin Shore and the danger had been neutralized, there would be only one thing left for him to do.

The best thing he could do for both Willa and the baby was to get as far away from them as possible.

Chapter Ten

Willa sat at the cozy kitchen table and ate the turkey and cheese sandwich Brandon had fixed for her. She wasn't actually hungry, but she forced herself to eat because of the baby.

Brandon's own sandwich lay untouched on the table across from her, and instead of eating, he was pacing while he talked on a cell phone. Since he'd been on the phone when she came out of the shower, she had no idea how long this conversation had been going on. But she did know that he was talking to Cash.

And Brandon obviously wasn't happy about the answers he was hearing.

"Now you think Dr. Farris could be responsible for the leak?" Brandon challenged. He didn't wait for an answer. He went to the laptop sitting on a corner desk and pressed some keys. "Because before we even met the doctor, Martin Shore found us at the safe house that SAPD provided."

He paused, and she could hear the faint sound of Cash's voice on the other end of the line. Unfortunately, she couldn't hear what he was saying.

"You do that," he told Cash. "You dig into Dr. Farris's

background, and I'll do the same. If the woman is dirty, I want her arrested."

So did Willa. She cringed because she'd actually been in the room with the person who might want her dead. And she'd trusted the doctor. Well, she'd trusted her enough to watch that DVD that had spurred her memory and almost certainly created more danger.

"Cash thinks the doctor is the leak?" Willa mouthed.

He shook his head and held his hand over the speaker end of the cell. "I think he's grasping at straws. He has no proof."

And they didn't have proof of Cash's innocence, either.

"Good," Brandon said several moments later, removing his hand so he could continue his call to Cash. The printer next to the laptop began to spit out something. "Because I'd like to talk with Dean Quinlan, too. Yes, you can do that. Have him call me at this number."

Dean Quinlan—the former CSI whose name had been on the files at the hospital. Willa didn't think she'd actually met the man, but like Brandon, she wanted to ask him questions about his involvement in all this.

"No, I'm not bringing Willa in," Brandon insisted. "And no, I'm not telling you where we are." He hung up. "Don't worry. Cash didn't send the fax. My deputy did, so Cash doesn't know we're here." He snatched the piece of paper from the printer.

"Recognize him?" Brandon asked, sliding the paper across the table toward her. It was a picture of a brown-haired man with a thin face.

Willa shook her head. "No. Who is he?"

"That's Dean Quinlan."

She took a harder look at the man who seemed to be at the center of everything. Was he the person who'd hired Shore to kill her? He didn't look like a killer, but Dean Quinlan could want her dead because she might be able to prove his involvement in the maternity hostage situation.

"He wants to talk to you?" she asked.

"Yeah. But don't expect Quinlan to confess to anything. Cash questioned him over the phone—Quinlan refused to meet with him—but the man claims he's innocent."

And he might be. But someone was guilty. "What about the actual lab samples at the maternity hospital? Did I tamper with them?" She shook her head, huffed. "Because I only remember hacking into them."

"Cash claims the test results were fine. They did a duplicate set of tests at another site and came up with the same results." He sat down across from her and met her gaze. "Of course, if you managed to tamper with the actual samples, then the duplicate test would give the same results."

Willa put her sandwich back on the plate and tried to recall any other details. But her mind just wouldn't let her go there.

"If I somehow contaminated or corrupted the samples, then how would I prove that?" she wanted to know.

"You can't. But it's possible they could exhume Jessie Beecham's body to get what they need. There were two

DNA samples in the files you accessed," Brandon explained. "They were taken from tissue found beneath Beecham's fingernails."

"Jessie Beecham," she repeated. "The club owner with ties to the mob who was found murdered."

Another nod. "But this wasn't a mob hit. Too messy for that. It appears Beecham had been in some kind of physical altercation with his killer before he was struck on the head with a blunt object. His wallet, gun and phone were all missing, so SAPD suspected the motive might be robbery."

Willa gave that some thought. "Or maybe it was meant to look like a robbery?"

"Yeah." And he paused again. "So, SAPD wanted a fast turnaround on the DNA they collected from his fingernails because they wanted a quick arrest. Beecham's allies were making a lot of noise and blaming Beecham's rival. SAPD thought they might have a mob war on their hands. Since the lab in Austin was out of commission thanks to the fire, they sent it to the secure area of the San Antonio Maternity Hospital."

Which had turned out not to be so secure thanks to the gunman, and her. "Who would have known the samples were there?" she immediately asked.

"Anyone in SAPD." Brandon mumbled some frustrated profanity. "Or someone who worked in the hospital lab itself."

In other words, there were too many people involved to narrow it down to one specific suspect. She already didn't trust Dr. Farris, Cash and this Dean Quinlan, but she would possibly have to add many more to her list.

Brandon took the photo from her and stared at it. "According to Cash, the DNA samples were held in a secure vault, and the handful of hospital staff who had access to that area all had the proper security clearances. They've all checked out and are no longer suspects."

"Well, someone gave the gunman the code to get into the vault area because it was written on the paper he took from his pocket."

"Cash believes the gunman could have gotten the info after the hostage situation started. A lab tech was killed within minutes after the gunmen stormed the hospital. It's possible the gunman threatened to kill the tech, and he coughed up the code."

"And the gunman killed him anyway," Willa supplied. Then she thought of something else. "The gunman tried to call Dean Quinlan."

"Quinlan denies that," Brandon grumbled. "But I don't buy it. Quinlan could have been bought off."

"By whom?"

"By Wes Dunbar, the rival club owner. Jessie Beecham and he were long-time enemies. They could have gotten into an altercation that resulted in Beecham's death." He dropped the picture onto the table. "But the DNA samples didn't prove that. The DNA belonged to a homeless man with a criminal record a mile long."

"So, this homeless man was arrested?" Willa asked.

"He was. And his court-appointed lawyer did a plea bargain. The guy's already in jail for manslaughter."

But he could be innocent. All of this, including the hostage situation itself, could have been orchestrated to put the blame for murder on a homeless man when the real killer was still out there.

It didn't take Willa long to come up with a possible identity for the real killer. "Wes Dunbar, the rival club owner, could have murdered Beecham and then paid off the CSI, Dean Quinlan, to tamper with the evidence."

Brandon nodded and pulled in a hard breath.

So, why was there the threat of another hostage situation? Had someone else decided to do the same thing as Wes Dunbar? If so, Willa's memory wasn't going to be of any help. That caused her to groan. As long as the danger was there, she was anchored to Brandon. Part of her—okay, her body—was all right with that. She wanted to sleep with him, and she was certain that was driving a lot of her other desires.

But it was clear that Brandon wasn't in this for a one-night stand or a happily ever after. She didn't need her memory to feel that he wanted to be out of her life. And that meant solving this case. The sooner that was done, the sooner they could both go back to the way things were before. That's what she wanted.

Willa repeated that.

It still didn't ring true.

She forced herself to focus just on the case. "Any suggestions as to what I should do next?"

Brandon's jaw muscles stirred, but before he could answer, his phone rang. Even though the cell didn't have caller ID, she figured it was Cash. Hopefully, the cop would have information that would help them.

Brandon didn't say a word when he took the call. He merely put the phone to his ear. A moment later, she saw the surprise, and then the concern, go through his eyes.

"Dean Quinlan," he said.

Though the sound of the man's name caused her heart to race, this was good news. Well, potentially good. Dean was the next step in getting information because even if he was simply trying to cover his guilt, he could still slip up and tell them if Wes Dunbar or someone else hired him to have those DNA samples tampered with.

"A meeting?" Brandon questioned.

Willa waited with her breath held. She didn't relish the idea of seeing this man, but again, it might be the beginning of the end to the danger.

"All right," Brandon said a moment later. "I'll meet you at my office in Crockett Creek." He paused again. "No, I can't be there that soon. I'm at least two hours out."

That was a lie, of course, to try to conceal their real location.

Brandon checked his watch. "I'll meet you there at three o'clock. And Quinlan, my suggestion is you'd better have answers. The *right answers*. Or I'll find a reason to arrest you."

It seemed as if Brandon was about to hang up, but he stopped. "What do you mean?" he demanded from Dean. "Who's trying to kill you?"

Whatever Dean said, it caused Brandon's jaw muscles to go to work again. He cursed when he slapped the phone shut.

"Someone's trying to kill Dean Quinlan?" Willa asked.

"Yeah." And that's all Brandon said for several moments. "He claims Cash wants him dead. And Quinlan says he has something to prove it."

Chapter Eleven

Deputy Pete Sanchez parked in front of the back entrance to the Crockett Creek sheriff's office. It was Brandon's usual parking space, but before today, he'd never felt like checking his too-familiar surroundings before he exited. Of course, that had plenty to do with Willa being with him.

Brandon tried to give her a reassuring glance before he got her out of the vehicle and hurried her inside. He'd already apologized a couple of times for having to bring her for what would likely be a high-stress meeting with Dean Quinlan. However, the alternative was leaving her alone at his place, and that wasn't going to happen. Brandon had no intention of letting her out of his sight.

Martin Shore was still out there somewhere. And even though it was Christmas Eve, the holiday season wouldn't stop the hired gun from striking again.

Brandon heard the voices the moment he stepped inside. He was already on full alert, but those voices upped his anxiety. One of the voices belonged to his other deputy, Sheila Gafford, a thirty-year law-enforcement veteran who didn't normally raise her voice. But that's exactly what she was doing now.

"I told you to sit down and wait," Sheila ordered.

"And I told you that I will see the sheriff *now*," the man responded.

Brandon didn't recognize the voice, but he sure as heck recognized anger when he heard it. This guy was outraged about something.

"Wait here with Willa," Brandon told Pete, and he left them in his office while he went to the front of the building. Sheila was there, staring down a tall man wearing a business suit.

The man looked past the deputy and glared when he spotted Brandon making his way toward them.

"A problem?" Brandon asked Sheila.

His deputy rolled her coffee-brown eyes and huffed. "This is Mr. Wes—"

"Dunbar," the visitor interrupted.

Well, Brandon hadn't had to go looking for the devil after all because here was his number one suspect, just a few feet away.

"Are you Sheriff Ruiz?" Wes demanded.

Even though he was rail thin, he had a booming voice, and everything about him screamed money. The suit was high-priced. Haircut, too. And judging from his perfect nails, the man had regular manicures. He didn't look the sort to do his own dirty work, but then Jessie Beecham had likely been killed in the heat of an argument.

"I'm Sheriff Ruiz," Brandon confirmed. "What do you want?"

"To talk to you. I heard about that former maternity

hostage, Willa Marks. She's connected to what happened in the hospital that day."

"Yeah? What makes you think that?" Brandon didn't intend to volunteer anything.

"Don't play stupid with me. Protect her all you want. She's not the reason I'm here. But I figure that sewer rat, Dean Quinlan, is dying to get to her, and since I'm dying to get to Quinlan, I figured the fastest way to do that would be through you."

Brandon glanced around to see if Dean was already there. He wasn't. Though he should have been. He was nearly a half hour late. Of course, maybe Wes Dunbar's impromptu visit had something to do with that. However, Brandon spotted an expensive black luxury sedan he didn't recognize. It no doubt belonged to Wes, and the man behind the wheel was probably his driver.

"Why do you want to get to Dean Quinlan?" Brandon asked.

"Simple. He's trying to pin Jessie Beecham's murder on me by claiming I'm the one who hired those idiots to take the maternity hostages."

"Dean told you this?"

"Didn't have to. I hear things, and I don't like what I'm hearing. Jessie's killer is already behind bars, and Jessie's in hell. Case closed."

Maybe closed but not necessarily resolved. "Did you try to kill Willa Marks?" Brandon didn't expect a straight answer, but he figured it wouldn't hurt to ask.

"I have no reason to kill her. As far as I can tell she's not blabbing to the cops that I'm Jessie's killer. Plus, I heard her head's all messed up. She doesn't remember her own name, much less what happened at the hospital that day."

Brandon wanted to punch that smug look off Wes's face. But while that might give him some temporary satisfaction, it wouldn't help Willa.

"You seem to know a lot about Ms. Marks," Brandon commented. It was a fishing expedition. He wanted to know if Wes was getting his info from anyone in SAPD.

But Wes didn't bite. A dry smile bent his mouth for several short seconds, and he aimed his finger at Brandon. "If Dean Quinlan gets in touch with you, my advice is not to believe a word he says."

"Why would he lie to me?"

"To cover his scrawny butt. I figure he screwed up something. He was a CSI after all. He screwed up something, and then tried to put the blame on anyone but himself." His finger landed against his own chest. "Well, that blame better not come anywhere near me. Got that?"

Wes didn't wait for Brandon's response. He turned and stormed out. Wes climbed into a sleek black limo waiting for him just outside and the driver took off.

"Never known a Christmas Eve like this one," Sheila grumbled. She pushed her dark, gray-threaded hair away from her face. "I swear, the phone's been ringing off the hook. Four messages in the past two hours—all from Dr. Lenora Farris."

Brandon cursed. "What does she want?"

"Same thing as the bozo who just left. She wants to talk to you. Says it's important. Says you're to return her calls ASAP." She lifted her hands in the air. "Don't these people have anything better to do over the holidays than pester us?"

Apparently not. "Did Dean Quinlan show up?"

"Not yet." She checked the clock on the wall. "Guess you want me to wait here until he does?"

"I do. Thanks, Sheila. But keep the door locked. I don't want just anyone waltzing in here unannounced."

The woman complained under her breath, as Brandon had known she would. She obviously didn't like being called into work on her off day, but she would stay. And she would do everything within her power to help him protect Willa. That was all he could ask for at the moment. But once this meeting with Dean was over, Brandon had to figure out his next move. It probably wasn't wise to stay around Crockett Creek now that both Wes and Dean knew he was there.

He walked back to his office where Pete was standing guard in the doorway. Willa was there, too, peeking out, and judging from her expression, she'd heard everything Wes had said.

"He's gone?" she asked.

Brandon nodded and tipped his head to Pete to get him moving as well. Pete went in the direction of the deputies' office on the other side of the reception desk.

Since Willa looked ready to collapse, Brandon pulled her into his arms. "Wes was just blowing smoke," he assured her. But the fact that he felt the need to blow smoke said a lot.

Wes was acting like a guilty man.

Of course, he had the strongest motive of all their suspects. If that had been his DNA underneath Jessie

Beecham's fingernails, then Wes could have been convicted of murder. Now, the question was had he killed
Beecham and then orchestrated the hostage situation
to cover it up?

If so, then Wes would almost certainly want Willa
dead.

Brandon was about to offer Willa more reassurances,
but movement stopped him. It hadn't come from the
hall but from Willa's middle.

The baby was kicking.

He pulled back slightly and looked down.

"Soccer practice," Willa joked.

There was certainly a lot of movement, much more
than he'd expected for an unborn child. And some of the
kicks were hard, too. He could actually see the thumps
against Willa's top.

Without thinking, Brandon slid his palm over her
belly. And he froze. He shouldn't be doing this. This
was something a real father should do, and it was far
too intimate. More intimate than the hot kissing session
they'd shared in his kitchen.

"Amazing, isn't it?" Willa asked.

Brandon made a sound that could have meant anything, and he jerked back his hand. "It must hurt."

"No," she insisted. She stared at him. "It's okay,
Brandon. A touch doesn't commit you to anything.
Kisses don't, either."

"But sex would," he mumbled before he could stop
himself. Hell. What was wrong with him? First he
couldn't control his hand, and now he couldn't control
his mouth.

"Depends on the sex."

His gaze fired to hers, and he expected to see another of those teasing half smiles. But no smile. She looked dead serious. Then, she huffed.

"Sorry," she whispered. "I guess there's no such thing as no-strings-attached sex when it comes to us."

"No," he agreed.

He wanted to explain that he wasn't the father his baby deserved, but Willa had already heard it. It obviously hadn't sunk in because he still saw the welcoming look in her eyes. For a woman who distrusted nearly everyone, it was a powerful, and touching, burden to place on him.

Brandon heard someone knock. The sound came from the back where Willa and he had entered. He drew his gun, motioned for her to stay put and went to look out the sliver of a reinforced side window.

Thankfully, the man looked exactly like his photograph so Brandon had no trouble recognizing their visitor.

It was Dean Quinlan.

Dean's gaze was slashing all around the parking lot as if he expected someone to jump out and attack. Which might be close to the truth. Brandon didn't see any sign of a weapon, so he opened the door.

"What was Wes Dunbar doing here?" Dean demanded.

Brandon didn't even try to relieve the man's nerves. "Looking for you, I think."

Dean tried to bolt inside, but Brandon stopped and frisked him. He wasn't carrying concealed, but he did have an envelope gripped in his left hand.

Brandon stepped aside so the man could enter, but he

kept himself between Dean and his office where he'd left Willa. Even though he was a good six inches shorter than Brandon, Dean tried to look over his shoulder.

"Did you tell Wes that I was coming here?" Dean asked. He continued to glance around, and there were beads of sweat on his forehead despite the chilly winter temperature outside.

"No. Did you?"

Dean looked at him as if he'd lost his mind. "Why would I tell a scumbag like him where I was? He could be the one who wants me dead." He paused. "Well, maybe it's him."

"You got more than one person trying to kill you?" Brandon asked.

"Maybe," Dean repeated and shook his head. "Look, someone's been trying to kill me, and I think it might be the same person who's after Willa Marks. There was a story in the newspaper about someone blowing up her house."

Brandon tried not to curse but failed. He was all for freedom of the press, but the less printed about Willa, the safer she might be.

"Who's trying to kill us?" Brandon heard someone ask. He groaned because it was Willa's voice and he heard her making her way toward them. He shot her a look, warning to go back to his office.

She ignored him and kept her attention pinned to Dean.

Dean studied her a moment and then handed Brandon the envelope. Brandon didn't put away his weapon, and he handed the envelope to Willa so she could open it.

There was a single black-and-white picture inside.

It was a grainy photo taken in what appeared to be a parking lot, and it took Brandon a moment to figure out that he was looking at a picture of three people.

Wes Dunbar, Dr. Lenora Farris.

And Cash.

Ironically, it was the face of his old friend that was the clearest.

"I've been keeping an eye on Cash and Wes," Dean explained. "I thought one or both of them might be trying to set me up to take the fall for that hostage situation."

"Why would they do that?" Brandon wanted to know.

"Because I think Wes did kill Jessie Beecham, and I think that DNA sample in the lab would have proven it."

Brandon couldn't argue with that. "But why would Cash want to frame you?" He handed the picture to Willa so she could see it as well.

Dean gave Brandon another are-you-out-of-your-mind look. "I've checked on you, and I know you and Cash are old friends. But Cash isn't the man you knew way back when. He's friends with Wes now—did he tell you that?"

No. Cash hadn't. And Brandon wasn't sure he believed Dean. Still, there was the photo.

"That picture proves nothing," Willa said, probably sensing Brandon's conflicting emotions.

"It proves the three of them were together," Dean countered. "And I think they were together for one reason—to figure out how they could cover up the fact that Wes killed his old rival."

Brandon could see one huge flaw in that theory. "Then why involve Dr. Farris? If Wes wanted someone to cover up his crime, he would go to Cash or some other dirty cop."

"You don't know?" But it wasn't really a question, and Dean seemed more than eager to dole out this tidbit. "Dr. Farris and Wes are old friends. But she was also friends with Jessie Beecham. She was having an affair with Jessie around the time he was murdered."

Brandon wanted to kick himself. He'd been so involved in keeping Willa safe that he hadn't given this case the time and work it needed. Hell. Even though this wasn't his specific case, he was a lawman, and he should have done better. If he had, this investigation might already be over and the danger gone.

He glanced at Willa to let her know he was sorry, but he only saw skepticism in her eyes. Brandon had that same skepticism, but what he couldn't doubt was that Dean appeared completely confident that he was telling the truth.

Brandon would check every detail to make sure he was.

"If Dr. Farris was having an affair with Jessie as you say, then why would she want to help the person who possibly murdered him?" Brandon challenged.

"Hey, I didn't say she was in love with the man. She's been going back and forth between Wes and Jessie for years. She might not have been sleeping with Wes at the time of Jessie's death, but from what I've learned about her, she wouldn't want him to be arrested for a murder rap."

Dean wasn't painting a very good picture of

Dr. Farris. And Cash must have known her background. Yet he'd brought her to that hotel suite to "help" Willa. Maybe the doctor had really come to see just how much Willa remembered. If so, that meant Dr. Farris could have been the one to alert Martin Shore.

"So, will you help me?" Dean asked. But he wasn't looking at Brandon, he was looking at Willa.

"Help you how?" she asked, wanting to know.

"Tell the cops that I had nothing to do with the hostage situation."

She shook her head. "I can't do that. The gunman—"

Brandon caught her arm to stop her from finishing. He didn't want Dean to know Willa had remembered the gunman trying to call him.

"It's time for you to leave," Brandon told the man.

"No." Dean volleyed glances between the two of them. "Not until she agrees to help me."

"She's not agreeing to anything." Brandon didn't wait for the man to concur. He let go of Willa so he could usher Dean out of the building. Brandon used more force than necessary, and he slammed the door in Dean's face and locked it.

Dean shouted out some profanity and threats, but he must have quickly remembered that only minutes earlier, Wes had been in the area. Brandon watched through the sidelight window as Dean scurried across the back parking lot and climbed into a white compact car.

Brandon turned to Willa to tell her they shouldn't stay put much longer, but she spoke before he could.

"I need access to a computer and the internet," she

told him. "I want to search some files and see what I can learn about all the things Dean just told us."

Brandon had a laptop at his house, but now that Wes and God knows who else knew they were in the area, it might not be safe to stay there. At least at the station, he had the two deputies who could back him up in case something went wrong.

"How long will you need?" Brandon asked, checking his watch.

She shook her head. "I'm not sure. I think I remember how to hack into files."

Brandon knew this was illegal, but he didn't care. Right now, he only wanted to get to the truth, and he wanted that truth in the shortest time possible so he could get Willa out of there.

"You can use my office," Brandon told her. "And while you're doing that, I need to make some calls." He had to do some checking on Cash so he could make sure his old friend hadn't betrayed him.

But first things first, he wanted to call the Texas Ranger crime lab in Austin.

After Willa dropped the photo Dean had given them on Brandon's desk, she sat at his computer and started to tap away on the keys. Brandon worked his way through the Ranger organization and contacted Sergeant Egan Caldwell, a Ranger he'd worked with on several cases. It took Brandon nearly fifteen minutes to get through the explanation and his request. He believed there to be a leak in SAPD and he was asking the Rangers to conduct an impartial investigation into the DNA results from Jessie Beecham's murder.

The request and Sergeant Caldwell's agreement

would no doubt cause waves. Now, the trick was to prevent those waves from placing Willa in any more danger.

Brandon made several more calls, searching for someplace to take her. He couldn't very well ask SAPD to provide a safe house, but he didn't have many options.

"I think I might have found something," Willa announced.

Brandon was about to hurry to the computer when he heard the knock at the front door.

"We're sure popular today," Sheila called back to Brandon a moment later. "Got two more visitors. Strangers at that. Should I let them in?"

"Not yet." Brandon drew his gun and started for the front, but he soon saw the two people standing on the other side of the reinforced glass door.

It was Cash and Dr. Farris.

Chapter Twelve

Willa was now certain of one thing. Nearly every one of their suspects knew where Brandon and she were. Martin Shore was the only one yet to make an appearance at Brandon's office, and she prayed he was far away from them.

She watched from the doorway of his office as Brandon "greeted" their latest visitors. Both Dr. Farris and Cash were visibly angry, but so was Brandon. Heck, so was she.

Especially after what she'd just learned about Dr. Farris.

Thank goodness her hacking skills were as sharp as ever. Willa might not remember key incidents of the past two months, but she obviously recalled how to worm her way into someone's personal information.

Now what she needed was some time to dig into the other suspects' computer files. So far they hadn't had much time to do that.

There hadn't been time for much of anything.

They had both showered and changed their clothes before Pete had arrived to pick them up at Brandon's house. Brandon had replaced his jeans with a clean pair and put on a black shirt and leather jacket. Hardly Christmas colors but neither was Willa's cream-colored sweater. She hadn't had anything else clean to wear, which meant she was either going to have to do laundry soon or buy something new. Heaven knows when she would get the chance to do either.

"Let us in," Cash demanded. "It's freezing out here."

It was, and that probably explained why Cash and the doctor were huddled together. Both had their heads lowered, but the sleet was starting to come down.

"Are you two friends again?" Brandon asked Cash and the doctor, not keeping the sarcasm from his voice. "Because just a few hours ago, you thought Dr. Farris here might be supplying bad guys with information about Willa."

The doctor turned that frosty look at Cash. "No. We're not friends. And we didn't arrive together. I had no idea he was coming here until I saw him pull into the parking lot."

"I'm a cop," Cash reminded her. "I have a right to be here." He aimed his attention at Brandon. "Any reason you wouldn't tell me where you were?"

"Yeah. The reason is Martin Shore and his repeated attempts to kill Willa." Brandon kept a tight grip on his weapon, and he didn't move out of the doorway so the pair could fully enter the station.

"I'm trying to stop another attack," Cash insisted. "That's why I've spent the past few hours looking for you. I got your address from the state database, but it wasn't in the GPS. I found the farm road and stopped and asked someone where your place was, but the person wouldn't tell me. He said it would be danger-ous for me to try to get to your house anyway because you keep attack dogs."

Good. Brandon would thank all his neighbors first chance he got for keeping the location of his house a secret.

"It's cold," the doctor reminded Brandon. She shoved her hands in her pockets and bobbed on her tiptoes in an attempt to keep warm.

"Then if you want to get warm, my suggestion is talk fast so you can leave fast," Brandon told them, and it earned him more glares from the pair.

Dr. Farris looked past Brandon, and the doctor's gaze met Willa's. She grabbed the photo Dean had given them and walked closer. She kept the picture facing toward her in case Brandon wanted to withhold it for some reason. But she wanted them to see, and more than that, Willa wanted an explanation about why the three had been together.

"You shouldn't have left without speaking to me," Dr. Farris warned her. "The therapy session wasn't over, and I needed to debrief you so you could put all that you remembered in perspective."

Willa stopped next to Brandon. "I'd had all the perspective I could handle for one day. Plus, Shore was in the lobby waiting for us when we left. I don't suppose either of you would know why he was there?"

The doctor and Cash exchanged glances again and then shook their heads. "I have no idea why he was there," Cash insisted. "But maybe it's like Brandon suggested on the phone—Shore could have been following your PDA."

"My PDA was several buildings away in a parked car."

Cash shrugged. "Maybe Shore had already followed you by then. Maybe he saw you go into the hotel."

Willa couldn't totally discount that, but she didn't intend to trust Cash, either.

"You need to come back with me," the doctor insisted. "Or at least let me finish the session."

"Willa's not going anywhere with you," Brandon informed her. He took the photo from Willa and put it right in Cash and the doctor's faces. "Got an explanation for this?"

Well, that got a reaction. The color drained from Dr. Farris's cheeks, and Cash cursed.

"Where did you get that?" Cash demanded.

"A concerned citizen. Now, would you like to tell me what was going on in this meeting?"

"Nothing," the doctor volunteered. "I was duped into being there."

"But Wes and you are old friends," Willa pointed out.

"*Former* friends," the doctor corrected. "I got a call from someone claiming to be Wes's assistant. The person—a man—told me that Wes had proof of who'd killed Jessie Beecham. I went, of course, because I wanted to know who was responsible so I could have the police arrest him. And when I arrived, Cash was there."

"I got a similar call," Cash continued. He stared at the photo. "So did Wes. It didn't take us long to figure out that we'd all been brought there under false pretenses. But we didn't know why someone would want to bring the three of us together." He paused. "Now, we know. It was to get this incriminating photo."

Again, that could be the truth, but Willa was glad Brandon wasn't letting them inside. It did make her wonder, though, if Dean Quinlan had set up the incriminating photo to throw blame off himself.

"Are you sure this meeting wasn't to figure out how to place the blame on the homeless man who's in jail for the murder?" Brandon asked.

Cash opened his mouth to speak, but it took him a few seconds to form the words. The anger tightened and twisted his face. "Brandon, you've got the wrong idea about me. I'm one of the good guys."

"Maybe," Brandon mumbled.

"There's more," Willa started and she glanced at Brandon to make sure it was okay to reveal what she had learned on her computer search. He had no idea what she knew, of course, since there hadn't been time to tell him, but Willa hoped that he would trust her not to spill anything that would only make this worse.

Brandon nodded.

And Willa met the doctor eye to eye. "Dr. Farris, you've come into a rather large sum of money recently."

The doctor placed her hand on her chest, and her mouth dropped open. "How would you know that?" But she shook her head and didn't wait for Willa to answer. "You invaded my privacy. You snooped on me. Well, it doesn't matter. The money was a gift from my grandfather."

"Really?" Willa questioned. "It came in seven different deposits, all just small enough not to alert the IRS. That's not usually the way people give gifts."

Cash and Brandon both gave the doctor a suspicious stare.

Dr. Farris huffed and made an adjustment to the collar of her coat so that it covered the back of her neck. "What? You think that money was some kind of payoff?"

"Was it?" Brandon asked. "Maybe Wes paid you off to keep quiet about him murdering your lover, Jessie Beecham?"

The doctor made a sound of outrage. "I don't have to listen to this. This conversation is over." And with that, she turned and started toward a sleek silver sports car that was parked just up the street.

One down, one to go.

But Cash didn't leave. Instead, his phone rang, and after glancing at the caller ID screen, he took the call. Brandon started to shut the door, but Cash held up his index finger in a wait-a-second gesture. Brandon did wait, but he leaned over and put his mouth to Willa's ear.

"We'll be leaving as soon as I'm done with Cash," he told her.

That didn't surprise Willa, but she had to wonder— where would they go now? Would it be safe enough to return to Brandon's house? Probably not. But then, she wasn't sure it was safe anywhere.

The baby kicked, as if in protest.

Cash ended his call and slapped his phone shut. "You

called the Texas Rangers," he said to Brandon in an accusing tone.

"Yeah, I did," Brandon readily admitted. "I want them to review Jessie Beecham's murder investigation, including the DNA samples."

"Those samples were tested after the hostage incident. They're clean."

"Then you should have no problem with them being tested again."

"You know I do." Cash's jaw was clenched so tightly that Willa was surprised he could manage to speak. "It'll make me look bad in the eyes of my superior officers." He cursed. "Hell, Brandon, you know how this works. Even if those tests hold up—and they will—there'll be questions about how I've handled this case."

Brandon took a step closer. "I need those questions answered. Willa and the baby are in danger, and I thought this was the fastest way to get to the truth."

"You could have come to me!" Cash practically shouted.

Brandon shook his head. "I'm not even sure I can trust you." He held up the picture to remind him of why. "Someone has been leaking info at SAPD, and I want to know who."

"Well, it sure as hell isn't me." Cash groaned and scrubbed his hand over his face. "Come on, we fought together side by side. I deserve the benefit of the doubt."

"No. I can't give you that. Not with Willa's safety at stake. And not until I know for sure who told Martin

Shore the location of the safe house where Willa and I were nearly killed."

Cash's gaze flew to Brandon's. "Dr. Farris. She could be the leak."

Willa didn't intend to look so skeptical, but it certainly seemed as if Cash was saying anything to try to save his own skin. "How would Dr. Farris have had access to the information about the safe house?" she asked.

Cash pulled in a hard breath. "She might have gotten it from my computer."

"What?" Brandon snapped.

"I didn't give her the information," Cash quickly defended himself. "But it's possible she got it when I was away from my desk. She showed up about the time we were making the arrangements for the safe house. She said she had the DVD for the therapy and she wanted to get in touch with Willa. I had to leave my desk for a couple of minutes to see someone, and when I came back, Dr. Farris was in my chair, waiting."

"Waiting?" Willa repeated. "Then what makes you think she accessed the location of the safe house?"

"Because it was on my computer screen." Cash continued to explain even over Brandon's loud groan. "I don't remember leaving the file open. In fact, I could have sworn that I closed it."

Brandon got in his face. "And why are you just telling me this now?"

"Because I forgot about it. I haven't exactly been twiddling my thumbs since then. I've been trying to figure out who's after you."

"I don't want your help figuring that out," Willa let

him know. She lifted her hand so Cash could see that she'd written Trust Brandon Ruiz on her palm. "Your name isn't on there for a reason. So, please, just leave me alone."

She thought Cash might argue with her. But he merely belted out some more harsh profanity, turned and walked away. Brandon immediately shut and locked the door.

"He's either innocent," Willa mumbled, "or he puts on a good show. Which is it?"

Brandon shook his head. "I wish I knew. But I don't regret calling the Rangers. In fact, I want to fax Sergeant Caldwell this photo that Dean Quinlan gave us and tell him it'd be in the best interest of the case to dig into Dr. Farris's financial records."

All of that was good, but a new investigation might take months to complete. She didn't have months. Her baby would arrive in about sixty days. Maybe it was some kind of early nesting instincts, but Willa wanted to be settled and soon.

But where?

And how?

She thought of the cash she had in several safety deposit boxes in San Antonio and Austin. She either had to get to one of them and start out some place new, or...

She had to continue to rely on Brandon.

"What?" Brandon asked, probably noticing the renewed concern on her face.

She stared at him and remembered the kisses. The hot attraction. Willa remembered how much she wanted him.

And how much he was trying to keep his emotional distance from her.

That helped with her decision.

She checked the time. It was too late to make it to San Antonio or Austin before the banks closed, and tomorrow was Christmas. It would be the day after before she could get to her cash.

"On the twenty-sixth, I'll need to go to a bank in San Antonio," Willa told him. "You think you can get me there safely?"

He studied her as if trying to figure out what was going on in her head. And he probably would, too. Brandon seemed to be in tune with that she was thinking.

He clutched her shoulders and looked her in the eye. "I'll protect you both until this is over."

Yes, he would. She didn't doubt that. But this would take a heavy emotional toll on both of them. Because the longer she was with him, the more she wanted him. The more she started to spin a fantasy of them being together to raise this child growing inside her.

Rather than start an argument with him, Willa merely nodded, but she would get to the bank the day after Christmas, and she'd go off on her own again.

And her heart would be broken.

But she would have to deal with that later, after she was sure her baby girl was safe.

"I need to pick up some things from my house," Brandon told her. "Let me send this fax, and we'll get out of here."

She turned, ready to go back to his office, but the sound stopped her. It came in an instant with no warning.

A loud blast shook the building.

Willa gasped and automatically ducked down. However, it wasn't a shot. It took her a moment to realize that there had been an explosion.

She looked out the glass door and saw the flames and the debris in the building directly across the street. Oh, God. She knew that sound and recognized the destruction.

A grenade had gone off.

Chapter Thirteen

"Get down!" Brandon yelled, not just to Willa but also to his two deputies who were still in the building.

Brandon pushed Willa to the floor and aimed his gun, but he had nothing to aim at. The diner on the other side of the street was in flames. Since it had closed early because of the holiday, there was no one inside. He couldn't see anyone milling around, either. That was the good news.

But someone or something had caused that explosion.

"You okay, Brandon?" Pete shouted.

"Yeah." Brandon glanced back at Pete who also had his weapon drawn. By his side, Sheila had done the same. "Call the fire department. I don't want that fire spreading to other businesses on Main Street. But tell them not to approach the area until they get an all-clear from one of us."

Brandon heard Sheila pick up the phone and do as he'd asked.

"There's a hired gun after Willa," he told them when Sheila had finished her call. "His name is Martin Shore.

He's six-two, stocky build and has a military-style hair-cut. He's armed and dangerous."

"I don't see anybody," Pete relayed, and with his gun pointed toward the burning diner, he inched closer.

"Look harder," Brandon insisted. He whispered for Willa to stay down, and he levered himself up so he could look as well.

There was still no one visible on the street, but that didn't mean the assassin wasn't there.

Because Brandon had his attention fixed on the burning building, he saw the second explosion at the exact moment that he heard it. The blast tore through the fiery debris and what was left of the diner, and it sent a spray of fire and ashes right at them.

"What the hell is going on out there?" Pete grumbled as he dropped to the floor.

Hell was the appropriate word for what Shore was creating out there. The assassin might be trying to scare them or draw them out, and he was tearing up the town to do it. Of course, Brandon had to consider that the next grenade would be launched at the sheriff's office.

"Help me!" someone yelled.

With her breath gusting, Willa looked back at Brandon. "That's Wes Dunbar."

Yeah. And his shout had come from the front door.

"Let me in!" Wes demanded.

Not a chance. Brandon had no idea if Wes and Shore were partners in crime or if these latest explosions were a result of Wes working alone. And he didn't have time to find out.

"Are we going out there to make sure we don't have any injuries on our hands?" Sheila asked.

That would be standard procedure. It would also be procedure to identify the assailant's location and stop him from doing any more harm.

But Brandon looked down at Willa.

She was shaking and pale, obviously terrified. She had her hands over her belly. He had to try to end this as quickly as possible and get her out of there.

"Call the sheriff over in LaMesa Springs and have him send us some backup," Brandon instructed his deputies.

LaMesa was the town nearest to them, but it was still a good half hour away. By the time backup arrived, it could be too late. Shore might blow up the entire town to get to Willa.

"Sheriff Tanner and his deputy are on their way," Sheila relayed several moments later.

Another blast rattled the windows and sent them all ducking for cover. Outside, Wes banged on the door again and yelled for help.

"The SOB blew up the feed store," Pete spat out.

That did it. Brandon knew this wouldn't end until he stopped it. He got up from the floor despite the fact Willa was trying to pull him back down.

"Martin Shore is a hit man," she reminded him. "The minute you step outside, he'll try to kill you."

That was probably true, but if Shore managed to get close enough to the sheriff's office, he'd kill them all. Or try anyway.

"Brandon, I don't usually argue with what you plan on doing, but I gotta argue with you now," Pete said.

He glanced at Willa. "If this hired gun is after her like you say, then this is where he's headed. It'd be best if Sheila and I go out back and see if we can spot him."

"And maybe kill him," Sheila added.

Pete nodded. "And if he gets through us, at least you'll be here to protect her. I've got no stomach for a pregnant woman being at the mercy of a man who likes to toss grenades. Stay here, boss. And protect that woman and her baby."

Brandon wanted to argue. He wanted it to be him who went out the door and put his life on the line. That was actually his comfort zone. But protecting Willa and the child was also his duty, and they had to come first. Because Pete was right—Shore was almost certainly headed this way.

Brandon finally nodded, giving his deputies the okay.

"We're going out back," Sheila said without hesitation. "If I get a shot at him, I'm taking it."

Good. Because Sheila had solid aim, better than Pete's, and Brandon trusted her to do her job.

"What should we do about the guy yelling out front?" Pete asked.

"Steer clear of him," Brandon warned. "He could be in on this."

Pete nodded, and after Sheila and he put on their heavy jackets, they headed for the back door. Brandon followed them and watched as they made their exit, locking the door behind them. Shore wouldn't be able to get in that way without Brandon hearing him, but the place had eight windows in all. Each had wire mesh running through the glass so that would make it harder for anyone to break in.

Unless Shore bashed through one of them with a grenade.

"Should we stay here or go to your office?" Willa asked.

Brandon glanced around, trying to determine the best place for them to make their stand. Behind the reception desk might be their safest bet. He could see both the front and back doors from that position, and the large reinforced window at the front allowed him to watch what was happening on Main Street. And right now what was happening was the two fires.

He caught the movement from the corner of his eye and automatically shifted his gun in that direction. It had come from the right of the burning diner.

Brandon tried to pick through the thick black smoke to see if it was Shore. But it wasn't. It was a tall man wearing a suit, and Brandon didn't recognize him.

"Over here!" Wes yelled. And the suited man responded by waving. It was Wes's driver.

But what the heck were they still doing in town? Wes had stormed out of his office at least twenty minutes earlier and should have been long gone by now.

"I'm driving over there to get you," the man called out to Wes. He headed for his car.

But he didn't get far.

Something must have alerted him because he swung around and took aim at the other side of the car. In the same motion, he dropped, using the vehicle for cover.

Beneath him, Willa waited, and he could feel her pulse in every part of his body.

They didn't have to wait long.

Brandon saw the movement. So slight. At first, he thought it was a swirl of black smoke. But then he saw the man's hand.

And the gun he carried.

The man stepped out from the cover of the building near Wes's car, and he didn't take aim at the driver who was now on the ground.

He took aim at the window of the sheriff's office.

Right at Brandon.

And he fired.

BRANDON PUSHED HER DOWN a split-second before Willa heard something slam into the window of the sheriff's office. She had no doubt that it was a bullet. She also had no doubt about who had fired it.

Martin Shore.

She'd caught just a glimpse of the assassin before Brandon had maneuvered her out of the semi-crouching position and flat on the floor. Well, as flat as she could manage. She was on her side with her hands covering her belly.

There was another thick blast, no doubt from another shot, but she didn't hear the sound of breaking glass. Maybe that meant the reinforced steel webbing was holding the window in place. It probably wouldn't hold for long, especially since Shore fired another shot.

She no longer heard Wes's frantic shouts for them to let him in. Maybe the man had wised up and gotten away from there.

Or maybe Shore had already killed him.

Until this attack, she had thought that maybe Wes

had hired Shore to come after her, but after hearing Wes's reaction to the explosion, either he was extremely good at faking fear, or he was an innocent bystander in all of this.

Another bullet slammed into the window, and this time she did hear the glass crashing to the floor. She also felt the cold air start to spill into the building. Brandon didn't return fire. Maybe that's because he would have to fire through the window as well, and he perhaps didn't want to create an opening that Shore could use to shoot at them.

"Let's go," Brandon told her. "But stay down."

She did stay down. He didn't. Brandon rushed them to his office and got her inside, but instead of coming in with her, he stood in the hallway and took aim.

He was right in the line of fire.

There was another shot.

Then, another.

Where were the deputies? Why couldn't they get to Shore and stop him?

Her heart was pounding now, and Willa tried to force herself to calm down. This fear and anxiety might hurt the baby. But she couldn't discount the fact that all of them might die here today. And for what? To cover up what she'd been forced to do while she had been a hostage?

Or was something else going on here?

Brandon had positioned her on the side of his desk, but she could still see out the single window in the center of the wall. Willa kept watch, but she knew that Shore was still at the front because she could hear his shots.

"Stay down," Brandon told her.

And he fired.

That meant Shore had either destroyed the window or was maybe already inside.

She wanted to tell Brandon to get down as well and to be careful, but the movement outside the window caught her attention. It wasn't the deputies. Or Martin Shore.

It was Dean Quinlan.

He didn't appear to be armed, but he had his back pressed to the building next to them. What the heck was he doing out there?

"Brandon," she warned. "Dean's outside."

He stepped back into his office, and his gaze slashed to the window. He didn't take aim at the man but instead kept his gun in the direction of the last shot that had been fired.

She heard the sound of more breaking glass, followed by a heavy thud. Someone was trying to kick in the door.

Oh, God.

Shore was breaking in.

Willa spotted more movement outside the window. It was Pete, the deputy, and he went to Dean and pushed the man to the ground. Pete, too, kept his weapon aimed in the direction of the front of the building. Maybe, just maybe, Pete could get off a shot and stop Shore.

At least that's what she thought until she heard the next bullet.

It didn't come into the building but rather the narrow alley where Dean and Pete were. Pete dropped to the ground as well, but Willa couldn't tell if he'd been hit.

Brandon slammed his door and caught her shoulder to move her deeper into the room, next to a metal filing cabinet. Willa no longer had a clear view of Dean and Pete, but she did see something else.

"That's Wes's driver," she told Brandon.

The man came out from across the street and he had a gun in his hand. He took aim but she couldn't tell who or what he was aiming at.

Pete got back to his feet as well and aimed in the same direction as Wes's driver.

Everything seemed to happen at once. She heard the front door crack and give way. Brandon threw open his own office door and stepped into the hall, ready to kill the intruder.

Willa heard herself call out to him, but her words were drowned out by the sound of the shots. There seemed to be so many of them, all coming from different directions, and the combined blast was deafening.

She closed her eyes for just a second and prayed that Brandon hadn't been hurt.

When she looked out, Brandon was still standing. Thank God. He had his gun pointed toward the front door. So did Wes's driver. And neither man was moving.

"He's down!" Pete shouted.

Did Pete mean Shore? Relief flooded through her, but Willa reminded herself that he could have meant someone else. There had been a lot of shots fired in the past thirty seconds, and there were other people outside, not just Shore.

She waited with her breath held.

"You okay, boss?" Sheila called out.

Brandon glanced at Willa first. "We're okay," he answered.

Willa tried to see what was going on, but everyone had left the alley. Brandon moved too and went toward the front of the station.

She followed him, terrified of what she might see and that Shore might still be standing out there ready to do what he had been hired to do.

The door was wide open, the wind battering it against the wall, and there were massive gaping holes in what was left of the window. She spotted Wes across the street. He was behind his driver. Or maybe a better word for the man would be *bodyguard* because that's what he seemed to be doing—protecting Wes. He had Wes positioned behind him as Brandon had her.

They inched closer, but Brandon didn't lower his gun.

Willa saw Pete and Dean to the right. Sheila was on the left. Both deputies had their weapons trained as well, but they were definitely converging toward the front door.

She soon realized why.

There was a pool of blood on the small concrete step directly in front of the door, and next to that pool lay Martin Shore.

"I had to shoot him," Wes's driver confessed. "He was about to put a bullet in your deputy."

Brandon stooped down and put his fingers to Shore's neck. Checking for a pulse. But Willa knew he wouldn't

find one. Shore's blank eyes were fixed on the dull
winter sky, and there was no life left in him.

No life and no breath.

And that meant he couldn't tell them who had hired
him to kill her.

This wasn't over.

Chapter Fourteen

Brandon couldn't get his mind to slow down. It was racing with the images and sounds of the latest attack. He could still hear the shots slamming through the glass, and the tremble of Willa's body.

And see the fear on her face.

Those were images that would stay with him for a lifetime.

Once again, she could have easily died, thanks to Martin Shore. And once again, Brandon hadn't been able to prevent her from being at the center of an attack.

His body seemed to be trying to keep up with his racing mind. He put himself on autopilot and tied up what loose ends he could at his office, but he was thankful when the neighboring sheriff, Beck Tanner, and his deputies agreed to take over the investigation so that Brandon could get Willa out of there. That couldn't have happened soon enough. He wanted the baby and her far away from the bullet holes, Martin Shore's dead body and especially away from the person who was responsible for sending Shore after her.

The problem was, Brandon still didn't know who that person was.

Even though Shore was dead and his body was on the way to the county morgue, they didn't know who had hired him.

And might never know.

He certainly couldn't eliminate any of their four suspects. Dean, Wes, Cash and Dr. Farris had all been in the area. And, yes, Wes's man had been the one to shoot and kill Shore, but Wes could have ordered him to do that so he could save his own butt. If Wes thought that Shore was about to be captured and taken into custody, he wouldn't have wanted to risk having the man spill his guts. No. Wes would have told his man to take Shore out.

That thought only caused him and his mind to race more, and when Brandon glanced down at the speedometer, he realized he was going a good twenty miles over the speed limit. Not a bright idea, since the sleet was making the roads slick. Worse, Willa had a whiteknuckle grip on the armrest.

"Sorry," he mumbled. And he eased up on the accelerator a bit. Still, he didn't dawdle.

"Don't be. I'm not exactly anxious to be out in the open like this."

Yeah. He knew what she meant. They were literally out in the sticks, nearly eight miles from town and the chaos he'd left there, but Brandon knew that chaos had a way of following them. That's why he had continued to check his rearview mirror throughout the drive.

"We can't stay at my house tonight," he reminded her.

And soon, very soon, he'd need to ditch the car since

it was the one Pete had used to pick them up earlier. Someone could recognize it. Unfortunately, it was the sheriff department's only vehicle that hadn't been hit with bullets in the attack.

"So where will we go?" she asked, checking the side mirror as well.

Brandon had considered several possibilities—including a drive back into Austin or San Antonio. The problem with that was the icy roads, and it was getting late. The sun was already close to setting, and that would drop the temperatures even farther. He didn't want to risk getting into an accident.

Plus, there was no one he truly trusted in either of those places.

If they went to either city, they would have to check into a hotel, and while he had the cash stashed at home to do that, paying with cash might alert a curious desk clerk who might in turn alert the police. Brandon figured if Wes had heard about the attacks on Willa, then it had likely been on the news. This latest attack and Shore's death would be reported as well, and the press would be able to come up with photos. Their faces could be plastered on the pages of every newspaper in the state.

And that brought him back to their temporary sleeping arrangements.

"There's a fishing cabin on the back part of my property," he told her. He turned on the road that led to his house, and he saw the dogs race out to greet them. "There's no electricity, but I do have a generator. We can stay there tonight and then figure out tomorrow where we should go."

"Or you could just drop me off somewhere and put some distance between us." She said it so softly that it took a moment to sink in.

"You think I'd leave you?" He hadn't intended to sound so angry, but damn it, that riled him.

"I think it would be smart for you to do that. Right now, the person who hired Shore is looking for *us*. As in the *two* of us. If we split up, he or she will be looking only for me." She shook her head. "And we both know it's me they're really after."

Brandon brought the car to a stop, not in front of his house, but he parked inside the garage, and he used the remote control to shut the door. While it ground to a close, he turned in the seat to face her. "Let's get something straight. I'm not leaving you." Well, not until he was positive she was safe.

The look in her eyes told him that she understood that last unspoken part.

He cursed and reached for the car door. "Come in with me to get some things."

Because he sure didn't want her waiting in the car alone. It had been chilly before, but it was bitterly cold now, and that along with the possible danger caused them to rush inside. He locked the door and set the security system even though he only planned to be there for a half hour or so.

"Don't turn on the lights, but if you want to wash up, you'd better do it here," Brandon let her know. He tried to take the anger out of his voice but failed. Hell. She had actually thought she could talk him into dumping her so he could save himself. "There won't be any hot water at the cabin."

No hot water. No heat other than the fireplace. No bed, just a single army-style cot. And no comforts of home. It wouldn't be an ideal place to spend what was left of Christmas Eve.

He grabbed his old duffel bag and headed to the linen closet so he could grab some bedding. The place wasn't exactly pitch dark, yet, but he had a little trouble locating the thermal blankets. When he finally got them, he shoved them into the bag and then started for the kitchen.

Willa stepped out in front of him.

"You're mad at me," she said, "but you have to admit I'm sort of like Typhoid Mary right now. There really is no reason for both of us to be in danger."

Oh, yes, there was. Brandon put his hand on her stomach to remind her. He'd intended for it to be a quick touch, but he held it there.

There was just enough light left that he could see her face. Willa stood there looking at him, and her right eyebrow lifted as if questioning him as to what he was about to do.

Brandon had no idea.

He just knew that touching Willa wasn't a good idea. Still, even with the danger and his anger, he didn't stop and didn't pull back. They both seemed to be waiting to see what would happen next.

And what happened next was that he snapped his arm around her, pulled her to him and kissed her. He wasn't gentle. He didn't give her a chance to change her mind and pull away. Brandon just took what was right there in front of him.

Maybe he meant this as some kind of reassurance

that he would be there for her. But Brandon cursed himself. This didn't have anything to do with reassurances. He'd been burning to kiss Willa since their last kissing session had ended. He wanted her, and there was no logical explanation for it other than she got him hot.

She curved her hand around the back of his neck and moved as close as she could get. Because of the pregnancy, they weren't exactly body to body, but they were plenty close enough for Brandon to deepen the kiss. He didn't taste the fear or the adrenaline from the attack.

He only tasted Willa.

Man.

That taste went straight through him.

Brandon realized he was trying to get even closer to her when Willa's back hit the wall. That stopped him a moment because he wanted to make sure he wasn't being too rough with her. But Willa merely latched on to a handful of his shirt and pulled him right back to her.

The kiss got even hotter.

They couldn't keep this up. Soon, very soon, their bodies would demand more. They would demand sex. And Brandon knew he had to try to keep a clear head. Plus, having sex with Willa wouldn't be fair since they would no doubt be going their separate ways.

Or would they?

Maybe the scalding kisses were melting his brain because Brandon realized they couldn't entirely go their separate ways.

Hell.

When had that happened?

When had he decided that he would want to see this baby after she was born?

He pulled back again, blinked. And he tried to gather the strength to stop this so he could think. But he saw Willa again. Her mouth was slightly swollen from the hard kisses, and her breath was fast and thin. But that wasn't a "let's stop" look in her eyes.

No way.

Those heavy-lidded eyes were sending out an invitation that his body had no trouble understanding. She wanted to have sex with him and she wanted it now.

Brandon wanted that, too, and there was no amount of willpower that would stop him from taking her mouth again. Willa made a sound of relief. Maybe even victory. And she melted into the kiss.

Her arms went around him, and she fought to get closer. Hard to do but not impossible. Brandon slid his hand between them and shoved up her sweater so he could touch her breasts. She was perfect. Full and round. He'd always been a sucker for a curvy woman, and the pregnancy had obviously left Willa's breasts ripe for the touching.

So, that's what Brandon did.

He shoved down the cups of her bra and circled her nipples with his fingers. Willa obviously approved because she made more of those sounds of pleasure and relief.

Brandon felt no relief. Every touch was like fire to his blood, and he felt that fire course through him. He was already hard and ready for her, but that need skyrocketed when he lowered his head and took her right nipple into his mouth.

"Yes," she mumbled.

That *yes* slammed through him as much as the kisses had done. Maybe more. His body began to demand that he do something about the powder keg that was building inside him.

His mouth went back to hers for a hard, punishing kiss, and he shoved his hand into the waist of her pants and into her panties.

He found her, hot and wet, and he groaned because that wouldn't help any shred of resolve he had left. No. It told him what he already knew.

That he was going to have her.

Here and now.

It didn't have to make sense. It didn't even have to be right. But it would happen.

Brandon scooped Willa up into his arms and headed for the bedroom.

WILLA WAS AWARE THAT she was moving, but she didn't care where Brandon was taking her. She only cared about one thing—finally making love with Brandon.

She'd been burning for him since the moment she laid eyes on him. Lust at first sight. But it seemed to be a lot more than just lust. She'd never felt this intensity. Never wanted a man more than her next breath.

However, Brandon seemed to have set a new benchmark.

Even though he hurried to the bedroom, he was gentle when he lay her on the bed. The old-fashioned feather mattress swelled around her, cocooning her in its softness. Brandon followed on top of her, using his forearms to keep his weight from bearing down on her belly. He wasn't soft. He was all sinew and muscle.

All man.

He continued to kiss her, and he set fires wherever his mouth touched her. On her neck. On the tops of her breasts. He kissed her through the fabric of her top. At first. But she wanted his lips and breath on her skin so Willa fought to shove up her top and open her bra.

Brandon took her exactly the way she wanted to be taken.

This foreplay was sweet torture, but the kisses only made her want more.

Since it would almost certainly take some maneuvering for them to have more, Willa turned, shifting their positions so that she was on top. Her sweater had to go so she peeled off both it and her bra and tossed them aside.

In the back of her mind, she considered that she probably didn't look very sexy, but that didn't seem to bother Brandon. He pushed down her stretchy pants, exposing her belly and giving him access to her panties.

He touched her again. Watched her. And while Willa straddled him, she watched him, too. Brandon was lost in the fire, his eyes hot with need. And that need only fueled hers. He had on too many clothes for sex, and she wanted him naked.

His coat came off easily, but she struggled with his holster and gun. Brandon stopped his own attempts to get her out of her pants so he could help. His hands and fingers that had been so clever touching her now seemed rushed and awkward. Willa felt awkward and cursed when she couldn't get his jeans unzipped.

Brandon placed his hand over hers, sliding down the zipper so that Willa could touch him the way he had touched her. Even though the lights were off, she could still see his face. She could see what her touch did to him, and even though she hadn't thought it possible, she burned even hotter for him.

He was clearly ready for sex so Willa saw no reason to wait. She couldn't wait. Her mind and body were racing, pushing her toward the relief that suddenly felt as necessary as life itself.

His hands were rushed again. So was his breath. His breath gusted, his chest pumping as if starved for air. Brandon got her pants and panties off, and he didn't waste even a second of time.

Neither did Willa.

Since she was still straddling him, she was in the perfect position to move this to the next level. She lowered herself, taking him into her body. Inch by inch. Until she had him fully inside her.

The pleasure blurred her vision and sent her heart racing.

Over the past two days, her heart had been doing a lot of racing, but for the first time, it was due to pleasure and not fear. And there was no doubt about it—this was pleasure in its purest form.

She moved. Brandon did, too. He caught her hips to set the rhythm of the strokes inside her. It was too fast. Too frantic. Too intense to last. But Willa wasn't interested in prolonging this. Not this time, anyway. Maybe some other time they could have a long leisurely afternoon of lovemaking. But this time, she needed him too much to want anything but completion.

Brandon didn't try to slow things, either. He continued to take them both to the only place they wanted to go.

Willa locked gazes with him as their bodies found the perfect rhythm and pace to create exactly what they needed. He moved faster. Harder. The grip he had on her hips tightened and everything honed in on that one moment. That one prize that was just seconds within their reach.

"Do something about this," she heard herself mumble.

Brandon did something about it all right. He lifted his hips, pulling her down onto him for one last hard penetrating stroke.

And that was it.

That was all it took.

It was exactly what she needed to go spinning over the edge. Her body closed around him, as he pulled her to him. Close and tight in his arms.

With her heartbeat echoing in her ears and her breath filling the room, she still heard him. She heard what he said at the moment of his surrender.

Brandon whispered her name.

Chapter Fifteen

Even though Brandon's body wanted to stay put with Willa in his arms, the sane and logical part of his brain kicked in. Thank goodness. Because it just wasn't a smart idea for them to linger there and enjoy the moment.

And what a moment.

Later, and probably a lot sooner than he wanted, he would regret this. The timing was all wrong.

Hell.

The sex itself was wrong, too.

He shouldn't have taken Willa as if he had a right to do that. He had no rights. He'd given her no hope of a future, only the pity story of his biological father.

All of that seemed, well, pointless right now. But that was probably because he'd just had the best sex of his life. His body wanted to have her all over again. His body wanted him to stay inside her and stare up at her beautiful face.

But thankfully, his brain reminded him of the danger.

Brandon eased her off him, and Willa slumped onto the mattress. She was obviously trying to catch her breath, and he wondered if this had been too much for her. He didn't know anything about having sex with a pregnant woman.

"Are you okay?" he asked.

She smiled, maybe to soothe the alarm on his face and in his voice, and she slid her hand around the back of his neck to pull him to her for a kiss. It wasn't a peck. It was the kiss from a woman who was definitely interested in round two. Because that couldn't happen—well, not right now anyway—Brandon ended the mouth-to-mouth contact and got up from the bed so he could dress.

"We have to leave," he reminded her.

Willa groaned, and that sound went right through him. Resisting Willa was next to impossible. Still, he resisted. And Brandon put on his shorts and jeans before his body talked him into getting back in that bed with her.

She got up, too, and the smile didn't leave her face while she dressed. Well, it didn't until she caught him staring at her belly.

"Sorry," she mumbled, quickly pulling on her pants. "Sometimes, I forget just how big I am."

"You're not *big,* you're pregnant. You're supposed to be this size."

And because he thought they both could use it, he slid his hand over her stomach, over the baby, and he kissed her. Like Willa's kiss, it wasn't a peck, either. It turned hot way too fast, but Brandon ended it before it became the start of more mind-blowing foreplay.

"After what just happened, you must know I'm attracted to you," he said against her mouth.

"Even with the pregnant belly?" she questioned.

Especially with the pregnant belly. But since that made him sound like some kind of pervert, Brandon just settled for a nod.

"I need to pack us some food," he hurriedly added. *Keep your mind on the task and get your hands off Willa.* "When we leave tomorrow, there might not be any stores or restaurants open."

He put his holster and jacket back on and headed to the kitchen. Willa could probably use a few minutes alone anyway. To freshen up.

To deal with her regrets.

Brandon was sure she would have them eventually. After all, he might be her baby's father, but he had more baggage than she needed.

He grabbed a plastic bag from beneath the sink and filled it with some granola bars, apples and bottled water. It was hardly the makings of a Christmas dinner, but he hadn't planned on holiday food. If things had been normal, he would have settled for a turkey sandwich while covering the office so that Pete and Sheila could spend the day with their families.

Families.

That word caused him to take a deep breath. Soon, very soon, he had to work out what that meant to him as far as Willa and the baby were concerned.

While he slapped together two turkey sandwiches, Brandon glanced out the kitchen window above the sink. The sun had just set, but he could see and hear the sleet pinging against the glass. It would be a slow, hazardous drive out to the cabin, but there was no way he would make Willa walk the two-plus miles in this weather.

He heard a sound and first thought it was the rustling of the trees in the wind, but he looked closer. Despite the sleet, the oaks near the house were practically still.

An uneasy feeling went through him, and he set the bread aside so he could get a better look. However, he stepped back from the window. Far back and kept in the shadows. And he waited.

Brandon saw it then.

The car.

It was just up the road, probably no more than a hundred yards from the house. There were no headlights, and the car was dark colored. With the clouds covering the moon, he might not have spotted it at all if hadn't been for the vehicle's parking lights.

His stomach went to his knees.

This couldn't be good. If Sheila, Pete or any of the other townsfolk were coming to see him in this weather, they wouldn't have turned off their headlights. No. There was only one reason to do that.

So the driver could sneak up on them.

"Willa?" Brandon softly called out to her. He tried to keep his voice calm while he kept an eye on the car. It was definitely moving closer, inching along at a snail's pace.

But eventually the driver would arrive at the house.

Brandon was betting whoever that driver was, he or she would be up to no good.

"Yes?" Willa answered.

He heard her footsteps leading out of the bedroom and toward the kitchen. But what he didn't hear were the dogs. If anyone or anything had gotten close to the house, Butch and Sundance would have alerted him. They'd be barking their heads off.

So, why hadn't his dogs sounded the alarm?

Brandon wasn't sure he wanted to know the answer to that.

"Are we ready?" Willa asked, walking into the kitchen. But she froze the moment she saw Brandon. That was probably because he'd drawn his gun. "What's wrong?"

He really hated to tell her this. She'd already been through too much. But he couldn't exactly keep this from her, either. "Someone's out there."

She gasped, hurried to him and followed his gaze out the window. "Who is it?"

Brandon shook his head. "It's my guess that the driver isn't paying a friendly visit."

"Oh, God." And she frantically started looking around the kitchen.

For a moment Brandon thought she might on the verge of panicking, but he soon realized she was looking for a knife. She found one in the drawer and pulled it out.

"There's a gun on top of the fridge," he let her know. And while he didn't like the idea of Willa being armed, he didn't like the alternative any better.

Besides, things could turn ugly fast, and she might need to defend herself.

She fished around on the fridge and came up with the Smith & Wesson. It was loaded, and thankfully she treated it that way. She kept it pointed toward the floor.

"Where are the dogs?" she asked.

Brandon had to shake his head again. "I didn't hear any gunshots," he added. Though Willa likely knew that someone could have used a silencer.

It cut at Brandon's heart to think of someone harming his pets, but right now he had to put all his focus on protecting Willa.

"Check the security system panel by the front door and make sure the red light is on," he told Willa. "And stay away from the windows."

She scurried away and Brandon kept watch. The car came even closer but stopped just on the other side of his mailbox. The doors didn't open, and he saw no signs of the driver trying to exit.

It was possible that the person didn't know they were inside. After all, their car was parked in the garage with the door down, and they hadn't turned on any lights. Maybe, just maybe, if he could hide with Willa, the driver would assume the place was empty and leave.

Brandon wasn't sure he wanted that to happen. Part of him wanted to confront this SOB who could be responsible for hiring Shore to come after Willa. But if he could avoid a gunfight with Willa around, then that had to be his first option. No bullets meant Willa and the baby would be safe for another day.

Until the next confrontation.

"The red light is on, and the system is armed," Willa said, coming back into the room. "What do we do now?"

It was risky to stay inside because the person could

try to blow up the house. But it would be an even bigger risk to go outside.

Brandon considered the garage. They could get in the car and wait as they had at the safe house. But that wasn't without risks, either, especially since he would have to disarm the security system for them to go through the mudroom door and into the garage. Plus, there was a door at the back of the garage that led to the yard. He was certain he had locked it, but locks could be easily broken.

"For now, we'll wait here, inside," he whispered.

Brandon moved Willa to the side of the fridge and positioned himself in front of her. They were now out of range of the window, but he could see the back door, and if he peered around the fridge, he could see the front one as well. Thankfully, with the exception of the exterior garage, all the doors and windows were wired with the security system so it should go off if someone tried to break in.

If that happened, they would have to go with Plan B.

He would try to get Willa to the garage so he could take down this person who was hell-bent on trying to kill them.

Behind him, he could hear Willa's shallow breathing, but that, the sleet and the hum of the fridge were the only sounds in the room. Maybe that's why it wasn't hard for him to hear the car door. It was slight, as if someone was trying to ease it shut, but Brandon still heard it.

He braced himself for whatever was going to happen next. At best, the person might just leave or there'd be a knock at the door. Maybe it was someone lost and having car trouble.

But Brandon didn't think this was an "at best" kind of situation.

The seconds crawled by, and Brandon continued to wait. There were no more sounds of car doors. Not even any footsteps.

Still, he didn't relax.

Good thing, too.

The sound of the shot blasted through the house.

WILLA CHOKED BACK A GASP and took aim in case she had to return fire. But Brandon obviously didn't want her to do that because he pushed her even farther back so that she was against the wall.

With him in front of her.

Protecting her, again.

How many more times was he going to have to put himself in danger like this?

If she hadn't been pregnant, if she had only herself to worry about, Willa would have considered making her own stand. She was exhausted and spent from these attacks, and one way or another, she just wanted them to be over. But she couldn't just step out from cover. She had to think of her baby girl.

Brandon took his cell from his pocket and passed it back to her. "Call Pete. His is the first number."

Though her hands were shaking and she was trying to keep a firm hold on the gun, Willa made it to his list of recent calls and pressed the call button. She held her breath and waited for Pete to answer. She also waited for another sound from their attacker.

But nothing.

Not from their attacker. Nor from Pete. He didn't answer the call, and it went to voice mail.

"Pete didn't answer," she whispered, automatically moving on to Sheila's number who was next on the phone list. Willa tried it as well, but there wasn't an answer from Sheila, either.

Something was wrong. Even though it was Christmas Eve, one of them should have answered.

And why hadn't the dogs barked? As frightened as Willa was of them, she wished the Dobermans were there to protect them. They'd need all the help they could get.

"Sheila didn't answer?" Brandon asked, his voice barely audible.

"No. Should I try anyone else?" But as she was asking, she looked at the list of names and numbers. Since this was his prepaid cell, it obviously didn't include his normal list of contacts. With the exception of Cash, there wasn't anyone else, and they obviously couldn't call him.

Or anyone else in SAPD.

There was another shot and, while Willa had thought she was prepared to hear it, the sound still sent a stab of fear through her. Still, she wouldn't let that fear immobilize her. She had a gun, and even though she wasn't sure she knew how to use it, that wouldn't stop her.

"He's shooting at the lock on the front door," Brandon mumbled.

So that explained why there'd been no sound of breaking glass. And there were no indications of the door opening, either. That was something at least. The person hadn't actually managed to get inside.

So, who was out there?

Cash, maybe. Or Wes, Dr. Farris or even Dean. All of them had motive to keep her silent, and it was entirely possible that one or more of them had teamed up against Brandon and her. All four of them potentially had a lot to lose if she ended up testifying about what had gone on in that lab the day of the hostage incident.

Of course, she had to stay alive to be able to testify.

"Call nine-one-one," he instructed. "Ask for help from the county sheriff's office over in Saddle Springs."

God knows how far away that was, but they needed some kind of backup. She quickly pressed in the numbers, and the dispatcher answered on the first ring.

"I'm Willa Marks," she told the dispatcher. And then she realized she didn't have the address. "I'm at Sheriff Brandon Ruiz's residence near Crockett Creek, and we have an intruder. Send someone immediately."

Since she didn't want her voice to give away her location to the person trying to break in, Willa didn't hang up, but she didn't say anything else.

There was another shot, and this one was different from the other two. It sounded as if the bullet had smacked against something metal.

Maybe the lock? Or maybe it was just the brass doorknob.

The emergency dispatcher continued to talk, asking Willa for details about what was going on. Because the questions were coming from the other end of the line, they weren't loud. But they could still be heard. Willa closed the phone and hoped the dispatcher wouldn't have any trouble relaying the request for immediate help.

Willa heard the sound then. A slight creaking noise. She thought it might have come from the hinges on the door, but she prayed she was wrong.

But she wasn't.

Seconds later, she felt the cold winter air slice through the kitchen.

Oh, God.

Someone had opened the front door.

Chapter Sixteen

Brandon didn't take the time to curse himself for staying too long at his house. But he would do that later. Right now though, he apparently had a fight on his hands.

He eased a fraction away from the fridge so he could get a better look at the front door.

It was open.

He didn't see an intruder and didn't hear footsteps so that could mean the person was lurking on the porch. Bullets could easily come through the window and make their way to Willa and the baby.

Who was out there?

Who was doing this to them?

Brandon desperately wanted to know, but he didn't want that knowledge at Willa's expense. Nor did he want to start a gun battle. Right now, his best bet was to wait. To listen. And to try to get off the shot that would put an end to this.

He glanced back at Willa to make sure she was okay. She looked scared but determined, and she still had hold of the gun she'd taken from the top of the fridge. Good. Because he might need her help.

Finally, he heard the footsteps. It was hard to tell because of the wind howling, but he was pretty sure the intruder was still on the porch. For now, anyway. Those footsteps seemed to be leading straight into the house.

Brandon got ready, and took aim at the front door. He wouldn't have but a split second to identify the person and then shoot, and he couldn't risk not getting off the first shot.

He heard another step. Then, another. But he also heard something else.

A car engine.

He tried turning his ear to the sound, but he couldn't figure out if it was coming from the intruder's vehicle or if someone else had just driven up.

Hell.

He hoped this SOB hadn't brought an accomplice.

Brandon spotted the movement in the doorway, and his finger tightened just slightly on the trigger. He was ready. Too ready. Every muscle and nerve in his body was primed for the fight, but the intruder didn't show his face. He stayed there, in the shadows.

Waiting for Brandon to make the first move.

That wouldn't happen. He had Willa in a protected position right now, and he wasn't going to change that unless it was absolutely necessary.

The seconds ticked off again, but there were no more footsteps. No sounds of a car engine, either. Just the brutal wind and the central heating that had kicked in.

Brandon definitely felt the chill in the air, and behind him, Willa started to shake. Her teeth weren't chattering, yet, but it was close. It hadn't taken but a couple of minutes for the inside temperature to plunge, and with the front door wide open, there was no way the heat could neutralize all that cold air gushing in.

Of course, the intruder was out in the cold, too, and Brandon hoped like the devil that it affected the person's aim and judgment.

There was no movement. No warning. Definitely no footsteps. And even though Brandon was ready for an attack, the sound still surprised him.

A bullet came through the living room window.

The sound blasted through the entire house. So did the shattering glass. The bullet slammed into the kitchen wall by the sink. Not exactly close to Willa and him. A good six feet away. But it was close enough for Brandon to know he had to return fire.

He came out from cover and sent a shot right back through the front window.

Brandon didn't stay in the open. He couldn't. He had to move back into place so that he would be in front of Willa. And once he was there, he waited, praying he'd managed to shoot the intruder.

But there was no indication of that.

Definitely no moan of pain. No body dropping to the porch.

Several seconds later, another shot came roaring into the kitchen. There was no six feet of space this time. The shot came damn close to the fridge.

The third shot came even closer.

"Stay down," he whispered to Willa. Brandon didn't leave cover, but he sent two shots of his own right back at their attacker.

Glass spewed from what was left of the window, but that didn't slow the assault. More bullets came, each of them tearing through his house and coming right at them.

Brandon had no choice but to pull Willa to the floor.

The new position took him out of firing range since there was furniture in between his line of sight and the window. But that same furniture was in the way of the shooter as well. Brandon hoped it would be enough to keep Willa safe.

More bullets came. Four of them. Each were thick blasts that rocketed his adrenaline and put him in fight-or-flight mode. Unfortunately, he needed to take the flight option because of Willa. This person obviously wasn't going to come out in the open so that Brandon would have a clean shot, and this guy wasn't worried about running out of ammunition.

Brandon was.

He couldn't go bullet for bullet in this fight.

"Stay low on the floor," he whispered to Willa. "We're going to the garage."

Yes, it was a risk, but at this point, staying put seemed the biggest risk of all.

Brandon kept himself positioned in front of her, and Willa crawled to the other side of the fridge. He fired another bullet at their attacker and hoped the single shot would buy them a few seconds of time.

It worked.

The person didn't fire any other shots until Willa was near the mudroom door that led out to the garage. Brandon wasn't quite so lucky though. The shot came right at him, and even though he was low on the floor as well, the bullet sliced through the sleeve of his jacket. Well, hopefully it was just the sleeve. He didn't have time to look and see if the bullet had grazed him.

He hurried, trying to get Willa away from the kitchen window. Even though the attacker would have to run from the porch to that particular part of the kitchen, Brandon didn't want to wait around for another attack. He got Willa to her feet and opened the mudroom door so he could get her into the garage.

"What now?" she asked. She was still shivering, and Brandon prayed this stress and all the running around weren't harming the baby.

He glanced at the car and knew he had left the keys in the ignition. He could try to drive them out of there, but since the shooter was out front, that would almost certainly put them right back in the line of fire.

Plus, there was the possibility of a second vehicle. An accomplice who might be blocking the road to prevent them from getting away.

"We're going out back," Brandon whispered.

He tipped his head to the rear door that led into the backyard. Beyond that was a small barn and then the thick woods that made a semicircle around his property. If worse came to worst, there were plenty of hiding places in those woods. However, it would put Willa out there in the freezing night. Thank God she had on her coat, but that probably wouldn't be enough eventually.

No. He had to end this soon.

With his gun still drawn, Brandon unlocked and eased open the door. He peeked out but didn't see any signs of the shooter. He didn't want to wait to give the person time to get around the house, either. Or time to get to Willa and him. It was a good twenty feet to the barn, and the woods were another twenty feet or more beyond that.

"Let's go," he told Willa.

Brandon kept watch all around them. Or at least that's what he tried to do. Hard to cover all the shadows and places a killer could hide and launch a new attack. So, he focused on hurrying to get them to the side of the barn. They reached it.

Just as a bullet came their way.

Hell. The shooter had moved to the backyard and had a visual on them.

Brandon pulled Willa to the ground. The dirt was rock-hard frozen, so he tried to break her fall with his arm.

It wasn't a second too soon because the bullets slammed into the side of the barn. Not one shot but four before the gunman stopped.

Was he moving to a new position?

Brandon glanced out but couldn't see anyone. Worse, the wind was even louder outside so he wasn't even sure he could hear approaching footsteps. All he could do was wait and pray for a safe opening to get Willa into the woods.

"There," Willa whispered. Her voice was frantic enough that Brandon glanced at her to see where her attention and index finger were aimed.

She was pointing at the kitchen door, specifically at the small sidelight window.

He saw the movement. Inside the house.

Find, try & love
more books like this!

Visit millsandboon.co.uk

MILLS BOON®

You can find all Mills & Boon titles at our websit
millsandboon.co.uk

For a limited time only, we are offering you an **EXCLUSIVE 15% OFF** when you order online. Simply enter the code **15JAN12** at the checkout. But hurry, this offer ends on 31st January 2012.

PLUS, by ordering online you will receive all these extra benefits:

- 🌹 Purchase new titles 1 MONTH AHEAD OF THE SHOPS. Available in paperback and as eBooks!

- 🌹 Order books from our huge backlist at a discounted price

- 🌹 Try before you buy with Browse the Book

- 🌹 Be the first to hear about exclusive offers in our eNewsletter

- 🌹 Join the M&B community and discuss your favourite books with other readers

Terms and Conditions:
- Offer expires on 31st January 2012
- This offer cannot be used in conjunction with any other offer.
- Code can only be redeemed online at www.millsandboon.co.uk
- Exclusions apply
- Discount excludes delivery charge.

JAN12

Brandon shook his head. How the hell had the person gotten inside so quickly? Just seconds earlier, the shots had come from the right exterior side of the house.

Maybe this was an accomplice?

There was no way the county sheriff could have already made it out here.

Brandon's gaze fired all around, in case this was some kind of ploy to distract him. He damn sure didn't want the shooter sneaking up on them.

There was more movement from the sidelight window, and from the corner of his eye, Brandon saw the back door ease open.

With his heart in his throat, he levered himself up a little and took aim.

He didn't fire, just in case this was indeed the county sheriff. Instead, he waited.

Behind him Willa waited, too, and he thought he heard her mumble a prayer. Good. Because they might need divine intervention to get through this.

The door opened all the way, and Brandon saw the hand then. Whoever was in his kitchen was holding a gun.

Brandon watched as the figure stepped onto the porch.

It was a man, and like Brandon, he had his gun ready to fire.

"Brandon?" the man called out.

Hell.

And Willa obviously recognized him, too, because she cursed.

Sergeant Cash Newsome was on the porch.

That barely had time to register in Brandon's mind when the next shot rang out.

WILLA CAUGHT JUST A glimpse of Cash a split second before Brandon dropped back down in front of her. But a glimpse was all she needed to know that Cash was close enough to them to deliver a fatal shot.

If that was his intention.

Brandon fired in the direction of the shooter—still on the right rear of the house. The blast echoed in her ears. Because of her own pounding heartbeat, she was already having trouble hearing, and that certainly didn't help. However, Willa didn't need to hear to know that Brandon and she had to get out of there fast. With the shooter—and now perhaps Cash—they were out-gunned. Sure, she had a gun, but she didn't trust her shooting skills against a cop.

"Brandon, Willa, I'm here to help you!" Cash called out.

Thank God Brandon didn't buy that because he began to scoot her toward the back side of the barn.

Away from Cash.

Hopefully, away from the other shooter, too.

There was another shot, but because Brandon was in the way, she couldn't see where this one landed. However, she heard Cash curse. He said something, too, something drowned out by the next shot.

Was this some kind of ploy by Cash to make them think he was innocent, or was he under fire just like them?

Brandon didn't wait to find out.

He got them to the back of the barn, keeping them

right at the corner, probably so they could duck around the side if the shooter came at them from either direction. The problem with that was ducking to the side could put them in Cash's sight again.

"We're going to the woods," Brandon whispered. "Stay behind me."

The woods. Well, at least there were plenty of huge trees that could hopefully absorb the bullets—she had no doubts that shooter would continue to fire at them.

Maybe Cash, too.

She got behind Brandon as he asked, and they started to walk backward toward the woods. Willa kept her gun ready and prayed she could do some good with it if it came down to the shooter or them.

The wind howled and slapped at them, and it robbed her of what little breath she had left. Still, she tried to keep walking, hurrying, while she kept watch all around them. Brandon kept watch, too, and he kept volleying his gun between the porch where Cash was and the general area where the shooter had fired the last shot.

Willa felt something soft but solid bump against the lower back part of her leg, and she nearly let out a yelp. She also tried not to trip, especially when Brandon walked right into her.

She risked glancing at what was on the ground and spotted one of the dogs.

Oh, God.

At first, she thought he was dead, but then she saw his chest pumping. The Doberman was taking in quick, shallow breaths.

"Someone drugged him," Brandon mumbled. He

turned, caught Willa's arm and practically ran with her to the nearest tree.

They ducked behind it.

"Will your dog be all right?" she asked.

"Maybe." But he didn't sound very hopeful.

Neither was she. Anyone who would try to murder a pregnant woman probably didn't have much value for life in general.

"We'll help him later," Brandon said.

Willa latched on to that thought. There would be a later. They would get out of this safely.

Brandon peered out from behind the tree but immediately popped back into cover. Someone fired a shot, slamming right into the tree where his head had been just seconds earlier. She didn't think it was her imagination that the shooter had moved closer.

"Watch out, Brandon!" Cash shouted.

That sent Willa's heart pumping even more, and she turned, looking all around them, but she didn't see anyone.

There was another shot, but it didn't hit the tree. In fact, she didn't think it had even been fired in their direction.

A moment later, she heard Cash moan.

The man sounded as if he were in pain. And maybe he was. Maybe he had been shot. Of course, it could all be an act to draw them out into the open so he could kill them.

All around them were the sounds of the wind assaulting the trees, and she couldn't pick through that noise and determine what the heck was going on, but she had a horrible gut feeling that things were about to get worse than they already were.

"Should we stay put?" she whispered.

Her voice was beyond shaky, and that must have been the reason he glanced back at her. "For now." Unlike her, his voice was calm.

Reassuring.

She thought of their short time together. It came like images flying through her mind. She'd only known Brandon for two days. That was it. Under normal circumstances, she would have considered him practically a stranger. But he wasn't. He was the father of her child and the only person she completely trusted.

And she was in love with him.

It was the worst possible time for that to pop into her head. She couldn't tell him, of course. That wasn't such a bad thing. Willa wasn't sure *I love you* was something Brandon would ever want to hear from her.

Maybe it was that particular heartbreaking thought that distracted her. Or maybe she truly didn't hear the sound of the footsteps.

But there had been footsteps. Unheard ones.

Willa had no doubt about that when she felt someone knock the weapon from her hand. She also felt herself being jerked backward.

Into someone's arms.

And before she could even call out, that someone put a gun to her head.

Chapter Seventeen

Brandon sensed the movement behind him and whirled in that direction.

But it was too late.

Someone had Willa.

His breath vanished. His stomach knotted. Hell, his heart nearly stopped. Because this was his worst-case scenario come true. The SOB who had been trying to kill them, now had control of the situation.

Brandon couldn't see the person's face, only the sleeve of a thick coat and the gloved hand that held a gun pressed up against Willa's right temple. The person's body and face were hidden behind the tree.

He made a split-second glance at the porch, the last place he'd seen Cash.

The man was no longer there.

Brandon cursed again. He hadn't seen Cash get up and leave, but then he hadn't exactly had all his attention focused on the porch, either. He'd known there might be two possible attackers, and he hadn't wanted to watch only Cash and give the second person a chance to sneak up on them.

But that's what had happened.

Or else maybe it was Cash who now had Willa.

Brandon didn't care who it was. He only wanted to get Willa away from that gun.

"Who are you, and what do you want?" Brandon asked the gunman.

The person didn't answer. Didn't move. Neither did Willa. Her entire body seemed frozen in place, and the only movement was from the wind whipping at her hair. Her eyes were wide, her mouth slightly open. She was obviously terrified, and while Brandon wanted to assure her that everything was going to be okay, he knew she wouldn't believe him. He didn't believe it, either.

There were no guarantees that either of them would make it out of this alive.

"Let Willa go," he tried again.

And he would keep on trying because there was no alternative. Somehow, he had to talk the person into dropping that gun, or else he had to use force to take it away. The longer this went on, the higher the chances that Willa would be hurt.

Or worse.

"Willa doesn't remember everything that happened in the hospital lab," Brandon continued. "She has no idea who hired the men who held her hostage."

There was only about eight feet of space between them, but Brandon inched closer. He had to get within reach of the gun, and lunging for it wouldn't work.

"Think of Willa's baby. My *baby*," he added. Saying those words cut deep into his heart because for the first time, he saw the baby. Not Willa's pregnant stomach. Not the vague images he'd tried to keep pushing away.

Brandon saw what it would be like to hold his child.

His daughter.

And if this gunman took Willa's life, then his baby wouldn't have a chance. Brandon wouldn't have the opportunity to tell Willa just how much she and this baby meant to him.

"Don't do this," Brandon pleaded. "Please, just let Willa go."

At first he thought his words were useless, that they were having no effect on the person. But then, he saw the slight movement of the trigger finger. The gunman's index finger tensed as if there were some hesitation. Maybe because the gunman hadn't considered just how difficult it was to threaten a woman and her unborn child.

"Let Willa go," Brandon repeated. "And if you need a hostage, take me. Better yet, just leave. Just get back in your car and put an end to this now."

Of course, Brandon couldn't let the person just drive away as if none of this had happened. He would have to stop this once and for all, otherwise the danger would continue. But for now he would say or do whatever it took to get Willa out of the line of fire.

Because Willa was staring at him, he had no trouble seeing when she lifted her left eyebrow. She seemed to be questioning him about what she should do. Maybe she was thinking about trying to drop to the ground so that Brandon could get a clean shot.

But he only shook his head.

If the gunman fired, there wouldn't be time for Willa

to move out of the way. It was too big of a risk to take, especially since he seemed to be making progress.

"I can help you," Brandon told the gunman. "I have money inside so you can get away. You can leave now, and no one else will get hurt."

If it was Cash behind that gun, he probably knew that wouldn't happen. But the other three—Wes, Dean and Dr. Farris—they might believe it.

And even Cash might *want* to believe it if he was trying to rationalize a way out of this.

Martin Shore had been a cold-blooded killer, an assassin, but none of the four suspects had likely done a close-kill attempt like this before. Brandon had. During his time in the military, he'd been forced into violent situations. And he knew it wasn't something that most people could stomach.

"Here's what we can do," Brandon continued. It was almost impossible to keep his voice level and calm, especially while looking in Willa's eyes, so he focused on the gunman's trigger finger. "We both put our guns down. We just drop them. Willa and I will get on the ground while you walk away."

The seconds crawled by.

The gunman still didn't utter a sound, but the gloved trigger finger lifted just a fraction. That certainly didn't mean Willa was out of danger, not by a long shot, but he was making progress.

"I want to name our daughter Hannah," Brandon said. It wasn't exactly the first name that came to mind, but it was a name he liked. "She'll be born in February."

The movement on Willa's face caused him to glance at her. She was blinking back tears.

But the gunman didn't have a tearful reaction. The finger went right back on the trigger, and Brandon thought the person was shaking his or her head.

Damn.

He had to say the right thing or do something, and it had to happen now. But what? How could he get through to this would-be killer?

Brandon didn't have a chance to figure that out.

He heard the sound and then saw the movement cut through the darkness. Something came flying through the air.

A small tree branch.

And it smacked right into the back of the gunman's head.

Everything happened fast. Too fast for Brandon to do anything but rely on his instincts to react.

The gunman made a feral sound, part gasp, part outrage. But somehow, the person managed to hang on to the gun.

That didn't stop Brandon.

He latched onto Willa's arm and slung her out of the way. It worked.

Well, it got Willa out of the way.

However, it didn't stop the other things that had already been set in motion.

Their assailant turned. And fired. Not at Willa or Brandon. But at the person who had just delivered that blow with the tree limb.

But before Brandon could take aim and right his own position, it was already too late. He found himself staring right down the barrel of their attacker's Sig-Sauer.

"Move and you die," the person warned.

THE SOUND OF THE VOICE caused Willa's breath to stall in her lungs. She instantly recognized the person who'd just issued Brandon that death threat.

When all of this had first started, she had thought it was Cash or Wes who was holding her at gunpoint. But it wasn't either of the men.

It was Dr. Lenora Farris.

Willa stared up from the ground where Brandon had pushed her out of the way, and she looked around. The gun that Dr. Farris had knocked from her hand minutes earlier was there, on the ground. Willa reached out for it.

"Don't," the doctor warned. It was hardly the caring, empathetic tone she'd used in the hotel suite when she had shown Willa that DVD.

The doctor grabbed Willa again and put her in front of her. She curved her arm around Willa's throat. The position literally made her a human shield. It would make it nearly impossible again for Brandon to fire.

While keeping the gun aimed at Willa's head, the doctor kicked away the gun that Willa had tried to reach. She also used her foot to swat at something else. Something near the tree limb that had hit Dr. Farris in the head.

"Why?" Willa asked, trying to look back at her so she could make eye contact. "You're the one who tried to help me regain my memory."

She gave a weary, hollow laugh and shifted her

position so that her back was against the tree. "I didn't want to help you. I was there to find out how much you knew. How much you remembered." The doctor glanced at her. "You remembered too much, Willa."

"Obviously not. Because I don't have a clue why you're doing this."

"Dr. Farris is doing it because she's trying to cover up her guilt," someone snarled.

It was Cash, and he was on the ground to the doctor's left. He sounded as if he was in pain, but it was too dark for Willa to see if he'd been hurt. Though he probably had been. After all, Cash was the one who had tried to hit the doctor with the tree limb, and she had fired in that direction. It was also likely his gun the doctor had kicked out of reach.

But Brandon was still armed. And maybe that's why the doctor turned the gun back on Willa. "Sheriff Ruiz, do as I say, if you want her to live."

Dr. Farris shot a glance Cash's way and what she saw must not have alarmed her enough to finish him off. Instead, she kept her attention nailed to Brandon.

"She put a tracking device on your car," Cash continued. Yes, he was definitely hurt, and he paused to pull in his breath between each word.

God, was he dying? Willa prayed not.

"Why don't you want Willa to remember?" Brandon asked. He stepped closer.

The doctor shook her head and thrust her gun at Willa's stomach. "Stay put and drop your gun," she warned Brandon. "I'm calling the shots here."

"Yeah," Cash agreed. "She's calling the shots because she's a killer. I didn't trust her when I saw that photo Dean had given you. She set me up with that picture. She called, said she had evidence about the case, but I'm guessing she did that so she could get something incriminating in case she needed a fall guy."

If so, then all of this had obviously been premeditated.

"That's why I followed her when she started driving out here toward your place," Cash added. "I figured she'd try to kill you."

Too bad Cash hadn't been able to stop her.

"Put. Down. Your. Gun." Dr. Farris's teeth were clenched when she threatened Brandon.

Willa didn't want him to drop the gun so she tried to help. It was obvious the doctor was far from being calm and in control. Her hands were shaking, and she looked to be on the verge of killing them all.

"The gunman in the lab wanted me to tamper with some DNA files," Willa said. It worked. The doctor went still. "It was the DNA taken from beneath Jessie Beecham's fingernails the night he was murdered."

That last part was a guess. But it was obviously a good one because Dr. Farris groaned softly. "You do remember," she mumbled. Now, there was sadness, maybe even regret, in her voice. "The DNA would have sent me to jail for murder. Because it was my skin tissue beneath Jessie's nails. He scratched me, and I didn't have time to clean him up."

"You killed Jessie Beecham," Willa mumbled. The next question was why, but Willa didn't get a chance to ask her that.

A weary sigh left the doctor's mouth, and she loosened the grip she had around Willa's neck. Since she wasn't watching Cash, Willa hoped the man wasn't so injured that he was unable to do something to help.

Without warning, the doctor pulled the trigger.

The sound blasted through the night, and Willa braced herself to die.

But the bullet slammed into the ground next to her. In the same motion, she swung the gun back to Brandon. "Put down your weapon, or I'll kill you both right now."

Brandon stared at the woman. And then he shook his head and cursed.

He dropped the gun.

Willa's heart dropped with it.

That gun was the only thing protecting them, but Brandon had had no choice. Willa didn't know the doctor very well, but she could tell from the woman's tone that she wasn't bluffing. Of course, Dr. Farris intended to kill them anyway so this would only give them a few more seconds at best.

"I won't go to jail for killing Jessie," the doctor said in an almost whisper. "The man was scum and deserved to die."

Maybe. But now, the doctor was apparently willing to keep on killing.

"I'm sorry," Dr. Farris added.

Everything happened fast. Practically a blur. Dr. Farris lifted her hand, aimed her gun back at Cash. She fired. Two shots. Both slammed into something.

Cash, probably.

The doctor didn't waste even a second. She took aim at Brandon. She was going to fire. Willa had no doubt about that. The doctor was going to shoot Brandon at point-blank range, and he was helpless, standing there, because he couldn't risk coming at the doctor and hurting Willa.

But Willa could do something.

Yes, it was a risk. Anything was at this point. But she couldn't just stand there and let Brandon die.

Willa gathered the air into her lungs and let out the loudest yell she could manage. She threw all of her weight to the left, away from the doctor. The jarring motion worked because Dr. Farris's arm snapped back, releasing the grip she had on Willa's neck. At first, Willa wasn't sure why that had happened.

Then, she saw Brandon.

He had lunged across the space that separated him from the doctor. He was obviously trying to tackle her before she got off another shot.

But he was too late.

The blast, loud and thick, tore through the night.

Everything seemed to freeze, and the images clicked through her head as if someone was snapping pictures. Willa saw Brandon slam into Dr. Farris, and they both flew backward, tumbling onto the ground.

Then, Willa saw the blood.

It was everywhere. On Brandon. On Dr. Farris. Even in the evening light, she could see it on both their clothes.

"Brandon!" Willa called out. He had to be all right. He just had to be. She couldn't lose him.

She scrambled across the yard toward the scuffle. Brandon had the doctor in a fierce grip, his left hand locked around her arm, and his right hand gripped her weapon. And she was fighting back. Though not with much strength.

Willa soon saw why.

Behind Brandon and Dr. Farris, Cash was sitting up, and there was blood all over the front of his shirt. No doubt where Dr. Farris had shot him. He had a gun. The gun that the doctor had knocked from Willa's hand. And judging from the angle of the barrel, he had fired directly at Dr. Farris.

But Brandon had also been in that line of fire.

For one terrifying moment, Willa thought Cash might fire again. At her or at Brandon. But he simply gave a satisfied nod before he collapsed, the gun falling to his side.

Cash might be dead. That registered in Willa's mind. But she couldn't go to him until she helped Brandon. She couldn't let Dr. Farris use that gun to kill him.

Willa reached out to latch on to the doctor's arm so she could help drag the woman away from Brandon. But the arm she held was limp and lifeless.

Willa's gaze flew to Brandon. To his face. To his body. Yes, there was blood. But when he stood, she realized he hadn't been shot. Dr. Farris had been. Cash's bullet had taken out a killer.

And Brandon was safe.

He was safe.

The tears came, burning hot in her eyes, and Willa made it to him in one step. Brandon pulled her warm and deep into his arms and held on.

Chapter Eighteen

Brandon glanced at his watch. It was still five minutes until midnight. Five minutes until it was officially Christmas Day.

Not that they would go anywhere to celebrate.

He didn't intend to leave the hospital until Cash was out of surgery. After all, Cash had probably saved their lives, and Brandon wanted to thank his old friend. However, that didn't mean Willa had to be stuck in an uncomfortable chair in the waiting room.

"Sheila said she could drive you to her place here in town so you can get some sleep," Brandon reminded Willa. It'd been a generous offer from his deputy, but both Sheila and Pete were probably reeling from everything that had happened.

Brandon certainly was.

Judging from Willa's too-pale face and trembling hands, she was as well.

"No thanks," she answered. "I'd rather wait here with you until the doctor gives us an update on Cash."

Since Cash had already been in surgery for hours, Brandon had no idea how much longer their wait would be. So he slipped his arm around her and eased her head onto his shoulder. Maybe she would at least grab a nap.

Or not.

Her head came right back up, and her eyes met his. "Dr. Farris deserved what she got."

"Yeah." Brandon didn't dispute that. The woman had tried to commit premeditated murder, and from what he'd been able to figure out from the notes and emails that SAPD had found on the doctor's computer, she'd taken plenty of steps to do just that.

Thank God she hadn't succeeded.

But not for lack of trying.

In addition to hiring Martin Shore to find and kill Willa, she had spied on Cash's computer to find the location of the safe house where Willa and he had been attacked. Cash had been right about that. He'd also been right about the doctor planting a tracking device on Brandon's vehicle. And to insure that Brandon's deputies wouldn't respond to his call for backup, the doctor had planted a jammer at the sheriff's office where the deputies were wrapping up Shore's last attack and death. The jammer had prevented their cell phones from ringing. She had even drugged his dogs so they wouldn't alert anyone that she was on his property.

Dr. Farris had been thorough. And in doing so, she had created plenty of future nightmares. Brandon would never forget how close he had come to losing Willa and the baby.

Brandon heard the footsteps in the corridor and got to his feet. He also tried to brace himself for the worst. Cash had not only taken three bullets, he'd lost a lot of blood.

But it wasn't the doctor. It was Pete.

"Merry Christmas," the deputy greeted, though it wasn't very cheery. The fatigue was heavy in Pete's weathered eyes.

"Merry Christmas," Brandon and Willa mumbled back.

"SAPD just called," Pete explained. "They tried your cell first, but the call couldn't go through in here."

Brandon was aware of that. Because the waiting room was right next to radiology, the walls had been reinforced with steel, making reception poor at best. Still, he figured his deputies would keep him informed, and they had. During Cash's three hours of surgery, either Pete or Sheila had paid them a visit at least every half hour.

"SAPD found more stuff on Dr. Farris's computer," Pete continued. He shook his head. "That woman was something else. One of the gunmen who took the maternity hostages was her patient, so she learned about the hostage situation before it even happened. But she didn't lift a finger to stop it."

That sent a coil of anger through Brandon. Willa had gone through hell and nearly died while as a hostage, and it could have been stopped before it even started.

Of course, if it had, he might never have met Willa and known about the baby.

Ironic that Willa was here in his arms because of Dr. Farris and those hostage-taking gunmen.

"So, if she knew the gunmen, was she also the one who hired them?" Willa asked.

"I guess you could say she just paid them to do something extra. Their boss had already hired them to tamper with some evidence, and Dr. Farris just paid them on the side to do the same for her. She had her DNA replaced with tissue from the homeless man who was arrested for Jessie Beecham's murder."

"A murder that Dr. Farris committed," Willa mumbled. "Yes. That woman was indeed something else."

Brandon agreed. But this might not be over. "What about the other hostage situation, the one that's supposed to happen today?"

"It was a lie," Pete insisted. "Well, according to the notes SAPD found, it was. She hired Shore to kill Willa and to also get out the word that there'd be another set of hostages taken. But the story was just a ruse to draw Willa out of hiding."

Brandon cursed. The ruse had worked.

"There won't be any other hostages," Willa said. And she repeated it. The breath just swooshed out of her, and when she looked at Brandon, he saw her smile. It was, well, amazing and it lit up her entire face.

Suddenly, it felt like Christmas morning.

"Y'all need me to bring you anything?" Pete asked.

Willa shook her head, but she didn't take her eyes off Brandon. "It's really over. No more danger. No more hostages. I'm free."

"The danger and hostage parts are true. But what about your memory?" Pete asked.

She paused a moment, as if going through her thoughts. "Everything seems to be there. I'm free," Willa repeated. "For the first time in months, I'm really free."

Yeah. And that hit him like a sucker punch.

Brandon was sure he wasn't smiling, and that warm Christmas glow faded as quickly as it'd come.

Willa was indeed free, and that meant she could and probably would be leaving soon. Of course, that left Brandon with a huge question.

Was he going to let her go?

It took him about a split second to come up the answer to that.

No. He wasn't going to let her go.

Well, not without a fight anyway.

"I know I said I might not make a good father," Brandon heard himself blurt out. Not the best start he could have had for what would be the most important next few minutes of his life.

"But I'd like to try," Brandon added.

Willa blinked. Stared at him.

"Uh, I should probably go," Pete mumbled. And he didn't wait for either of them to acknowledge his exit. Being the smart man that he was, Pete left Brandon to fumble around with what he wanted to say to Willa.

"I'd like to try to be a good father," Brandon amended. He shook his head. That still wasn't right. "I'll do everything within my power to be a good father."

"To Hannah," she supplied, making it sound like more of a question than clarification.

"Hannah." He huffed. And then cursed when Willa looked hurt from that huff. "No. I didn't mean it that way. I used the name, Hannah, to make the baby more personal to Dr. Farris, so she wouldn't shoot you. It's a hostage negotiation technique to personalize the crisis situation."

Great. Now, he was babbling.

"But I do like the name Hannah," he added when Willa just stared at him.

Still babbling.

So, Brandon changed tactics. He cradled the back of Willa's neck and pulled her closer. He kissed her. Really kissed her. He put his mouth to hers and took in the softness of her lips. Her taste. That taste soothed him, fired his blood and reminded him just what was at stake here.

Everything was at stake.

"I'm in love with you," he said against her mouth.

He braced himself for her shock and expected her to pull back and stare at him some more. After all, he'd given her no indication of that love. Hell, he hadn't realized himself until he saw Dr. Farris point the gun at her. Then, in that moment, he knew this wasn't about protecting Willa and the baby.

It was about loving them.

Willa didn't pull back, but he felt her smile form on her lips. "You love me?"

Well, this answer was easy. "I do."

"Good." And she kissed him long and hard and stopped only when both of them remembered they needed to breathe. "Because I'm love in with you, too."

The breath he'd just taken in stalled in his throat. His entire body seemed to stop, so he could grasp what she'd just said.

"You love me?" he clarified.

"God, yes. I thought that was way too obvious."

Now, it was his turn to smile against her mouth. But

Brandon did ease back because he wanted to see her face. Her eyes. That incredible smile. Willa took his breath away again, and he didn't care if he ever got it back.

Maybe it was because he was totally lost in the moment that he didn't hear the footsteps until they stopped right next to him.

Brandon caught the movement out of the corner of his eye and automatically reached for his weapon. But no weapon was necessary. It was Dr. Ross Jenkins, the surgeon who had been operating on Cash.

Both Brandon and Willa got to their feet, and Brandon tried to interpret the surgeon's poker face. He couldn't. He could only stand there and wait.

"Sergeant Newsome took three bullets to the chest cavity. He's lucky. Damn lucky. Other than a collapsed lung and some broken ribs, he should be fine."

The relief was instant, and Brandon grabbed Willa and hauled her into his arms for a celebratory kiss. Cash was going to be all right. Dr. Farris hadn't succeeded in any part of her plan to kill all three of them.

"I'll keep him sedated most of the day," the doctor continued. "No visitors until tomorrow. So, you two might as well go home." His attention dropped to Willa's belly. "Do I need to call in the OB?"

"No," Willa quickly answered. "No contractions. And Hannah's kicking like crazy. She's fine."

The doctor nodded, pulled on his surgical cap and ambled away.

Willa smiled again, but there were tears in her eyes. "Cash is going to be okay," she mumbled.

Brandon understood those tears. They were of the

happy variety. And even though the timing wasn't the best, he decided to see if there was another level of happy to be had here.

But before he could utter a word, Willa pulled back her shoulders and stared at him. "Are you going to ask me to marry you?"

He had been about to do just that, but Brandon hadn't expected her to jump the gun. And he couldn't tell if it was a question she wanted him to ask. The tears were still there in her eyes, but she was no longer smiling.

She was waiting.

It was a risk because if she said no, she might feel too awkward to hang around. She might say they needed space, time or some other thing that Brandon was sure he didn't want.

He wanted Willa.

He wanted their daughter.

And he had never been so sure of anything in his entire life.

To increase her chances of saying yes, he snapped her back to him for a kiss. He made it long, French and hopefully as mind-numbing as he could manage. Willa added some mind numbing moves of her own and pressed herself against him. Hard against him. In such a way that reminded him that he could spend at least part of Christmas day making love to her.

But first, he needed to ask the question.

And get the answer.

He caught on her shoulders and looked her straight in the eyes. "Willa, will you—"

"Yes," she interrupted. She grabbed a handful of his shirt and dragged him right back to her.

But Brandon wasn't sure exactly what question she was answering. "Yes?" he quizzed. He stepped back a little so he could keep a clear head.

Her smile returned. So did the kiss. "Yes, I'll marry you, Brandon. I'll be your wife. Your lover. The mother of your children. Yes to all of it."

That was the only answer he wanted.

So, Brandon pulled her to him and kissed the start of their new life together.

* * * * *

COWBOY SWAGGER

BY
JOANNA WAYNE

All the characters in this book have no existence outside the imagination of the author, and have no relation whatsoever to anyone bearing the same name or names. They are not even distantly inspired by any individual known or unknown to the author, and all the incidents are pure invention.

First published in Great Britain 2012
by Mills & Boon, an imprint of Harlequin (UK) Limited,
Eton House, 18-24 Paradise Road, Richmond, Surrey TW9 1SR

© Jo Ann Vest 2010

ISBN: 978 0 263 89493 6

46-0112

Harlequin (UK) policy is to use papers that are natural, renewable and recyclable products and made from wood grown in sustainable forests. The logging and manufacturing processes conform to the legal environmental regulations of the country of origin.

Printed and bound in Spain
by Blackprint CPI, Barcelona

Joanna Wayne was born and raised in Shreveport, Louisiana, and received her undergraduate and graduate degrees from LSU-Shreveport. She moved to New Orleans in 1984, and it was there that she attended her first writing class and joined her first professional writing organization. Her debut novel, *Deep in the Bayou*, was published in 1994.

Now, dozens of published books later, Joanna has made a name for herself as being on the cutting edge of romantic suspense in both series and single-title novels. She has been on the Waldenbooks bestseller list for romance and has won many industry awards. She is also a popular speaker at writing organizations and local community functions and has taught creative writing at the University of New Orleans Metropolitan College.

Joanna currently resides in a small community forty miles north of Houston, Texas, with her husband. Though she still has many family and emotional ties to Louisiana, she loves living in the Lone Star State. You may write Joanna at PO Box 852, Montgomery, Texas 77356, USA.

To all my readers who love cowboys.
To my grandsons, who have taught me what it means to
totally lose your heart to a child—though they
are growing up fast.
And to my hubby who will spend many hours driving
me around the beautiful Texas Hill Country to research
the setting for the books in the SONS OF
TROY LEDGER.

Chapter One

Murderer's kid! Murderer's kid! Murderer's kid!

The taunts reverberated inside Dylan Ledger's brain as he approached the Mustang Run Elementary School. Seventeen years after his father's conviction, distant echoes of the mocking still tied knots in his stomach.

Or maybe it was the significance of the day that brought the old rancor home to roost. His father's homecoming. The murderer's return to the scene of the crime, as one radio news announcer had so bluntly put it.

Dylan slowed and stared out the window of his truck. The flagpole was topped with the American colors, and just below that the Lone Star State banner waved in the gentle breeze. Cows grazed the fence line that kept them off the playground.

Kids were filing out of the building to board the yellow school buses that had lined up in front of the building. It was late May, but apparently classes were still in session.

Cars formed another line, mothers waiting to take their children home. Memories flooded his mind. He and his brothers had waited in that line on the fatal day eighteen years ago this September. His mother had never come.

He grimaced and pushed the memories back to the

dark crevices of his mind, the way he'd learned to do years ago.

Only now that he was back in the town where his life had been ripped apart, he realized he wasn't nearly as detached from the past horrors as he'd thought. Even worse, he wasn't sure why he'd come back or what he really hoped to gain from this.

The traffic light in front of the school turned red. His gaze drifted to a woman who'd just stepped from her vehicle and was waving frantically, probably trying to get the attention of her kid. The woman's hair was so red it looked like fire in the bright sunlight.

She turned his way for a second. His gaze was riveted on her, not only because she was a knockout. She reminded him of someone, though he had no idea whom.

The light turned green. He lowered the truck's window as he drove slowly through the town and then turned onto the narrow dirt road that led to the family ranch. The odors of earth, grass and even the occasional whiff of manure were a welcome change from the smells of car exhaust and fish from the open market a few steps from his tiny apartment back in Boston.

Rolling hills stretched in all directions as far as he could see. A grouping of magnificent horses stood in a fenced pasture, mingling with a few young colts. A cluster of persimmon trees gave shade to some longhorns. A dog barked in the distance, and a flock of coal-black crows cawed noisily from their perch atop a weathered gate. In a few miles he'd be home.

Who was he kidding? He had no real home. Not in Texas and certainly not back in Boston where he'd never really fit in.

A tractor bounced and rumbled along the road in front of him. Dylan slowed. The driver of the tractor pulled to the edge of the road and gave a two-fingered wave as Dylan passed him.

A minute or two later, a red Jeep Wrangler bore down on him from behind, passing the tractor and riding the tail of Dylan's truck for a minute before passing him, as well. The driver of the vehicle appeared to have a cell phone glued to her ear. He couldn't be sure due to the mass of wild, red curls that tumbled to her shoulders.

Same hair. Same vehicle. It had to be the woman who'd captured his attention at the school, but there was no child in the Jeep. Her car disappeared around the next curve. She was in a damn big hurry to get somewhere.

Another vehicle came up behind him, chased Dylan's bumper around a curve and then passed him. The van had the name of an Austin TV channel emblazoned on the door. It hit Dylan then that they were rushing to the same place he was heading. The media were once again gathering at the Ledger ranch with teeth bared.

Fury burned in Dylan's veins as he drove the rest of the way. Did the media never have the decency to just back off?

The metal gate was propped open. The wheels of his truck rattled over the cattle gap, and he kept driving. There was no need to latch the hook; the varmints were already inside.

A sense of gruesome déjà vu attacked him as he drove the quarter of a mile to the house. But he wasn't a kid any longer. He'd handle whatever came his way.

COLLETTE McGUIRE GAVE UP on finding a decent parking spot and left her Jeep in a grassy area just north of the house. She grabbed her camera, then pushed through the dozen or so reporters and photographers who were clumped around the front door of the Ledger ranch house.

A lot like vultures, she thought, guilt surfacing that she was one of them.

She shivered and looked around her, always wary, hating the unfamiliar fear that had crawled inside her over the past few weeks.

"There you are. I've been looking all over for you."

She turned to find her friend, Eleanor Baker, maneuvering through the restless reporters and heading her way.

"Thanks for answering my SOS," Eleanor said.

"Next time could you give me a little more notice? I had already told Alma I'd pick up Georgia from school on my way home and take her shopping. Her eleventh birthday is this weekend."

"Your niece is already eleven?"

"Yes. Can you believe it?"

"Not really." Eleanor glanced around. "Where is she?"

"I got to the school in time to have her catch the bus. I postponed the shopping trip."

"You can take her when we're through."

"There won't be time. I'm working a wedding tonight. Georgia is not happy. Both you and Melinda owe me big-time."

"Get me some great shots of Troy Ledger arriving at the little house of horrors and we'll both be in your debt."

"So the infamous Mr. Ledger hasn't arrived yet?"

"No sign of him, but according to reports of when he left the prison, he could drive up any minute."

"What happened to Melinda?"

"She's on assignment in Austin for her real boss. You know, the guy who actually pays her. She thought she'd be back in time to help me out, but got stuck in traffic."

"So that's why I got drafted."

"Which reminds me, do you mind if I camp out at your place tonight? I have an interview scheduled with a developer just outside Mustang Run at an ungodly hour in the morning."

"You want my house *and* my expertise with the camera? That will cost you," Collette teased.

"Let's hope this turns out to be worth it."

"Take the left side of my garage tonight. I'll park on the right."

"I remember. You know, you may actually be better at this assignment than Melinda."

"Not likely. Ghosts are not within my area of expertise," said Collette.

"No, but you're local. That should be worth something. Pictures of Troy Ledger inside the haunted house would catapult *Beyond the Grave* to the hottest paranormal magazine on the racks. And then I could actually pay Melinda—and myself."

"Local or not, fat chance I'll get inside that house. I'll be lucky if I get a shot of him entering the door."

"Then I guess Melinda and I will be forced to break in the house the first time Troy Ledger leaves."

Collette covered her ears. "Don't confess planned illegalities to me. I'm the sheriff's daughter."

"Like you'd turn us in to him. You barely speak to the man."

"Yes, and let's keep it that way."

"Speaking of illegalities, are you still getting calls from that weirdo?"

"Occasionally. The calls are pretty lame, but they're starting to get to me."

"Sic the sheriff on him."

"I don't know what he could do since the guy only

spouts harmless utterances of devotion. What are you hoping to get today for the article?" Collette asked, changing the subject.

"I'm thinking the tag will be 'Troy Ledger returns to the house that drove him to murder,'" Eleanor said, holding up her hands as if framing the article.

"Last I heard, he was still claiming his innocence. And he was released from prison." Collette removed her camera from the case and adjusted the lens.

"Sure, but released on a technicality," Eleanor countered.

"The prison psychiatrist interviewed on the morning news claimed Troy Ledger has never shown one sign of violent behavior since his conviction. She said she's certain of his mental stability and even went so far as to say that she wouldn't hesitate to trust him with her own son."

"Shrinks, what do they know?" Eleanor glanced at her watch. "Do you think he killed his wife?"

"My opinion doesn't count for much. I was ten at the time."

"Your dad must think he's guilty. He arrested him." Eleanor stretched for a better look as a commotion ensued at the back of the crowd.

A black pickup truck approached, driving up to the front door and sending the reporters who'd gathered there flying to get out of the way. A sexy hunk of a man in boots, worn jeans and a Western hat climbed out, a man who was decades too young to be Troy Ledger.

He looked around and shook his head before stamping to the door. Once there, he pulled a ring of keys from his pocket and poked one into the lock.

"Holy Smoley," Eleanor said lustfully. "I'd sleep with

ghosts any night as long as that cowboy was in the bed with us. Do you know him?"

"He could be one of Troy Ledger's sons. I think he had four."

"Five," Eleanor corrected. "Dakota, Tyler, Dylan, Sean and Wyatt."

"You've done your homework."

"And a couple of major investigative articles on the crime. FYI, I think Troy Ledger is as guilty as sin and I renege on any offer to sleep with one of his sons, not even if it guaranteed me a picture of ghosts."

Collette aimed and started shooting, still looking for something familiar to help her identify the stranger. She'd known a few of Troy Ledger's sons, but that was years ago when they were mere boys.

The guy pushed open the door but didn't go inside. Instead he scanned the crowd as if looking for someone. Flashbulbs popped, and he blinked and squinted in defense. Reporters started yelling questions and trying to stick mikes in his face.

"Are you a relative of Troy Ledger?"

"Is Troy coming back to the ranch?"

"Will he move back to Mustang Run?"

The cowboy put up a hand as if to quiet the group. Amazingly, they obliged him, though Collette was certain the cooperation wouldn't last long unless he gave them something they wanted.

"You're trespassing," he said. "And looking for a story that was milked dry seventeen years ago."

"Who are you?" a reporter yelled from the back of the group.

"Dylan Ledger, son of the convicted murderer." He tipped his hat as if mocking them and propped a hand on the door frame.

Dylan. She remembered him more than the others. He had been a year ahead of her and had ridden the same bus to school and back. Even then he'd been cute, but he'd aged to perfection.

Someone pushed a mike into his face. "Have you forgiven your father for killing your mother?"

"My relationship with my father is none of your business."

"Is your father going to live here on Willow Creek Ranch?"

"I have no idea what my father's plans are for the future. End of story, so you may as well go out and find yourselves some real news."

He scanned the crowd again. When his gaze fixed, Collette was certain that he was looking right at her. She felt the impact of his stare right down to her toes, a kind of heated awareness that set her on edge.

Eleanor poked her in the ribs with her elbow. "He recognizes you."

"No way. I was scrawny and wore braces when he saw me last."

"And now you're gorgeous and you've acquired breasts. You've got his attention. Ask him a question."

"I'm a photographer, not a reporter."

"He doesn't know that." She took Collette's free hand and waved it in the air. "Ask him if he thinks the house is haunted."

Again, Dylan stared straight at Collette. "I'll grant one interview," he conceded, as if it were an afterthought. "In private. The redhead in the jeans and yellow shirt," he said, pointing at Collette.

Eleanor slapped her on the back and pushed her forward. "Go get 'em, girl. But don't forget the pictures. And be careful."

Collette panicked. She didn't represent a legitimate news organization, and she'd never conducted a real interview. She was terrific at what she did, but that was photography, usually for weddings or at least happy family occasions.

Eleanor gave her another shove. "What are you waiting on?"

Collette gave up and pushed her way through the crowd. Some reporters moved out of her way to make it easier for her. A few guys deliberately blocked her path, and two made sexist comments about her looks doing her work for her.

She had a couple of words for them, too, but she managed enough restraint to keep them to herself. When she reached Dylan, he escorted her inside and closed and locked the door behind them. Her stomach rolled, though she couldn't blame the uneasiness on the house's aura. It looked and felt like any other sprawling ranch house, except for the musty odors that came from years of being closed off from life, wind and sun.

Dylan's hand brushed the back of a worn leather couch as he walked past it. "At least the air conditioner works."

And worked well, she noted. The house was pleasantly cool and free of dust and the myriad spiderwebs that would have given it a true haunted look. Someone had obviously readied the place for Troy Ledger's arrival.

Dylan walked to the kitchen. She followed him.

He opened what appeared to be a new refrigerator. "There are soft drinks, bottled water and beer," he said. "What's your pleasure?"

"Water would be nice."

He handed her a bottle of water and took a beer for himself. She nodded her thanks.

He unscrewed the top from his beer. The silence grew awkward.

"Why me?" she finally asked.

"You passed me back on the road."

"That's not much of a reason."

He took a long swig of the beer. "Guess I just wanted to know why the hurry. Is news that scarce in Mustang Run?"

"Frankly, yes."

"Must be an exciting town."

"About the same as when we were at Mustang Run Elementary School."

His eyes narrowed. "Should I recognize you?"

"I'd worry if you did. I've changed a lot since fifth grade. I'm Collette McGuire. I was a year behind you in school."

He nodded as if he'd just had an ah-ha moment. "Collette the tattletale. You're right. You've definitely changed. Is your father still sheriff?"

Her only claim to fame. In this case, it would work against her. "Yes, he is."

"Is he part of the welcoming committee waiting outside?"

"I didn't see him out there. As far as I can tell, the mob is all media sharks."

"Like you?"

"Not exactly. I mean I am with the media today, but I'm not a reporter."

His eyebrows arched.

"I'm a photographer—with *Beyond the Grave*," she added hesitantly. "It's a magazine that explores the paranormal."

His muscles bunched, and his lips pulled into a tight

line. "Let me guess. You want to help me connect with my dead mother."

Ire burned in her veins. "I don't communicate with the dead." Or some of the living, either, she silently added.

He took another swig of the beer and leaned against the counter. "So why is *Beyond the Grave* interested in Willow Creek Ranch?"

"Word around town is that your house is haunted."

"You people need to get a life."

In theory she agreed with him. That didn't keep his arrogance from rubbing her the wrong way. He'd been gone for years. What did he know of their town or her? But she should probably cut him some slack considering the reason he'd come back to Mustang Run. Besides, Eleanor and Melinda did need those pictures.

She placed her camera case on the kitchen table. "I realize the timing is not the greatest for you, but since you invited me inside, why not let me take a few pictures? And if there's anything you want to say for the magazine, I can see that you're quoted accurately."

"I've nothing to say. But go ahead. Take your pictures." He glanced at his watch. "Make it fast. My father will be here any minute now, and I seriously doubt he'll be as accommodating as I'm being."

"Thanks for the warning." She started snapping pictures of the kitchen. Try as she might, she couldn't find a way to make the place look spooky. She fared no better in the family room. The space just looked lonesome and bereft of human touch.

Intent on working quickly, she didn't notice that Dylan had joined her in the family room until she caught sight of him in her viewfinder.

Her heart skipped a beat or two from the sheer masculinity of the man against the backdrop of the huge stone fireplace. The slow burn he ignited crept to her cheeks. She lowered the camera without taking the shot.

Dylan propped a booted foot on the low hearth and an elbow on the mantel. "What makes people say the house is haunted?"

"Some claim that they've seen a woman in white out by the gate when they pass it at night. She tries to wave them down as if she needs help. If they stop, she disappears."

"Is that it?"

"Not quite. Some claim to have seen a woman standing at one of the windows."

"Superstitious fools." Dylan raked his fingers through his hair, parting the sandy locks into deep grooves that quickly filled back in place. "Are you one of them?"

"One of the superstitious fools? No. I have too much trouble with the living to worry about ghosts."

Her cell phone rang. Probably Eleanor with instructions as to what photos she wanted for the magazine. "Excuse me," she said, reaching for her phone.

"No problem."

"Hello."

"I saw you go inside the house with Dylan Ledger."

Apprehension ground in her stomach. The lunatic who'd been stalking her must have followed her to Willow Creek Ranch.

She walked back to the kitchen, hopefully out of Dylan's hearing range. "I told you to stop calling me," she whispered.

"I can't do that. We're soul mates, Collette, meant to be together."

She took a deep breath, hoping it would settle her shaky nerves and shakier voice. "I'm not anything to you, and if you don't stop harassing me, my father will arrest you, throw you in jail and lose the key."

"I'm not afraid of your daddy, Collette. But I have a message for him. Tell him I'll soon be sleeping with his precious daughter. And you'll like it. I promise you that."

Her skin crawled. As much as she dreaded the thought, she was going to have to get a gun. This guy was nuts.

She broke the connection and rejoined Dylan. "I'm sorry for the interruption."

"You look upset. Is something wrong?"

"It was a nuisance call." She tried to take another picture, but her hands shook and she had trouble holding the camera steady.

"Are you sure you're okay?" Dylan asked.

He was far too astute to buy her feeble excuses. "Yeah, I'm okay. It's just that there's this guy who's bothering me. I'll deal with it."

She went back to taking pictures, and this time her hands remained calm. She finished in record time and walked to the kitchen. Dylan was staring out the window, his face a hard mask that revealed no emotion. She felt a weird connection with him, as if growing up in Mustang Run were a bond in itself.

She stepped closer. "It must be tough coming back after all these years. It's a nice thing to do for your father."

He shook his head. "I'm not sure I'm doing it for him."

So things weren't fully settled between them, which made his inviting her in even more strange. "Did you stay in touch with him over the years?"

He shrugged. "Does it matter?"

Which meant he considered it none of her business. Fair enough. Only he was the one who'd started with the questions. "Why did you really let me in to take the pictures, Dylan?"

"You looked familiar. I just realized it's because you look like your mother."

"You remember my mother? I wasn't even aware that you'd met her."

"She came over the day my mother was murdered. She cooked dinner for my brothers and me. My memories from that night are sketchy, but I remember her telling us that no one would hurt us and that it was all right to cry. She stayed until my grandparents got here."

"Where was your dad?"

"Being questioned by the deputies—and your father."

Yep, that pretty much defined her parents. Mom had always been there to comfort. Her dad was always there to find fault and uncover the hidden sins.

"How is your mother?" Dylan asked.

"She had a stroke and passed away a few years ago."

"I'm sorry, "Dylan said. "Go ahead with your pictures. My father won't like it, but the skeletons have been rattling around in this house for too long already. Might as well shake a few out for your readers."

His voice was gruff and his tone edgy, an attempt, she suspected, to hide his emotions. Dylan was all man in every way that showed, but somewhere deep inside him, there must be some remnant of the boy who lost not only his mother to a brutal murder, but life as he knew it.

The clatter of voices outside rose to a crescendo. She joined Dylan at the window. A white truck was speeding down the road to the house.

"The return of Troy Ledger," Dylan said.

Troy Ledger, not his father. That said a lot. His father might have gotten a get-out-of-jail-free card, but he obviously wasn't getting a pass from Dylan. Maybe she had more in common with Dylan than she'd thought.

Surprising herself, she pulled out a business card. "If you need to talk, I'm available. You can call my photography studio or my cell number. Or you can stop by anytime. I live in the old Callister place. It's the yellow house just past the Baptist church."

"Your husband might not appreciate that."

"What makes you think I'm married?"

"I saw you at the elementary school when I passed."

"I was there to pick up my brother's daughter, or rather to tell her I couldn't pick her up and that she should ride the bus home."

Their eyes met again as he took the card from her. His were tempestuous, yet mysteriously seductive. "I hope this works out for you," she said.

"Yeah. Same for you. Be careful with the jerk who's giving you a hard time." He handed her the camera case and then walked her to the front door just as the back door swung open. "See you around."

"Yeah, cowboy. See you around."

She had a feeling he wouldn't be looking her up. That was probably for the best, she told herself. He was far too complicated. She'd seen that in his intense, brandy-colored eyes. And she had complications and problems enough of her own.

Oddly, though, she found herself hoping that he'd call.

Chapter Two

He kept his distance, remaining unnoticed from his position behind the woodshed and sheltered by the low branches of a spreading live oak tree. Lifting his binoculars to his eyes, he watched as Collette McGuire walked out of the house and squeezed through the mob of reporters who were all but wetting their pants over the arrival of what looked to be the infamous Troy Ledger.

The wind tousled her hair like a lover might, lifting and teasing the fiery red curls before letting them fall to her narrow shoulders. Collette McGuire was both beautiful and spunky. Neither altered the outcome, but they had changed the game, likely even prolonged it.

She was a woman who could tempt any red-blooded male, even one as scarred and damaged as he was.

Too bad she had to die.

Chapter Three

Dylan dried the plate and put it away. The dishes were old, probably the same ones they'd eaten off of when he was a kid. Still, they were as unfamiliar to him as the man standing next to him.

Troy Ledger was tall and gaunt with slight bags under his tortured eyes and wrinkles that dug deep furrows across his brow. His nails were chewed down to his flesh, and a jagged scar ran along his right cheek and down to his breastbone. His forearms were muscled. He'd likely be a tough contender in a fight.

Fifty-five years old but he looked like a man who'd lived through hell. He acted only half alive, as if he'd been reduced to going through the motions, except that twice that afternoon he'd seemed to be in the grip of a mood so intense he could barely control it. One of those times, he'd clutched the glass he was holding so tightly that it shattered in his hand.

Dylan would have liked to ask what he was thinking at that moment, but his dad had set the rules of engagement from the moment he'd walked into the house. They'd shared a quick handshake and greeting, and then his dad had withdrawn so deeply into himself, Dylan might as well have been invisible.

They'd spoken briefly since then—about the steaks

Dylan had grilled for their dinner, about the price of beef these days, about the weather. The closest they'd come to anything personal was when the formidable Troy Ledger had asked Dylan if he was married. He'd said no. His dad had only nodded. Who in hell knew what that meant?

His brothers had been right. Coming here was a mistake. But now that he was here, he'd stick it out at least a few more days. No reason to hurry off. No one was waiting for him anywhere.

"What are you going to do about the ranch?" Dylan asked when the dishes were all put away.

"Raise cattle, same as other ranchers."

"Cattle cost money."

He was pretty sure his dad didn't have any. They were never rich, and the little Troy would have been swallowed up by lawyers' fees and taxes on the ranch.

Dylan had learned that much from his father's attorney who'd handled the estate—the estate consisting of the ranch and this old house. The attorney had contacted Dylan and his brothers when their father's release had become imminent and suggested they welcome him home. Dylan had been the only one who'd accepted the proposal. At his father's request, the attorney had mailed Dylan a key to the house.

The family of Dylan's mother was in much better financial shape. His and his brothers' inheritance from their grandparents had gone into a trust fund that had put them all through college.

Uncle Phil had been upset when Dylan decided to go into the army after graduation instead of joining his uncle's extremely successful advertising firm. Dylan had wanted to do something for his country and he'd needed adventure. The army had offered both.

Troy stuffed his hands in the back pockets of his jeans. "Able Drake's backing me for a start-up herd."

"Do I know him?"

"Not likely. Lives up in Dallas now, but he's from these parts."

Dylan couldn't help but wonder if Able was someone Troy had met in prison. As far as he knew, no one on his mother's side of the family had ever mentioned the man, but then they hadn't even spoken his father's name in years. They were all convinced he'd killed their beloved Helene.

Dylan had acted as if he believed it, too. But he hadn't. The father who lived in his dreams and imagination could never have killed his mother.

"Is Able the one who readied the house for you?" Dylan asked.

"He had it done." His father looked around as if noticing the place for the first time. "Not much of a house, is it?"

"Structure's okay," Dylan said. It was the only positive thing he could think of.

"Used to look better," his dad said. "Back when…" He stopped midsentence, looking as if pain was digging into his ruddy flesh like sharp nails.

"Yeah," Dylan agreed. "It used to be better."

His dad rubbed the old scar. "I'm beat. Think I'll head on off to bed."

And avoid any more feeble attempts at conversation with the son he hadn't seen since the day he'd been convicted. All the boys had been there that day to say goodbye, against their grandparents' will.

Dylan tried to muster up a bit of resentment for his father's eagerness to escape his company. It didn't come. Truth was, he wasn't up to talking tonight, either. The chasm that separated them after years of zero communication was too deep and wide to be bridged by a steak and a few attempts at meaningless small talk.

"I'll take the back bedroom," his dad said.

Not the big bedroom he'd shared with Dylan's mom, though Dylan had spotted him standing at that door earlier, staring into the room, his muscles strained and his expression as pained as if he'd been kicked in the gut by an angry bull.

Dylan sure as hell wasn't sleeping there, either. "I'll take my old bedroom. I checked earlier and it looks like all the beds have new sheets on them."

"Guess the old ones would have rotted by now."

Troy walked away, leaving Dylan standing alone in the kitchen. Memories gathered around him like a suffocating fog. His mom stirring big pots of stews and soups at the range. Her singing while she worked. Trays of fresh-baked cookies cooling on the counter. Her long hair flying when she'd grab him and dance about the kitchen. Her fragrance when she'd pull him into a hug. Her arms around him when he'd had a nightmare.

Returning footfalls in the hallway yanked him from the bittersweet reveries. He swallowed hard and turned to see his dad's tall, lean body filling the open doorway.

"Thanks for being here, Dylan."

The words were husky, as if they'd been pushed through a scratchy throat. His dad's eyes looked moist. Dylan's started to burn.

"Sure thing," Dylan said. "We'll talk more tomorrow."

"Yeah. Tomorrow."

He turned away as his dad's retreating footsteps echoed down the hallway. The connection had been brief, but it had been there. It was a start.

Dylan searched the cupboard for a real drink, something strong enough to fight off the memories and regrets. He found a bottle of whiskey. Not his brand but now was not the time to be choosy.

He poured a couple of fingers of the amber liquid into a glass, swirled it around and then sipped it, welcoming the burn that trailed down his dry throat. He pushed through the back door and into the gray of twilight. Too restless to sit, he finished the drink, left the glass on the back steps and walked to his truck.

He'd be back, but right now he had to get out of here before the ghosts from his past made the woman in white who appeared for the superstitious think she was living in a freakin' mausoleum.

COLLETTE RAISED THE CAMERA and framed the image of the bride dancing with her preadolescent nephew, an adorable red-haired lad who was stepping all over the hem of her gorgeous gown. The bride, Isabelle Smith, barely twenty-one herself, showed no sign of irritation.

This was her day, and the glow of love emanated from her like stardust. The only bad thing about stardust was that it had such a limited shelf life.

Not that Collette had anything against marriage. She might even take the plunge one day—just not any day soon. She liked her independence and had never met a man who'd tempted her to become a "we" instead of a "me." But she had to admit, the bride did look ravishing and blissfully in love.

Collette had known Isabelle and her whole family for years. They went to the same church that Collette had grown up in, and Isabelle's father had helped Collette raise a prize-winning pig back in her 4-H days. Her own father had been too busy enforcing the law and making inane rules for her and her mother to follow.

She also knew the groom and his family. Carl Knight's dad owned the local hardware and feed store. His mother taught at the new consolidated high school. Carl was in the Marines and had worn full-dress uniform for the ceremony. He'd be shipping off for Afghanistan soon.

Even as she'd taken pictures of the couple exchanging the vows, Collette had prayed he'd return safely. She suspected many of the guests were doing the same.

She moved to another corner of the dance floor that had been set up beneath the white tent. The country band switched from a lively two-step to a romantic ballad, and Isabelle's grandparents joined the group on the dance floor. Collette couldn't help but smile as she got a couple of great shots of them snuggled in each other's arms and swaying to the music.

Setting her camera on a nearby table, she checked her watch. The reception would start winding down soon, but she was sure that she had enough formal and candid shots to satisfy the bride and her family. At least she would once she captured the newlyweds leaving for their honeymoon.

"Care to dance?"

She spun around at the unfamiliar voice.

"Sorry. I didn't mean to startle you."

"You didn't," she lied. "I just didn't know anyone was behind me." Stupid response considering they were beneath a rather crowded tent. She hated that the recent phone calls had made her so apprehensive that she sometimes jumped at her own shadow.

"I'm Brady Collins, friend of the groom."

He extended his hand. A nice hand, she had to admit, attached to a slim blond guy with cobalt-blue eyes and an enticing smile. There was no spark when his hand wrapped around hers. Obviously, he was no Dylan Ledger.

"I'm Collette McGuire, the photographer."

"I noticed. You've been doing a heck of a job, but I'm sure the happy couple would forgive your abandoning your post for one dance."

"The offer is tempting, but not in my contract."

"Ah, the prettiest woman at the reception would have to be a woman of principle."

"Thanks," she said, "though we both know the prettiest woman at the wedding tonight is unquestionably Isabelle."

"Only because she has the unfair advantage of the wedding glow."

Carl picked that moment to rescue his bride from the awkwardly energetic nephew. Collette reached for her camera. "Your friend Carl looks pretty happy himself. Now, if you'll excuse me, I really do have to get back to work."

"Can't blame a guy for asking."

She didn't, but even if she hadn't been working, she wasn't really interested in meeting anyone tonight. Working the wedding had helped, but the stalker's call this afternoon had left her more nervous than usual. Not only that, but try as she might, she hadn't been able to fully shake Dylan from her mind.

She doubted he'd call, but instead of turning her cell phone off completely as she usually did when working an affair, she'd left it on vibrate tonight. There was no rational explanation for how he'd affected her. All she knew was that she wanted to see and talk to him again.

She took a few more pictures and then stepped outside the tent, walking a few yards away for a breath of fresh air. Silvery strings of moonlight filtered through the trees, and the music that had been loud and vibrating inside the tent was softly romantic in the background.

She took out her phone and called her house, not that she had any doubts Eleanor had made herself at home once Collette had left for the wedding. Eleanor was outgoing and resourceful, no doubt part of the reason for her success as a freelance investigative reporter. And they had been friends since their first year at the University of Texas.

The phone rang until the answering machine picked up. Disappointment swelled. Eleanor must have decided to drive back to Austin instead of spending the night after all.

Ordinarily, Collette was fine going home at night to an empty house. Her stalker had infiltrated those feelings of safety, replacing them with irritating spurts of apprehension. If the calls kept up, she was going to have to break down and buy a gun or maybe get a dog. A big, ferocious-looking dog who'd bark like crazy if anyone came sneaking around the house she rented from the Callisters. Maybe she'd get both.

Mustang Run was a peaceful town, but it hadn't totally escaped violence. She'd been reminded of that quite vividly while taking pictures inside the Ledger home today.

She wondered if a dog or a gun would have saved Dylan's mother. Not likely if Troy Ledger was actually guilty of killing her.

Thoughts of Dylan crowded into Collette's mind. She did her best to push them aside. She didn't need a guy with a tortured soul in her life. But impulsively she slipped her hand into her pocket and let it slide across the leather case that held her cell phone.

The phone remained still and silent.

DYLAN TIPPED THE BOTTLE of cold beer to his lips and took a long swig. Mack's Haven was exactly how he would have pictured a typical small-town Texas bar. Smoky. Loud. Friendly. A down-home kind of place. A worn wooden sign pronounced, "No Dancing on the bar with your spurs on."

Smoky and loud didn't bother Dylan. Nor did the sign, since he not only didn't own a pair of spurs, he had no plans for dancing on the bar. Neither was anyone else at the present time, though the cozy dance floor was crowded.

The friendly part of the equation was the drawback. Far too many of the patrons had felt it their duty to introduce themselves and make the stranger welcome.

Dylan probably came across as antisocial, but explaining who he was would have led to questions he couldn't answer about his return to Mustang Run. So far he'd managed to give only a first name and resist the invitations to dance by a couple of affable young women. Another beer and he might not be so inclined.

He hadn't planned to end up here tonight, but when the musky memories from the day his mother had been killed began to pound inside his skull, he'd spotted the bar and seen it as a temporary escape.

The buxom blonde waitress in a seductive cotton T-shirt and a pair of denim shorts returned to his table. "Want another of the same?"

"Better not." He pulled out his wallet. "What do I owe you?"

"Two beers—ten dollars and eighty cents."

He gave her a ten and a five.

"Thanks." She took the money but didn't walk away as he stood to leave.

"Are you new to the area or just passing through?"

"Most likely passing through. You take care," he said and walked away before she followed up with another question.

He climbed in his truck, revved the engine and started back to the ranch, slowing as he passed the house he'd already identified as the one in which Collette McGuire lived. Lights were on. She was still up, though not necessarily alone.

Still, she had said stop by anytime.

He pulled in the driveway and kept his truck running. There was no sign of Collette's Jeep, but she could have parked it in the garage.

He wondered what the hell he was thinking driving up to somebody's house this time of the night. Not to mention that he'd be opening himself up to a barrage of intrusive questions.

He should turn the truck around right now before Collette spotted him. But the dread of going back to the ranch tonight got all mixed up with the crazy desire to see Collette again. She'd been easy to talk to, almost like running into an old friend in the midst of an enemy camp.

He shut off the car and, just as he killed the lights, he caught a glimpse of movement behind the house. It could have been a large dog or possibly a deer, but it had sure looked like a person. He turned the headlights on again, but whatever it was had disappeared into the trees and shadows.

An owl hooted in the distance as he got out of the truck and walked the uneven concrete path to the steps. Light from inside the house gave a soft glow to the wide porch.

Pots of blooming flowers lined the three steps. A swing half-filled with colorful pillows hung at one end of the porch. Two white rocking chairs and more potted plants lined the other side.

The house looked as if it should belong to a family, not a feisty, single professional like Collette. He hesitated before he knocked, listening for voices. The house was silent. He rang the doorbell and waited. No response. Either she wasn't home or didn't want to see him.

Still, he couldn't quite dismiss the figure he'd thought he'd seen running from the house. That left him with an uneasy feeling, and he'd learned it was always best to trust his instincts for danger. One of his commanding officers had claimed that Dylan sniffed out trouble the way a bomb dog trailed the scent of explosives.

His muscles tensed and he hammered his fist against the door. "Collette? Are you in there?"

He called her name again as he turned the knob and the door swung open. He stepped inside. The foyer opened into a dimly lit living room. The illumination came from a lamp and a cluster of candles resting in a copper dish. Magazines were scattered about the sofa, and a glass of wine sat on the coffee table. Nothing was amiss.

"Collette?" he called again. "It's Dylan Ledger. Are you here?"

His call went unanswered.

Lights were on in the back of the house, but all was quiet. He started down the hall. And then he saw the blood. Just a trickle, creeping past an open doorway ahead of him. Curses and panic rattled his skull as he followed the crimson trail into the kitchen.

And to the body lying face down in the middle of the floor.

Chapter Four

The body was not Collette's. Relief merged with dread as Dylan studied the scene.

The victim was fully clothed in jeans and a UT T-shirt. Blood oozed from a cut on the back of the head. A golf-ball-size knot had swelled around it. The blood that spilled across the floor came from a stab wound to the woman's right shoulder, but the bleeding that must have spurted at first had all but stopped.

A bloodied knife lay a few feet from the body. A small skillet stood on its edge against a table leg.

Dylan knelt to check for a pulse. It was rapid, but weak. Her skin lacked the clamminess and paleness that indicated shock, but other than the uneven and shallow rise and fall of her back, she wasn't moving or responding.

Afraid to chance compounding her injuries or starting the bleeding all over again, he left her on her stomach as he took out his phone and called 911. Thankfully, telling the 911 operator to send an ambulance and law enforcement to the old Callister place near the Mustang Run Baptist Church was all the address he needed to give.

"You're okay," Dylan whispered as he covered her with a checkered cloth he'd yanked from the table. "I've called for an ambulance."

She wasn't worried. She was out cold.

Possibilities raced through his mind. Had that been her attacker Dylan had seen running from the scene? Or could the killer still be in the house? He might even be holding Collette hostage.

Dylan struggled to stay calm so that he could weigh the options. He should have paid more attention when Collette had talked of the lowlife who was harassing her. He should have asked questions. Should have…

Hindsight. Always 20/20 and totally worthless.

Muscles tense and hard as stone, he stepped to the counter and took a clean knife from the block.

Leaving the kitchen, he explored the rest of the house, room by room. There were two bedrooms, two baths and a small, uncluttered office. One of the bedrooms had clothes spilling from an open piece of luggage. The other was neat except that the yellow shirt Collette had been wearing today was draped over a wooden rocker.

There was no more blood and no sign of Collette. He went back to the kitchen and checked on the victim. She was still breathing, but still out.

He heard the hum of a motor and the crunch of tires as a vehicle pulled onto the driveway, the same way the attacker must have heard him when he drove up.

Dylan rushed to the front door and spotted Collette exiting her Jeep. Alone and safe. Suddenly his body felt as if he'd been released from a killing chokehold.

He opened the door and waited for her.

"Dylan. I wasn't expecting you."

"I took you up on your invitation to stop by anytime."

"Eleanor must have let you in. I was afraid she'd gone home when she didn't answer the phone. I guess she told you I was working a wedding tonight."

"I haven't talked to Eleanor."

"Then who let you in?"

There was no good way to tell her this. "There's a problem, Collette."

A siren sounded in the distance.

"What kind of problem?"

"An attack."

"On whom?" Her eyes widened. "Where's Eleanor?"

"In the kitchen. She's hurt. I've called an ambulance. They should be—"

Collette bolted toward the kitchen. He followed her, feeling helpless when she went ghostly white and fell to her knees beside her friend.

"Eleanor. Eleanor, say something. Who did this to you? Talk to me. Please talk to me."

"I've called 911." As the wail of the sirens grew louder, Dylan knelt beside her and explained what he knew and how he'd come to find the body.

She shuddered and leaned against him. He put his arm across her shoulders, feeling awkward. He'd never handled emotion well.

She pulled away as the ambulance stopped in front of the house and a rush of footsteps sounded on her front porch. "It was him, Dylan."

"Who?"

Her eyes were moist, but her tone was harsh and accusing. "The man who keeps calling me. He must have come here looking for me, but he found Eleanor instead."

"I wouldn't jump to conclusions." He stood and tugged her to her feet as the room filled with paramedics. By the time they had Eleanor inside the ambulance, more sirens sounded and two squad cars arrived on the scene.

Four armed men in khaki uniforms got out. Two of the deputies had guns pulled, both aimed at Dylan. For the first time, it hit him that he'd put himself into a very compromising position.

The oldest uniformed man glared at him before stepping between him and Collette. "What happened here?"

"My friend Eleanor was spending the night with me. Someone broke in and attacked her while I was photographing Isabelle Smith's wedding. She was hit at least once on the head and stabbed with one of my kitchen knives. The ambulance just left. They're taking her to the hospital."

"Did she name her attacker?"

"She was unconscious. She'll be afraid when she comes to. I need to go to the hospital so that I can be with her."

"You'll need to answer a few questions first."

Dylan stepped forward. "I'm the one who found the body. I can probably tell you more about the situation than Collette can."

The man turned toward him. "Who the hell are you?"

"Dylan Ledger."

The lawman rested his hand on the butt of his holstered gun. "And I'm Sheriff Glenn McGuire, so you better have a damn good explanation for what you're doing in my daughter's house."

COLLETTE CRINGED at her father's reaction to Dylan. Could he for once just listen to the facts before going off half-cocked?

"Dylan is here because I invited him here."

"I hope you have a hell of a good reason for doing something that stupid."

"Did you ever think that he might have saved Eleanor's

life by arriving when he did? He may have saved mine, as well."

"Right now I'm thinking how the Ledgers are back in town one day and we already have a brutal attack. What's Eleanor's last name?"

"Baker. Eleanor Baker. You've met her before, Dad. She visited our house frequently when we were in college."

The sheriff rubbed his chin. "Eleanor? Isn't that the reporter who writes about ghosts?"

"Yes."

"I warned you about hanging out with the likes of her and Melinda Kingston. Kooks attract other kooks. One day you're gonna start listening to me."

Dylan walked over to stand next to Collette and slipped a hand to the small of her back. "You might want to cut Collette some slack, Sheriff. It's rough enough that her friend was attacked."

"I don't need advice from the offspring of a murdering son of a bitch." He turned back to Collette. "Do you know of anyone who had it in for her?"

Collette took a deep breath. "I don't think she was the intended victim. I think the man was here because of me."

His brows arched. "Why would anyone want to hurt you?"

"I'm not sure that's what he intended, but some man has been calling and harassing me over the past few months. He claims to be in love with me, but I don't even know him."

The sheriff glared at Collette. "You've been stalked by a psycho for months and you never bothered to mention it to me?"

"He never threatened to hurt me."

She couldn't tell if it was anger or frustration that

pulled her father's face into deep lines and caused the veins in his face and neck to pop out.

"I should have told you," she said, "but you've told me before that there's not much you can do if there's no threat of violence."

"Did you at least change your phone number when he started calling?"

"I couldn't very well do that. My cell is the only number clients have to reach me. It's on my business cards and my Web site."

"Did he always call you on your cell phone?" the sheriff asked.

"Always."

"Let me see the phone."

"It won't help," Collette said, handing the phone to her father. "The caller ID always said Unavailable or Out of Area."

The sheriff checked out the phone before handing it back to her.

"There are only two vehicles parked outside," the sheriff said.

"Eleanor's car must be in the garage. Mine would be, too, except that I stopped out front when I saw Dylan's truck."

"Check the garage, Brent," he told one of the deputies. "Be nice if the perp stole the victim's car, so we'd have a known vehicle to chase." Sheriff McGuire turned to Dylan. "Where was Eleanor when you arrived?"

"Facedown on the kitchen floor."

The sheriff led the way with the deputies a step behind. Dylan and Collette followed.

"Don't let my father intimidate you," she whispered to him.

"Don't give it a thought. As long as he goes after the lunatic attacker, the rest is insignificant."

She liked Dylan more by the second.

Her father stepped over the stream of blood. "Tell me exactly what you found."

Dylan described the scene as best he could.

The sheriff stooped to get a better look at the knife and the skillet as he listened. When he'd heard enough, he stood and rocked back on the heels of his boots.

Brent joined them in the kitchen. "There's a blue Ford Mustang in the garage."

"That's Eleanor's," Collette said.

The sheriff nodded. "Brent, wake up the CSI team and tell them I want a full workup on the scene. Chuck, put the state patrol on alert. Tell them we've got a dangerous nut on the loose and may need some help tracking him down. He can't have gotten too far away from this location yet."

"I'm on it," the middle-aged deputy said.

"Good. I'll get with them shortly with whatever pertinent details we can come up with. The rest of you stand guard here and make sure none of the evidence is tampered with until we get prints and any other evidence they can find."

The men jumped to do his bidding.

"We'll talk on the porch," her father said to Collette. "I need more information on your stalker before you leave for the hospital. And, Ledger, don't even think of cutting out before I get through with you."

DYLAN STOOD AT THE EDGE of the porch staring at the scene that had completely changed since he'd arrived at Collette's less than half an hour ago. The quiet had evolved into a chaotic grind of activity, talk and barked orders.

The "ifs" and "buts" of the situation roared though his mind with the same frenetic energy. If he'd left the bar a few minutes earlier, he might have arrived in time to save Eleanor from being attacked. If he'd chased down the figure running from the house, he might have caught the bastard. If Collette had arrived a few minutes earlier, she might have been the one assaulted.

Collette collapsed onto the porch swing and wrapped her arms around her chest although the night was warm. He turned toward her, struck by how incredibly vulnerable she looked.

She hadn't fallen apart even in the first shock of seeing her friend's condition, but she looked as if she was on the verge of it now.

She needed a pair of strong arms wrapped around her, but probably not his. Her father had made it plain that Dylan was the outsider here, persona not grata just by virtue of who he was.

"I should have never let Eleanor spend the night. If she'd driven back to Austin after we left your ranch, she wouldn't have been hurt."

Dylan thought it best not to point out the possible fallacy of that statement. Collette was certain that the man who'd made the disturbing phone calls to her was behind the violence. That wasn't necessarily so. Eleanor might have enemies of her own.

He leaned against the support post near the edge of the steps. "How well did you know Eleanor?"

"We've been best friends since college. The two of us and Melinda Kingston met our first year at UT. We hit it off from the get-go. The three of us shared an off-campus apartment from our sophomore year right through graduation."

"Where does Melinda live now?"

"In Austin, in the same apartment complex as Eleanor. Along with their regular jobs, Melinda and Eleanor are the editors and owners of *Beyond the Grave*. I was helping them out when I met Eleanor at your ranch today."

"Is Eleanor married? Divorced? In a relationship?"

"Not married and no steady relationship. She's a workaholic and a much-sought-after freelance investigative reporter. She'll do whatever it takes to get her story."

And that kind of fervor likely earned her all kinds of enemies, he thought. "Any particular reason why she stayed overnight instead of driving back to Austin?"

"She was interviewing a man just outside Mustang Run early tomorrow morning. She thought it would be easier to just stay here instead of driving back to Austin. She hadn't counted on running into a lunatic."

Not in what seemed to be a quiet, rural Texas town. It had probably seemed even quieter and more peaceful almost eighteen years ago when Dylan's mother had been murdered in similar fashion mere miles away. That time the perpetrator had used a gun.

Damn!

He'd been doing a good job of keeping his own dark memories out of this, but now that he'd acknowledged them, they slunk into his consciousness like a pack of howling coyotes. But this wasn't about the past or him.

"I know you're going to the hospital to see Eleanor, but I don't think you should come back here by yourself after that."

"I live here."

"That doesn't mean you have to spend the night here tonight."

She put her foot flat on the porch to stop the gentle swaying of the swing. "Are you suggesting I stay at your ranch?"

He'd definitely not been suggesting that. "Haunted houses make for a lousy night's sleep," he said, keeping it light.

She shrugged. "I'll be fine, and once my father gets tired of interrogating you, you should go home and get some sleep."

He should. He probably wouldn't. "Your father obviously doesn't approve of our being friends."

"He seldom approves of anything I do. I like it that way."

And yet she still lived on his turf, in the same small town she'd grown up in.

She pulled her cell phone from the pocket of her full skirt. "I should call Melinda. She'll want to know about the assault. And then she can get in touch with Eleanor's mother in Houston."

He nodded and waited.

By the time she broke the connection, he could see new frustrations setting in. "Was there a problem?"

"Melinda was spaced-out on her migraine drugs. She insisted she call Eleanor's mother and she offered to call a cab and go to the hospital, but I told her to stay home. She's a zombie when those headaches set in."

He walked over and dropped to the swing next to Collette. She rested her head on his shoulder and his need to pull her into his arms jumped into overdrive.

This was not the time to have these feelings. And Collette was definitely not the woman to be having them for. It was also not the time to be a jerk, so he slipped a comforting arm around her.

The front door swung open, and the sheriff stepped onto the porch. He stood like a stone statue, scowling as if he'd caught them in some immoral act. His censure of Dylan couldn't have been clearer.

Screw him, Dylan thought. Yet he stood and moved away from the swing.

The sheriff continued to stare him down. "I have plenty of questions for you, Dylan Ledger, but first I want to hear from my daughter."

The sheriff walked to the edge of the porch and spit a wad of tobacco into the dirt before turning to Collette. "What do you know about this stalker and why haven't you come to me about this before now?"

Chapter Five

Her reasoning seemed futile now. Could it be that she'd let Eleanor face this because of her own stubborn resentment toward her father?

Collette took a deep breath and tried to put her guilt aside for now. She needed her full powers of concentration to recall every detail she'd gleaned from the madman's phone calls. That was the least she could do for Eleanor.

She clasped her hands in her lap. "I didn't come to you because the man's calls were never threatening. At first I thought they were a joke."

"A joke? Someone was stalking you and you took it for a joke?"

"At first," she admitted. "He'd say how beautiful I was and that he couldn't get me out of his mind. I figured one of my friends had put him up to it."

"What else did he say?"

"I can't remember word for word. The first few times, it was as if he was flirting. He'd say how much he looked forward to meeting me. When I asked why he didn't tell me who he was, he'd say he was waiting for the right time."

"I take it that progressed."

"Yes. A few weeks ago, he started freaking me out.

He'd describe how I looked in a specific dress or outfit, talk about how I'd worn my hair, comment on the errands I'd run that day. He seemed to know everything about me, what I did, where I went. That made me increasingly nervous."

"But he never asked you to meet him?"

"Not once, though he kept saying we'd meet soon and that I'd like him."

"What about his voice? Did it remind you of anyone you know?"

"No, that was the creepiest part of the calls. His voice sounded strained, croaky, as if he had a perpetual case of laryngitis. I'd recognize that voice anywhere. That's why I'm almost sure I've never met him."

"When did this start?"

"A few months back."

"Be more specific."

"Sometime around mid-March, I think. I was working late in my studio." She'd taken it so lightly that first time, but it made her skin crawl now to think that even that night he might have been snooping around, watching her every move.

"Damn it, Colley. What were you thinking? You should have called me immediately."

Colley. He'd reverted to his childhood name for her. She'd hated it, thought it made her sound like a dog. Eventually, he'd dropped it, but tonight it felt right.

He started to pace. "Think, Colley. Had you met someone new who'd come on to you, maybe while photographing a wedding or a party of some kind?"

"No."

"Are you sure?"

"How can I be sure? People talk to me all the time.

I don't think about the possibility that they could be stalkers."

"Don't get riled with me. I'm just asking."

"I know. I'm sorry. This is just so hard when I don't even know how badly Eleanor is injured."

But her father's questions kept coming, on and on until her head felt as if someone were pushing needles into her brain.

When she could take no more, she buried her face in her hands and tried to regroup. She knew her father needed something specific to go on, but there was no consistent pattern to the stalker's calls. All she knew of the man was his voice and the way it had started to creep inside her stomach and turn it into knots whenever he'd call.

Drowning in guilt wouldn't help. She gripped the chains that held the swing and raised her head, finally looking at her father. "I realize now that I should have reported the phone calls, but I've heard you say yourself that there's little law enforcement can do when an unidentified stalker fails to make physical threats."

"I'm your father, Collette. I would have found a way to track down the son of a bitch."

"Then do it now," she said, her nerves stretched to the breaking point.

"Your daughter's had a rough night," Dylan said, interrupting the conversation for the first time since her father had started grilling her. "Maybe you should give the questions a rest for now."

"When I want your advice, I'll ask for it, Ledger."

His continuous brusque treatment of Dylan was uncalled for, and it grated on Collette's already raw nerves. "Dylan's right, Dad. I'll keep trying to think of anything

I can to help, but we're wasting time here and Eleanor might need me."

Her dad nodded and spit again, wiping his mouth on his sleeve before walking over to the swing where she was sitting. "Okay, but I don't feel good about you being alone while the lunatic who attacked Eleanor is still on the loose."

"I won't be alone. I'm going straight to the hospital."

"Get your things and Brent can drive you there. When you're finished, he can take you to Bill and Alma's to spend the rest of the night."

Always with the orders. But this time she would do as he said—or almost as he said. "I'll take my own car. I don't like being stuck anywhere without it."

"Dumb move with a lunatic on the loose who has made it his business to follow you around. But if you insist on having your car, Brent can drive you to the hospital and I'll have one of the other deputies drive your car to Bill's."

"Okay." Too bad Dylan hadn't invited her to his place for the night. Her father would have thrown a fit, but it would have been a lot easier than going over all of this again with her brother and his wife.

And she really hated the thought of bringing Georgia into this. Not that they could keep it from her. Nothing stayed secret in Mustang Run.

When she stood to go inside, her father put a hand on her shoulder. The touch was discomfiting for her and no doubt for him, as well. She'd accepted long ago that he was guarded with his emotions. Instead he gave orders and criticized.

And drove away the best things in his life.

"We'll get the son of a bitch, Colley." He patted her on

the shoulder and then stepped back. "You get your things together. I'll go tell Brent the plan."

When he walked away, Dylan took his place at her side and took her hands in his. "None of this is your fault, Collette. Don't let anyone make you think that it is."

There was no awkwardness in Dylan's touch. He was practically a stranger, yet it was easier to turn to him for comfort than to her own father.

"Thanks," she murmured. "For everything."

"Glad I could help."

"Keep that thought while my father is trying to break you the way he would a wild steed. That's what you get for coming to the aid of the sheriff's daughter."

"I'm not worried about him, but I can see why he's suspicious about my showing up here tonight. Just for the record, why did you tell me to stop by anytime?"

She had no answer that made sense even to her. "I guess I just wanted to see you again." She pushed through the door, then stopped and turned back to face Dylan. "Why did you come?"

"Two beers. Dread of going back to the ranch." He leaned against the door frame. "And I wanted to see you again."

She could really grow to like this man.

DYLAN WOKE and opened his eyes at the smell of brewing coffee drifting from the kitchen. The predawn darkness outside his window told him daybreak was at least a half hour away. He couldn't have slept more than a few hours.

Punching his pillow, he rolled to his stomach. A pain attacked just below the small of his back. The mattress on his boyhood bed was likely the culprit, either that or the strain of the previous evening.

He'd assumed it would be the memories of his past that messed up his mind when he returned to Mustang Run. Now there were new dilemmas to consume his thoughts and rob him of sleep.

The only good news was that Collette had called him from the hospital last night to let him know that her friend Eleanor had regained consciousness and was in stable condition, though too groggy from pain medication to answer questions.

She'd suffered a concussion and needed to undergo surgery today to repair damage to her shoulder. But luckily the injuries were not life-threatening.

Nonetheless, Collette sounded panicky about her friend's condition.

The floorboards squeaked when he threw his legs over the side of the bed and planted his size-ten feet. Fatigue still clung to him like soap scum to a shower door, but he might as well face the day ahead and his dad.

Dylan grabbed the jeans he'd worn yesterday from the chair where he'd tossed them last night. He'd shower and change after coffee. He didn't bother with shoes or a shirt. He did stop at the bathroom, take care of business, wash his hands and rake his damp fingers through his hair.

When he stepped into the kitchen, his dad was standing at the back door looking out and seemingly studying the skulking shadows made by branches swaying in the slight breeze.

"You're up early," Troy said, not bothering to turn around.

"I smelled coffee."

"Yeah. I started a pot once I figured out how. Even appliances have changed a lot in seventeen years."

Dylan hadn't considered that there would be so many common everyday things his father hadn't done while he was in prison. Even moving around his own kitchen must seem strange.

That was another reason Dylan probably should have given him some time to adjust on his own before barging in as a welcoming party of one. But the attorney had felt it important that at least one of Troy's sons be there for his homecoming.

"You were out late last night," Troy said.

Dylan nodded. When the coffee indicator flashed green, he took two mugs from the cabinet and filled both of them, handing one to his father.

"No place better to party than Texas," Troy said.

"Actually I was late because I ran into a problem."

The tension factor in the room increased. "What kind of problem?"

"A young woman was viciously attacked. I was the first one on the scene."

Troy winced as if the words had been blows. His free hand clenched and unclenched a couple of times before he pulled a chair from the kitchen table and sat down.

"It won't involve you," Dylan said. "I can handle this on my own. I've already explained all I know to the sheriff. I just wanted you to know what's going on."

"Sheriff Glenn McGuire?"

"Afraid so. I think he's a fixture in Mustang Run."

"One that should have been replaced and junked years ago. How about starting at the beginning and telling me how and where you stumbled upon this crime?"

Dylan joined him at the table, though he'd have preferred to stand and occasionally pace. He'd been diagnosed with ADHD a few years after his mother had died. He'd supposedly outgrown the problem, but sitting still when his mind was going a mile a minute remained a challenge for him.

Dylan went over the details, leaving nothing out. By the time he'd finished, the situation seemed far more confusing than it had last night.

Troy worried a small glass saltshaker that had been left on the table from the night before. "If the stalker knew as much about Collette as his calls indicated, then he surely wouldn't have mistaken Eleanor Baker for her."

"That's just one of the factors that don't make sense."

"What are the others?"

"Motivation for breaking and entering and assaulting the friend of someone you claim is your soul mate."

"I'm sure Glenn McGuire is way ahead of you on that."

No doubt. Dylan sipped the hot brew while he tried to refit the puzzle in his mind. "It's possible the perpetrator wasn't Collette's stalker," he said, thinking out loud. "The man might have been after Eleanor."

Troy leaned forward and propped his elbows on the table. "Or it could have been just a random attack of violence. But you said Eleanor had regained consciousness. She may be able to clear this up."

"Hopefully soon, but last I heard she was too woozy from pain meds and too weak to question. What worries me most is if the man who's been making the harassing phone calls to Collette is responsible for the attack, he is one sick bastard."

"Or just a normal man who snapped," Troy said. "It happens."

The same way people said it had happened with Troy when he'd killed Dylan's mother. "I don't agree that normal people just snap into violence," Dylan said, needing to get that much off his chest. "Losing control is just another form of cop-out. But if Collette's stalker is guilty of the attack, then Collette is in real danger."

"Her father's the sheriff. I'm sure he realizes that and has the resources to keep her safe until the nutcase is apprehended."

Meaning Collette wasn't Dylan's responsibility. He got that. It didn't do much for relieving the anxiety that was eating away at him now.

"I'll get some more coffee," Dylan said, needing a break. He took their mugs to the counter and refilled both of them.

Troy hunched over his cup. "Tell me exactly what the sheriff said when he questioned you alone, Dylan. Word for word or as close as you can remember it."

"There's not that much to tell. Most of the questions were redundant and a waste of time."

"He was hoping you'd mutter something he could use against you."

"I'm not a suspect, Dad. He might wish I was, but he's got nothing on me."

"Don't underestimate Glenn McGuire. Did he question you about your reasons for being at Collette's?"

"Yeah, and he clearly didn't like that his daughter was mixed up with a Ledger."

"Did he ask about your personal life?"

"For an hour, but other than a couple of speeding tickets, I'm clean as a whistle. Besides, if there's any doubt about me in the sheriff's mind, Eleanor will clear that up as soon as she can talk."

Any question of his guilt was a nonissue in Dylan's mind, but Troy was growing increasingly agitated. The muscles in his bare arms bunched as if he were about to slug someone.

"Get a lawyer, Dylan. Today. Before the sheriff comes calling with more questions."

"There's no call for me to get lawyered up. I didn't do anything wrong."

"Guilt or innocence doesn't matter to McGuire. He makes his own rules. The evidence is what he says it is. Take my word for it. You need an attorney."

His father's reaction was too intense for this to just be about last night. It had to track back to Troy's experiences. Was he convinced that the sheriff had built a murder case against him when no evidence existed?

If so, his anger and frustration were justified.

"You need an experienced attorney who's on top of his game," Troy said. "I'll ask Able Drake. He'll know who's who in the legal world."

"I appreciate the offer, but I can't afford that kind of counsel. And I don't need it. If anything, I'm the hero here. I may have frightened off the attacker before he finished the job of killing Eleanor and then waited around for Collette."

He could tell by the look on his father's face that he wasn't convinced by Dylan's logic.

Troy pushed back from the table. "At least give it some thought. Now, how about some bacon and eggs?"

"That, I could use."

His father broke some eggs into a bowl while Dylan peeled the bacon from the package and fit it into the frying pan. He surveyed the refrigerator and found butter and blackberry preserves.

Whoever Able Drake was, he'd done a good job of getting the cupboard stocked and the house ready. If it turned out Dylan needed an attorney, he'd keep Able in mind. But he didn't expect to need one.

"Did the sheriff give you any warnings, like not to leave the state or the county until he gave you clearance?" Troy asked, obviously not quite ready to drop the subject.

"Only one, and it was more an order than a warning."

"What was that?"

"Stay away from his daughter."

COLLETTE'S BROTHER grabbed a hot biscuit from the pan his wife had just taken from the oven, juggling it until it was cool enough to handle. He took the seat that was catty-corner from Collette at the table. "Did you eat, Sis?"

"No. My stomach would rebel."

"You look worn. You should go back to bed and catch a few more z's."

"I couldn't sleep."

"Exhaustion won't help anyone."

"You couldn't have gotten much sleep yourself. You were still up when I arrived during the wee hours of the morning."

"I'd been asleep. Dad talked to Brent when you two left the hospital. He called here and wanted me to make sure you got here safely and didn't leave again."

"Good old Dad."

"He doesn't want you seeing Dylan Ledger again. I agree. Stay away from him."

Alma joined them in the kitchen, still in her robe but with her bobbed brown hair combed and her make-up on. "Bill, do you have lunch money for Georgia? The smallest bill I have is a twenty."

"I gave her enough for the week on Monday."

"She had to pay for some supplies she needed for art class."

"Lunch money is for lunch."

"And while you're at it, I need money for Sukey."

"The cleaning woman's fees are supposed to come out of your household budget."

Alma went to the pitcher of fresh-squeezed orange juice and poured herself a glass, ignoring his complaints. Bill pulled out his wallet and divvied up the money, ones for Georgia, twenties for Alma to pay Sukey. He was dressed impeccably, blue-striped suit and silk tie in a muted pattern, standard attire for the insurance company he owned and managed in Mustang Run.

"Thanks for letting me barge in on you in the middle of the night," Collette said.

"Glad to have you," Alma said. "The extra bedroom is yours for as long as you want it."

"I appreciate that." Actually she'd already stayed as long as she wanted. It wasn't that she had issues with her brother. It was more that they weren't from the same planet. He was all about rules and routine and handing out advice. Not as adamant as their father was, but enough so that Collette with her free-spirited approach to life was never totally in her comfort zone at his house.

She liked Alma, but there was a disconnect factor there, as well. On the other hand, Collette absolutely adored her niece. Georgia was not only intelligent and outgoing, she was energetic and upbeat.

"I'm playing tennis at the country club this morning," Alma said. "Why don't you join us, Collette? The exercise and fresh air will do you good. I mean, if there's nothing you can do for your friend who was attacked."

"I need to clean my kitchen."

Alma made a face. "You don't want to clean up blood. If I ask, I'm sure Sukey can fit you in this week. I have a key to your house that I can let her use. That way you can put last night's incident behind you."

Last night's "incident," as if Eleanor's near-fatal assault

was a spilled drink or a bit of vomit that had soaked into the carpet.

Georgia picked that minute to walk into the kitchen, her school backpack slung over one shoulder. She tossed it onto an empty chair. "Good. You're awake, Aunt Collette." She gave Collette a quick hug. "Dad told me about what happened when he got me up for school. You must be bummed to the max."

"To the max," Collette agreed.

"I'm really sorry. Was the woman who was attacked the woman you were going to meet when I saw you after school yesterday?"

"She was."

"Dad said Grandpa will get the man who attacked her."

Collette wondered what else her brother had told Georgia about the attack. He hadn't wanted to tell her anything, but Collette had persuaded him that it was better coming from one of them than from the kids at school. News of violence traveled fast in a tight-knit community like Mustang Run.

"It's okay if you can't take me shopping this week," Georgia said, "but I hope you can make the party on Saturday."

"I wouldn't miss it."

"Are you afraid that man might break into your house again? Is that why you're staying with us?"

Bill brushed a crumb from the front of his shirt. "Stop bugging your aunt, Georgia. Grab you lunch money and your book bag and I'll give you a lift to school."

Georgia gave Collette another quick hug and her mother a peck on the cheek before following Bill to the car.

"She's a good kid," Collette said.

"But impressionable," Alma added. "The less she hears

about the brutality the better. I know she'll question you, but—"

"I never planned to go into the gritty details with her," Collette interrupted, irritated that Alma might think she would. "I'm going to get dressed and then I'll get out of your hair."

Her cell phone rang as she started back to the guest room. Melinda's name came up on the caller ID. Collette ducked into the room and closed the door before taking the call.

"I'm glad you called," Collette said. "Have you heard from Eleanor this morning?"

"I just got off the phone with Mrs. Baker. She said they'll be taking Eleanor into surgery any minute. I offered to come up and sit with Mrs. Baker, but she said it wasn't necessary."

"Is Eleanor talking?"

"Very little. Her mother says she's still confused about what happened to her. The doctor thinks it's likely due to the pain medication."

"I'm sure my father is driving them crazy wanting to question her about the attack."

"Your father is the real reason I called. Can you give him a message for me? He gave me his cell-phone number, but I can't remember what I did with it."

"Sure. What's the message?"

"I located the two articles he asked about."

"What articles?"

"Ones that Eleanor wrote about the Ledger murder and trial. I can fax them to him if he'll give me a fax number."

Collette sank to the bed. "My father called you this morning to ask about those?"

"Yes, but I don't mind. I told him that I want to help

find the man who tried to kill Eleanor in any way I can."

Collette's stomach churned. How dare he do this? "The Ledgers have nothing to do with last night's attack on Eleanor."

"I hope you're right, but with Dylan's being there and Troy Ledger just getting out of prison, I can see why Sheriff McGuire wants to check this out."

So could Collette, and a surge of anger whipped though her like a riled rattlesnake.

"I'll give Dad the message, Melinda."

When they broke the connection, Collette yanked a pair of jeans and a teal-blue pullover sweater from the duffle she'd thrown together last night. She dressed quickly, gave her disheveled mass of hair a couple of careless brushes and tinged her lips with gloss.

"Where are you going in such a rush?" Alma asked when Collette passed her in the hallway.

"To pay a visit to Dylan Ledger. Be sure and tell my father that if he calls."

Chapter Six

It was just after eight in the morning when Dylan stepped out the back door. The sky was cloudless, and already the sun was warm on his back. He walked toward the old storage building just behind the garage.

Mockingbirds were having a lively banter in the branches of the mulberry tree just past the back steps. A spattering of weedy yellow wildflowers he couldn't name dotted the pasture that stretched into the distance.

It was a typical, serene pastoral scene, but the thoughts playing havoc with Dylan's mind were anything but tranquil. Collette McGuire was at the center of his mental chaos. He wasn't sure if her stalker had anything to do with the attack, but he couldn't shake the feeling that she was in danger.

The good sheriff didn't want Dylan anywhere near his daughter. Not that Dylan would lose sleep over what Glenn McGuire wanted. He would stay away from Collette, but only because she didn't need him. The sheriff was a hotheaded, arrogant blowhard, but he was in the perfect position to protect Collette.

Dylan would only bring complications and excess baggage to the table. The murderer's kid all over again. Obviously, some things never changed.

Standing around stressing over a situation he could

do nothing about wasn't helping, either, he told himself. He might as well take a drive around the ranch and see what kind of work his father was looking at if he actually planned to get the spread up and running again.

Not that his father had asked for or given any indication that he wanted Dylan's input. He'd left while Dylan was in the shower with not so much as a scribbled note as to where he was going or when he'd be back.

Before Dylan reached his truck, he heard the rumble of a vehicle bumping its way along the rutted ranch road. He recognized Collette's Jeep the second it came into sight. A surge of unwelcome anticipation pulsated along his nerve endings.

By the time she'd come to a complete stop, he was opening her door for her. She jumped out, eyes blazing as if she were showing up for a gunfight.

It worried him how much he wanted to pull her into his arms. Instead he closed the door after her. "More trouble?" he asked.

"For you."

He tensed a little. "Care to explain?"

"My father's out to get you."

So her concern was for him. He relaxed a little, even liking the fact that she'd gotten this fired up on his account.

"Is he bringing his rope over to hang me?"

"More likely his gun to shoot you in the back, and this isn't funny, Dylan."

He found it amazing that she could be that angry and look that good. "I'm not amused. I'm just thankful you weren't upset about something more serious."

"You don't think involving you in a felony is serious enough?"

"The sheriff is just blowing off steam because he

doesn't like the fact that you invited a Ledger to your house. As soon as Eleanor talks, he'll have to eat crow."

"You do not know my father. He called my friend Melinda this morning wanting her to look up some articles that Eleanor had written about your mother's murder."

At least he wasn't going around town leading the chorus of "murderer's kid." "If I went around attacking every journalist who'd ever written about our family, I'd be busy from morning until night."

"That's not the point."

"So, what is the point? That your father doesn't like me? Big deal. That he thinks all Ledgers should be hung on general principle? He's probably not the only one of that opinion."

"But he's not just someone with an opinion. He's the sheriff and he has no conscience when it comes to destroying people."

"Is this still about me? Because it sounds a lot like personal father bashing."

"I'm trying to warn you about him."

"I'm not afraid of your father, Collette."

"You should be."

He stepped to his truck and opened the passenger-side door for her. "Get in."

"Why? Where are we going?"

"For a ride around the ranch and a chance for you to cool down so that we can talk about this rationally." He stepped back. "Unless you agree with your father and you're afraid to go off with me."

"If I were afraid of you, Dylan Ledger, I wouldn't be standing here right now." She climbed into the truck to prove her point. "But I do need to call and cancel my appointments for the day." She pulled a day planner out of her handbag and started making calls.

She might not be afraid of him, but he was afraid of her. Afraid of falling for a woman in a town that had spit him out years ago and showed no signs of wanting him back. He didn't mind playing bad boy, but he wasn't going to spend a lifetime sticking out his face just to get his teeth kicked in.

He climbed behind the wheel. She leaned forward and her gorgeous red hair tumbled in front of her, falling over her spectacular breasts. She threw back her head and shoved a tangle of curls behind her ears. Her green eyes sparkled like fiery emeralds when she looked up to find him staring at her.

"Are we going to sit here all day, or are you going to drive?"

Man, did he hate gorgeous, feisty redheads with svelte bodies and killer smiles. If he told himself that enough, he might even start to believe it sometime.

About the time he believed that Texas was going to secede from the Union and bulls were really sweet-natured creatures who'd just gotten a bum rap.

COLLETTE BUCKLED HER seat belt as Dylan shifted into Drive and gunned the accelerator. Fifty yards past the house, the ranch road became little more than tire grooves cut into the hard, dry earth. Overgrown pastures and broken fences stretched endlessly in front of them. They were totally alone.

If she had any fear of Dylan, it would surely surface now. But there was none. She knew next to nothing about him yet she'd felt a connection with him almost from the moment he'd arrived at the ranch. She'd hoped he'd call, had been excited when she'd seen his truck parked in front of her house last night.

Admittedly, he was cocky and a bit arrogant and even

had a cowboy swagger about him, though his hands were too smooth to belong to a rancher. Yet he'd been protective and sensitive last night, supportive, but not overwhelming.

Dylan lowered the driver's window and propped his arm on the door. "It's been five years since anyone's run cattle out here and it shows."

"I didn't realize anyone had been here since your father…"

"Since he went to prison? You can say it, Collette. I won't be offended by the truth."

"Sorry. It just seemed callous to put it so bluntly."

"No one's lived in the house," he explained, "but a man named Tom Hartwell rented the land. I'm assuming he used it for cattle. I don't see any signs it's been used for anything else."

"I know the Hartwells. His wife cuts hair at a salon on Main Street. Tom lost his arm in a hay-baling accident about five years ago. I heard he cut way back on his herd after that."

"I never heard that, but guess it explains why he quit renting the pastures of Willow Creek Ranch."

"Some people around here expected one of the Ledger sons to come back to run the ranch once you were grown."

"We talked about it," Dylan admitted, "but neither my brothers nor I were excited about the prospect of living in Mustang Run."

"Does that mean you're not staying?"

"Don't plan to, nor have I been invited. Now that my father's out of prison, the ranch is his to run as he sees fit."

"Do you have a position to go back to?"

"No. I joined the army right after I graduated from the

university. When I was discharged six months ago, I gave working for my uncle's advertising agency a shot. The job and I were not a fit. It required far too many hours shut up in an office."

Dylan turned to face her. She met his gaze and felt his penetrating stare vibrate though her. Even with all that had happened over the past few hours, she couldn't escape the fact that he stirred something a bit primeval and feral in her.

Dylan took a left that put them on a dirt road leading over a crest and then started downhill. "You seem calmer," he said. "Now do you want to talk about what happened last night?"

"I came here to let you know what my father is up to, not to rehash the attack."

"Your father is a smart man, Collette. He may not trust me, but he can't manufacture a case against me. If he's arrogant enough to try, Eleanor Baker will nullify the strategy as soon as she's able to describe her real attacker."

"Assuming she got a good look at the man before he hit her over the head with the skillet."

"I say we go on that assumption until we find out differently. Better yet, let's operate on the assumption that your father has a lead on your stalker by now. I'm sure he's checking your phone records. It's amazing how close they can pinpoint the origin of calls these days."

"If he has valid information, he hasn't given me any of it."

"Have you had any more calls from the stalker?"

"No."

"And there's a good chance you won't. He's likely afraid to call now, for fear the sheriff already has a lead on identifying him."

Dylan stopped beneath an oak tree sporting its new cover of green leaves. A creek that was practically overflowing from the spring rains rushed past them.

"Is this the ranch's namesake?" Collette asked.

"This is it. Willow Creek."

"I don't see any willows."

"There are black willow trees along the northern edge of the creek. My brother Sean and I used to sit beneath them and fish for bream." Dylan opened his door and climbed out of the truck. The scene in front of her was too tempting not to join him.

She walked to the edge of the creek. "Did you ever swim in the creek?"

"We had a better spot for swimming, though I'm not sure I can find it anymore, at least not by truck. None of us boys were driving then, so we went by horseback."

"Is it part of the creek?"

"Better. It's a spring-fed pool, cold year round, but the water felt great in July and August. I got in trouble more than once for sneaking off to swim before I'd finished my chores."

"And I'll bet your brothers were right behind you."

"Wyatt was usually leading the way."

Dylan had known the life every Texas boy dreamed of and then he'd lost that and both parents. One to death. One to prison. It was difficult to believe that after all that, he'd become the confident, easygoing man he seemed today.

"You must have missed life on the ranch terribly when you had to move away."

He shrugged. "For a while. I hated city life. Uncle Phil said I was a cowboy who fell out of the saddle and then lost the horse. At first it made me mad when he said that, but then I figured it was pretty much how things were."

"Who is Uncle Phil?"

"My mom's oldest brother, the one who owns the advertising agency. He and Aunt Sylvie were elected to take me in when my grandparents divvied us up."

That surprised her. "I just assumed you and your brothers went to live with your grandparents."

"Nope. They said five was too many for them to handle, so they shared the wealth. And don't give me that look, Collette. I hate that look."

"What look?"

"That oh-you-poor-dear look. So my life wasn't ideal. Whose is? And that was all years ago."

"Point made." She slipped out of her sandals and rolled up the legs of her jeans. Stepping cautiously to avoid sinking in a muddy spot, she made her way to the edge of the creek.

Slowly she dipped a toe into the water. The cold slapped against her. She stumbled backward.

Dylan's arms wrapped around her and held her steady. Her breath held at the gentle pressure of his fingers on her stomach and the strong cushion of his chest at her back. She inhaled the musky, woodsy scent of him and something stirred deep inside her, an ache that was both sweet and painful at the same time.

His arms tightened around her, and his lips touched the back of her neck. A tingle danced through her, leaving her weak.

He exhaled slowly and released her. "Gotta watch those slippery slopes."

Too late. She was falling. And it had nothing to do with the water or the mud. She'd just have to make sure she didn't fall so hard she couldn't move on when Dylan left Mustang Run.

Once out of the water, she wiped her damp feet on the thick carpet of grass and then slipped back into her sandals. Dylan waited and walked at her side as they started back to the truck. If the moment of closeness had gotten to him the way it had her, he showed no signs.

Her cell phone rang. Part of her hoped the caller would be her stalker. She'd like to tell him that she knew he'd attacked Eleanor and that he would pay for it. Still, the dread stabbed at her composure as she took the phone from the leather holster attached to her low-riding jeans.

The ID read Dad. The dread turned to fury. She didn't bother with a hello. "Why did you call Melinda this morning and ask her to look up Eleanor's articles on Troy Ledger?"

"I'm working an investigation, Collette. The woman who was attacked is a reporter. I can't rule out the fact that she pissed off somebody and they came after her."

"Not somebody, Dad. You asked about Dylan in particular. I told you this isn't about Eleanor, and it's definitely not about Dylan Ledger. Leave him out of this."

"Don't start telling me how to do my job, Collette. What kind of crazy stunt do you think you're pulling by going to the Ledger ranch?"

"I figured someone should warn Dylan what you were up to."

"You did, did you?" Anger chipped at his words so that each syllable was sharp and spiked.

"Yes. I'm with Dylan now, as a matter of fact."

"I'm not ruling out anyone and you can stop acting like Dylan's attorney. You don't even know the man you're defending and cavorting with. I'm sending Brent to pick you up and drive you back to Bill's."

"I'm not cavorting. And don't bother sending Brent. I'm capable of taking care of myself."

"You're as pigheaded as—"

"You, Dad." She broke the connection before he could

say more. Her heart was pounding, but she knew what she had to do. Not for her but for Dylan. He'd been through enough in this town without her father shoveling more crap on top of him.

Dylan opened the truck door for her. "I take it that was the sheriff."

"Yes, and as genial as he always is if someone dares to cross him."

"You don't have to defend me to him, Collette. I fight my own battles, and I don't want to come between you and your father."

"You're way too late in the scheme of things to do that."

She considered her options on the drive back to the Ledger house. Staying with Bill and Alma wasn't the answer. It would only disrupt their lives and Georgia's.

Staying alone in her house and thinking about Eleanor lying facedown in her blood every time she walked into the kitchen didn't sound like a good idea, either.

There was another choice. It would piss off her father, but he'd surely get the message that he couldn't tell her whom she could befriend and whom she should reject.

She shifted so she could face Dylan. "How do you think your father would feel about a houseguest his first week back in Mustang Run?"

"So far, he's not overly excited."

"You're not a guest. You're family."

He shot her a dubious look. "Am I missing something here?"

"My father thinks I need a protector. I'm thinking you'd fit that bill to perfection. You have a big house. I'd stay out of the way. You'd hardly know I was there."

"Your father would go ballistic."

"That's what makes this a win-win."

She'd just have to be careful on those sensual slippery slopes of attraction. Surely she could handle that.

TROY HAD SPENT most of the morning driving aimlessly, down one blacktop road after the other, trying to come to grips with what it meant to be back in Mustang Run. He'd thought he could handle it, but eighteen years had done nothing to erase the pain of losing Helene.

Every detail was still burned into his mind. The choking humidity that had slowed down his progress at setting a new row of fence posts and made him late getting home for lunch. The smell of burned peas. The voice of Mariah Carey singing about love on their old stereo system. Helene had loved Mariah Carey.

He closed his eyes tight as the pictures slipped from their hiding places in his mind and returned to torture him. Helene's beautiful body bloodied and nearly naked stretched out on the living-room floor. Her head was lying on the cold, hard stones of the hearth. Her long, dark hair was matted with her blood.

Life had ended for him that day. He'd kept breathing and walking, going through the motions. But he'd stopped living. His attorney had accused him of not fighting hard enough to prove his innocence during the yearlong ordeal of questioning and trial. The truth was he hadn't fought at all. Dead men had no fight left in them.

He'd let down his sons. Helene would never forgive him that.

He left the old farm-to-market road and turned into a section of town that had been ranch land the last time he'd seen it. Big houses of brick or stucco with two- and sometimes three-car garages filled every lot. Mostly commuters or retirees, he imagined. Mustang Run did not have the jobs to support that style of living.

Leaving the suburbs behind him, he made his way to the old part of town. Main Street had become a strand of antiques shops and coffeehouses. The only establishment that bore any resemblance to a place he remembered was Abby's Diner.

Abby had been working at her father's dry cleaners when Troy moved to Mustang Run to work as a wrangler for the Black Spur Ranch. He'd dated her a couple of times. They'd never clicked as a couple, but later, after Abby had opened the diner, she and Helene had become good friends.

Troy had mostly roamed the rodeo circuit before settling in Mustang Run, working just enough to earn entrance fees. He'd found the wrangling job through a newspaper ad, and the New York owner of the Black Spur had hired him via a phone call. The guy had taken more interest in using the ranch for a tax write-off than making money.

Troy made him money anyway and that's when ranching had gotten into his blood.

Impulsively, Troy pulled into a parking spot a few stores down and walked to the diner. The smell of coffee, cinnamon and spices greeted him when he stepped though the door.

The chairs at the bar were mostly occupied by older guys, none of whom he recognized. Several looked up, though only one made eye contact. Troy nodded as the chatter in the small diner diminished into an uncomfortable hush.

He made his way to a booth, slid in, removed his Western hat and set it on the seat beside him. The hat felt strange on his head, the same way his new boots and jeans felt, as if he were a pretender who should still be in a prison jumpsuit.

A pretty, slim waitress with a nice smile and the whitest teeth Troy had ever seen stopped at his elbow. Her badge said her name was Jenny.

"Just coffee?" Jenny asked, when he gave his order. "Abby makes the best biscuits and gravy in town."

So Abby was still around. At least something in this town had stayed the same, other than the arrogant sheriff. "I've already had breakfast," he said. Even then his appetite had been dulled by the new developments with Dylan.

He didn't see the son he remembered when he looked at Dylan. The son he remembered was a scrawny kid who loved to watch cartoons on TV and hated homework. Dylan was a man now—with his mother's eyes.

That got to Troy, made him realize that his sons were all he had left of her. And they were strangers. None of the others had even bothered to contact him since he'd been released from prison. He understood why, but it didn't make it any easier.

"I wondered how long it would take you to face your adoring public."

Troy looked up as Abby wiped her hands on her white apron, slid into the booth across from him and pushed a mug of steaming coffee his way. Evidently, Jenny had reported they had an infamous celebrity in the house.

The years hadn't been nearly as hard on Abby as they'd been on him. If anything, she looked better than she had before. She'd picked up some weight. Her bones no longer poked at her skin.

"My admirers don't seem all that excited to see me," he said.

"Because they bought into the prosecutor's lies. Your refusal to cooperate with your attorney didn't leave them a lot of choice."

"Let's not go back there."

"Whatever you say." She reached over and straightened the envelopes of sweetener. "I heard Dylan came back to town to help you get settled in."

"Word gets around."

"You don't need Facebook or Twitter to keep up with the gossip in Mustang Run."

"Good. I don't even have a computer as yet."

"I'm glad Dylan came, Troy. The boys need to get to know you. They're older now. They can make up their own minds about you and not have everything filtered through Helene's family."

"I'm not expecting miracles."

"Maybe you should. You're out of prison. That's a miracle in itself."

"You could call it that." And he wouldn't waste the opportunity that provided him. He had a score to settle. He'd never rest easy until he did.

Abby spread her hands palms down on the table. "Sheriff McGuire was in the other day."

"The man probably knows a good cup of coffee when he tastes it."

"You were the topic of his conversation. He's not going to make your return easy on you."

"I wasn't expecting him to throw a party."

"I'm serious, Troy. He said he planned to watch you like a hawk. Cross any line and he'll come down on you like misery on Job."

"I'll keep that in mind."

"Make sure you do."

The bell over the door rang and a middle-aged woman with frizzy brown hair and a rail-thin body stepped into the diner. A tall guy, muscled, with thinning hair and a tattoo on his left bicep, followed her in.

The woman stared openly at Troy before sliding into a booth.

Abby gave her a friendly wave and then leaned across the table. "Do you know who that is?" she asked, keeping her voice low.

"Can't say that I do."

"Edna Granger. You have to remember her. Five or six years younger than us. Wore her sweaters super tight. All the guys had the hots for her."

"I'm guessing I didn't."

"I forgot. Once you met Helene, you didn't know any other woman existed."

"Who's the guy?" Troy asked, making conversation and pretending he cared.

"I have no idea. I've never seen him before, but I can't believe he's a love interest. I've seen corpses that had more life in them than Edna."

"She looks like she's had a tough life," Troy agreed.

"You better believe it. Her husband got gunned down in Brownsville in some kind of drug turf war a couple of years ago. That's when she moved back here. Her addict daughter was shot last fall while she was high on crack cocaine. Losing her only child destroyed what was left of poor Edna."

"Does this story have a point?"

"Edna's lost her daughter and that turned her into a bitter woman. But living with nothing but anger and regret won't bring her daughter back."

He was beginning to see where this was going. He took a long sip of his coffee and waited for it.

"Helene wouldn't want you to give up, Troy. She'd want you to be a father to her sons even if they are grown. She'd want you to keep living and ranching."

"And eating pie?"

"Yes. And eating pie. Just don't dry up like Edna."

He had no intention of drying up, not until the dirty bastard who'd taken Helene's life paid with his own. "Don't worry about me, Abby. I've got things under control."

"If you ever need a friend, my number's in the book."

"I'll keep that in mind."

"I won't be holding my breath. Now I've got to get back to the kitchen before the crusts on my cherry pies turn from gold to black."

"I'll be back to try them one day soon."

"Bring Dylan. I'd love to see him. And watch out for McGuire."

McGuire's riding herd on him was the least of his worries. Taking it out on his son—on Helene's son—was a horse of a different color.

Troy had gone to prison because Glenn McGuire had twisted every speck of evidence against him. He would not get the chance to do that to Dylan.

If Troy had learned anything in prison, it was how to take care of business—by whatever means it took.

Chapter Seven

The blonde bitch hadn't died. Not that he'd meant to kill her originally, but since she'd fouled up everything for him, it would make him feel better to know she was no longer breathing.

Once again, he'd screwed things up. But there was no way he could have known the blonde would be there or that the guy in the black truck would show up.

He'd tracked Collette McGuire's every movement. She lived alone. She didn't date. No one had spent the night in that house except her for the past three months.

Ordinarily he could back off now, give things a chance to settle down, provide some damage control.

Not this time. Days, maybe hours, could make a difference.

Take one life to save another.

He'd killed for a lot less.

Chapter Eight

Dylan had balked at first, not wanting to start a war between her and her father, but Collette had persisted, and he'd finally agreed to let her stay at the ranch. His only stipulation had been that she tell her father beforehand.

She'd taken care of that a few seconds ago—after she'd asked how the investigation was going. There was no way she could have had a rational discussion with her father after telling him she was sleeping on murderer's row. His description, not hers.

Dylan turned into the drive that led to her house. Like most of the rural homes, this one sat well back from the road. Every other week, a neighbor kid cut the grass for her on his riding mower.

"Any word on fingerprints?" he asked Collette.

"The only matches were mine, yours and Eleanor's. I knew he had my and Eleanor's fingerprints on record. He made a point of getting them when we headed to Florida for spring break our freshman year at UT after telling us horror stories about women who were abducted by strangers. We figured it was to frighten us away from cute college guys we met on the beach."

"Did it work?"

"Until we met the first hunk. Did he take your fingerprints last night?"

"He did. It's routine, so don't go getting bent out of shape about it. Did your father say if they'd gotten any info from your wireless provider?"

"No, and I'm not sure he'll be able to get that information. When the stalker phones, my caller ID always indicates Out of Area or Unavailable. I think he uses prepaid phones."

"Even with those, you can get some information. The general location where the call originated. Whether or not he always used the same phone." Dylan killed the engine and opened the truck door. "Give me the name of your provider and I'll see what I can find out."

She told him and then jumped out of the truck and met him on the walkway that led to the front porch. "You're not a cop. How can you get info on my calls?"

"I have connections. My oldest brother, Wyatt, is a police detective in Atlanta."

"I see."

"That's one of the advantages of having five brothers. You have a wide range of expertise to call on when you're in a jam."

"Are you close?"

"Not so close that I can tell you the name of Wyatt's current squeeze or what he ate for dinner last night, but close enough that I can ask a favor."

"When was the last time you saw Wyatt?"

"About four years ago when my grandmother died. All five of us were there for the funeral. The Ledger contingent was in full force that day."

Collette took the key from her handbag but didn't open the door. "How often do you all get together?"

"We tend to avoid reunions. When the five of us congregate, the topic of conversation tends to center around the things we all have in common. Mother's murder. Having a father in prison."

"But you're still family." Not that she had room to talk about failed family relationships. Collette unlocked the front door and pushed it open. The house felt cold and hostile, as if the aura of violence had attached itself to the very walls. It struck her that the Ledger home must feel a thousand times more frosty and intimidating to Dylan.

And she'd be sleeping in that same house tonight, with Dylan, his father and all their haunting memories of what used to be. She shuddered at the thought.

Dylan's hand came to rest on her shoulder. "Are you okay?"

"I will be when I get the house back in order. You can wait here if you like while I go change into work clothes."

"In that case, I think I'll make that call to Wyatt."

DYLAN PUNCHED IN WYATT'S cell-phone number. He had all his brothers' phone numbers programmed into his phone, though he seldom called them.

"You're on." Wyatt answered with his typical offbeat greeting.

"It's Dylan. Did I catch you at a bad time?"

"It's always a bad time around here. What's up? Problems in paradise already?"

"A few."

"Is Troy all right?"

It was never Dad with Wyatt.

"About what you'd expect."

"I have no idea what I'd expect."

"Dad's home. Quiet. Withdrawn, but talking about getting the ranch up and running again."

"Interesting. How are things working out for you?"

"They could be better."

"So, what's the problem?"

"I need some information."

"Sure. Can you hold on a minute?"

Dylan waited while Wyatt held a hurried conversation with someone else. There was loud talking in the background.

"Sorry," Wyatt said when he came back to Dylan. "I'm at the precinct. It's crazy around here."

"I won't keep you but a minute. I was wondering if you could get me the details on calls made from one cell phone to another in the Mustang Run area."

"Is some idiot harassing Troy already?"

"No. It's for a friend of mine. I'm guessing she could get the data herself but I figure you can get it a lot faster."

"A woman, huh? You're a fast worker."

"It's my killer charm."

"Must run in the family. So what's going on with her?"

"Her house was broken into last night and a girlfriend of hers who was there alone was attacked. Some guy's been making anonymous, harassing phone calls to my friend and she thinks he could be behind the assault."

"How serious were the victim's injuries?"

"He stabbed her in the shoulder with a kitchen knife. There was considerable blood loss and the wound required surgery. He also hit her in the head with a skillet. She suffered a concussion, but no major complications to this point."

"Sounds as if she was fighting him off and he missed his mark with the knife, or else he didn't mean to kill her. Either way, he's dangerous. The police should be handling this."

"They are."

"And you should be staying far away from this situation, Dylan. The Ledger name alone could make any attempt to help backfire on you."

Wyatt didn't know the half of it. "Can you get the info?"

"I'll need your friend's name, cell-phone number and her wireless provider."

Dylan obliged him, giving the name last.

"McGuire," Wyatt repeated. "Any kin to Sheriff Glenn McGuire?"

"His daughter."

"How in hell did you... Hold on a second, will you?"

This time Wyatt was back on the line in a matter of seconds.

"Things are hopping. Gotta run, but I'll get back to you. In the meantime, my advice is to run from this like you've got a couple of wild hogs chasing you."

"I'll keep that in mind. Thanks, bro."

Thanks for reiterating what he already knew. Being with Collette was a mistake. Having her stay at his place against her dad's wishes was downright masochistic.

Dylan didn't see Collette when he walked through the house, but he could hear noises and music with a Latin beat coming from her bedroom. He stepped into the kitchen. The blood was still on the floor along with the mess the investigation team had made searching for evidence.

Dylan knew little about working a crime scene, but he figured they'd surely taken DNA samples. They'd also have taken the bloodied knife and skillet. Hopefully some concrete evidence would come of it. And Wyatt was right. They didn't need Dylan's help.

Still, he walked to the back door to check the lock. It was evident that it had been tampered with. His guess was that the man had come in and left that way. Dylan's first instinct about seeing a figure run from the house was probably right on target. He'd mentioned that to the sheriff during the interrogation session, but he had no idea if the sheriff had checked it out.

Dylan walked out the back door, across the porch and down the steps. The grass was high, probably due to be cut soon. There was no sign of footprints.

He scanned the area, looking for a protected spot where the attacker could have parked his car hidden from the road. There was a cluster of oak trees about fifty yards behind the house, but there were no tire tracks leading in that direction. If he'd parked there, he hadn't gotten there from Collette's driveway.

Dylan made his way to the trees, though he wouldn't wander far. Not that he expected trouble today. The attacker would have to be insane to chance coming back to the scene of the crime with Dylan's truck parked in the drive—the same truck that had most likely frightened him away last night.

The grass gave way to bare earth as Dylan reached the heavily shaded area. He knelt for a closer look at what appeared to be prints of rubber-soled shoes. The prints weren't totally distinct, but there was enough there to tell that the man had walked this way toward the house and then run back to his car. He held his foot next to one of the prints. He'd guess the attacker's shoe size at an eleven.

And just beyond the trees, there were well-indented tire tracks. He followed them just far enough to determine that the driver had cut across from a partially overgrown dirt road that ran behind the Baptist Church. The stalker had done his homework.

But he'd likely made a few mistakes. He'd have assumed Collette's car was parked in the garage, would have seen the shadows behind the blinds and mistook them for Collette's. And then Eleanor had surprised him, and he'd panicked and attacked her.

Had it been Collette alone inside the house...

Sick possibilities wreaked havoc with his mind.

Had the stalker come as he'd promised to convince Collette he was her soul mate? Or had he come to claim her against her will?

He'd love the stalker to show up now. Love to slam a fist into his face over and over until the man was mush.

He didn't know how he'd become this attached to Collette so quickly. All he knew was that he had to keep her safe.

Collette was on her knees in the kitchen when he returned to the house, scrubbing the blood stains with a terrycloth rag. The harsh odor of chemicals in the cleanser clogged his nostrils.

"Do you mind opening another window?" she asked without looking up.

He opened several and left the back door ajar.

"Thanks." Her yellow rubber gloves made a crinkling sound as she dipped the rag in the bucket of water and squeezed out the excess.

He watched her work, mesmerized by the movement of her body in the denim cutoffs and the soft pink T-shirt she'd changed into. She had a natural way about her that made her far more enticing than any glamour queen he'd ever seen. She was sensual without trying, feminine yet feisty and independent.

And what she did for a pair of denim cutoffs and a cotton shirt was affecting him in ways he didn't need right now. He had to find something to do besides stare at her derriere.

"Why don't you let me work on those stains while you go get your things together," he said.

"About that…" She dropped her rag into the bucket of soapy water and pulled off the gloves, dropping them onto the floor. "I've given that more thought. I can't intrude on you and your father when he's trying to adjust to life outside of prison and you're trying to reconnect with him. It wouldn't be fair to either of you."

He reached for her hand and pulled her to her feet. "Fine. Then I'll stay here with you."

"I can't ask you to do that."

"You didn't ask. I'm offering."

"And I'm turning you down. I have to move back into this house sooner or later."

"I'm not leaving you alone, Collette. Your place or mine. They're the only options, unless you want me to rent a hotel room for both of us."

"You're not making this easy, Dylan."

"It sounds easy enough to me."

"I can't take you away from your father. He needs you, probably even more than I do."

"Then it's settled. Get your things. You and your vivacious energy are probably exactly what the Ledger house needs." A new thought occurred to him. "Unless you're afraid my father is dangerous or that the house is haunted."

"From what I read in the newspaper yesterday, your father is exceptionally nonviolent. And I'd take ghosts over real live villains any day."

"Then it's settled. You pack. I'll clean."

"Forget about the scrubbing. I think I'll take my sister-in-law up on her offer to send her housekeeper my way for a day."

"Good. I hate scrub-pail hands."

He mussed her hair as if she were a kid, letting his fingers delve into the thick richness of it. "This should be fun. I haven't had a sleepover in years."

"A houseguest," she corrected him. "Sleeping in separate bedrooms."

He smiled. "Of course. Just a slip of the tongue."

He was far too smart to share a bed with Collette. He'd be out of here in a week or two, and she was going to be hell to get over as it was. Not that he had any idea where he was going. He only knew he couldn't go back to being cooped up in an office.

IF SOMEONE HAD TOLD Collette yesterday that she'd be staying over at Troy Ledger's house tonight, she'd have thought them daft. Dylan made the difference. They were still virtual strangers, yet she'd connected with him in a way that defied the odds.

Her heart had jumped to her throat when she'd accidentally caught him in the viewfinder yesterday, and being around him didn't lessen the impact. But if the attraction were purely physical, she'd have put him on the back burner while she dealt with her stalker and his attack on Eleanor.

But Dylan was protective without being patronizing. He hadn't lectured her about dealing with the stalker on her own or even hinted that this could be her fault.

And he'd discovered the footprints and tire tracks behind her house. She assumed her father had as well, but, of course, he wouldn't bother to mention any of that to her. Now all they needed was a good description of the rat from Eleanor.

"Do you mind driving to the hospital before we go back to the ranch?"

"Not at all. If Eleanor's talking, she could provide a lot of missing details."

"Maybe I should call first. If she can't have visitors yet, there's no reason to waste time on the drive."

She retrieved her cell phone and punched in the number for Eleanor's private room. She immediately recognized the voice that answered. "Good morning, Mrs. Baker. This is Collette."

"I'm glad you called. I was so stressed last night I don't know if I thanked you for staying with Eleanor until I could drive over from Houston."

"I was glad to do it, though Eleanor never knew I was there."

"Your father has already been in this morning. I'd heard a lot about him from Eleanor but had never met him. I feel a lot better after talking to him. He assured me he'll get to the bottom of this and arrest the thug who tried to kill Eleanor."

"I'm sure he will," Collette agreed. "How is Eleanor?"

"The doctor said the shoulder surgery went well. He doesn't expect any complications. I'm just glad you found her and got her to the hospital as quickly as you did."

"Actually, Dylan called for the ambulance even before I got home."

"Dylan?"

So her dad had failed to mention him. She'd love to know the reason for that. Likely more of his diabolical plan to put Dylan on the hot seat and keep Collette from trusting him.

"Dylan's a friend of mine and he arrived at the house just before I did. It's possible the attacker ran from the scene when he heard Dylan drive up."

"Oh, my. I didn't know. Please thank him for me, as well."

"Is Eleanor up to having visitors? I'd love to stop by for a minute and say hello."

"I think it best if you wait. She's taking pain medication and the doctor wants her to get as much rest as possible. I wasn't in the room when the sheriff tried to question her, but he said she was still too groggy to respond coherently."

"Then she wasn't able to describe her attacker?"

"I'm not sure she even knows she was attacked. She keeps asking what happened to her."

"I understand. Please tell her that I called."

"I'll be sure to."

They said their goodbyes, and Collette broke the connection just as another call rang in.

"My dad," she announced to Dylan, "hopefully with news that he's made an arrest."

"Or at least identified a suspect other than me," he replied.

"Hi, Dad." She tried to keep her voice amicable even though she doubted he'd do the same. He didn't disappoint her.

"Have you come to your senses yet or are you still chasing after Dylan Ledger?"

"I'm with Dylan."

"You're putting yourself in danger for a man you know nothing about."

"Is that what you called to tell me?"

"No, I called to tell you that when I mentioned Dylan's name to Eleanor Baker, she became agitated and looked fearful."

"That's odd. I heard she was too groggy to talk to you. Dylan didn't attack her, Dad. The man who did left his footprints and the imprint of his tires behind my house. Dylan's truck was parked in the driveway."

"I suppose Dylan pointed those tracks out to you."

"Does it matter?" Collette said. "Just check them out and see for yourself."

The silence lasted too long.

"You already knew about the tracks, didn't you?"

"My deputies found them this morning after daylight, which would have given Dylan plenty of time to put them there himself to throw us off."

Unbelievable. "Do you really think Dylan is a suspect, or is all this just to keep me away from a Ledger?"

"You don't want to get mixed up with the likes of him."

Which pretty much answered her question. Anything she said at this point would only make matters worse. The barriers that separated them had grown almost impenetrable.

"Find my stalker, Dad. When you do, you'll have the man who attacked Eleanor."

"I'll find your stalker. Make no mistake about that. Your wireless provider was more than willing to work with us. I should know the second the pervert calls you—if he calls again."

"I'm glad to hear that."

"If you hear from him, act as if nothing has changed and keep him on the phone as long as possible. As soon as we get a lock on his location, I'll send the closest deputy to arrest him, hopefully even before he breaks the connection."

"Then you agree the stalker is the major suspect in this case?"

"He's a suspect. I haven't ruled out anyone as yet. I

shouldn't need to remind you that your friend Eleanor's articles have made her more than a few enemies."

This was going nowhere. She shifted and moved the phone to her other ear. "Is there anything else I should know about the case?"

"Just that you're trusting the wrong man with your safety."

Her head began to pound at both temples. Why did everything with her father have to be so difficult? Resentment swelled inside her, not so much for the present as for the past.

If he'd ever been attuned to anyone's feelings but his own, her mother would still be alive.

DYLAN DODGED A LARGE turtle making its way across the road leading to the ranch house while Collette adjusted her visor to block the worst of the early afternoon rays. "I still think you should have given your father some advance warning that you're bringing the enemy home with you."

His lips cracked into an incredibly seductive smile that reached all the way to his mesmerizing eyes. "You're not the enemy."

"I doubt your father will see it that way."

"What could he possibly have against you?"

"How about the fact that Sheriff Glenn McGuire is determined to make you a suspect in a felony for no other reason than you're my friend?"

"It could be that your father is just doing his job."

"Are you always so generous in your opinions of people?"

"I'm not generous. I give people the benefit of the doubt. Until they prove me wrong."

Which made sense considering that was exactly what

he was doing with his own father. Dylan was giving Troy Ledger a chance to be the father he hadn't been in eighteen years.

The circumstances of Troy Ledger's release on a technicality had been covered ad nauseam in the local media, but she'd ignored most of it. That left her a little fuzzy on the details. As she understood it, the reversal involved some supposedly coerced testimony. The prosecutor at the time had since retired and moved to a Caribbean island, so she doubted they'd ever get the full story.

Nonetheless, some, like her father, would always see Troy Ledger as guilty and hold that against Dylan, as well. Others, like the cute young waitress at Abby's Diner, obviously couldn't care less.

She'd flirted with him shamelessly when they'd stopped there for lunch before driving to the ranch. And Abby herself had seemed genuinely happy to see Dylan. She hadn't even let them pay for their meals.

Abby had claimed it was worth it seeing the way Dylan appreciated her food. More than appreciated, he'd devoured the noonday special of chicken-fried steak smothered in cream gravy with mashed potatoes, pinto beans and corn bread on the side. He'd topped that off with Abby's famous coconut pie.

Collette had choked down half a burger and a tall glass of iced tea. It churned in her stomach as Dylan stopped his truck in front of the Ledger ranch house. To her surprise, what looked to be an almost-new horse trailer was parked in the driveway.

Looking past that, she spotted a tall but muscular man standing on the front porch, nonchalantly leaning against a support post and peeling an orange. His hair was the same dusty brown color as Dylan's but without the sun streaks that gave Dylan the appearance of a real cowboy.

The man's lips looked as if they'd been pulled tight for so long that a smile might crack them.

"I'm not sure what the horse trailer's about," Dylan said as he jumped out and grabbed her bag from the backseat of the double-cab pickup.

"Your father may have bought some horses."

"Anything's possible." He sounded doubtful.

Collette stepped from the truck and into a muddy patch where a water hose had recently run, likely to water the horses. Thankfully, she'd taken a quick shower after her scrubbing routine and changed into a pair of black slacks and a pair of Western work boots. She'd even tamed the wildest locks of her thick red hair.

Troy stared at her as if she were trespassing on sacred ground. A deacon at their church, a man she'd known all her life, stepped from the house just as she and Dylan reached the porch. She considered his appearance a reprieve as she sucked in a gulp of fresh air.

"Well, look who's here," Bob said in his booming voice. "Collette. And you must be Dylan." He stuck out a hand in Dylan's direction. "Bob Adkins. If I have my Ledger brothers straight, the last time I saw you, you were claiming bragging rights about a catfish that got away."

Dylan set her bag down on the porch. "I hate to say that I don't remember you, but nice to meet you."

"Wouldn't expect you to remember me. Good to have you back in Mustang Run. Good to have your father back, too."

Collette was relieved that Bob had come over to welcome Troy Ledger home. He was one of the most respected men in town, and his acceptance would go a long way. Even the hard-nosed sheriff would not attempt to tell Bob whom he could befriend.

"Bob brought over a couple of horses," Troy said.

"Yep." Bob grinned and nodded. "I thought you could use them to ride your land and see what kind of shape the outbuildings, pastures and fences are in. Keep the young fillies as long as you need. They need to be ridden anyhow. The roan's Lady, the chestnut is Ginger. If I forgot any tack that you need, give me a holler."

"Great," Dylan said. "I can't wait to give them a workout."

Bob turned his attention to Collette. "I heard you had some trouble at your place last night."

"Someone broke in and attacked my friend. That's why I'm here with Dylan. He's volunteered for bodyguard service until the perpetrator is apprehended."

"Good idea. Any guy who earned a silver star in Iraq passes muster in my book."

That was more information she didn't know about Dylan, and she wondered how Bob did.

"I'd love to chew the fat a little longer," Bob continued, "but I'd best get back to the ranch. By the way, Ruby Nelle told me to tell the both of you that she wants to have you over for dinner as soon as you get settled in."

Troy set his half-eaten orange on the porch railing and wiped his hands on his jeans before stepping to the edge of the porch with Bob. "Thanks," he said. "Your friendship means a lot. Ruby Nelle's, too."

"Think nothing of it. We go way back, Troy. Long as I got a biscuit, you got half."

They waited on the porch until Bob drove away, pulling the horse trailer behind him.

"Collette's going to be staying with us for a few days," Dylan said.

"I kind of figured that, what with you carrying a bag."

"Unless it's a problem," Collette added quickly.

Troy's expression stayed fixed into the grim stare. "Might be a problem for the sheriff."

"I'm an adult. My father doesn't make my decisions."

Troy shrugged. "Then you're welcome to stay. Place isn't much to brag about. Bare necessities, that's about it."

"I'm sure it's fine."

To Collette's surprise, Troy picked up her overnight bag. "I'll show you to the guest room so you can put your things away."

She followed Troy down the hall to an extension that jutted off the back of the house. The bedroom was at the end of that short hallway. A queen-size mahogany four-poster covered in a blue-and-white quilt dwarfed the cozy area and matched the antique dresser. Beside the bed was a large hook rug, worn but spotlessly clean.

On the far wall, double windows opened to the remains of a long-neglected English garden that fit between this and a matching extension off the other side of the house, providing a sunlit area protected from the wind.

Vines climbed over odd-shaped rocks and around flowerbeds that were overgrown with weeds. A few lone daffodils had fought their way through the dense foliage. A stone wall at the back of the garden made the area seem totally private, yet open to the heavens.

Collette stared in awe. "What a terrific spot for a garden."

"Helene designed it and the extensions to the house. Our bedroom was in the opposite extension so that the garden could be the first thing she saw when she woke in the morning. As overworked as she was caring for five boys, she spent hours tending those flowers."

Sadness sank so deep into his voice that Collette had to swallow hard to fight back tears.

"Guess it's not that great a view now." With that, Troy turned and strode away, leaving her alone to stare at Helene's forsaken oasis.

The stories of ghosts haunting the house crept into her mind. Maybe the ghost of Helene Ledger did still live inside these walls, waiting all these years for Troy and her boys to come home.

The piercing ring of Collette's cell phone startled her back to reality. She checked the caller ID. Unavailable.

Chills froze her breath and stilled her heart. As always, the living were far more frightening to her than the dead.

Chapter Nine

"I'm glad you answered, my sweet. I've been worried about you."

Collette's stomach turned at the term of endearment, but she had to play this cool. "Why would you be worried about me?"

"I heard that someone broke into your house and attacked your guest. You should use more care in choosing your friends."

"What is that supposed to mean?"

"Your friend obviously has enemies. Everyone adores you—as I do."

He was playing this to the hilt, further proof of how vicious and callous he was.

"You know nothing about me."

"Ah, but I do. I know and love everything about you. Even your scent intoxicates me. It's Cartier, isn't it?"

Her stomach swirled in nauseous waves. Had he been that close to her without her knowing it? Or had he been inside her house before last night, touched her things, or done God only knew what else?

"Either tell me who you are, or get out of my life."

"I'm only trying to comfort you and keep you safe. Hanging out with Dylan Ledger is not helping with that."

She stared out the window, imagining him somewhere beyond the stone wall that bordered the old garden. Her senses teemed with urgency, as if he might appear in the flesh at any second.

She should never have come here, never have pulled Dylan and his father into her entanglements with a madman.

"I must go now. Keep safe, my love, until we talk again." Then the line went dead.

The conversation had been short, as always. He might have suspected from the first that his location was being traced. She punched in her father's cell number. When there was no answer, she left a message.

Just because the sheriff hadn't answered didn't mean a deputy wasn't already aware of the stalker's call. If the monster was on or near Willow Creek Ranch, deputies could be speeding this way even now. She should alert Dylan and Troy.

Before she could, there was a tap at the open bedroom door.

"Come in."

Dylan stepped inside just as her father returned her call. "Give me a moment," she said. "I have to take this."

Dylan nodded and stepped closer. His presence wrapped around her even though they weren't touching. There was no ignoring his rugged virility, but it was the calm, understated support he gave so naturally that she needed most right now.

Never one to mince words, her father jumped in as soon as she'd answered. "We've got the general location he was calling from."

"It's Willow Creek Ranch, isn't it?"

"Not even close."

She exhaled sharply in pure relief. "So where is he?"

The answer shot a new surge of terror straight to her heart.

DYLAN WATCHED Collette's guard come crumbling down as she tossed her phone on the bed. He reached for her and pulled her into his arms. He tensed when her face burrowed into his chest. He was overstepping the boundaries of their tenuous relationship.

But she didn't pull away, and he didn't want to let her go. He liked the feel of her in his arms, liked the fragrance of her hair and the sensation of the curling locks beneath his chin.

"I take it that was bad news," he said, once she'd gathered her resolve and pulled away.

"My stalker called again."

That confused him. "I assumed from the conversation that you were talking to your father."

"I was then, but that was the second call. Dad called to say that they'd tracked the stalker's call."

"Wouldn't that be a good thing?"

"The stalker is somewhere inside Carlton-Hayes Regional Hospital."

He muttered a low curse. No wonder Collette had taken an emotional dive. The brutal rat was now stalking Eleanor as well, walking the halls of the hospital where she was recovering from his almost-deadly assault.

"What does your father plan to do?"

"The hospital is out of his jurisdiction, but he can have the local police chief provide round-the-clock guards for her room, at least for the time being." She wrapped her fingers around the bedpost. "The perverted brute must know that Eleanor can identify him and he plans to kill her before she can."

That seemed the most logical conclusion, except that if he'd attacked Eleanor when she surprised him in the house, why not finish her off last night?

Still, he hated to see Collette so upset. Dylan took both her hands in his. "It sounds as if your father has the situation under control. I'm sure they're not going to let this guy into Eleanor's hospital room, and she's not going anywhere. She'll be safe."

"I wish I felt as sure as you sound."

So did Dylan. "What do you say we go take a look at the horses? Better yet, we could take a ride and see if I can still find that old swimming hole."

"Tired of hearing me whine?"

He squeezed her hands. "Tired of seeing you look as if the world just came crashing down on top of you."

She nodded. "Give me a minute to lather on some sunscreen. I burn at the mention of sunshine."

"Take your time. I'll be in the kitchen—unless you need help with the sunscreen," he teased.

He was rewarded with the first real smile he'd seen on her gorgeous lips. But that was only because she didn't realize how much he'd actually enjoy rubbing in the lotion.

He found his father in the kitchen, staring out the window the way he seemed to spend half his time. Dylan wondered what went on in his mind during those zombielike sessions. Whatever it was, the thoughts planted a haggard look on his father's face and sucked the life from his somber eyes.

"I guess I should have called you before I brought Collette home with me." Home. The word sounded strange on his tongue yet it had slipped out effortlessly.

Troy stepped away from the window and leaned against

the counter. "No need. It's your house, too, long as you want to stay."

"Thanks."

"I'm more concerned about what's going on between you and Collette," Troy said.

"I told you. She needs protection. I've got nothing better to do."

"And her being single and gorgeous has nothing to do with it?"

"Makes the job more pleasant."

"Just watch yourself, Dylan. The sheriff will make trouble for you eight ways to Sunday if he thinks there's anything going on between you two. I'm not saying she wouldn't be worth it. I'm just warning you."

"I barely know her."

"Love doesn't always wait for that. I knew from the first day I met your mother that there would never be anyone else for me." He worried the scar on his face with his right hand. "There never was."

Ever since the murder, Dylan had been brainwashed by his grandparents, aunts and uncles to believe that his father had committed the brutal, despicable act. He'd never bought into it.

He was even more convinced of his father's innocence now. However, that didn't end the issues between them.

"Do you mind if Collette and I take the horses for a ride?"

"Bob brought them over to be ridden. Check out the condition of the ranch while you're at it. I'm looking to buy a starter herd of cattle next week. I can't hack this sitting around doing nothing. Even in prison, we kept busy. If we hadn't, I'd have gone insane."

"Hard work won't hurt you," Dylan agreed.

"Guess you had plenty of that in the service. Eight years, wasn't it?"

Dylan nodded. Eight years, and he'd walked as close to death as a man could get and still come out in one piece. Never once had he heard from his father. Not then and not when Dylan was younger and had sent Troy countless letters and pictures. Photographs of Dylan playing varsity football, running track and swaggering around in his first pair of authentic Western boots since moving away from Willow Creek Ranch. He'd been sixteen at the time and had bought them with money from his first summer job.

A letter or a phone call from his dad back then would have meant the world to Dylan. Better late than never might not be enough to cut it at this stage in his life.

"I guess Bob Adkins told you about my time in the army when he stopped by today?"

"Yep. You turned into quite a man."

With no help from you.

The old anger and rejection kicked up inside Dylan, and he knew that if he didn't get out of this house right now, he'd explode.

"Tell Collette I'll be outside."

COLLETTE TOOK THE beautiful cinnamon-colored roan to a full gallop, loving the feel of the wind in her face and the warmth of the sun on her back. Her mother used to claim that spring in the hill country was like a rhapsody, the melody a perfect blending of scents, colors and sounds that made just breathing seem like a rebirth.

Collette couldn't claim rejuvenation in the midst of all her problems, but the ride through the rolling hills with new growth budding all around her had lulled her anxiety to a more wieldy level.

Dylan's mount was a flaxen chestnut, a bit more nervous than hers, but quite regal. Dylan had calmed her with a steady voice when approaching and saddling her, and the filly had quickly settled down. He clearly had the same knack for charming horses as he did her.

He had that deliciously laid-back cowboy way about him even when she knew coming home to face his father after all these years had to be stirring up an emotional storm inside him.

Dylan slowed the chestnut to a trot. He pointed to his left as she reined in her spirited mount so that she could ride beside him.

"That's the legendary Ledger swimming hole where my brothers and I used to escape our chores every chance we got."

"I can see why."

The vista was breath-stealing. Beautiful willows dotted the banks, and the clear blue water sparkled like dancing jewels in the bright sunlight. A silvery fish jumped in the middle of the pool creating a circle of widening ripples. A stately blue heron stood on the bank, looking so still and perfect it could have passed for a statue.

She brought the roan to a dead stop to watch a fawn that studied them from beneath the spreading branches of an oak tree on the other side of the pond. When Dylan slid from his saddle to the sea of grass, the animal turned and disappeared into a cluster of scrubby oaks, rough-leaf dogwoods and underbrush.

She pushed her sunglasses to the top of her head for a better look. "It's so peaceful out here."

"Which is not at all the way I remember it."

Lady pawed the ground, ready to be off again, but Dylan took the reins while Collette dismounted.

"It was never quiet back when my brothers and I

were out here together. See that old rope hanging from the oak near where that deer was drinking before we startled it?"

"I see it."

"It's a bit gnarled and shredding now, but that was our version of a water park in the good old days."

The good old days, before brutal violence had stolen his youth. She hurt for that boy even though she marveled at the man he'd become. He led the horses to the edge of the water for a cooling drink after their vigorous run.

"Did you really earn a silver star in Iraq?"

"Can't say that I did, at least no more than anyone else who served there. I just happened to get noticed and they presented me with one."

"Methinks you're a bit too modest."

"No, just honest. You don't really think about your actions in the heat of battle. You just do what you're trained to do and try to keep yourself, your combat buddies and innocent civilians alive."

When the fillies had drunk their fill, he tied the reins to a low-hanging branch of one of the willows. That done, he proceeded to unbutton his long-sleeved blue Western shirt. Anticipation hummed through her senses as the shirt opened, revealing well-defined abs and a dusting of hairs on his tanned flesh.

He shrugged out of the shirt and spread it on top of the prickly blades of grass, then motioned for her to have a seat. Giddy with desire, she dropped to the shirt and pulled her knees up to her chest.

Stretching beside her, he propped himself up on his elbow to face her. The closeness was intimate, and the temptation to lie back and press her body against his was all but irresistible.

Dylan tugged on the brim of his Stetson, pulling it

lower to block some of the sun's rays. Even then, stray locks of his dusty brown hair escaped to fall over his forehead.

"Tell me about Eleanor," he said.

The statement cooled the desire she'd almost succumbed to and brought the real reason for their being together back into sharp focus.

"I told you all I know. We've been friends since college. She's a go-getter investigative reporter who also likes to have fun. And she and Melinda are fascinated with the ghosts and spirits. That's probably the one thing I don't have in common with them."

"Investigative reporting can gain a person lots of enemies."

"No doubt it does, but what got her attacked was showing up at my house on the wrong night."

"Still, I'd like to know more about her and any enemies she might have."

"The stalker was harassing me, and he called from the hospital where she's recovering. Isn't that proof that Eleanor is just a victim of circumstance?"

"It would seem that way, but when you're sure the enemy is dead ahead and things are under control, you'd best watch your back."

"Meaning you think there's more to this than the obvious?"

"I'm not saying that your analysis of the situation is wrong, Collette. I'd just like a better scope of the landscape. Do you have Internet access at your house?"

"Yes, but both my desktop and my laptop are at my studio. Why?"

"I'd like to research Eleanor's recent articles and determine which ones could be considered incendiary."

"Incendiary, as in the articles Dad decided made you

a suspect. I don't think we should go down that road, Dylan."

"It won't hurt to check them out. Where's your studio?"

"In the old section of town. It's only a couple of blocks from Abby's Diner."

Thank goodness, he let the subject drop. Silence melded into a gentle truce, and when he reached over and trailed his fingers down her arm, her need for him became a shimmering heat of ribbon that corded around her heart.

"Tell me about yourself, Dylan."

"I'm overeducated, unemployed and unattached. I'm a steak-and-potato kind of guy who prefers beer to champagne and would rather be tied and flogged than stuffed into a suit and tie. I'd say that pretty much sums me up."

If so, he was much more than the sum of his parts. But it was the unattached part that intrigued her at the moment. "Have you ever been married?"

"No."

"Engaged?"

"No. I have had sex before, though. As best I remember, I liked it a lot."

As best she remembered, she hadn't been all that impressed with the act itself. She had an idea that conclusion wouldn't hold with Dylan. A burn crept to her cheeks, and she turned away to keep him from seeing it.

"What about you?" Dylan asked.

"I've never been married, but I was engaged once. It didn't work out. The fire died before the ink on the wedding invitations dried."

"His loss."

"It was a long time ago. I'm sure he's forgotten all about me."

"That's doubtful."

His fingers left her arm to climb the column of her neck and entangle in her hair. Her pulse spiked. How could she possibly react to his touch this way when her life and Eleanor Baker's were in a state of chaotic danger? Nonetheless, desire grew red-hot inside her. She stretched out beside Dylan, spread her hand over the bare hardness of his chest and pressed her lips against his.

He kissed her back, tentatively at first, but then ravenously, as if he couldn't get enough. She trembled in his arms as the hot, deep, slow kisses awakened a throbbing passion inside her.

His hands roamed from her neck and hair to her abdomen. His thumbs rode upward until they brushed the swell of her nipples, the movement arousing and titillating through the thin cotton of her shirt.

She knew if they didn't stop soon, they wouldn't stop at all. Her inhibitions kicked in, and calling on all the restraint she could rally, she pulled away.

He had to be a bit sexually frustrated at the abrupt halt, but still he managed a smile that sent her senses soaring again.

"Never had that much excitement at the swimming hole before," he teased.

"And with your boots on."

The flirtatious interplay was disrupted by the tones of Dylan's cell phone.

The delicious moment faded into oblivion as she watched his expression turn grim. Cold chills replaced the warmth in her veins and reality returned with a punishing vengeance.

Chapter Ten

"My gut feeling is that this is far more complicated than an overzealous stalker and that Collette McGuire is in imminent danger."

Wyatt's words couldn't have gotten to Dylan more if they'd been delivered by a fist to the gut. "Did you come to this conclusion just from checking her phone records?"

"That and past experience. I've dealt with this type of stalking behavior before."

"So you think we're dealing with a psycho nutcase?"

"No. I think you're dealing with a cagey, calculating male who knows exactly what he's doing."

"Were you able to identify the caller?"

"No. That's part of the problem. He used prepaid cell phones that couldn't be traced and in some instances, he stole phones and made the calls before the owner discovered they were missing and stopped the service. Your run-of-the-mill nonviolent stalker seldom goes to that extreme to remain anonymous."

"You said that was one of the problems. What are the others?"

"He made the calls from different places and at different times of the day so there's no way we can pinpoint his schedule. One was made from Willow Creek Ranch yesterday."

"Collette was inside the house with me when he made that one."

"I suspected as much. He's following her. I'm not convinced it's love or even lust that is motivating his actions."

"What motivators are you considering?"

"Jealousy. Revenge. Betrayal—or perceived betrayal. Those are the most common."

"Collette seems certain she doesn't know the caller."

"I'm just throwing out possibilities."

"What do you make of the most recent contact, the call made from the hospital where Eleanor Baker is being treated?"

"That must have occurred after I got the report. How did you learn about it?"

"Sheriff McGuire called Collette. He's convinced she's in danger, too. Of course, he thinks being with me is adding to her peril."

"Don't underestimate Glenn McGuire. As for the call from Eleanor's hospital, that definitely adds a new layer to the case. You need to be really careful, Dylan. Criminals don't follow rules of engagement."

"Neither did terrorists."

"Good point. Do you want me to fax you the data I collected?"

"You could, if I had access to a fax machine."

"I have one in my studio," Collette interrupted. She gave him the number, and he relayed it to Wyatt.

"One other thing," Wyatt said.

"Hit me with it."

"Are you totin'?"

"I have a Glock .45 in my truck's glove compartment. Wouldn't travel without it. And I have a rifle on the truck's gun rack. When in Rome…or in this case Texas."

"Keep them handy, but don't go trying to steal the sheriff's job. I can understand your trying to keep his daughter safe—well, actually I can't, but that's your business. Apprehending criminals is the sheriff's business."

"Got it."

"Good. Take care, bro, and keep me posted."

"Will do. Thanks."

Dylan broke the connection, already dreading going over this with Collette. Wyatt's info further complicated the ideas he'd already considered and added a couple of new alternatives to the mix.

Welcome to Texas.

THE COZY, USUALLY QUIET office in Collette's photography studio was a whirlwind of activity. The fax machine hummed as it spit out page after page of calls made to and from her cell phone over the past few months. Dylan's fingers tapped against the keyboard of her desktop. Water dripped through the grounds and into the Thermos belly of her automatic coffeemaker.

Against this backdrop of purposeful activity, Collette was reduced to doodling meaningless scribbles on the edge of the notes she'd made while talking to Eleanor's mother.

Eleanor was alert but had no memory of the attack. The last thing she remembered was walking into the kitchen to return her empty dinner plate. Temporary memory lapses after a concussion were not unusual occurrences, the medical staff had assured the family. In most instances the patient regained full or at least partial memory of the event causing the injury.

Bottom line, they couldn't be sure when or if she'd be able to describe her attacker. In the meantime, there was nothing to do on that front but wait.

Dylan was using her desktop computer to surf the Net for articles written by Eleanor. Collette looked over his shoulder for a minute, then picked up her laptop and took it to the sitting area where she normally discussed prices and picture packages with clients.

Dropping to the most comfortable of the chairs, she turned on the computer and started to type in *Eleanor Baker,* changing her mind before she reached the second *e.* She changed the search criteria to *Troy Ledger's murder trial.* Hundreds of choices lined up on the screen.

She clicked on the most promising and started reading an account of the evidence presented against him during the course of the trial. She scanned one article after another. The mild irritation she experienced at first became a tightening in her chest and then a sickening surge of disbelief.

Troy Ledger had been sentenced to life in prison based on conjecture, circumstantial evidence and the testimony of his dead wife's parents, Collette's father and a few other locals.

In contrast, the defense had claimed that Sheriff McGuire never searched for the real killer once Troy Ledger had been confirmed as a suspect. The sole focus of her father's investigation was said to be collecting evidence to convict Troy, who had publicly criticized the sheriff's handling of a previous investigation involving two migrant workers accused of stealing from their employer.

Helene's parents had testified that Troy protested when they tried to give their daughter and their grandchildren money or nice gifts and trips, even though he couldn't provide them. Character witnesses for Troy had said that while he was stubborn and independent, he was a non-violent man who loved his wife and kids and provided the necessities.

The conviction clinchers had been the fact that Helene was shot with Troy's pistol, coupled with his unwillingness to cooperate in his own defense and the testimony of one of Helene's best friends who said she'd stopped by the Willow Creek Ranch the morning of the murder and found Helene packing a bag. When she'd asked her where she was going, Helene had said to her parents', that she'd let things go on too long.

Troy Ledger had claimed his innocence, but for the most part, he'd seemed angry and sullen or else totally detached from the trial proceedings. When he'd finally taken the stand, he'd broken down and cried. One of the articles claimed that the jurors had apparently seen that remorse as guilt.

The family of the murdered wife had cheered at the conviction. Dylan and his brothers were not present for any of the proceedings except the sentencing.

Collette leaned back in the chair and studied Dylan's profile as she mentally reviewed the findings about his father. Deep in thought as he was, the tiny wrinkles that creased Dylan's eyes when he smiled were all but invisible. The muscles in his arms weren't flexed, but they still pushed at the fabric of his shirt. He was as tough and independent as his father must have been.

She wondered if Dylan would ever find out the truth about what had really gone on at Willow Creek Ranch the day his mother had been murdered. Unless Troy Ledger was innocent, she hoped he never did.

Knowing that your father had destroyed your mother was a cross she'd never wish on anyone.

Exhausted, she leaned back and stared at the clock on the wall opposite her. It was half past nine in the evening, and she'd gotten very little sleep last night. No wonder she was fading. She closed her eyes, but now it was her own mother's tragic death that weighed heavy on her mind.

"I CAN'T BELIEVE you hired an attorney after I told you I didn't want one."

Dylan spoke through clenched teeth, determined to keep his voice low enough that Collette would not hear the argument from wherever she'd disappeared to in the house. She'd escaped the table and the tension right after Troy had announced that he'd hired an attorney to represent Dylan before the sheriff came up with an arrest warrant.

Troy held a bowl beneath the faucet and rinsed away remains of the beef stew he'd cooked for dinner. "You'd think differently if you knew the sheriff the way I do."

"There is no evidence against me."

"I told you this morning. The evidence is whatever Glenn McGuire says it is. Believe me. I know."

"This isn't about you. It's not even about me. It's about stopping a lunatic before he kills someone."

"And if he does, you'll find yourself behind bars so fast, you won't even have time to think about what happened. And she'll be dead. That's all you'll know."

His father's hands began to shake, and the glass he'd just picked up slipped from his soapy fingers and hit the floor, sending slivers of glass in every direction.

Seeing his father like this stole the thunder from Dylan's anger and resentment. His release from prison would have been traumatic enough without being hurled back into his past by an assault that had nothing to do with him.

Drops of blood dripped from Troy's thumb as he cleaned up the broken glass with his bare hands. Dylan handed him a paper towel and tried to think of something to say to a man who had become a virtual stranger to him. Too many years had passed. Too much had gone unsaid.

"I wish we'd have connected sooner," Dylan said.

"Now's a fine time to think about that." Troy picked up the towel, brushed tiny shards of glass from his hand and walked away.

The last words had sounded like an accusation. The irony of that set Dylan on edge. Never had a kid needed a father more than he had. But he didn't pursue it.

"I noticed first-aid supplies in the hall bathroom," he said instead. "Take care of the cut. I'll finish up here."

"The cut's nothing."

Fine by him. Dylan walked away and went in search of Collette, though he hoped she'd gone to bed. She'd dozed in the chair back at her office, but she needed more than a catnap after what she'd been through.

Instead he found her on the front porch, sitting on the top step, her gorgeous hair tousled by the wind, her face tinged with moonlight.

His muscles grew relaxed. His need for her grew heady. Two days and he'd already fallen harder for her than he'd ever fallen for anyone. The situation probably had something to do with his letting himself get so close so quickly. But it was Collette who made it feel so right.

"Sorry to bring you into that father/son moment."

"No need to apologize. I just thought you needed a little privacy."

Dylan sat on the steps beside her. "I actually think he means well, but he can't separate this from what happened to him."

"Can you blame him? I mean if he's innocent, then he was wrongly convicted. It's only natural he'd worry that the same could happen to you. He lost eighteen years of his life."

"Seventeen," Dylan corrected, though it didn't make much difference.

"Eighteen," Collette repeated. "The year he spent waiting for the trial must have been the most horrific of all. He'd lost his wife to violence and his kids to a family that hated him."

"You're right. I came here to see if there was a way we could forge a bond, but on some level, I think I'm trying to start a fight."

"Forging bonds takes time." She leaned back against the porch railing and faced him. "My being here doesn't help."

"It helps me," he said. "At least when you're here I know you're safe." He reached for her hand. He liked how it felt in his and knew it wouldn't take much for him to lose control with her. A few kisses like they'd shared this afternoon, and his hunger for her would explode like a grenade.

They sat without talking for five minutes or more while the night wrapped around them. The hum of crickets and the high-pitched chirping of tree frogs created a soothing backdrop for the fireflies that darted among a patch of povertyweed.

Dylan stretched and leaned against the post at the top of the steps. "I don't remember it ever being this quiet. Mom used to say we kids made enough racket to raise the dead. Dad always countered that it's when we were quiet that he worried."

Odd how that came back to him now when he hadn't thought of it in years. Back then he hadn't had a care in the world. If his parents had, they'd hidden it well. He'd heard them argue, but not that often. Instead, they'd laughed a lot. On nights like this, they'd held hands in the porch swing while he and his brothers had played chase or wrestled in the grass.

Collette scooted closer. "I always envied my friends who had large, boisterous families."

"How many siblings do you have?"

"Just my brother, Bill, and we were never that close. He's too much like my father for us to get along."

"Is he in law enforcement, too?"

"No. He has an insurance agency, but he's adopted my father's opinionated and domineering ways."

"You must have taken after your mother. I know you look a lot like she did."

"Unfortunately, that's the only way we're alike. Mom was patient and far too submissive for her own good. I may have inherited just a streak of my father's stubbornness."

"You?" he teased.

"A tiny streak."

"What happened to your mother?" he asked. "And feel free to tell me it's none of my business if you don't want to talk about it."

"She had an accident. After that she had several strokes before her body just shut down."

"I'm sorry."

"So am I."

Collette seemed to pull inside herself, and Dylan slipped an arm around her shoulder. "How long has it been?"

"She died the week I graduated from UT. I gave up the position I had waiting for me in D.C. I needed time to get over the grief. By the time I did, I realized I liked the flexibility of owning and operating my photography business and living here in Mustang Run."

"You must miss her a lot."

"I do." She stretched and massaged the back of her neck. "I'm really tired. I think I'll call it a night."

"Good idea. It's almost midnight."

He stood and tugged her to her feet as headlights from an approaching vehicle bounced off the trees and shot rays of illumination across the terrain. Dylan jumped up and raced to his truck for his rifle. Before he reached it, a sleek sports car sped into view.

"My brother," Collette announced, "no doubt here to deliver a new set of orders from on high."

Dylan left the gun in the truck. He offered a hand when Bill started up the walk. Bill ignored it and walked right past him. Dylan resisted the temptation to teach him a few manners in a way that would have Bill McGuire rolling on the ground in pain. It wouldn't be a fair fight. Bill's muscles looked as if the heaviest thing he'd lifted in years was his briefcase.

Collette stood her ground at the top of the steps, her shoulders back and her hands propped on her slender hips. "I suppose Dad sent you."

"It doesn't matter who sent me. Coming out here is totally irresponsible. Get your things and get in the car."

"I'm not going with you, and you owe Dylan Ledger an apology for barging in here like a mad bull."

"Dylan had no business bringing you to his ranch. Surely you didn't expect us to sit by while you shack up with the son of a murderer."

Dylan's blood began to boil. "If you have concerns about Collette being out here, that's fine. But don't act like she's doing anything inappropriate. Got it?"

That's when the twerp made a big mistake. He shoved Dylan.

Dylan grabbed Bill's arm and felt his fingers dig into the man's flabby bicep.

Collette stamped her foot and inserted herself between them. "Would you both please just stop this? I don't need rescuing or defending. I'm capable of deciding where I want to be and, yes, Bill, even whom I want to shack up with if I so choose."

Dylan exhaled sharply and let go of Bill's arm. Pulverizing Collette's brother wouldn't help the situation. Even letting the guy know that he could would serve little purpose except to vent his own anger.

"Go home, Bill," Collette ordered. "If Dad has anything to say to me, he knows where I am."

"This isn't like your usual fights with Dad, Collette. This time your obstinacy could get you killed."

"It's my life. I'll take that chance."

"Fine. I'm washing my hands of the situation." Bill glared at Dylan, then turned and stormed to his car without looking back.

Dylan reached over and pushed a wild lock of red curls from Collette's face, tucking it behind her ear. "Are you sure? I'd worry about you but I'd understand if you wanted to go with him."

"I'm sure, Dylan. I'm not going anywhere without you."

Her eyes locked with his, and the desire to keep her safe melded with a need so earthy and primal that he felt it inside every cell of his body.

He'd never wanted a woman more.

Which meant he'd best not stand here staring into her bewitching eyes another second.

He fit a hand to the small of her back. "Let's go inside. It's been a long day and we both could use some rest."

But it wasn't rest he was craving when he followed her inside and down the hallway to her room.

DEEP PURPLE SHADOWS merged into bizarre shapes that danced eerily across the ceiling. Collette stared at them, enthralled by the shifting patterns. She'd fallen asleep immediately only to wake again before dawn. Her eyes were heavy, her mind captured in that state of drowsy confusion, somewhere between sleep and wakefulness.

Slivers of moonlight filtered through the curtains at the window painting shimmering strings of light across the blue coverlet. Collette closed her eyes only to open them again when a frigid chill infiltrated the room. She shivered and pulled the quilt to her neck, but the frost was bone deep.

A figure coalesced, dressed in a white gown with tattered remnants that swirled about the room as if they had wings of their own. Collette watched, mesmerized, rapt by the essence of the ghostly image.

Fear suffused her senses, but she couldn't bring herself to try to escape or even to look away.

"Are you Helene Ledger?" she asked, unsure if she was whispering the words or if they were being pulled from her mind by the ghostly vision.

"Get out of my house," the apparition ordered.

Frosty swirls drifted from the figure and from Collette's breath. The chill was real. So was the ghost.

"Why should I leave?"

"You bring danger to yourself and to my boy."

The figure grew translucent, and the swirls of white disconnected for a few seconds, then reunited again on the other side of the room.

"I would never hurt Dylan. But he's not a little boy,

Helene. He's a man, a very brave man, and he's trying to help me."

"Leave my house. Go to your father. He's the one who brought the trouble on you. He will destroy my family."

The words echoed in Collette's mind, but if the spirit haunting her was Helene, why would she appear to Collette instead of to Troy or Dylan?

"You must leave this house, but be very, very careful. Death is bearing down on you."

But death wasn't talking. The ghost was. "Did your husband kill you, Helene? Is that why you're trapped in this house?"

"Go, before you bring danger to the ones I love."

The tiers of white snapped as if they'd been cracked like a whip. A second later the spirit vanished, and the room grew so hot, Collette was afraid it might burst into flame.

She jumped out of bed and tore off her pajamas. But the temperature changed again, leaving the room chilly but not frigid. She grabbed the emerald-colored cashmere robe she'd brought with her and pulled it tight around her naked body.

A nightmare, though she hadn't realized she'd drifted off to sleep.

That's all it could have been. A frightening reaction to all that had happened over the past two days.

Just a vivid dream. Yet even now it seemed infinitely more real than the present. Helene's words obsessed her, playing over and over like a mantra.

He's the one who brought the trouble on you. He will destroy my family.

Collette's father couldn't be responsible for her stalker, but he could have been behind Troy Ledger's arrest and conviction.

Now he was nursing a grudge against Dylan that would grow stronger as long as she stayed at Willow Creek Ranch.

Perhaps she should call Bill to come back for her first thing in the morning, before she actually did bring danger into this house that had already seen too much bloodshed.

No. She was being foolish. The phantom had been a figment of her overwrought imagination. Helene Ledger was as dead as the flowers in her forsaken garden.

But if the ghost was real, then so were her warnings. Death was bearing down on Collette.

She forced herself to stay in bed until the sun peeked over the horizon and dropped golden rays of light into the garden outside her window.

Sliding her bare feet into her slippers, Collette opened the door and stepped into the hall. The house was silent except for the ticking of the large clock in the family room and a vibrating snore coming from one of the bedrooms.

She stopped in the kitchen for a glass of water and tried to shake the sense of imminent doom. When that didn't help, she opted for the serenity she'd found on the front porch before her brother had shown up with all his bluster and threats.

She closed the door behind her and shivered at the howls of a pack of coyotes in the distance and a rustle in the grass just beyond the porch. She followed the sound with her gaze and spotted a family of skunks parading by, no doubt returning from a night of scavenging. She stayed perfectly still until they'd disappeared from view and the chance of inciting an odorous attack had passed.

A black spider crept by her foot. She stepped over it and walked to the edge of the porch. The wind had picked up, and the limbs in a nearby tree creaked like an old man's bones.

All of a sudden, she had the crazy feeling that she was being watched. She'd best get a grip before she saw ghosts coming at her from all directions.

Shoving her hands in her pockets, she took one last look into the scrubby brush where the skunks had disappeared. Another rustle, much louder that the first, came from somewhere near the woodshed. She stared in that direction and spotted a glint of sunlight bouncing off metal.

Collette turned to go back inside just as the crack of gunfire shattered the early morning quiet.

Chapter Eleven

Dylan woke instantly at the sound of gunfire, jumping from the bed as adrenaline rushed through his veins and triggered his battle instincts. Only this time he wasn't in a combat zone. His senses became razor sharp, his mind sizing up the situation as he grabbed the pistol he'd left on his bedside table and tore down the hall in his underwear. The scream had come from outside, though he had no idea why Collette would be outside this early in the morning.

By the time he reached the front door, Collette was inside and leaning against it. Her robe was open enough that he could tell she had nothing on beneath it. His senses reeled, but his gaze was drawn to the blood trickling down her cheek and the ghostly pallor of her face.

He stroked the injured cheek with his free hand. Her skin was icy cold, but the injury was no more than a scratch, likely made by one of the splintered wood fragments that clung to her robe. "Are you hurt?"

"I don't think so," she said, her voice quivering. "But someone just tried to kill me."

"Did you see the shooter?"

"No, but a split second before the shot, I saw a glint of sun off metal out by the woodshed. I think what I saw was a gun."

She yanked her robe tightly around her just as Troy joined them, still zipping his jeans.

"Was that gunfire?"

"Someone's on the property," Dylan said. "Take care of Collette. I'm going after him."

"No, Dylan, please," Collette pleaded. "Call 911. He has a gun."

That made two of them. "Stay inside," he ordered and rushed out the door. Fury drove him, but his brain and training kicked into autopilot. He jumped from the porch and raced to the tree line that stretched almost to the old woodshed.

There was more gunfire, and one of the bullets ricocheted off the trunk of a pine tree just in front of him. Dylan ran even faster, staying in the cover of trees, his bare feet almost silent in the thick grass.

His breathing came hard as he neared the woodshed. The last few yards he'd be in the open. He needed to draw the shooter out so he could get a clear shot to take him down, hopefully without killing him. Dead men didn't talk and he wanted answers.

An engine sputtered, knocked and backfired. Damn. The shooter was back in his vehicle, giving up and making a run for it. Dylan dashed toward the shed, but before he reached it, he spotted a man on a motorbike heading for the east pasture. Unless Dylan came up with a better plan, the son of a bitch was going to get away.

He sprinted back toward the house, stepping in a patch of stickers that punctured his skin. The sharp pains only urged him faster.

Troy was on the porch, holding the rifle he must have retrieved from Dylan's truck. "He escaped on a motorbike," Dylan yelled. "I'm going after him."

"Take this with you." Troy started toward the truck with the rifle.

"You keep it in case he doubles back here," Dylan called.

"I don't need it," Troy said. "I have a shotgun inside the house." He opened the passenger-side door of Dylan's truck and left the rifle with Dylan.

Dylan didn't know if Troy's having a firearm was legal under the circumstances of his release, but he didn't have time to worry about that now.

Collette came running out of the house still in her robe.

"Get back inside," Dylan ordered.

She kept coming, jumping into the truck and grabbing the rifle as he fired the ignition. She slammed the door. "What are you waiting on? Hit the gas before the dirty rotten coward gets away."

"Buckle up," he said, knowing there was no time and probably no use to argue with her. "And for God's sake, don't shoot yourself or me with that rifle."

COLLETTE'S FRIGHT was swiftly replaced by the need to keep the rifle and her body from bouncing off the roof as Dylan's truck rumbled and rocked across the bumpy hills. The would-be killer had a head start, but he couldn't be too far ahead of them.

"That way," Collette yelled, pointing to the left when she noticed a downed fence.

"Good work."

Dylan drove through the break, dragging down more fence posts before cutting across empty pastureland at breakneck speed. The bent and broken grass blades made the shooter's trail easy to follow, but there was still no sign of the motorbike.

In spite of the danger and the gravity of the situation, exhilaration rushed Collette's system like a drug.

"I never realized riding shotgun through empty pastures would be this exciting."

"Don't get used to it," Dylan said. "It's hell on the tires."

They came to another downed fence, but this one opened to the blacktop road that ran behind the ranch. Tracks from the motorbike's tires led right up to the road and then swerved right.

Dylan turned left.

"You turned the wrong way," she squealed.

"My guess is he knew I'd follow and he was trying to point me in the opposite direction."

"Okay, makes sense," she admitted and wondered why she was so naive when it came to the criminal mind.

"Besides, going left would get him to the highway a lot quicker," Dylan added.

They drove another ten miles without any sign of the bike. When they reached the highway, Dylan slowed to a stop, muttering a few choice curses under his breath.

"Sorry for the soldier talk," he said. "It's just aggravating to lose the guy when we all but had him in our sights."

"Are you giving up?"

"For the moment. The guy could have gone in any direction or cut off across someone else's land. We could keep going but we'd just be chasing rabbits."

"Instead of the rat we need." She felt the frustration herself, but sitting here in the truck at daybreak, holding a rifle steady with one hand and trying to keep her robe together with the other, she couldn't help but see the humor in this. Her smile drew an instant reaction.

"You could have been killed back there, Collette. Exactly what is it you find amusing about this?"

"Us. You in your underwear. Me riding shotgun half-naked. You have to admit we make an unusual crime-fighter team. Maybe we should try for a TV reality show."

He snaked an arm around her shoulders. "You, Collette McGuire, have gone mad from your wild and daring ride."

"No, Dylan." She reached over and circled his navel with her index finger. "I'm giddy from the excitement of you."

He leaned in close, his lips brushing her eyelids, her nose, her cheeks, as her thrill quotient went soaring to a new high. When his lips finally took hers, she was almost to the point of begging.

He ravaged her mouth, the kisses frantic at first and punctuated by tantalizing thrusts of his tongue. Finally the kisses grew deeper, and she melted into them, savoring the salty sweetness and the passion.

Her robe opened. Dylan slipped his hand inside and she tensed at the delicious thrill of the touch of his fingers on her bare skin. She arched toward him as he cupped her breasts and let his thumbs massage her taut nipples.

Soft moans of pleasure emanated from deep in her throat. Heat rushed to her core and she entangled one hand in the hair at his temples and splayed the other across his abdomen.

"Who knew?" she whispered.

"Knew what?"

"That having a private protector could feel this good."

"It's not supposed to. Definitely not supposed to." He

pulled away and ran both hands through his hair as if he were annoyed, or just plain frustrated.

"We better get back." His words were husky, his breath ragged.

"Did I say something to upset you?"

"No, but I need my mind clear to keep you safe and my mind is never going to be clear when I'm this turned on by you."

Dylan had put her on a sensual high the moment he'd shown up back in Mustang Run, but he was right. They should back away from each other, but not for the reason he thought. Nightmare or reality, Helene had warned Collette that she was pulling her family into danger. Nothing proved that more than the fact that Dylan had gone after a madman.

Collette had not only dragged Dylan into her perilous mire but she was entangling him in complications that couldn't be good for him or Troy. No matter how crazy she was about Dylan, the best thing she could do for him and Troy was to get out of their lives until her stalker was behind bars.

TROY TOYED WITH the 30-06 bullet he'd dug from the support post with his new pocket knife. The knife was another staple Able had provided, same as he'd supplied the shotgun. Guns, knives, ropes, machetes, all just tools of the trade to a rancher, but foreign and illicit to a prisoner.

When Able had first handed him the gun, Troy had broken out in a cold sweat. Even handling the knife seemed strange after all these years, and it had taken him several minutes to angle the blade and work the bullet from the wood.

The bullet had burrowed in just about head high. Had

it struck Collette, her brain would have splintered and sprayed the porch the way the slivers of old wood had. The shooter had been aiming to kill.

Memories flooded Troy's mind, trapping him in the horror and the nauseating visions he'd never even tried to escape. To let his pain and wrath dim would negate the gravity of the crime and devalue Helene's life. He would never let that happen, and he would never let his heartbreak heal until whoever had killed her paid for the crime.

Helene had been home alone when her killer had come calling, and the hooligan hadn't shot her from a distance. He'd walked inside the house and shot her twice in the head and once in the chest at point-blank range. Three shots when any one of them would have killed her.

Excessive brutality indicated a crime of passion, the prosecutor had said when he'd argued the case against Troy. His wife had been leaving him and taking their sons with her. Faced with the loss of all that he loved, Troy had given in to his darker side.

The side of him his mother-in-law had claimed Helene knew all too well. That's why Helene had warned her parents that under no circumstances were they to confront Troy about anything to do with the ranch or money.

The accusations hadn't fazed Troy then. Nothing had. The pain had deadened him to everything except the knowledge that he'd never see Helene again, never hold her slender, beautiful body in his arms. Never hear her sing when she was working around the house or in her garden, never dance with her under the light of the moon or two-step her around the kitchen.

Never be able to whisper how much he loved her and have her whisper the words back to him.

Some lunatic had robbed him of that.

Now another lunatic was after Collette. But why? The stalker story didn't hack it. Not when two days ago the anonymous caller was professing his love for Collette, and now he was shooting at her.

He could be someone who didn't stand out but faded easily into a crowd. A man whom Collette might have seen many times in passing and never really noticed. Even in prison there had been guys like that, the ones who didn't attract the attention of the guards or the bullies.

Those were the lucky ones.

If this guy was that nondescript, it could take weeks or months to expose him.

In the meantime, Dylan was putting his life on the line, and not just from the sniper who'd tried to take him and Collette out this morning. If Collette had taken that bullet, Glenn McGuire would have battered Dylan with questions until he was too weary to think, would have focused on every idle word he uttered and every dubious act he'd ever committed.

All that for no reason except that Dylan was the son of Troy Ledger.

But Troy would not let Dylan become another sacrificial lamb to Glenn McGuire's need for revenge. He'd make damned sure of that. For now he just wished Dylan and Collette would get back here so he'd know they were safe.

Too restless and anxious to sit back and do nothing, Troy headed toward the woodshed.

He scanned the area as he covered the distance. A large black rat scurried over the top of a pile of rotting firewood stacked outside the dilapidated shed. A loose strip of tattered metal hung just above the wood, the remains of an old sign advertising a cleaning product that hadn't been manufactured in years.

Just below the sign, Troy spotted a smear of color.

Fresh blood from a scratch the stalker had gotten from the prickly brush that had overgrown the shed? Or from the rusted metal of the sign?

Possibly.

His spirits lifted. He just might have discovered the shooter's DNA.

Other than having Dylan at home, it was the most positive thing that had happened since he'd returned to Mustang Run. Even Glenn McGuire with all his ploys and vindictiveness couldn't ignore DNA.

SIX DEPUTIES CAME barreling down the ranch road shortly after Collette and Dylan returned from the chase. Her father was not with the group, and she suspected it was because he hadn't been informed of the situation. Fortunately, both she and Dylan had had time to slip into more appropriate attire before the lawmen arrived.

Troy had called in and reported the shooting and the fact that he had found what was likely the culprit's blood near his woodshed. If it turned out the DNA was in the FBI's CODIS base, they'd have the identity of the shooter. It was the most promising development since the attack.

At a quarter past nine the second piece of welcoming news arrived via cell phone. Eleanor was alert, cognizant and asking to see Collette.

By eleven, she and Dylan were standing just outside the door to Eleanor's private room. The young police officer on guard introduced himself as Clay Sevier and flashed his badge.

"I'll need to check your IDs before you can enter Room 612."

They each gave Clay their driver's licenses. He studied

them carefully. "Are you related to Sheriff McGuire?" he asked as he handed the license back to Collette.

"He's my father."

"A good man. I met him yesterday when he came by to talk to the patient."

She nodded, avoiding comment.

The guard frowned as he returned Dylan's driver's license. "Collette is cleared to visit Ms. Baker, but I'll have to ask you to wait outside."

"That's better anyway," Collette assured Dylan. "Eleanor will feel more comfortable and free to talk if I'm by myself." She turned back to the officer. "Is anyone in the room with her now?"

"Not at the moment. Her mother was in there most of the morning, but she left about ten minutes ago. I believe she was going to get something to eat."

"I could use a cup of coffee and a newspaper," Dylan said. He put a hand on Collette's shoulder. "I'll make a quick run to the cafeteria and then come back and wait on you here."

"Take your time, but cross your fingers that we leave the hospital with a description of Eleanor's attacker."

"They're crossed, but don't count on too much. The doctor said it could take days—or even longer—for her to remember everything."

"I know."

"Call if you need me," Dylan said.

"I will." She tapped lightly on the door to Eleanor's room. When there was no answer, she pushed it open and walked inside.

Collette's heart sank to her toes when she saw how wiped out Eleanor looked in the oversize hospital gown. Her eyes were closed, but rimmed in dark circles. An IV fed into one arm. The opposite shoulder was bandaged.

Eleanor's hair had been combed and pushed behind her ears, but it looked flat and dull, lacking its usual shine and vibrancy. The same could be said of Eleanor. Except that Eleanor hadn't *lost* hers. It had been stolen from her by the thug she prayed Eleanor was about to describe.

Eleanor groaned and slapped at the cover without waking. Collette stepped to the side of the bed, not sure if she should disturb her. A nurse walked in the room, saw Collette and smiled.

"Look, Eleanor. You have company."

Eleanor opened her eyes as the nurse checked her pulse. Her gaze settled on Collette and she managed a weak smile.

Collette fit her hand on top of Eleanor's. "Hi, girl. You're looking good. Nice gown."

"You think? I can probably filch you one."

"I'd take you up on that if it were my color."

The nurse finished her check. "You two have a good visit, but don't tire out my patient," she cautioned as she left them alone.

"Guess I made a mess of your house," Eleanor said. "Teach you to befriend an investigative reporter."

Her words came slow and slightly labored, but her wit was intact. Collette was certain that was a good sign.

"I'm so sorry you were attacked," Collette said. "If I'd had any idea you were in danger at my place, I would have never invited you to stay over."

"Not your fault. Just luck of the draw."

Collette seriously doubted that. "Do you feel like talking about the attack?"

"I feel okay. They have good drugs in this place."

"I'll bet."

Eleanor shifted and winced. Obviously the meds didn't relieve all the pain.

"I was in the living room, drinking wine and watching CSI reruns. Had the volume too loud, I guess. Didn't hear him break in."

"Did he come into the living room?"

She shook her head, a slight movement, but enough. "I'd made myself a BLT. I took my empty plate back to the kitchen and there he was."

Lurking in Collette's kitchen the way he'd been lurking in her life. Collette felt that sinking, violated feeling again. Eleanor had to feel that, too, along with her pain. "Did he say anything before he attacked you?"

"I'm not sure. The attack is still fuzzy. I remember screaming and him diving at me with a kitchen knife." Eleanor squinted and then closed her eyes for a few seconds before opening them again and looking right at Collette. "I'm lucky to be alive."

"Yes, you are. Thank God for that." But the monster might not have given up on killing her yet. He could be in the hospital this very minute, walking the halls, waiting for any opportunity to kill Eleanor before she talked. He had to be stopped.

"Did you get a good look at the man?"

"I must have, but all I can remember is that he was tall. And burly. You know, muscled."

"Was he wearing a ski mask or gloves?"

"Gloves. He was wearing gloves. Black ones. I'd forgotten about that."

So Eleanor's memory did respond to coaxing. Collette would have to keep wheedling unless Eleanor grew stressed by her attempts.

"Was he wearing anything over his face?"

"Maybe. I can't remember. I had to have seen him, but I just can't remember."

"What about his hair? Was it long or short?"

Eleanor sucked in her bottom lip and touched a finger to her chin. "I don't know. I just don't know."

"Any idea if he was young, old, middle-aged?"

Finally she smiled again. "Not old enough. I could have beaten up an elderly man."

"I'd have paid to see that," Collette teased, though she wasn't ready to let up on the pressure completely just yet. "Was he older than I am?"

"Could have been older. But he was strong. Really strong."

"Do you remember anything else about him? Scars, tattoos, a beard?"

"It happened fast. Wham, bam."

"What did he say to you?"

"Nothing. I don't think he said anything. He stabbed me. I was on the floor—for a long time, I think. Then we heard you drive up."

"Is that when he hit you over the head?"

"No. He had a gun. When you drove up, he had a gun."

"There was a vehicle," Collette explained, "but it wasn't mine. Dylan Ledger drove up in his truck. He got there before I did. He's the one who found you unconscious on the kitchen floor."

"Dylan Ledger, the murderer's son?"

"Dylan Ledger, my friend," Collette corrected.

"Why was he there?"

"I invited him."

"Huh?"

"I invited him to stop by anytime," Collette repeated. "He took me up on the invitation."

Eleanor shook her head. "Don't trust him."

"I do trust him." She was even starting to trust Helene. Eleanor and Melinda were probably the only two people she knew who would believe her tale about conversing with a paranormal spirit, but she didn't want to say anything now that might further confuse Eleanor.

"What happened after he pulled the gun?" Collette asked.

"He was going to kill you. I had to stop him."

"How?"

"With the skillet. It was still on the range. I pulled myself up and grabbed it."

"Did you hit him with it?"

"I'm not sure. The skillet was in my hand. That's the last thing I remember."

"He may have taken it away from you and hit you instead. That would explain the concussion and the knot on your head."

"He was strong."

"Are you sure he didn't say anything? Do you remember a gravelly, gruff voice?" She was leading the witness, but it wasn't as if she was in a courtroom. She was trying to find a villainous pervert.

"I don't remember. I'm sorry, Collette." Eleanor closed her eyes and turned away.

Collette had pushed as hard as she dared. "Don't try to think about the attack for now, Eleanor. Just rest and take care of yourself."

Eleanor didn't respond. The meds were doing their work, and she was drifting off to sleep. "It will all work out," Collette whispered before she made her way to the door. But if it didn't work out soon, the guy was going to strike again.

He'd gone along for months with nothing but phone calls, but now it seemed he'd become desperate. There had to be an explanation for that.

Her father was steps from Eleanor's door when Collette

exited, in a quiet but animated discussion with the cop on guard duty. She was tempted to march right by him without speaking, but the situation they were in was too serious to let the long-held resentments interfere.

"There's your daughter," Clay said.

Her father turned to face her. "So it is, though she hasn't acted much like a daughter of late."

"I just talked to Eleanor," she said, refusing to fight with him here. "She's conscious, but still under the effects of the medication."

"Did she give you a description of the perp?"

"Only that he was tall and muscled. She just drifted off to sleep, but I can tell you everything she said."

"Then the information would only be hearsay."

Dylan walked up and joined them, newspaper tucked under his arm and coffee in hand. Her father glared at him, clenching his fists as if preparing to throw a punch. Subtlety wasn't in his repertoire.

She was sure Dylan noticed, but he gave no indication that he cared.

"Good morning, Sheriff."

Her father ignored his greeting and pointed a condemning finger at Collette. "I see you're still playing your silly little games and putting yourself in danger. You just can't listen, can you, Mildred?"

Mildred. Collette swallowed hard as the mistake sent a new round of resentment swirling inside her. He'd not only called her by her mother's name but used the same tone he'd used with her mother so many times before.

She turned and strode away before she said what she was thinking and caused a scene. Dylan caught up with her just as she stepped into the crowded elevator.

"What was that about?"

"Too much to go into now."

The elevator stopped on the fourth floor, and two men and a woman stepped on. The doors were already closing behind them when Collette heard a hoarse, croaky voice coming from outside the elevator. Her blood ran cold. She'd know that voice anywhere.

Chapter Twelve

Collette tried to reach through a cluster of people to hit the Door Open button, but it was too late. The doors had closed tight, and the elevator had already begun its descent. When the elevator stopped at the third floor, she grabbed Dylan's arm and tugged him off even while a lady with two young children was pushing into the car.

Dylan's brows arched. "Change of plans?"

"The gruff voice. That was him. My stalker."

"You heard his voice?"

"Yes, just as those people were getting on at the fourth floor." She looked around for stairs.

Dylan spotted the stairwell sign first, took her hand and took off running.

Once in the stairwell, he let her take the lead, only jumping in front of her when they reached the door to the fourth floor. He pushed it open and waited for her to exit.

"The elevators are right there," Dylan said, pointing to his right.

The hallway was empty. Disappointment settled like a bowling ball in her stomach. "If he was waiting for an elevator, he may have already boarded one and disappeared."

"But we don't know that he was getting on an elevator,

only that he was close enough that you heard his voice. Do you have any feel for the direction the voice came from?"

"I thought it came from the left, but I can't be sure."

"Tell me how Eleanor described him."

"Tall, muscled, strong. That's it."

With little to go on, they hurried down the halls but saw no one who looked or sounded suspicious. Collette's confidence in finding the man was sinking fast.

"Let's try the sixth floor," Dylan urged.

"But I heard him on this floor."

"Saying what?"

"'Excuse me.' He said, 'Excuse me,' and then he coughed."

"He could have been on another elevator, one stopped on the fourth floor on its climb to the sixth."

Of course. She should have thought of that. And right at that very moment he could be on his way to Room 612. "Let's go."

They took the stairs, and Collette was panting by the time they'd run the two flights. Again, the hall near the stairwell was empty, and no one was waiting at the elevators. They hurried toward Eleanor's room, where the guard was chatting up a pert, young nurse with ample curves.

Collette breathed a little easier. If there had been trouble, surely he wouldn't be carrying on a flirtation.

"Go wait with the guard while I check out the men's room," Dylan told her. "If I see someone who looks suspicious, I'll ask him a question and see if he croaks like a bullfrog."

"It's not quite that bad," she admitted. "But if he sounds like he has a cold, nab him."

The nurse walked away from Clay Sevier, and Collette

quickly caught up and fell in step with her. "My friend was supposed to meet me here ten minutes ago—a tall guy, gruff voice."

"I haven't seen him. Who are you here to visit?"

"Eleanor Baker."

"If I see a guy who looks lost, I'll send him that way."

"Thanks." Collette's frustration built.

Dylan met up with her before she reached Eleanor's room. "No luck," he said, "but I do have an idea."

"Good. I'm desperate for one."

"Assuming your father is still with Eleanor, you need to let him know what's going on. He can initiate a room search to see if anyone's on the floor without a legitimate reason."

"Why didn't I think of that?"

"If you thought of everything on your own, you wouldn't need me."

She was certain that she would.

The guard smiled as they approached him. "Back so soon?"

"Yes, I need to discuss something with my father."

"He's with the patient, and he said I was to keep visitors out until he was finished questioning her."

"What I have to tell him concerns the attack and it can't wait."

"Orders are orders," the guard said.

"This is an emergency. I'll take full responsibility for the consequences." She hurried past him and eased open the door to Eleanor's room.

"But you admit you were warned to stop digging into the murder. Who else but one of the Ledgers would be alarmed by what you planned to write?"

"Someone with something to hide," Eleanor murmured.

"Or someone trying to protect the guilty," the sheriff said. "A son, maybe."

"Like Dylan?"

"Exactly."

Collette started to shake. How dare he try to frame Dylan for the attack when he knew her stalker had called from this very hospital just yesterday.

The guard propped a hand over the door frame. "Step away from the door."

"I have to see you, Dad," she called out, ignoring Clay.

The sheriff left Eleanor's bedside. "What's the problem here?"

"I have to talk to you about the case. It's urgent." Her voice vibrated with rage that he'd been going after Dylan. She struggled to get it under control until the current emergency was handled.

The sheriff nodded to the guard. "It's okay. She can come in."

"We can't talk in there," Collette protested. "We need privacy."

"What's this about?"

"Please, just step outside with me."

He followed her into the hallway. When he saw Dylan, he stiffened, but this time he gave the sarcasm a rest.

She led him a few feet away so that they had a small degree of privacy. "I'm almost certain my stalker is in the hospital now and probably hiding somewhere on this floor."

"Do you have evidence to that fact, or is this some tomfool idea you got from Dylan?"

"I heard his voice. I think he was on a different elevator, going up when we were going down."

"A lot of voices sound the same, especially at a distance."

"It was him, Dad. As many times as I've been tormented by that voice, I'd know it anywhere."

"Okay, take it easy. I'll look into this. You do realize I'm out of my jurisdiction."

"It's not out of Clay Sevier's. He or his supervisor could have the staff check all the patient rooms and supply closets or any other place the goon might be hiding."

"Are you telling me how to do my job now?"

"No, of course not." She knew better than to try and tell him anything. Beg or inveigle, he loved that. But never tell.

"I'll handle this, Collette. Feel free to leave and take Dylan Ledger with you."

"I need to be here," she insisted. "I'm the only one who can identify the voice."

"Then have Dylan take you to the coffee shop. If something comes of the search, I'll call you."

More proof that he didn't actually consider Dylan a suspect or a danger to her. Yet he was determined to make Dylan's stay in Mustang Run so exasperating that he gave up and left. Or maybe it was Troy Ledger he wanted to run out of town.

"Fine," she said. "Find the stalker and you'll have Eleanor's attacker."

"If he's here, I'll find him. As for his arrest solving the assault case, that's yet to be determined. Bear in mind that the stalker called for months without resorting to violence. The attack came the very day the Ledgers moved back to town."

COLLETTE AND DYLAN chose the hospital's multilevel atrium instead of the coffee shop. Live plants and sunshine were far more conducive than caffeine to releasing the stress and lowering the levels of adrenaline rushing through her veins.

They strolled for a minute and then Collette dropped to an ornate wooden bench that faced a sparkling fountain. Dylan sat next to her, resting his arm along the arched back.

"It's beautiful here," she admitted, "but I'd rather be on the sixth floor in the middle of the action."

"That makes two of us, but even if we were there, we wouldn't be allowed access to any area but the restrooms and the halls."

She leaned back and Dylan let his hand fall to her shoulder and his thumb trail the tight tendons in her neck. It was amazing how in sync she felt with him when he'd only dropped into her life two days ago. Great for her. Not so terrific for him.

"You must wish you'd waited until next week to arrive in town," she said. "Then you would have missed the chaos."

"Nope. I'm glad I arrived exactly when I did."

"Me, too. After talking to Eleanor, I've even more convinced that you saved both our lives by showing up at my house when you did."

"I can't take a lot of credit for that. I was just coming by to intrude on your evening."

"Timing is everything." She'd promised herself last night that she'd gracefully bow out of his life before she dragged him into more danger. That was probably even more critical today with her father determined to make things hard on him.

Helene Ledger's ghost would no doubt be happy about

Collette leaving Dylan's life. She suspected that Troy Ledger would as well, though he'd made her feel welcome and even cooked her breakfast this morning while she'd dressed for her run to the hospital.

"I still fear that spending so much time with me gives you very little time to bond with your father," Collette said.

"I'm not sure how much bonding we'd be doing anyway. He spends most of the time staring out the back window or standing at the door of the bedroom he shared with my mother."

"He's been away from the ranch and cut off from society for nearly eighteen years. The readjustment must be difficult for him."

"I'm sure it is. Readjusting to civilian life after eight years in the service was difficult enough. Actually dealing with the stalker situation has crystallized a couple of decisions about what I'd like to do next in my life."

If one of the decisions was to run as far as he could from Mustang Run, she didn't want to hear it. Still, she had to ask. "What decisions have you made?"

"I definitely don't want to go into any type of law enforcement."

"Had you been considering that as a career option?"

"I'd talked about the possibility with Wyatt. He loves it and thought I should give it a try."

"All law-enforcement officers are not as intolerable as my father if that's what's holding you back."

"No. I've just had enough violence and bureaucracy— all of the things that would go with the job. I gave a hundred percent during my eight years in the service. I'm glad I was able to do that for my country, but I'm ready to move on."

She experienced a plummeting sensation that didn't

mix well with the chaos of the morning and the interminable wait to hear news from her father.

"To move on as in away from Mustang Run?"

"Not necessarily. I'm thinking of going into ranching, either here with Dad or on a spread of my own. I have a small inheritance from my maternal grandfather and I saved most of my salary while I was in Iraq."

"You made that decision after only two days?"

"It doesn't take long to know when something's right."

His tone made her think he could be talking about more than just ranching. Warmth seeped into every pore. It could just be infatuation, but her feelings for Dylan were growing stronger by the second.

Dylan shifted and moved away from her. She wondered if he, too, was feeling the heat.

"Guess I've always been a cowboy at heart," he said.

"I could have told you that from the moment I met you."

"Really, Miss Personality Expert. How's that?"

"You had that cowboy swagger when you walked up on the steps of the ranch house and tipped your hat to the waiting sharks. Besides, you know the old adage, don't call him a cowboy until you see him ride. I saw you ride, and you're a natural with horses."

"How am I doing with you?"

"You've got potential," she teased.

Dylan pushed up his shirt sleeve and looked at his watch. It finally hit her that the conversation over the past few minutes had been designed to keep her mind off the drama playing out on the sixth floor.

It had worked for a few minutes, but the anxiety had just come crashing down on her again.

She stretched her legs in front of her, crossing her

ankles and flexing her toes to release the coiled strain to her muscles.

"I really appreciate all you've done for me, Dylan, but the best thing I can do for you and your father right now is to get out of your lives."

"I thought we were past that."

"I thought so, too, but things with my father will just continuously get worse for you until this case is solved."

Dylan turned to her and cupped her face in his hands, forcing her to look in his eyes.

"Get this straight in your head right now, Collette. I've faced enemies whose idea of destruction was blowing me into a thousand pieces or cutting off my head and hanging it from a pole. I'm not afraid of your father. Your walking out of my life is the last thing I need or want. If it's what you want, I'll live with it, but don't even think it would be best for me."

He dropped his hands from her face, then took one of her hands in his. "What is it with you and your father? Every meeting between the two of you is charged with hostility. You can't even talk about him without getting edgy and tense."

"We've had our differences."

"It must have been a hell of a difference to leave you this bitter."

"You don't want to go there, Dylan."

"You don't have to tell me anything you don't want to, but it would help me get a grip on what's going on."

She took in a deep breath and exhaled slowly. "Okay, Dylan, I'll dish the dirt, but I have to warn you. My family history is sordid and heartrending."

Dylan squeezed her hand. "Welcome to my world."

Chapter Thirteen

"The accident that led to my mother's stroke could have been avoided."

Dylan kept hold of Collette's hand, knowing the worst was yet to come. Yet if she didn't get the rage and resentment out in the open, he feared she might explode, especially with the incidents of the past two days no doubt setting her nerves on a short fuse.

"Mom asked me to come home for spring break my senior year, saying there was something important she needed to tell me," Collette continued. "I knew from her voice that something was seriously wrong, but she refused to say more on the phone. I immediately thought cancer or some type of risky operation, and I canceled my Florida plans. I was a wreck the rest of the week."

"Had she been diagnosed with a life-threatening condition?"

"No. Our visit turned into a true-confessions session for which I was totally unprepared. I knew living with Dad's belligerence wasn't easy. He and I had clashed on many occasions, but he never seemed to get to Mom the way he did me. That's why I was totally unprepared for the bomb she dropped on me."

"The divorce bomb?"

"How did you guess?"

"I witnessed it more than once in the service with guys who had never seen it coming. One day they're telling you about the wonderful wife and kids back home, the next they're reading Dear John."

"Mom said that she'd had all she could take of my father and that she'd only stayed with him the last few years because of me. She wanted me to graduate and be on my own before she left him."

Which basically made Collette the scapegoat for her mother's bad marriage. Talk about piling on the guilt. And Dylan could imagine all holy hell breaking out when Glenn McGuire found out he was being dumped.

"How did the sheriff react to the prospect of divorce?" he asked her.

"Mom hadn't told him and didn't plan to until she was ready to walk out the door. She said she knew he would explode and that there would be no living in the same house with him after that."

"So you were the first to know?"

"I think so, but that wasn't the half of it. She said my brother was conceived out of wedlock and that even after Dad had said he loved her and asked her to marry him, he'd still been writing to an old girlfriend begging her to take him back."

"How did she discover that?"

"Apparently the woman returned all the letters to Dad with a note asking him to stop writing. Mother found them in the attic when she was going through some of Dad's college yearbooks. The letters were important enough to him that he kept them all those years, and believe me, Dad is not the sentimental sort."

"What did he say when she confronted him?"

"She didn't. That's my Mom. She hated conflict and avoided it at all costs, but I think the letters were the real impetus for deciding to leave him. She insisted I read the letters."

"And did you?"

Collette shook her head. "They were Dad's property. I wouldn't have felt right. I refused to take them, but she stashed them in my luggage without my knowing it before I went back to UT."

"What did you do with them?"

"I still have them. I've thought of returning them to Dad, but that would mean having a conversation with him about them, and I've never wanted to deal with that."

"How do the accident and strokes fit in with her wanting a divorce?"

Collette's shoulders sagged, and she dropped her head to stare at the toe of her right boot that she was twisting as if putting out a lit cigarette.

"I only know the rest from what Dad told me. I heard about the accident just as I'd finished my last final. Dad had gone in to work early that day to deal with a case of vandalism at the high-school football stadium. He'd gotten caught in a sudden spring thunderstorm and had gone home to change into dry clothes. When he got there, Mom was packing her bags."

Rotten way to find out your wife was leaving, Dylan thought. He wouldn't even wish that on a hardheaded, cantankerous guy like the sheriff. Not that he was taking sides.

"Dad confronted her and they had an argument. His story is that he tried to grab her arm to keep her from leaving before they had a chance to talk things out. She slung a duffel at him and slipped in the process, falling down the steps and banging the back of her head against the heavy antique bell stand in the corner of the landing.

When they got to the hospital the doctors told him she had a concussion. From there it went from bad to tragic."

"Was your mother conscious?"

"No, and when she was still unconscious the next day, they did a CAT scan that showed brain contusions. I rushed home from Austin, though they were still telling us she'd be okay."

Collette's voice grew shaky. Her hands had grown clammy, and she pulled them from his and wiped them on her jeans.

"We can finish this conversation later," Dylan said. "I should have never asked when you have so much else to deal with."

"I'd like to finish it now," she said, her gaze straight ahead. She pulled her arms tight around her chest. "I've never talked about this with anyone else, not even Bill. I think maybe it's time."

"Then I'm glad I'm here."

"Thanks." She propped her elbow on the arm of the bench and supported her head with her hand. "Mom remained in the ICU and they kept her sedated so that her brain could rest. When she came to, she recognized me and Dad and talked to both of us, though she avoided mentioning her fall or the divorce. But then, so did we. It didn't seem the right time for it.

"I left the hospital that night, thinking all was well, but then she slipped into a coma during the night. An MRI the next morning indicated vasospasms."

"I'm not familiar with that."

"Constriction of the blood vessels that limit blood to the brain. As a result of that there were clear signs that she'd suffered multiple strokes."

Dylan had known several guys who'd had brain contusions, both on his high-school hockey team and in the service. None had ever had strokes or any lasting complications. "Are strokes normal after brain contusions?"

"No, the neurologist said he'd seen it occur after aneurysms, but it's extremely rare after contusions. But it does happen. It *did* happen. Mom never recovered. She died a few days later."

Collette's head fell against his shoulder, and she cratered against him as the emotional strain drained her body of strength. The friction between her and her father made sense to him now. She blamed him for the accident and her mother's resulting death. She had never let herself forgive him.

Dylan was far from an expert on family dissension, but he'd lived with it for years. That's how he knew that family ties could hold against most anything the world threw at them. Those ties were why he was back in Mustang Run. They were why he was trying to find some way to connect with his father.

They were why Collette needed to let go of the blame and hostility and go on with her life. Unless she believed the fall wasn't an accident.

"I know Dad didn't intentionally push Mom down the stairs," Collette said, as if reading his mind. "But—"

Her cell phone rang, yanking them both back to the problem at hand. "It's Dad," she said, sitting up straight and pushing her back against the wooden slats of the bench. She answered the call with a question. "Have you found Eleanor's attacker?"

Dylan didn't have to hear the answers to get the gist of them. Disappointment and frustration were written all over Collette's face. Sitting around, doing nothing while they waited for the next attack was never good battle strategy.

Fortunately, Dylan had a plan.

IT WAS JUST AFTER two-thirty when Collette and Dylan pulled up in front of her house. They'd stopped for lunch at a roadside restaurant on the way back from the hospital. As usual, she'd nibbled at her meal, leaving more than half of the Texas-size bacon/jalapeño burger on the plate.

Dylan had devoured all of his along with a side of onion rings, and washed it all down with a tall glass of iced tea. She liked watching him eat. He did it with such relish.

In fact she liked everything about him. It was completely out of character for her to fall this hard, this fast. But then she'd never met a man like Dylan Ledger.

Tough as nails, yet thoughtful. Protective, but not domineering. And so incredibly sexy and virile that he took her breath away even in a crisis.

"We can just pick up your appointment book and take it back to the ranch if you'd rather clear out of here," Dylan said.

She pushed her key into her front-door lock. "I usually keep it with me, but in all the confusion, I forgot it when I changed handbags yesterday. I'm fine to work here. I don't see Sukey's car, so she must be done with the cleaning."

Collette opened the door, and they were greeted by a house that was so clean it sparkled and was fragrant with the fresh scent of flowers. She didn't have to look far to find them. A huge bouquet of spring blossoms in brilliant pink, snowy white and vivid red sat in the middle of the antique chest that served as coffee table. She recognized the vase as one of her own.

"Alma must have sent the flowers with Sukey," Collette said, walking over for a better look at the bouquet. "It's not something Bill would think to do."

Dylan grabbed her arm as she reached for the card.

"Let me get that for you."

"I'm not help—" She broke off the sentence as she

saw him carefully touch only the edges of the card. He thought they could be from the stalker. But the man had never sent flowers or gifts before.

Dylan murmured a couple of choice sentiments under his breath. That told her all she needed to know.

"They're from *him,* aren't they?"

"Yeah. He's either a complete psycho or there's method to his madness."

"Which would you guess?"

"The latter," Dylan admitted.

He held the card so that Collette could read it without touching it, just in case there were fingerprints. She doubted there were. The man had outfoxed them at every turn. No reason to think he'd screw up now.

So sorry about your friend. I can't sleep for thinking it could have been you. I couldn't bear to see you in pain. Take care, my sweet Collette. We'll talk soon.

Her blood boiled. "I can't believe his gall to just walk in and out of my house like this."

"Wait here," Dylan said.

Her pulse quickened as he rushed past her and to the back of the house. Did Dylan think the stalker was still here? What if he was?

What if he'd come straight here from the hospital and arrived while Sukey was cleaning? What if Dylan found her lying on the floor in a pool of blood?

Collette rushed toward the kitchen. Dylan caught her on his way out and pulled her into his arms.

"It's okay," Dylan said. "Everything's in place. There's no sign that he's been inside the house. Do you have Sukey's phone number?"

"No, but I can get it from Alma."

"Do it and then call Sukey and see if the flowers were here when she cleaned."

"Maybe they were delivered while she was here," Collette said. "If he delivered them himself, she could have seen him."

"Don't count on that."

"We're past due for a break." She called Alma on her cell phone, interrupting a pedicure. A few minutes later she had Sukey on the phone.

"The house looks great," Collette said, not wanting to alarm her.

"Thank you. I dropped your key off with Mrs. McGuire when I finished."

"Thanks. I'll get it from her." After a moment's hesitation she asked, "Did someone deliver flowers while you were here?"

"They were sitting by your door when I got there and were starting to wither. I put them in the vase of water for you and tied the pretty pink ribbon that held them around the vase. They looked better right away."

"Yes, they're lovely. I just thought you might have seen the man who delivered them."

"No, but whoever sent them must like you a lot. It's a really big bouquet."

Someone must really like her, all right. They'd like her dead. They must also think she was a moron.

She disconnected the call after thanking the woman again, then turned to Dylan. "Could this man possibly be so arrogant that he believes a bouquet of flowers will make me think he's not the man who attacked Eleanor?"

"You wouldn't know it with such certainty if we hadn't discovered that the last call was made from the hospital. No reason for him to think he's not still calling with impunity."

"And free to roam the hospital conniving to get into Eleanor's room and kill her."

"Maybe not," Dylan said. "He may have found out that she's been talking to the sheriff and assumes she's already given a description of him. But we still need to move quickly."

"Agreed. I'll get my daily planner. We can work at my kitchen table. That will give us more room to spread out." Besides, she couldn't avoid the room forever just because it reminded her of the attack.

Dylan followed her down the narrow hallway and explained his plan. "I'll start going through the phone records and circle all the ones that could be from the stalker. Hopefully we'll find a pattern between his calling and where you'd been and who you'd seen on those days."

And if there was a pattern, that would at least give them a place to start. If the pattern involved a specific location—stores, banks, offices—the sheriff's department could confiscate the appropriate security footage and see if anyone appeared to be following her.

Success was iffy, as Dylan had said when he'd proposed his plan, but doing something was far better than waiting for the next vicious drama to unfold. Or for the results of the DNA testing.

A minute later she returned to the kitchen and set her planner on the table near Dylan's elbow. "I'm having a diet cola. Would you like one?"

"No, thanks, but water would be good," he said, circling in red another suspect call from the list of numbers.

She got him a glass of water and then pulled the soda from the fridge and popped the cap.

"Did you make note of the dates or times of any of the

stalker's calls?" Dylan asked as she slid into a chair next to his.

"I didn't the first few times, but I started keeping track of all of them about three weeks ago. I received the first call from him around the middle of March."

"How about March twelfth at ten-thirty in the evening?" Dylan asked. "That's the first indication I see of a call from a number that can't be traced to an individual account."

"The time sounds right. I know I was working late in my studio the first time he called."

She checked her calendar for that day. "I had a sitting with the Clerys for their adorable daughter's first-birthday pictures, a consultation with the Aldings of Marble Falls for an upcoming wedding, and I'd gone to Betts Cummings's real-estate office to photograph her at her desk for a new Web site she was having designed."

"You do stay busy."

"And I can't keep canceling appointments the way I've done this week. Let's see, there was also a late-afternoon dentist appointment for my semiannual cleaning."

She checked the date for the following weekend. The gallery showing was marked and highlighted in yellow.

"That could have well been the date of his first call. I know I was framing some photos I'd taken of lightning bolts during a recent storm."

Dylan looked up from his list. "You take pictures of storms?"

"Sometimes. I'd been experimenting with various shutter speeds and that night I got it right. The clarity of the streaks of light was remarkable. One of the Austin galleries was having a big show that coming weekend and had asked to include some of my nature photographs so I was working extra late."

"I'd love to see some of your work."

"The first chance we get, as long as you promise to be duly impressed by my offerings."

"I can't imagine not being impressed by anything you do."

A preposterous burn crept to her cheeks. At twenty-seven, she shouldn't blush at a casual compliment. Had the comment come from anyone but Dylan, she'd have paid it no mind. This was just more of the sensually decadent effect he had on her. And reason enough to keep her mind on the task at hand.

"If I'd any idea the calls would lead to this, I would have kept excellent records. But who expects this kind of trouble in Mustang Run?" She realized as soon as the words were out of her mouth that Dylan was not the person to have said that to, not after what had happened to his mother in this town. And that had been when the population was much smaller than it was now.

"Nowhere is totally safe these days," Dylan said. "If someone's motivated to commit crimes, they find a way."

Motivation was the key. What was the motivation for stalking her or for wanting her dead?

"What about March eighteenth?" Dylan asked. "You received another suspicious call on that day, this one at 1:10 p.m."

She checked the calendar. "That was a Saturday. My to-do list says pick up nails to fix a loose shutter and meet Melinda and Eleanor in Austin for an early dinner."

"Where did you shop for nails?"

"At Knight's Hardware. It's just a couple of blocks from my studio." Her memory kicked in with a gasp of insight. "That's also where I got the bronzed metal paint for the frames I made for the lightning bolts. I stopped by there on my way back to the studio that night. Mr. Knight was just locking up, but he waited for me to purchase what I needed."

"How often do you visit Knight's Hardware?"

"Maybe once a month, but I pass it every time I walk down to Abby's or Joyce's Soups and Salads for lunch. That's at least a couple of times a week."

"Tell me about the employees at the hardware store."

"There's usually just Larry Knight, his nephew Kingsley and sometimes Larry's wife, Jane. Larry's the owner."

"What do you know about Larry?"

"Larry Knight is a family man, hardworking, active in his church and works with the Boy Scouts. I was photographing his son Carl's wedding the night Eleanor was attacked. Believe me, Larry has not been stalking me. Besides, I know his voice."

"What about Kingsley?"

"He's still in high school, a senior, I think. He only works part-time. He's always friendly and helpful when I go in, but he's never been into any trouble that I know of. Again, I know his voice and his cheerleader girlfriend. You can rule him out, too."

"Do they have security cameras inside the shop?"

"Probably inside and out. Everyone does these days, except me." She'd remedy that soon. Mustang Run was not as safe as she'd believed.

"I say we call your father and have him put someone on checking that footage."

"I doubt we have to wait on the sheriff's department. If we explain the situation to Larry, he'll probably hand over the disk to us, or at least let us view the footage. I'm sure he's already heard about Eleanor's attack, or at least some version of it."

"Then let's do it," Dylan said. "We can check out the rest of these numbers and dates later at the ranch."

At the ranch. So he assumed she was staying again. She'd vowed not to. But that was to keep him from getting involved with her problems, and he was already in neck deep. Besides, if she didn't go back to Willow Creek Ranch, there would be no chance of a repeat visit from his mother's ghost.

Not that she believed in ghosts, but just in case she was wrong and the house at Willow Creek Ranch really was haunted... Helene might be the only one who had a clue what was behind the stalker's madness.

"Let me pack a few more things."

Picking up her drink and her planner, she went back to the bedroom. She tossed a small overnight bag onto the bed and unzipped it. The first panties she pulled from the bureau were a pair of white briefs. Impulsively, she dropped them back to the stack and chose a lacy red thong and a black lace bikini panty.

She gathered some jeans and T-shirts and pulled out a pair of white shorts while she was at it. The weather was getting warmer, or at least she was.

Once everything was in the overnighter including her appointment book, she zipped the bag, slung it over her shoulder and stepped over to close the closet door.

She hesitated and then reached onto the top shelf of the closet and removed the plastic shoe box marked Personal. Opening the luggage again, she fit the box of letters inside. If she was already being haunted by ghosts, maybe it was time to let the secrets in her closet come out of hiding, too.

"NICE HORSES AND thoughtful of Bob Adkins to let you use them. I guess you'll find who your real friends are day by day."

"I suspect I can count them with the fingers of one hand." Troy scratched the nose of the flaxen chestnut filly who'd come to the pasture fence to check them out. "I didn't expect you to be among the number."

Ruthanne propped the heel of a stylish Western boot on the bottom rung of the recently repaired fence. "Helene was my best friend, Troy. I trusted you, as well. You know that. I was just too shocked and stunned by the murder to reason it all through back then."

"So you went with the tide of popular opinion and shunned me like the rest."

Which was why he'd been so surprised to see her at his door a few minutes earlier. He'd recognized her at once. In fact, she didn't look all that different than she had almost two decades ago. Ruthanne Foley had always been beautiful. She still was. Money had a way of softening the edges of a woman and keeping the wrinkles at bay.

She reached over and ran her fingers through the horse's thick mane. "I wanted to testify to your character at the trial, but Riley was dead set against it. He thought I was too close to the situation to see it clearly."

"He thought your befriending me would cost him votes." Troy had never been one to dance around the truth. "Does Riley know you're here now?"

"He doesn't know or care where I am anymore. We separated last year. He stays in Austin full-time now. I moved back to the family ranch."

"Your choice or his?"

"The divorce or the ranch?"

"Either. Both."

"It was his choice to take a mistress, a blonde young

enough to be his daughter, all very clandestine, of course. It was my choice to leave him and move back to the ranch."

"How are the kids?"

"Marilyn's teaching kindergarten and living at the ranch with me. Ellie is modeling in New York. She's the one I worry about. I heard Dylan is here with you."

"For the time being."

"I also heard that he's gotten mixed up in some trouble involving Collette McGuire."

Troy's muscles grew taut. "He and Collette are old friends. He's doing what he can to help her."

"That's not the way Glenn sees it."

Glenn. He took that to mean they were close enough that her information had come straight from the sheriff's mouth. "You got something on your mind, just say it, Ruthanne. If I ever had the knack for small talk, I lost it in prison."

"There's no love lost between Glenn and you, Troy. You know that. You'd best warn Dylan to watch his step very carefully."

"Is that what you stopped by to tell me?"

Ruthanne put her hand on his arm and leaned in so close he could see the rise of her breasts inside her white shirt and feel her silky black hair against his flesh.

A slow burn crept though him. It had been eighteen years since he'd been with a woman, and he was human. Too human. But even if she was offering, he couldn't be with Ruthanne without thinking of Helene.

And the ache inside him for Helene would be too devastating to let him even go through the motions. He had to have some kind of closure first, had to get justice for Helene. Then maybe he could move on, but he would never stop loving her.

"I need to get back to work," he said.

"Is that my signal to disappear?"

"If you've finished saying what you came to say."

"I've finished. But take my warning seriously. If Glenn can find a way to run Dylan out of town and away from Collette, you can be sure he will."

"Right, and you can tell the sheriff for me that I will not stand by and let him railroad my son the way he did me."

"I'll be sure he gets the word. If you want to talk some night, call me. I'd like that."

"I expect to be busy for a long time."

DYLAN WAS RELIEVED that Larry Knight had been eager to help. He not only provided the disks containing the security-camera footage for both days, but let them use his office and both his laptop and desktop computers to view them. His wife had even brought in bottles of water and cups of coffee.

Dylan chose the footage for March 12. In the desktop he loaded the disk from the camera closest to the front door. He put the one that scanned aisles beyond the checkout counter into the laptop. He fast-forwarded both files to just before six o'clock, Larry's usual closing time.

One man checked out at five minutes before six. Other than Larry Knight, he appeared to be the only person in the shop. Kingsley was either not working or was in the back.

"The man checking out is Skip Wakefield, the principal of the high school," Collette noted. "He's short and I can probably bench press more than him, so that pretty much rules him out as tall and muscled."

But Larry was both tall and muscled. Dylan decided not to mention that for now.

At two minutes before six, the film showed Collette walking through the door.

Larry smiled and motioned her to come in as she opened the door. Once she was inside, he took a key ring from his pocket and locked the front door.

"I think I asked if he was ready to close," she said.

"Obviously, he didn't want any additional customers."

"Probably not, though I have been in after the posted hours when he was still open for business. I think it all depends on what he has to do on a particular night."

"No sign of Kingsley tonight," Dylan commented. He'd hoped to see what the guy looked like. He might not be able to judge a book by its cover, but he could tell a lot about a guy by looking at him, especially if he could look the guy in the eyes.

Collette and Larry stepped out of view of one camera and into the view of the other. They were looking at small cans of paint.

"I wanted to give the frames an aged look," she said. "To do that, I distress the wood and use an antiquing rub. Larry stocks lots of different colors."

But Dylan's attention had moved to the other computer. A tall, muscled man wearing a T-shirt and faded jeans walked up to the door, tried it, but didn't move away when he discovered it was locked.

Instead he cupped his hand over his eyes and pressed his head to the glass as if he were trying to peer inside. He stayed a couple of minutes and then walked away. Dylan ran it back.

"Do you recognize this man?"

"No. I don't think I've ever seen him before. But that means nothing. New people are moving into the area all the time."

"The timing is right for him to get to the door if he was following a half block or so behind you. Ask Larry to take a look at the film to see if he recognizes the man."

Dylan blew up the image and printed out two copies on the laser printer while Collette went for Larry. The printed images were a bit grainy, but clear enough.

Larry returned with Collette and studied the film. "I don't know him, but he looks vaguely familiar. He may have been here before. Let me get my wife and have her take a look."

Unfortunately, Mrs. Knight didn't recognize the man, either.

Dylan switched files to March 18. At 11:43 in the morning, Collette entered the store and went straight to the shelf where nails were stocked.

Exactly three minutes later, the man whose image he'd printed walked into the store. He stopped at the same aisle as Collette and looked—or pretended to look—at a display of electric screwdrivers. More than once his gaze scanned the aisle in Collette's direction. At one point he looked directly into the nearby camera and then quickly moved out of view.

Dylan got that buzz in his veins he used to get in Iraq when they were about to close in on the enemy. His gut instinct was that he was looking at Collette's stalker.

The film showed Collette leaving a few minutes later with her nails. Shortly thereafter, the guy walked out. He was not carrying a bag.

Dylan hadn't realized Collette had clued in on his suspicions until he felt her fingers digging into his arm.

"You think that's *him*, don't you?" she asked.

"I think it could be."

"If it is, then I don't think this was ever about his lusting after me or thinking I was his soul mate."

"Why is that?"

She shuddered. "The way he looked at me. Go back and run that part again. Only this time enlarge his face."

Dylan did. Even in black and white, the man's stare was cold and calculating.

"I think he's planned to kill me all along."

COLLETTE CALLED her father's cell-phone number on the way back to the ranch and left a message for him to call her. The sooner they got this picture in his hands, the sooner he could run a search and see if the man had a mug shot on record. She realized that could take a while. Everything seemed to take too long.

"Do you think your father has been home alone all day?" Collette asked once they were inside the gate of Willow Creek Ranch.

"Yes, but I don't think he minds it. I think he may need the time alone to adjust to freedom and to come to grips with the past."

"It must be heartbreaking for him," Collette said. "Before the murder, he had a working ranch, a beautiful wife and five young sons."

"Now he just has empty pastures, rundown outbuildings, worn equipment and me," Dylan said, finishing her topic for her, though not in her words.

"He's lucky to have you, Dylan. And your brothers will come around. It just takes time."

"I know why I think he couldn't kill Mom, but what makes you so convinced he's innocent when a jury declared him guilty?"

Because I've talked to Helene.

Collette didn't dare say that out loud. She knew that Dylan would think her ghostly encounter was a nightmare or a hallucination. She thought so herself. She just wasn't as sure of it as she'd been before she'd seen and talked to Helene's ghost.

But that wasn't the only thing that convinced her of Troy's innocence. "When your father talked of your mother's garden, I could hear the grief and melancholy in his voice. He loved your mother. You don't destroy the person who holds your heart."

"My mother's side of the family was convinced that he did."

"What about your dad's family?"

"There is none. His mother died when he was a baby. His biological father had cut out long before that. He was raised in a series of foster homes. That's all I know about it. We were never encouraged to talk about our father once my grandparents had removed us from the ranch."

"They'd lost their daughter. Grief can instill the need for revenge at all costs."

Who knew that better than Collette? And Helene.

They topped the last hill and the Ledger ranch house came into view. The sheriff's vehicle and one additional squad car blocked the driveway. Her brother Bill's car was parked behind them. They wouldn't be out here for her, not after she'd refused to go with them last night.

Panic struck like one of her lightning bolts. "They must be here about Eleanor. The stalker must have found a way to get to her."

Dylan reached for her hand and squeezed it. "You don't know that."

"Why else would everyone be here except to deliver the bad news?"

She jumped from the car the second Dylan stopped, and raced toward her father's car. He was standing beside it when she reached him. The look on his face was grim.

One hand rested on the mirror of the car, the other on the butt of the pistol at his waist.

"Please tell me Eleanor is okay."

"Eleanor's fine," he sputtered. "Why wouldn't she be? She's under protective custody."

Dylan had walked up behind her, his presence calming her in spite of her father's callous attitude.

"Then why are you here?" Dylan asked.

"To see you and to give you a ride down to my office." He opened the back door of his squad car. "Get in."

Chapter Fourteen

Dylan needed a minute to think, but the situation was fast barreling out of control. Collette was livid and in the sheriff's face letting him know about it. A horse neighed in the distance. There was no sign of his father, but Dylan was certain he'd show up and join the circus at any minute.

"What reason do you have for taking Dylan in?" Collette protested. "He told you everything he knew right after the attack."

"He's a person of interest. Now get your things and Bill will drive you to his house. This lamebrain game you're playing with Dylan Ledger has gone on long enough."

"I'm not playing games. I'm as aware as anyone how serious this is. That doesn't give you the right to harass Dylan."

"This is law business, Collette, and none of your affair."

"So let's just get the show on the road," Dylan said, not wanting to pit Collette against her father any longer. "Go with your brother, Collette. I'll call you as soon as the sheriff finishes the *law business*."

"I'm not going anywhere. I'll be waiting right here when you return."

"No daughter of mine is staying alone in a house with a convicted killer."

The sheriff was pushing it now. Dylan had to fight the anger that swelled inside him. He might have to settle things with the sheriff one day, but right now his total focus had to be on keeping Collette safe, and he couldn't do that from a jail cell.

Dylan put an arm around Collette's shoulders, knowing that would irritate her father even more, but he couldn't leave her without some kind of assurance.

"I'll be fine. The sooner I talk to the sheriff about the evidence we discovered this afternoon, the sooner he can follow up on it."

The sheriff narrowed his eyes and glared at Dylan. "What evidence is that?"

"We checked out security footage from the hardware store and we think we may have spotted Collette's stalker."

McGuire turned back to Collette. "Is he talking straight?"

"Yes. The man on camera appeared to be following me on two different occasions on days that corresponded with the first two phone calls I received. We printed out his picture."

The situation was beginning to diffuse when Dylan spotted Troy walking back from the horse barn. Troy picked up his pace when he spotted the squad cars, his shoulders squared and his gaunt face looking as if he was about to climb in the ring with a killer.

Dylan had no idea what his father was capable of when he was fighting mad, but he figured they were about to find out.

"What's going on here?" Troy demanded.

"No problem, Dad," Dylan said, hoping to keep Troy out of this. "The sheriff just wants me to come in and answer a few more questions about the attack."

Troy's body clenched as if he was about to explode. "Do you have a warrant?"

"No," McGuire said. "He's not under arrest. He's just a person of interest."

Troy bristled. "Same as I was, Glenn, when you framed me?"

"Don't ride that road, Troy, not if you expect to come back and live in this town."

"You don't own the town. And there's nothing you can do to me that's near as bad as what's already been done. But I won't sit back while you railroad my boy. He'll talk when there's an attorney present and not before. I've already hired one."

Dylan had the good sense to realize this was no longer about him. The enmity between Glenn McGuire and Troy Ledger was rooted in the past. Theirs was a fight that was probably long overdue.

But Dylan was his own man. "I'm going with the sheriff. I have information he needs."

"Information that Dylan and I spent the day tracking down," Collette threw in. "I'm staying here until Dylan returns. If you're worried about my being here without him, Dad, then I suggest you make the questioning session short. And then get on with finding the stalker."

"Do as you please." McGuire was so furious his mouth could barely form the words. He turned his back on his daughter and got into his squad car.

The sheriff had won the battle he'd come here to fight, but he may have lost the war with Collette.

DYLAN HAD BEEN GONE for just over an hour when Collette picked up the dreaded stack of letters her mother had given her and walked to the weeds, briars and thorns that had once been Helene's beloved garden.

After being shot at on the porch the other night, she didn't trust any outside area open to sniper fire. Tucked between the stone wall and two added extensions of the meandering ranch house, the garden felt safe and protected. On the other hand, the letters she held felt like explosive contraband.

Using a tissue from her pocket she brushed leaves and dirt from the rusting metal bench and dropped onto it. Nothing she held in her hand would bring her mother back. Yet the yellowed letters that had stayed in the top of Collette's closet for years without notice were suddenly begging to be opened and have their secrets revealed.

The larger envelopes were all addressed to Helene Martin.

Collette's chest constricted painfully as she stared at the name. Helene Martin, Dylan's mother. Surely her father had not been involved with Helene. Her hands began to shake, and she struggled with a wave of nausea.

Below the stack of letters, one note-size square envelope was addressed to Glenn McGuire in neat, precise penmanship. Dread eating away at her, Collette opened it first, took a deep breath and started reading.

Dear Glenn,
Please do not write me again as it is time for both of us to move on with our lives. I never meant to lead you on. We had great times together, but it wasn't love, at least not for me.
I know you feel that both Troy and I have betrayed you since he was your friend long before you introduced him to me. But if you must blame someone, blame me. It was I who pursued him.
I love Troy with all my heart, and I know that he loves me, too. We're getting married in May, as

*soon as graduation is behind me. I am returning
your letters so that you can destroy them and put
that part of your life behind you.*

*I wish you all the best in life and hope that
one day you and Troy can be friends again. I know
he would like that.*
Warmly,
Helene

Collette trembled as full awareness of what she'd just
read seared into her mind. That friendship had clearly
never come to be. But had the perceived betrayal led to her
father framing Troy Ledger for Helene's murder while he
let the real killer go free? Nagging suspicions ground in
the back of Collette's mind. She had to know the truth.

An unexpected chill settled deep inside her as she
reread the letter, and she had the eerie sensation that she
was no longer alone in the garden. Could it be that Helene
was reading over her shoulder? Oddly, the possibility did
not disturb her.

She read the rest of the letters one by one, feeling her
father's loss, yet hurting for her mother. She could imagine
her mother's heart breaking at the vows of love Glenn
McGuire had written to another woman mere months
before they were married. Tears burned and filled Collette's eyes until she could barely make out the words.

The letters were full of the angst her father was expe-
riencing, but they were also informative enough to give
her an idea of the circumstances surrounding his breakup
with Helene.

Her father had also been a senior at UT at the time.
Apparently he and Helene Martin had been dating for
over a year when Glenn brought her home with him for
the weekend. He'd introduced to her his best friend, wild

and reckless Troy Ledger, a cowboy who hadn't gone to college and who was riding the rodeo circuit and saving every cent of his winnings to buy his own spread. That trip was the beginning of the end for Glenn and Helene and the beginning for Troy and Helene.

There was not one mention of Collette's mother in the letters, though judging from the dates, Glenn must have turned to Mildred during this time. No wonder Collette's mother had been so hurt when she read them. She became pregnant with Glenn's child while he had been touting his love for another woman and begging her to take him back.

And yet Collette's parents had made a life together— until a frayed stack of yellowed letters and a tragedy had ended it.

Footsteps on the old stone walkway startled Collette. This time the visitor was flesh and blood.

"I cooked some stew," Troy said, staring at her red-rimmed eyes, but not asking her what was wrong. "I can't vouch for its quality, but food with any flavor tastes like gourmet to me."

"I should have offered to help," she said.

"You're a guest."

"Some might say an intruder," Collette countered.

Troy didn't argue the point. He was surely no more enamored of her relationship with Dylan than her father was, albeit for different reasons.

"I'm sorry my father is being so hard-nosed about this," she said, hoping to smooth the moment.

Troy didn't respond, but she could see his features harden.

"If the sheriff has issues with me, he should take them up with me, not with my son."

"I agree, but I can't speak for my father."

"Right, so let's just drop that subject. Now what's this about new information that you and Dylan tracked down?"

Collette explained the findings. "I think all of the talk of love and soul mates may have been a ruse. I think the stalker's real motives may stem from something else."

"Did he try to blackmail you?" Troy asked.

"No. He just seemed to delight in upsetting me. I think he could be seeking revenge."

"Who would have that kind of grudge against you?"

"I think the grudge may be against my father." Even now in the garden haunted by Helene, Collette didn't mention that the ghost of Troy's dead wife had put her on that track. She definitely didn't mention the letters she'd just read.

"I suspect there are lots of people with grudges against your father." Troy reached down and pulled one weed from the multitude that clogged the beds. "I should get this area in shape. Helene would hate seeing it this way. She liked pretty things. I provided so few, but she never complained. She claimed she didn't need trinkets or luxury to be…"

A gravelly quake in his voice swallowed the last of his words. Coming home to life without Helene was clearly tearing him apart. "She had you and the boys," Collette said. "That's worth far more than inanimate possessions."

"Her parents never saw it that way. They wanted her back in Boston to be part of the elite circles they moved in. They wanted her to have expensive clothes and jewels and to send the boys to private schools."

"If Helene's family was from Boston, how did Helene end up at the University of Texas?"

"She was a bit rebellious, wanted to live where it was

warm and she liked cowboys." Finally, Troy smiled, deepening the creases around his eyes. "The real miracle is that she ended up with me."

"The miracle was love."

A love so strong that all these years later Collette could still feel it in this garden. Feel it as surely as she could feel the breeze that tousled her hair and danced across her cheeks.

She'd never really believed in that kind of love before. Now that she knew it existed, she wanted it. She could see herself having it with Dylan.

But Dylan could never love a woman whose father had been instrumental in sending the only parent he had left to prison for a crime he didn't commit.

DANGER WAS IMMINENT. The reality of that echoed in Dylan's mind as he stepped from the deputy's car and walked toward the ranch house. He had a sixth sense about looming disaster. It had saved his life more than once in Iraq.

Like the time he'd been leading his squad into a trap. At the last minute his instincts for pending catastrophe had forced him to pull back. Only later had they discovered how close they'd come to being blown to bits.

This time the fear was for Collette, and he had more than his gut feeling to rely on. He had the land mines she'd narrowly missed.

She'd missed being attacked and likely killed the other night by a matter of minutes—possibly because he'd stopped by her house on an impulse. She'd missed having her brains splattered over the porch by a matter of inches. The man who was masterminding the situation with claims of infatuation and gifts of flowers wanted

Collette dead. There was no reason to think he wouldn't strike again.

If Dylan was going to keep her safe, he had to stay out of jail himself. The sheriff had other ideas, and his reason for wanting to discredit Dylan was clear: for protection Collette had chosen the "murderer's kid" over her sheriff father.

Yet McGuire had taken the photo from the security-camera footage, and Dylan was sure he'd check it out. The man was vindictive to a fault, but he wanted his daughter safe.

Troy was waiting on him in the kitchen when Dylan walked in. A sheaf of papers was sitting on the table in front of him.

"How'd it go?" Troy asked.

"In redundant circles."

"That's McGuire's way of trying to trip you up."

"I don't trip," Dylan said, "and the sheriff doesn't have a shred of evidence against me. He just wants me out of Collette's life."

Troy pushed his chair back from the table. "It is strange that Collette's turned to you when she hardly knows you."

Dylan had no answer for that. All he knew was that he and Collette had connected instantaneously from some kind of uncanny chemistry that defied reason. And right now he couldn't wait to see her again. "Has Collette gone to bed?"

"She went to her room after dinner. I saved you some stew. I'll heat it for you while you take a look at those printouts."

Dylan scanned what looked like articles downloaded from the computer. Surely Troy hadn't left Collette here alone and unprotected while he went somewhere to get on the Internet.

"Where did you get these?"

"My friend Able Drake looked it all up for me. He forwarded it to Bob Adkins who was nice enough to print it out and run it over to me."

"You've been busy while I've been out."

"Collette suggested the stalker's motivation could be a grudge against her father," Troy said. "That makes sense to me. These are names of people and reasons why they might seek payback against McGuire."

Seeing Collette would have to wait a few more minutes. Dylan had to read the articles. "Thanks, Dad. And the stew sounds good."

He dropped to the chair and started reading, making note of the people who looked the most suspicious. Billy Sikes topped the list. He'd been arrested ten years ago for running a car-theft ring, stripping the vehicles and selling the parts. He'd been released from jail this past January and arrested again in March for robbing a liquor store. He was now out on bail and claiming that he was being framed by McGuire.

Alan Riggins was also suspect. He'd been accused of stalking the daughter of one of McGuire's deputies. He'd been nonfatally shot by said deputy. He'd filed charges against the deputy and the sheriff, saying McGuire had covered for the deputy, calling it self-defense when it was a clear case of police brutality. The deputy and the sheriff were cleared of all charges.

Then there was the case of Fancy Granger. The sheriff's office had been called by a neighbor to settle a domestic dispute in the mobile home Fancy shared with her live-in boyfriend. The anonymous neighbor reported screaming and feared the argument had grown violent.

Sheriff McGuire took the call along with one deputy. When he tried to arrest the boyfriend who was high on cocaine, Fancy Granger, also stoned, had pulled a gun on the sheriff. Gunfire had ensued, and Fancy Granger had been killed.

Dylan continued down the list. Eighty percent of the people in the county might love Glenn McGuire for being tough on crime, but he definitely had his share of enemies, especially among the criminal population.

He talked of the suspects with his father while he finished off the stew. His father was clearly concerned about him and willing to go to a lot trouble and the expense of hiring an attorney when his funds had to be extremely limited.

All of this now that Dylan was an adult. Yet he'd never once contacted Dylan or his brothers when they were growing up without him.

No excuse would satisfy Dylan, but still he needed to hear some kind of explanation for why Troy had denied him all those years.

He stood up and carried his bowl to the sink. "Why didn't you ever answer my letters?"

Troy twisted around in his chair. "What are you talking about? I answered all your letters, all nine of them. I wrote you and your brothers every week for years until Wyatt wrote and told me that none of you ever wanted to hear from me again."

"I never received a letter from you. Not one, Dad. Not one. Neither did Wyatt or any of the rest of us."

Troy banged his right fist into his left palm, over and over, as if he were kneading bread with his knuckles. "I wrote, son. The letters were mailed to your grandparents every week. I never knew you didn't receive them."

"Why would you mail the letters to them? Only one of us ever lived with them after the trial."

"I was under court order to go through them anytime I corresponded with any of you. I even tried to call whenever I had phone privileges. They never allowed me to speak to you. They said you didn't want to talk to me."

Troy walked over and put an arm about Dylan's shoulder. "I'm sorry, son. I should have pressed for more information. I should have tried harder. But your grandparents were right. I really didn't have anything to offer you but grief."

"They weren't right," Dylan said. "We lost Mother. We were kids. We needed our dad."

"I failed you. I'm sorry. I don't know anything else to say."

There was actually nothing to say. The hurt was still buried deep inside him. He'd missed his mother so much, he'd wanted to die. And then when he hadn't heard from his father, he'd felt lost and betrayed. He'd tried so hard to be strong. He never had been.

Maybe that's the real reason he'd joined the army, from a need to prove himself a man when he ached for the boy he'd never gotten to be.

"I'm sorry, Dylan. I kept up with you. I kept up with all of you. I knew when you graduated college and when you joined the army. I prayed for you every day. But I let you down. I should have found a way to get past your grandparents."

"You should have." He stared at his father, part of him wanting to lash out at him for not being the father he'd needed. Lashing out wouldn't change anything.

To get past this would take time. Yet for the first time in eighteen years, Dylan believed he and his father would find a way to be a family. He gave his father a hug, one that felt as if they were reaching across a huge gulf. Bridging it would be hard, but for now, this was enough.

"I wish we could start over, Dylan, but now is all I can offer."

"It's okay, Dad. It helps to know you tried. It doesn't erase the pain, but it helps. We'll get there in time, but right now we should probably get some sleep."

But instead of going to bed, Dylan went in search of Collette.

COLLETTE HAD JUST STEPPED from the shower when she heard the soft tapping at her door.

"Are you decent?"

Dylan. Her pulse quickened at the sound of his voice. She quickly pulled on her robe and then grabbed a towel to turban around her dripping hair.

"Come in."

He stepped through the door. Fatigue had settled in his broad shoulders. Her first impulse was to step into his arms, but knowing what she had to tell him held her back.

"Was the interrogation tedious beyond endurance?" she asked.

"Let's just say I'm not your father's favorite citizen. We Ledgers have a fearsome reputation."

And a history of trouble that started with the sheriff long before Helene's murder. "How did Dad react to the photo taken from the security footage?"

"He reminded me I'm not an officer of the law and have no business requesting security-camera evidence." Dylan mocked her father's stern tone.

She smiled in spite of the anxiety that was pulsing

inside her. "Does nothing drag you into despair, Dylan Ledger?"

"The Cowboys losing a playoff game."

"You grew up in Boston."

"But I was born a Texan." He sat on the edge of the bed. "However, I get the feeling that something is bothering you."

She walked to the dresser, reached into the top drawer and removed the telltale correspondence. "I read the letters Mother gave me."

He took her hand and tugged her down beside him. "Do you want to talk about it?"

"I think I should."

His hand roamed her back. "Only if you want to."

"They could affect you, too."

He looked at her questioningly. She dreaded hitting him with this tonight, but with all her father was throwing at him, he deserved to know the full truth.

She met his gaze, and the quake inside her shook her control. "The woman my father was in love with when he married my mother was Helene Martin." She pressed the handwritten note into Dylan's hand.

He winced as he started reading. By the time he was finished, his shoulders were squared, his back ramrod straight.

"I know what you're thinking, Dylan. I had the same thoughts, but nothing in those letters proves or even suggests that my father misused his power as sheriff when he arrested Troy."

"When my father went to prison, it didn't just steal seventeen years of his life, Collette. It ripped me and my brothers from him, from our home and from each other. Losing our mother broke our hearts. Losing our father as well destroyed our childhood and life as we knew it."

"I know. I'm so sorry." Tears burned her eyes. She stood and walked away from the bed.

"I don't blame you for any of this," Dylan said, "but if I learn that Glenn McGuire framed my father for murder because of a college crush he had on my mother, I'll find a way to make him pay, Collette. I couldn't live with myself if I didn't."

"I understand." Tears slid from her eyes and ran down her cheeks. "I'm not even sure I can ever forgive him for robbing my mother of the love she deserved. I know I have to talk to him face-to-face."

"When this is over."

"No, Dylan. I can't wait that long. I'm going to his house first thing in the morning."

"I can't see him confessing to anything."

"But I'll know," she said. "If I'm there, looking him in the eye, I'll know if he's lying."

"What a disgusting web this has become," Dylan said. "I thought I'd seen the worst of what life could throw at me when I was a kid and then again in Iraq. But it just keeps coming."

"Coming to my rescue certainly didn't help you."

Dylan crossed the room to where Collette stood staring out the window. He wrapped his arms around her and pulled her back to his chest. "This isn't our doing, Collette."

"Yet we're entangled in it."

Dylan's lips pressed into her neck, and the heat from the kiss sank deep inside her. But she couldn't give in to the need for him that swelled inside her, not when so much anguish was pushing them apart.

"Tell me about you," she said, pulling away.

"There's nothing to tell. What you see is what you get."

"How did you earn your medal?"

"Does that matter?"

"I need to concentrate on something besides the family mess that we're in."

"Fair enough." He went back to the bed and perched on the edge, his left hand circling the bedpost. "We were on a search-and-rescue mission in a small Iraqi village where an earlier battle had gone bad.

"We got trapped by the enemy and had to pull back and wait for more tanks and firepower. We were pretty much secure for the time being when a mother came running from a house shouting that her little girl had been hit by gunfire and begging someone to help."

"Was she bait to lure you into danger?"

"We couldn't tell, but when she got hit by a rain of bullets from her own people, she just kept yelling for someone to save her daughter."

Dylan averted his gaze, staring at the wall. "To make a long story short, I got what coverage I could get from my guys, went into that bombed-out house and carried the daughter to safety. While I was there, I found three American Marines in the wreckage, injured but still alive. By some miracle outside my doing, I got them out and back behind our lines."

Dylan was so much a man. He never saw himself as a hero. She'd never see him any other way. Her heart was so full of Dylan Ledger right now that she could barely breathe.

She walked over, stepped in front of him and put her arms around his neck, pulling his face into the cushion of her breasts. "I can see now why you're so tough."

"That didn't make me tough, Collette. It made me human."

He stood and tugged the towel from her head, letting

her damp hair hang free. "Tough would be offering to walk away from you right now."

She loosened the belt of her robe and let it slide off her shoulders, leaving her standing naked in front of him.

"Let's go for human."

Chapter Fifteen

Dylan rocked back on his heels, crazy with the need roaring inside him. If he acted on his instincts now, he'd pick up Collette, throw her onto the bed and ravage every inch of her. And likely scare her away for good.

He had to take this slow. Savor every delicious touch. Pleasure Collette until she ached to feel him inside her with the same rampant, agonizing hunger he was feeling now.

He cupped her beautiful breasts, letting his thumbs pebble the nipples until they were hard and erect. He wrapped his lips around one, sucking gently and teasing with his tongue. She moaned softly and arched toward him. His erection grew so hard he thought it might burst from the worn denim.

When he reached down to unzip his jeans Collette's fingers intertwined with his. She reached her hand inside his briefs and slid her finger around the wet tip of his burgeoning staff. His control was losing steam. The rest of him was hotter than an explosion.

Still, he held back. His first time with Collette had to be as near perfect as he could make it for her. It struck him then that he'd never felt this way about a woman before. Never thought about the future and that he wanted her not just now, but time after time, day after day.

That should scare him. It didn't. His brain was numb with desire.

She stroked him as he shucked his jeans and shrugged out of his shirt. Passion engorged him and sent blood rushing to his already raging erection. He fell back on the bed, tugging Collette with him as they stretched across the crisp, white sheets.

The sight of her naked body bathed in the filtered shimmer of moonlight touched his soul. The sweet, salty taste of her lips as he took her mouth with his set him on fire.

"You're the one thing I never expected to find in Mustang Run," he whispered as they came up for air.

"Is that what took you so long to get here?"

He didn't answer. He was too lost in the primal cravings that throbbed in his body and deadened his mind.

COLLETTE CLOSED HER EYES, afraid to open them even to look at the enthralling hunk of a man who was touching her in the most private of places and sending spikes of pleasure deep into her core. She'd been intimate with men before. She'd never made love like this, never had a raw hunger for anyone possess her this completely.

She trailed her hand down the length of Dylan's erection. He captured her hand with his and slipped them both between her legs so that she felt her own slick heat. The uninhibited sharing of their bodies made her want him that much more, and when he lifted himself to straddle her, her heart began to pound like a primitive drum.

Dylan put his mouth to her ear, nibbling and sucking her ear lobe. "Guide me in, baby. Make me yours."

She'd never wanted anything more.

Wrapping her hand around the hard length of him, she led him to her, holding her breath until she felt him thrust deep inside her. Exhilaration vibrated through her, sending her pulse skyrocketing and creating a river that flowed from her core with liquid fire.

Dylan's thrusts became a crescendo, the rhythm building until there was no holding back. He rocked her with him as she exploded into an orgasm so intense she thought her heart might burst free of her body.

Only then did she feel Dylan let go of the tight rein he'd held on his body. Calling her name, he let the orgasm overtake him, his erection throbbing within her. She milked him with her hips, drawing out every last drop of pleasure. Reveling in the moment, she let her hands trail down his back to his buttocks, memorizing every muscle and sinew.

Moments later, Dylan rolled over and pulled her into his arms. But even as the golden symphony of afterglow began to hum through her, it was still difficult to breathe.

The words *I love you* echoed in her mind, though she didn't dare say them out loud. She shouldn't even think them this soon, but she knew they were true. Maybe a woman always knew.

The euphoria wouldn't lessen the problems that waited for them at the first light of morning. But for now, she found heaven here in Dylan's arms, and no matter what the future brought, she'd hold these memories for the rest of her life.

MORNING CAME TOO SOON and even the sweet ache in Collette's thighs wasn't enough to ward off the anxiety about facing her father with the letters and accusations.

"You could still wait to do this," Dylan said, as he followed her directions to the small house her father had moved into after his wife's death. "Confronting the sheriff might be easier on you after the stalker is behind bars."

"I'd consider postponing the inevitable if Dad wasn't trying to run my life and ruin yours."

"Don't make me the issue here, Collette. This is between you and him. I have my own issues with your father, but I'll deal with them my way when the time is right and I have all the facts."

"I just want an explanation. I know it won't change anything, but I have to brazen out the confusion."

"Don't expect too much," Dylan said. "Men don't always grasp all the emotional implications the way women do."

"I don't expect a defining resolution, but I deserve to know if he ever loved my mother or if he destroyed her for the sake of some cruel charade."

"Do you want me to go in with you?"

"No. I have to face him alone. The house is on the right, second one from the end of the block."

"I don't see his car," Dylan said.

"He parks it in the garage."

She reached for the door handle as Dylan stopped in front of the two-bedroom brick in one of Mustang Run's older subdivisions. Dylan reached across the seat, put his arm around her shoulder and pulled her close for a kiss. It was tempered with restraint but still she felt the impact curl around her heart.

He brushed a lock of curls from her forehead. "Good luck."

"Thanks."

She marched up the walkway, her fingers clutching the strap of the handbag that held the letters. She pushed the doorbell twice and waited. Seconds later she pushed it again.

"Hold your horses," her father shouted. He was barefoot and buttoning his shirt when he opened the door. "Look who's here and dying to get in." He stood back for her to enter. "Come to your senses, did you?"

"I came to talk."

"If it's to convince me Dylan is an innocent saint, you can save your breath. I have no use for the Ledgers. Never have. Never will."

"And now I know why." She unzipped her handbag and took out the letters.

Her father bent over for a better look, then staggered backward. "Where did you get those?"

"Mother gave them to me a few weeks before she tried to leave you."

He murmured a low curse and pressed his fingertips against both temples. "How in tarnation did she get her hands on those?"

"She found them in the attic, in an old chest of yours. The question is why did you keep them instead of destroying them?"

"Who knows why I did anything back in those days? I was a know-it-all college student with a chip on my shoulder."

She wasn't convinced he'd changed all that much.

"There's no telling what was up in that attic," Glenn stammered. "None of it means anything anymore. Mildred, of all people, should have known that." He padded back to the living room, not seeming to notice or care if Collette followed him.

When she got there he'd dropped into his worn recliner and was cradling his head in his hands.

If he thought she was going to drop this, he was wrong. "Do you remember what you wrote in those letters to Helene Ledger?"

"I don't care what's in the damn letters. And she was Helene Martin back then. She wasn't married. Neither was I at the time I wrote them."

"But my mother was pregnant with Bill."

"From a stupid mistake one night when—"

Anger roared through her with such force she had to grip the back of the couch to hold steady. "Don't call my mother a mistake."

"I never have." His voice cracked. "The pregnancy was a mistake. I married Mildred. We made it right."

"But you were still in love with Helene."

Glenn threw his hands up in frustration. "I loved another woman thirty years ago, Collette. She dumped me for Troy Ledger. Is that what you want to hear?"

"No, I want to know if you ever loved my mother."

"How dare you ask me that?" Glenn raked his weathered fingers through his thinning hair. His eyes were moist, his lips pulled tight. "I loved your mother from the first day she laid that red, squalling brother of yours in my arms. She had to know that."

"How would she, Dad, when all you did was scowl and complain? When you constantly issued orders like a drill sergeant and made light of her wishes?"

"That's who I am. She knew that. I loved her. I didn't tell her enough, but she knew. She had to know." His shoulders shook. "If she'd only come to me with those stupid letters. If she'd only given me a chance to explain…" He dabbed at his eyes with the cuff of his shirt.

Seeing her father like this hurt more than Collette would have ever imagined. It was as if they were burying her mother all over again. She ached to go to him and tell him that she believed him, that in spite of all the antagonism of the past, she still loved him.

But the hurt went too deep to just sweep it away like

yesterday's dirt. And there was still the matter of Troy and Dylan Ledger.

Glenn stood and finished buttoning his shirt. "I'll burn the letters," he said, "the way I should have done thirty years ago. It's all I can do."

"I just have one more question," she said.

Finally he met her gaze straight on. "You seem to be the one in control here. Ask away."

She didn't need the control, not anymore. She'd learned more about her father in the past few minutes than she had in the twenty-seven years of her life. He was a blustering bear, but there was more to him. The tender and loving part of him was just hidden so deep inside that few people ever saw the real him. She prayed her mother had, for her sake and for his.

Unless…

The remaining question twisted inside her and tore at her heart.

"Did you frame Troy Ledger for his wife's murder?"

The transformation in her father was immediate and dramatic. His features hardened to granite. His eyes became a fiery storm.

"I put my life on the line any time it's needed in order to keep the citizens of this county safe, Collette. I don't back off from criminals, the politics or the media. I might have bent the strict restraints of the law from time to time, but by God, I have never framed any man or woman to get a conviction."

"Not even a man you admit to hating?"

"I didn't have to. The evidence did that. A jury sent Troy Ledger to prison for brutally murdering his wife and the mother of his children. I would have given him a death sentence. Feel free to tell both Dylan and Troy that."

Her father turned and walked out of the room, leaving

Collette to deal with his response any way she saw fit. She believed he was telling her the truth, but any chance of reconciliation between them would have to wait.

The would-be killer who spoke of love and soul mates but dealt in death wouldn't.

Chapter Sixteen

Tommy Jo Benoit stared out the window of his grandson's room on the third floor of Carlton-Hayes Regional Hospital and for the first time in his perverted life contemplated death. Forced to watch his eight-year-old grandson slowly lose his grip on life, Tommy Jo no longer saw death as a vague stagnation existing in grays and black, but as a predator who rode in on a blazing chariot in violent shades of red.

Tommy Jo would have gladly given his scarred, broken body and devil-owned soul to save the boy's life. But fate didn't bargain. Neither did the insurance company.

Now time was running out and Tommy Jo's well-laid plans were swirling down the toilet. When the clock was running down with the team behind and the time-outs depleted, someone had to come through with the game-winning play.

It didn't have to be pretty. It didn't have to be safe. It just had to work.

Tommy Jo reached beneath his jacket and touched his hand to the .45 resting in his shoulder holster. He'd made the deal. He'd see it through, though all the odds were against him now.

One life for another.

The pretty daughter of the sheriff would have to die.

Chapter Seventeen

The sixth floor was a din of clattering breakfast trays and rolling carts when Collette and Dylan stepped off the elevator.

"A new guard," Collette commented, as they neared Eleanor's room. "The nurses will be disappointed."

"He looks like he can handle the job to me."

"But he's not nearly as cute as the one on duty yesterday."

"I never noticed."

"I'd worry if you did."

Collette had been shaken and fighting tears when she'd climbed inside Dylan's truck after talking to her father. He'd let her talk, listening as he always did without passing judgment on her or her father. Though she still had a lot to sort through on that emotional front, Dylan had drastically improved her mood.

She had to admit now that it was possible that finding those letters had simply ignited a bout of insecurity in her mother, a meltdown that she would have recovered from without killing the marriage once she and Glenn had talked.

True, her parents hadn't had the kind of mutual esteem and equality in their union that Collette wanted, but that didn't mean it hadn't worked for them. She'd never know for sure, but it helped to realize that in his own way the domineering, stubborn and sometimes downright arrogant sheriff had loved his quiet and compliant wife. She just hoped her mother had found some happiness in the relationship, as well.

Eleanor's door opened and a man in a lab coat walked out followed by two nurses. Collette picked up her pace. "I hope that's just routine physician rounds and not a sign of complications."

"You'll find out soon enough," Dylan replied. "Did you mention to your father that you were planning to show Eleanor our hardware-store suspect's picture?"

"It didn't seem the ideal time for that. He doesn't like even a hint of us usurping his authority."

"As he made clear to me last night."

They stopped at the guard and Collette presented her ID.

"You're on the all-clear list," the guard told her.

"Does the patient have other company?"

"Melinda Kingston. She's on the list. Another guy stopped by here not ten minutes ago and tried to talk me into letting him in."

Collette felt a surge of apprehension and knew from the change in Dylan's stance that he felt it, too.

"Who was it?" Dylan asked.

"Some friend of the family. He left when I told him he wasn't on the list."

Collette pulled the photo from her handbag. "Is this the man?"

The guard studied it for a good half minute before handing it back to Collette. "No. The guy I talked to was ten to fifteen years younger than this man. But that guy in the picture looks familiar."

Dylan hooked his thumbs in the back pockets of his

jeans. "Do you have any idea where you might have seen him before?"

"No, but I'll give it some thought. Check with me when you finish seeing Ms. Baker."

"I'll do that," Collette said. "But if you see him, don't let him near the patient."

"I'm not letting anyone near the patient unless they have proper ID and are on my list."

"Good man." Dylan turned to Collette and took her hand.

Even here, amidst all the trepidation and qualms, his touch both soothed and stirred her.

"Call me the second you leave Eleanor's room and I'll meet you here."

"Will do."

She slipped the picture back in her handbag and stepped into Room 612. This time Eleanor was sitting up in bed, sipping orange juice through a straw and watching a morning news show on the television.

Melinda was propped in a chair by the window. She jumped up and gave Collette a hug as they exchanged greetings. "Eleanor was just saying she hoped you'd stop by today."

"Can't keep me away." Collette walked to Eleanor's bedside. "You look a bit livelier than yesterday."

"They took that annoying IV out of my arm and I can actually go to the bathroom instead of using a bedpan. I'm sure those things should be outlawed as an inhumane form of torture."

Collette fluffed Eleanor's pillow. "Yep, you're on the road to recovery." Even her speech was clearer, though there were still enough meds in her to give her words a slight slur.

"A couple more days and I'll be ready to help your

father go after the bastard who put me in the hospital," Eleanor said.

"How many times has Dad been up here to see you?"

"At least two that I was conscious for. Yesterday right after you left and again in the afternoon. Thankfully, I could finally give him what he wanted."

"The articles?"

"No, I finally remembered the whole attack. Didn't he tell you?"

"As a matter of fact, he didn't. What did you remember?"

"That the attacker was wearing a mask, one of the rubber ones that kids wear at Halloween. It was hideously ugly, like some creature who'd come back from the dead and was covered in mud and blood. I guess that's why I'd blocked it from my mind."

Eleanor had described her attacker, and yet Collette's father hadn't mentioned that to her or to Dylan when he'd come calling at the ranch last night. If the man had been wearing a mask when he attacked Eleanor, then there was no way she could have recognized him, no way he'd need to come back to kill her.

So what was the stalker doing at the hospital?

Melinda reached for the remote and muted the television. "Your father is worried about you, too, Collette, especially with that strange alliance you've formed with Dylan Ledger."

Eleanor took the last sip of juice and set the empty carton back on her tray. "We're all worried about you, Collette. I mean, the guy chooses you out of dozens of reporters to invite into the Ledger house."

"You insisted I go in."

"Right, and don't think I don't regret that. But I didn't tell you to invite him to your house."

"I feel kind of responsible for all of this, too," Melinda said. "If I'd shown up to take the pictures, you'd have never been drawn into this or even talked to Dylan Ledger."

And now she'd made love to him and couldn't wait to do it again. Imagine what they'd think if they knew that.

"Dylan had nothing to do with the attack," she said, though she felt no real need to argue the point.

Eleanor rolled her eyes. "You, Collette McGuire, are much too naive."

Collette straightened Eleanor's sheet. "What did you tell Dad about Dylan?"

"I just voiced my concerns."

"Such as?"

"I received several threatening letters when I was investigating Helene Ledger's murder for a series of articles I was doing."

"What did the letters say specifically?"

"I don't remember specifically. Something about keeping my nose out of the murder if I wanted to die of natural causes. You know, the usual kind of threats investigative reporters get."

Fortunately, she didn't know. "I don't see how or why you'd connect those with Dylan."

"He could have been trying to protect his father."

"His father was already in prison for the murder," Collette reminded her.

"But he could have known the attorney was looking into a release based on a technicality."

"I didn't think investigative reporters gave credence to unproven hypotheses."

"Okay, I admit I have no idea who attacked me," Eleanor admitted. "I just think you should stay away from the Ledgers."

Not if Collette could help it, but there was no reason to try and reason with these two now. She slid the photograph from the outside pocket of her handbag and handed it to Eleanor.

"Have you ever seen this man before?"

Eleanor squinted and held the picture toward the light over her bed for a clearer view. "No. Should I have?"

"I think he could be my stalker." Collette passed the picture to Melinda. "How about you?"

"Never seen him before. Do you know his name?"

"Not yet. Dad's working on it, but for now he's what the cops on TV call an unsub."

Collette visited a few more minutes. When her cell phone vibrated, she checked the ID. It was her sister-in-law. She ignored the call for now and kept chatting with Melinda and Eleanor.

When Eleanor appeared to be growing tired, Collette said her goodbyes. Dylan wasn't waiting, so she decided to grab a diet soda and return Alma's phone call before calling him.

A nurse was chatting with a couple of visitors in the hallway outside Eleanor's room. She stopped talking long enough to point the way to the nearest refreshment room, which was just down the hall, not even out of sight of the guard on duty at Eleanor's room.

Collette retrieved her drink from the machine and was about to open it when the door to the room closed behind her. Before she knew what was going on, a large, misshapen hand covered her mouth and she was shoved against the drink machine.

"Finally we meet, my precious Collette."

DYLAN STEPPED into the first-floor coffee shop. He scanned the area, fully alert for any sign of the Hardware Stalker, as he'd come to think of him.

He picked up a black coffee to go at the counter, paid for it and was about to leave when a woman at the back table turned in his direction and waved. It took a second before he realized it was Abby from the diner.

He walked over and sat down next to her. "I almost didn't recognize you without your floured apron."

"I get out of that kitchen every once in a blue moon. I'm not too keen on these hospital trips, though. They're too depressing. Just before you came in I was talking to a man whose grandson is dying from some rare disease that has no cure."

"That's rough."

She nodded. "Especially since the insurance company won't pay for some high-priced experimental drug that just might send the disease into remission. Poor guy. He said he was playing an option, though, and he was leaving to take care of it right then. Whatever that means."

"Hopefully it means the grandson will get the drug."

"The man looked familiar, but he said he'd never been in my diner. Claimed he'd never even driven though Mustang Run."

"I hope you told him he was missing out on the best coconut pie in all of Texas."

"Darn right I did."

"So what brings you to Carlton-Hayes?" Dylan asked.

"My neighbor had surgery last week. Not too serious. Got her gallbladder out, but she needed someone to drive her back for a checkup."

"And you're the Good Samaritan?"

She smiled at the compliment. "Better than hearing

her whine about taxi fare. What brings you over from the ranch?"

"I drove Collette McGuire to visit a friend."

"Oh, yes. That friend who got attacked in her house, I bet. I heard you were the one who found her." Abby set down her cup and gave him a pat on the back. "Just returned to town and already the hero."

"I don't think calling an ambulance qualifies as heroic."

"I bet that's not what Collette is saying."

He got a strange buzz at the mention of Collette's name, partly from an anxiety that had grown steadily stronger since they'd walked into the hospital. His prelude-to-danger instinct was on high alert.

But he owed part of the buzz to the way Collette was burrowing inside him. Making love to her had been everything he'd imagined it would be, but instead of giving him release from the hunger that stirred at every touch, it only made the craving worse.

He wasn't sure if what he felt for her was love. In his lifetime he'd experienced lust and infatuation, but what he felt for Collette was on a whole new level. It would have to happen in the town where he'd always be known to some as the "murderer's kid" and with a woman whose father he might have to settle a score with one day soon.

If he was smart, he'd just leave town as soon as Collette was safe, before his heart got trampled into the hard Texas earth.

His cell phone rang. The caller was Sheriff McGuire. "Excuse me for a minute, Abby. This could be important." Or it could be more of the same garbage the sheriff had thrown at him last night.

"We've identified the man from Knight's Hardware," McGuire said as soon as Dylan answered. "He's got a rap sheet long enough he could use it for a blanket. Since you're supposedly protecting Collette, I thought you should know."

"I appreciate that. What's the full scoop?"

"His name is Tommy Jo Benoit. He was never prosecuted but he was a hit man twenty years ago for the Chicago mob. He fouled up a hit and the story is the mob messed him up real bad and put him out of the business for good. The Feds kept him under observation for years, but finally dropped him as a harmless has-been."

"How much damage did they do to him?"

"For starters they turned him into a steer."

"Ouch."

"They also fractured the bones in his gun hand and left him with iron plates in his head and screws in both arms. And they permanently damaged his vocal chords."

"Sounds like we've got our man."

"Closing in on him, anyway," Glenn admitted. "I've put out an APB on him. If he's still in the area, we'll get him. If he's not in the area, we'll still get him. It just might take a while longer."

"Thanks for the heads-up."

"Yeah. Good work on fleshing him out."

The compliment left Dylan dumbstruck.

"Take care of Collette," the sheriff said before breaking the connection.

That was a given.

Abby had finished her coffee by the time he put his phone away. She stood and then sat back down as if she'd just remembered something important. "Either that guy I was telling you about has a twin brother or he lied to me."

"What makes you think that?"

"I just remembered where I've seen him before—in my diner with Edna Granger."

Edna Granger. A local widow whose daughter was shot by McGuire. Alarm bells clamored in Dylan's brain. "Did the man happen to have an extraordinarily raspy voice?"

"Now how did you know that?"

The danger instincts had been right on target. Dylan took off in a dead heat with disaster.

COLLETTE STRUGGLED to free herself from the man's grasp until she felt the hard barrel of a pistol pressed into the base of her skull. "Make one sound and I pull the trigger."

The sandpaper voice was all too familiar. They wouldn't need to search for her stalker any longer. He'd found her.

She shivered, and cold sweat trickled down her face.

"Control yourself," he ordered. "We're going to take a short walk, Collette, just you and me. Two close friends in a hospital hallway. You will not do one thing to make anyone suspicious."

Adrenaline kicked in. So did hope. He wasn't going to shoot her here. She would find a way to escape.

He removed his hand from her mouth and let her turn so that she could see him. The gun remained lodged in the soft, fleshy spot beneath her brain.

Dylan had called it right. The stalker and the hardware suspect were one and the same. And now Dylan was somewhere inside the hospital, waiting on her to call the second she left Eleanor's room. Had she done that, she wouldn't be in this predicament.

But somehow this man would have found a way to get her. The cold, sick truth of that was in his eyes.

"Why are you doing this?" she asked him.

"No time for talk now. Just listen. I have six bullets in this gun, and I never miss my mark. Do anything to draw attention to us and the first bullet is for you. The rest are for innocent bystanders or fools who rush to your aid."

"You'll never get away with this. When the bullets are gone, they'll kill you."

"They did that twenty years ago," he whispered. "I have nothing to lose. So walk beside me quietly or you and five innocent bystanders will die. You're too noble and pure to let that happen, Collette."

"You know nothing about me."

"I know everything about you and about your lover. There will be no silver stars for Dylan Ledger this time. No chance to be a hero."

The man reached over and opened the door. "Now walk."

The short barrel of the pistol slid from the back of her head as he went through the doorway, marching her beside him into the hallway.

She didn't feel the gun now, but his arm was linked with hers, and she knew the gun was close at hand. She could take her chances if it was only her, but she couldn't risk his shooting innocent victims.

It could be a bluff, but she couldn't be sure. Mass murders of innocent victims had become all too frequent of late. She had to stay calm, search for a way to make a clean break, perhaps just as they reached the armed guard.

Only they turned and went in the opposite direction down the hallway. A nurse passed them and smiled. Collette kept walking, one step at a time, a psycho dressed in a nice sports shirt and creased khakis holding on to her arm with one hand, a gun in the other hand with a bullet carrying her name.

They turned a corner. An arrow and sign indicated they were heading toward the X-ray center. The glass doors ahead of them were marked for entrance by hospital personnel only. He surely wasn't a doctor. Someone would notice and call security. This would all be over soon.

Only he stopped before reaching the double doors, in front of another doorway marked Maintenance. The hallway remained empty as he pulled a key ring from his pocket and tried three keys before one fit, and the door opened.

The man was shrewd and collected, as if he did this sort of thing every day, as if he knew he wouldn't make a mistake. When the door opened, he shoved her inside and she nearly stumbled over a mop and pail. Her heart began to pound. Whatever this man wanted, he was not going to let her leave this room alive.

She lunged for him, tearing at his face with the fingernails of one hand as she went for his gun. He knocked her against the wall so hard that her brain seemed to rattle like a baby's toy. Acute pain shot up her shoulder and once more the barrel of the gun pressed against her flesh, this time at her right temple.

"I told you no games," he croaked.

Blood trickled from her mouth where she'd cracked it on the mop stick. She wiped it away with the sleeve of her cotton sweater. "Who are you? What do you want with me?"

"Right now I want you take off your clothes. All of them, but do it slowly so that I can get the full effect."

"Don't rape me," she pleaded. "Please, don't rape me."

He laughed, a growling vibration from deep in his

throat. "If only I could. I told you. They killed me twenty years ago."

"Let me go," she pleaded.

"I said undress. Start with the sweater."

"No."

He laughed again. "No? You are a feisty one, aren't you?"

"If you want to kill me, do it, but I won't perform for you, you pervert."

Anger contorted his face and his eyes glazed over. "Very well, Collette. We'll do this the quick way. It's probably for the best anyway. Who knows when Dylan Ledger will come riding to your rescue and then I'd be forced to kill him, too. Not that I would find that offensive." He placed the gun on the shelf at his elbow while he pulled a pair of rubber gloves from his pocket.

It was now or never, she decided.

Instead of going for the gun, she reached for a bottle of bleach on the shelf beside her. In one quick motion she twisted off the cap and slung the bottle at him. Unfortunately, he ducked in time to miss the most of it.

He sputtered vile curses, but came at her with his eyes squinting from the caustic liquid. He pinned her against the wall, and his big hands closed hard around her neck.

"Thanks for the favor. I always preferred killing slowly with my bare hands so that I could watch the victim's faces as they realized they were dying. And you have such a pretty face, Collette."

She tried to fight him with her hands and feet, but her lungs were burning. She struggled for air.

"If it helps any, you're not dying in vain. Edna Granger will get her retribution. A daughter's life for a daughter's life. She's willing to pay well for that revenge, enough to buy the drugs that may save my grandson's life."

Collette couldn't make sense of the man's mutterings. She closed her eyes and tried to block his voice from her mind, so that his face and voice would not be the last things she saw or heard.

Forcing the evil into the dark corners of her fading consciousness, she let Dylan's face play in her mind. She pictured him stepping onto the porch of the ranch house that very first day and the way he'd looked when he'd smiled and tipped his Stetson to the waiting reporters. Cocky, virile, rugged, handsome. A cowboy to build a dream on.

She should have told him that she loved him last night. Now it was too late.

Chapter Eighteen

Someone, probably the Hardware Stalker, had tampered with the elevators, leaving all of them stuck on the top floor. Dylan raced up the six flights of stairs, his endurance training paying off big-time.

He knew that Tommy Jo Benoit was in the hospital with his sights set on Collette, but Dylan's cell phone hadn't rung, which meant Collette was still with Eleanor. She was safe, he assured himself.

Adrenaline was still pumping through him like water rushing from a dam break when he reached the sixth floor. He scanned the hallway before he approached the guard.

"Is Collette McGuire still with the patient?"

"No. She left a few minutes ago."

Dylan checked his cell phone. No missed calls. No messages. "Where did she go?"

"I didn't ask. She didn't say, but she walked off in that direction." The guard pointed toward the other end of the hall.

The assurances Dylan had fed himself on the staircase fell flat. He had to find Collette. She had to be okay. But why go off without calling him?"

A nurse's strident voice caught his attention. "I told you

the bathroom in Room 614 needs cleaning. The patient vomited all over the floor."

Dylan turned to see a burly orderly defend himself.

"I lost my keys or someone took them," the man said. "I can't get to my supplies."

"Find someway to get to your mop bucket now," the nurse ordered.

Again Dylan felt his impending-danger signal vibrate through his body. He rushed to the orderly taking the verbal abuse. "Where do you keep your supplies?"

"In the closet down the hall. I had the keys hanging from my belt a few minutes ago, and now they're gone."

"Take me to the closet. And hurry."

The panic in his voice must have sounded convincing. The orderly started walking at a brisk pace.

"On the double," Dylan ordered in military fashion. "This could be life or death."

The orderly obeyed and started jogging down the hall.

"That's the closet," he said, "but I don't have the keys."

Dylan tried the door. It didn't budge, but he heard a scraping and bumping noise inside. "Open up," he ordered.

When no one did, he stood back and took a deep breath. "We have to break it down."

"No way, man. I'll end up having to pay for the repairs."

"Then get the hell out of the way."

Dylan threw his shoulder into the door, and the wood frame splintered. The orderly jumped into the act and on the second hit, the door came crashing down.

Dylan's worst nightmare faced him. Collette was scrunched into a corner, her eyes glazed over. Tommy

Jo Benoit stood over her, the gun in his hand pointed at Collette's head.

The orderly backed away.

"Stay where you are," Benoit ordered.

Dylan sized up the situation. Collette's neck was red and her lips had a blue cast. Benoit had been choking her, killing her slowly, for his own pleasure. He was a trained assassin for the mob. Had he wanted, he could have broken her neck with one quick movement. Instead, he'd dragged it out, no doubt getting off on the sick pleasure of watching her die.

"Let Collette go," Dylan said. "This is Edna Granger's battle, not yours. If you kill Collette, you won't walk out of here alive. A paycheck isn't worth dying for."

"Sometimes it is. Say goodbye, Collette." Benoit poised to shoot.

Collette slumped into the corner. "I love you, Dylan. Please, don't be a hero. Not this time. Save yourself."

The words were so soft and hoarse that Dylan could barely make them out. He'd never set out to be a hero, but he could not let Collette die.

"You stinking, woman-killing coward," he spat. "They should have slit your throat instead of chopping off your tool."

Benoit shuddered in rage, and moved the gun so that it was pointed at Dylan's head. Dylan liked those odds a whole lot better.

That split second was all the opening he needed. He kicked the gun from Benoit's weakened hand, sending it clattering across the closet.

Brave now that Benoit was unarmed, the burly orderly tackled him to the floor while Dylan recovered the gun. He handed the weapon to the orderly. "If he makes one wrong move, shoot him."

Dylan fell to the floor beside Collette and gathered her in his arms. He held her close while he called for help, his heart still beating erratically.

Had he been a few seconds later... Had he found Collette dead...

He couldn't bear the thoughts; so he held her close, thinking that he'd never let her go.

"And Dad said you were nothing but trouble," she murmured.

"Like I said before, your father is a very smart man."

Epilogue

Three months later

Eleanor lifted her glass of chardonnay as if she were toasting. "I love this garden."

"It was Helene's private oasis originally," Collette said. "I wanted to revive it as a tribute to her love for her family."

Melinda sat down on the ornate bench that had been spruced up with new paint. "Did you do all the work yourself?"

"No. Troy dug up the weeds and tilled the new beds. Dylan's been busy with repairs to the ranch, but he helped me mend the stone wall. I planted, watered and fertilized."

Eleanor did a pirouette, a bit awkwardly since she was wearing incredibly high heels with her belted pencil skirt. "I think this would be a beautiful spot for a wedding."

"You can borrow it anytime you want to tie the knot."

"I'm thinking of you and Dylan. You love him, so what's the holdup?"

"He's busy helping Troy get the ranch up and running."

Melinda looked perplexed. "So you're just going to keep living at the old Callister place indefinitely?"

"It's a nice house, and I have my photography business," Collette protested. "It's not as if I need a wedding ring to have a life."

She avoided the painful truth that although Dylan seemed as much in love with her as she was with him, he'd never once mentioned marriage.

Collette stooped to pull a new weed. "Aren't you two the same friends who were telling me how bad Dylan was for me just a few months ago?"

"We were wrong," Eleanor said. "We admit it. Which reminds me, what's the latest on your crazed stalker/ assassin?"

"He's in jail awaiting trial. So is Edna Granger. When she started spilling her guts in hopes of a lesser charge, Benoit decided to follow suit. She hired him to kill me to get back at Dad for killing her daughter in the drug-induced domestic mayhem."

"I read about that," Melinda said, "but I still don't get the stalker routine."

"That was originally Edna's idea, but Benoit elaborated on the scheme. They decided that if I told everyone I was being stalked before I was killed, that would mislead the investigators and keep them from suspecting that Edna or Benoit had a hand in my death."

"It might have worked if Dylan hadn't shown up in time that very first night." Eleanor said.

"Exactly." Collette swatted at a mosquito that had landed on her arm. "Benoit had knocked you unconscious and was waiting for me to arrive so that I could watch him kill you before he killed me. He has a taste for the macabre." She shuddered, despite the summer heat. "Good thing Dylan showed up and knocked a giant hole in his plans."

"So all's well that ends well?" Eleanor asked.

"At least it ended as well as could be hoped for Benoit's ill grandson," Collette said. "After his story received so much publicity, the insurance company decided to pay for the drug after all. He's in remission and back home with his parents in Marble Falls."

Both Eleanor and Melinda cheered that news.

"And how are things between you and your father?" Eleanor asked.

"Making progress."

"Great," Eleanor said. "He lacks tact when questioning victims and he doesn't mince words, but I like the old buzzard."

"You would," Melinda said.

The talk turned from crime to the increasing sales of *Beyond the Grave* and their appreciation for Troy's letting them feature the house in the next edition. They'd taken dozens of pictures today.

An hour and a glass of wine later, they were ready to leave.

"I hate to lie to our readers," Melinda said as Collette walked them to Eleanor's car. "But this place is too peaceful to be haunted."

"Agreed," Eleanor added. "Too bad. If I were a ghost, I'd want to haunt a house just like this one."

If they only knew.

But they wouldn't hear it from Collette. It was a secret shared only by her and Helene.

DYLAN RODE UP on his recently purchased majestic black steed just as Collette was climbing into her Jeep.

He looked every inch a cowboy, a deliciously intriguing cowboy.

"Leaving so soon?" he asked.

"I've been here all afternoon. Where were you?"

"I wanted to give you time with your friends. I didn't expect you to leave before I got back."

"A man should never keep a woman waiting indefinitely."

I'll try to remember that. Now that I'm here, why don't we take the horses for a ride and catch the sunset by the creek?"

The offer was too tempting to resist. "I guess I can stay awhile longer."

"I'll saddle Lady for you."

"Good. I'll get my boots from the trunk and meet you at the horse barn."

In minutes, they were galloping across the east pasture with endless stretches of hilly grassland stretching in front of them. She could have ridden like that forever, but when they reached the creek, Dylan slowed to a trot and then stopped beneath the sketchy shade of a lonesome pine tree.

A row of willow trees lined the creek bed. A blanket was spread out beneath them topped with a picnic basket and a cooler of champagne. She flushed with pleasure, then did her best to hide it.

Dylan helped her dismount and then took her hand and led her to the edge of the creek where the picnic was waiting.

For the first time since they'd met, he seemed awkward and a bit unsure of himself. Whatever he'd brought her here for, he obviously wasn't sure she'd like it.

Her heart plummeted. He was going to tell her that he'd done what he came to Mustang Run to do. He'd bonded with his father. He'd gotten the ranch up and running. It was time for him to move on.

He'd never promised her forever, but how would she ever live without him? She loved his voice, his humor, the way he swaggered, the way he made love with her. She loved him.

She wanted to lash out and beat her fists against his chest and beg him never to leave. That had never been her style. Instead she propped her hands on her hips. "Sure of yourself, aren't you, cowboy? Planning a picnic without asking first. I could have said no to your invitation for a ride."

"I'm glad you didn't. I wanted you to see this spot just before the sun dips below that strand of trees off to the west. It casts a magic glow over the area."

Dylan was all the magic she needed.

"I'm thinking of building a house here," he said. "What do you think?"

Her heart jumped to her throat. "Does that mean you're staying in Mustang Run?"

He took off his Stetson and tossed it onto the blanket. "All depends."

"On what?"

"The answer to my next question." He reached in his pocket and pulled out a gold band circling a solitary diamond. "I love you, Collette. I think of you all day when I'm working the ranch. Nights I don't see you, I go crazy with wanting you. For the first time in eighteen years, I feel like I'm where I belong. I'm thinking that means we should get married."

Her heart pounded. All she'd ever wanted from life was standing in front of her in the person of a heroic, protective, gorgeous cowboy. "Oh, Dylan. I love you, too. I have from the first moment we met."

"But do you love me enough to marry me? Think before you answer. Becoming a Ledger means being branded with that name and all the suspicions that go with it for the rest of your life. So will our children—unless you don't want children."

"Of course I want children, lots of them. Well, three, at least. And I'll make sure they are proud to be a Ledger, proud to be your sons or daughters."

"Is that a yes?"

"That, Dylan Ledger, is definitely a yes."

Dylan pulled her into his arms for a kiss that promised a lifetime of love.

Tears of happiness burned in Collette's eyes as she thought of Helene and knew that somehow she was watching and that all heaven was cheering for the son of Troy Ledger who'd found his way home.

* * * * *